...f writ...
...of a brilliant...

...onard and George V. Higgi...

...haps the greatest living American c... ...iter'
Stephen King

'A bloody, brooding thriller of rare authenticity'
Evening Standard

'This is gold-standard character-driven crime writing that few will ever match. I can't wait for the sequel'
Financial Times

'George Pelecanos writes hard-boiled fiction with heart'
Sunday Telegraph

'Pelecanos has a perfect ear for the rhythms of life and language in his beloved Washington – not the nabobs of Capital Hill, but the ghettoes and the immigrant communities he knows so well'
Guardian

'Once again Pelecanos scores high . . . American crime writing at its finest'
Independent on Sunday

'He is, we reckon, the best American writer working at the moment. And no, we don't just mean in crime fiction'
Herald

'Pelecanos has a rare gift of creeping inside the heads of his characters and making them real'
Time Out

George Pelecanos is an independent-film producer, an essayist, the recipient of numerous international writing awards, a producer and an Emmy-nominated writer on the HBO hit series *The Wire*, and the author of a bestselling series of novels set in and around Washington, D.C. He is currently a writer and producer for the acclaimed HBO series *Treme*. He lives in Maryland with his wife and three children.

GEORGE PELECANOS
NICK'S TRIP

An Orion paperback

First published in the USA in 1993
by St. Martin's Press
This paperback edition published in 2013
by Orion Books,
an imprint of The Orion Publishing Group Ltd,
Orion House, 5 Upper St Martin's Lane,
London WC2H 9EA

An Hachette UK company

1 3 5 7 9 10 8 6 4 2

A CIP catalogue record for this book
is available from the British Library.

ISBN 978-1-4091-2705-5

Printed and bound in Great Britain by Clays Ltd, St Ives plc

The Orion Publishing Group's policy is to use papers that
are natural, renewable and recyclable products and made
from wood grown in sustainable forests. The logging and
manufacturing processes are expected to conform to the
environmental regulations of the country of origin.

www.orionbooks.co.uk

TO MY SON NICHOLAS,
AND TO LOU REED

NICK'S TRIP

ONE

THE NIGHT BILLY Goodrich walked in I was tending bar at a place called the Spot, a bunker of painted cinder block and forty-watt bulbs at the northwest corner of Eighth and G in Southeast. The common wisdom holds that there are no neighborhood joints left in D.C., places where a man can get lost and smoke cigarettes down to the filter and drink beer backed with whiskey. The truth is you have to know where to find them. Where you can find them is down by the river, near the barracks and east of the Hill.

An Arctic wind had dropped into town that evening with the suddenness of a distaff emotion, transforming a chilly December rain into soft, wet snow. At first flake's notice most of my patrons had bolted out of the warped and rotting door of the Spot, and now, as the snow began to freeze and cover the cold black streets, only a few hard drinkers remained.

One of them, a gin-drenched gentleman by the name of

Melvin, sat directly in front of me at the bar. Melvin squinted and attempted to read the titles of the cassettes behind my back. I wiped my hands lethargically on a blue rag that hung from the side of my trousers, and waited with great patience for Melvin to choose the evening's next musical selection.

Melvin said, "Put on some Barry."

I nodded and began to fumble through the stack of loose cassettes that were randomly scattered near the lowest row of call. The one I was looking for was close to the bottom, and its plastic casing was stained green with Rose's lime. It was Barry White's first recording, "I've Got So Much to Give," from 1973. The cover art showed the Corpulent One holding three minia-turized women in his cupped hands.

"This the one, Mel?" I palmed it in front of his face. Mel nodded as I slipped the tape in and touched the PLAY button.

Mel said, "Let me tell you somethin' 'bout my boy Barry. You done been on a bad trip with your girlfriend—you put on Barry. Barry be talkin' real pretty and shit, all of a sudden you sayin', 'I learned, baby. I sweeeear I learned.'" The bass of the Barrance came through the grilleless Realistic speakers, and Mel sensually joined in: "Don't do that. Baby, pleeease don't do that."

Melvin Jeffers had just sunk his fifth rail martini. He had begun to sing and in all probability would continue to sing for the remainder of the night. I eyed my options down the bar.

Buddy and Bubba were in place at the far right corner, seated next to the Redskins schedule that was taped to the wall, the one with the placekicker booting the pigskin through goal-posts shaped suspiciously like long-necked bottles of Bud. Buddy was short and cubically muscular with an angular face and white blond hair. Like many men who took up body build-ing for the wrong reason, he had found to his dismay that having a pumped-up physique did nothing to diminish the huge chip that was on his shoulder. His friend Bubba also considered him-self to be an athlete but was simply broad-shouldered and fat.

Bubba had the pink, rubbery face that some unlucky alcoholics get and then keep after their thirtieth birthday.

I moved down the bar, picked up Buddy's mug, and with my raised brow asked him if he wanted another. Buddy shook his head and made sure I saw him look me over. I turned my attention to Bubba.

"How 'bout you, Bubber?" I asked in my best whiny, mid-sixties Brando. "You want one?"

Bubba said, "Uh-uh," then looked at his friend inquisitively, something he did every time I addressed him in this manner. In *The Chase*, a film that barely contained one of Marlon Brando's most eccentric performances, the legendary actor continually mispronounced the name of Bubba, Robert Redford's character, as "Bubber." It was a film that the Spot's Bubba had obviously missed.

I left them and, as I passed, avoided eye contact with the only remaining customer, a cop named Boyle. Buddy and Bubba were one thing, rednecks wearing ties, but I was in no mood to open that particularly poisonous, psychotic can of worms named Dan Boyle.

Instead I turned my back on all of them and began to wipe down the bottles on the call rack. I caught a sliver of my reflection in the bar mirror between liters of Captain Morgan's and Bacardi Dark, then looked away.

ALMOST A YEAR HAD passed since I had taken my first case, a disaster that had ended with a close friend being numbered among the dead. I emerged relatively unscathed but had caught a glimpse of my mortality and, more startling than that, a fairly obvious map for the remainder of the trip. I had three grand in the bank and a District of Columbia private investigator's license in my wallet. In my license photograph I sported a blue-black shiner below my left eye, a trophy I had earned in a Eurotrash disco while on a particularly ugly binge. Clearly I was on my way.

Though my tenure in retail electronics was over (I had made the poor career move of staging a gunfight in my former employer's warehouse), I began the year with energy. I made the yellow pages deadline, listing myself as "Nicholas J. Stefanos, Investigator," even stepping up for the boldfaced type. I bought a used pair of binoculars and a long-lensed Pentax, printed report forms and business cards, and hooked myself up with an answering service. Then I sat back and waited for the cases to roll in.

When they didn't, I began to take long, daily walks through D.C. I visited galleries and museums, spending more than one afternoon studying the large paintings of Jack Dempsey and Joe Louis in the National Portrait Gallery at Eighth and F. Several times on these visits I was followed through the cavernous halls by suspicious security guards, something I attributed to their boredom and to my progressively hangdog appearance. When I had exhausted the museums, I went to the Martin Luther King Jr. Memorial Library and renewed my card, then spent the next week in the Washingtoniana Room on the third floor, mainly in the company of street people who slept silently at the various tables with newspapers wedged in their hands. In that week I read most of the *Washington Star*'s morgue material printed between 1958 and 1961, in an effort to get a feel for those years of my life of which I had no recollection. I then discovered the European reading room at the Library of Congress and read modern history for two weeks in a row, sitting across from an ultrawhite eunuch who wore a bow tie every day and never once looked in my direction. One day I walked the pale yellow tunnel from the Jefferson Building to the Madison Building and stumbled upon the Motion Picture and Television Reading Room on the third floor. I spent the month of March in that room, reading everything from scholarly works on the spaghetti western to André Bazin to something called *A Cinema of Loneliness* by a guy named Kolker. Though the room was reserved for professionals, no one questioned my presence or bothered me in any way. In fact, no one spoke to me at all. Spring came and I began to haunt the parks and gardens of the city, returning with frequency to the Bishop's Garden at the National Cathedral. Some days I would walk through cemeteries finding them a curious combination of the enigmatic and the starkly real. The Rock Creek Cemetery, with its Adams Monuments, was a particular favorite.

Sometime in May I was suddenly overcome with the natural feeling that it was time to "do" something. The next morning I tied my first Windsor knot in five months and rode the Metro to Gallery Place, where I walked to the offices of Bartell Investigative Services on Eighth at H, located smack in the middle of Chinatown.

I had picked them out of the phone book at random, preferring to work in that section of town, and was surprised upon entering and filling out an application that they would interview me on the spot. But as I stood in a reception area at the front of the office, I studied the other operatives at their desks, beefy guys in tight gray suits with prison haircuts who had the appearance of aging high school linemen, and decided it wasn't for me. I stuffed the application in my breast pocket, thanked the nicotine-throated grandmother type at the desk, and walked out into the street.

I had been all right up to that point, but the experience made me aware of just how irrevocably far from the mainstream I had strayed. I entered the Ruby Restaurant around the corner and had a bowl of hot and sour soup and some sautéed squid. Then I walked to Metro Center and boarded the Orange Line for a short trip to the Eastern Market station. I crossed Pennsylvania and headed down Eighth Street.

On the corner was the bar in which I first met my ex-wife Karen. They had changed both the ownership and the decor, from early eighties new wave to rustic Wild West saloon. I looked in the plate-glass window and saw cigarette-smoking Cambodians shooting pool and arguing. One of them had a wad of ones grasped tightly in his fist, his features taut as he shook the bills in his opponent's face. I kept walking.

I passed carryouts and convenience stores and cheap ethnic restaurants. I passed the neighborhood movie theater so hopelessly run down that it was no longer advertised in the *Post*, and a record-and-drug store. I passed two bars that catered to lesbians. I passed a bus stop shielding loud groups of young men wearing L.A. Raiders caps and red jackets, and quiet older folks who could no longer laugh, even in cynicism, at their surroundings. Karen and I had lived in this neighborhood during the early days of our marriage.

Toward the end of the street an MP in full dress was directing traffic near the barracks. I crossed over and headed to a bar whose simple sign had caught my eye: THE SPOT. Other than the rectangular glass in the transom, there were no windows. I pushed on the heavy oak door and stepped in.

There was a room to my right painted dark green, housing a few empty deuces and four-tops. Beer posters were tacked to three of the walls and on the fourth was a dart board.

I stepped down into the main bar, which was to the left and ran the length of the room. There were two hanging conical lamps, which dimly illuminated columnar blocks of smoke. A blue neon Schlitz sign burned over the center of the bar. Billie Holiday was singing in mono through the speakers hung on either side of the room. There were a couple of regulars who didn't glance my way and a redheaded woman behind the bar who did. I had a seat at the stool in front of the area she was wiping down.

"What can I get you?" she asked, seeming mildly interested to see a new face. She was in her twenties but had crossed the line from youthful optimism to drugged resignation.

"I'll have a Bud," I said, breaking my daytime drinking resolution.

She pulled a long-neck from the cooler and popped it with a steel opener that looked heavy as a weapon. I waved off a glass as she set down the bottle on a moldy coaster touting Cuervo Gold. After she did that she didn't walk away.

"What's your name?" I asked.

"Sherry," she said.

There was more silence as she stood there, so I pulled a Camel filter from my jacket and lit it. I blew the smoke down, but some of it bounced off the pocked mahogany bar and drifted in her direction. She still didn't move. I thought of something to say, came up blank, then looked up at the cursive neon tubes above my head.

"So," I said lamely, "you sell much Schlitz here, Sherry?"

"We don't sell it at all," she said.

"I thought, you know, with the sign and all..."

"We put up whatever the liquor distributors give us," she said, then shrugged and gave me a weak smile. "Fuck it. You know?"

Yeah, I knew. It was my kind of place and I was due. I returned there every day for the next two weeks and drank with clear intent.

In those two weeks I got to know some of the regulars and became a familiar face to the small staff. Sherry was, predictably, looking for other work, as was the other shift bartender, a stout-faced, square-jawed German woman named Mai who had married and then left a young marine as soon as her green card had come through. There was an all-purpose busboy/cleanup man named Ramon, a little Salvadoran with a cocky, gold-toothed smile who didn't understand English except when it had something to do with quiff or his paycheck. The cook, Darnell, worked in a small kitchen to the side of the bar. Mostly I saw his long, skinny arms as he placed food on the platform of the reach-through.

Phil Saylor was the proprietor of the Spot. He came in for a couple of hours in the afternoon and I presumed at closing time to do the book work. Saylor was an unlikely looking—short, soft in the middle, wire-rim spectacles—ex–D.C. cop, originally from South Texas, who had quit the force a couple of years earlier and opened this place. He seemed to make a living at it and to enjoy it. Certainly he enjoyed his abominable bourbon and Diet Cokes, which as owner he inexplicably opted to drink with Mattingly and Moore, the house rotgut.

Saylor's past explained the unusually large percentage of detectives on the D.C. squad who were regulars. Though the Fraternal Order of Police bar in lower Northwest was still popular with D.C.'s finest, this was a place where cops could drink without restraint and in private. And unlike at the FOP, where they were expected to unwind with "a few" after work, they could do their unscrutinized drinking at the Spot while still on duty. In fact, in my two weeks spent with bent elbows at the bar of the Spot, it became obvious that this was a place where serious drinkers from all across the city came to get tanked in peace, without the presence of coworkers, hanging plants, brass rails, or waitresses who overfamiliarly (and falsely) addressed them as "gentlemen."

One Monday late in May I watched the bar as Sherry and Saylor retired to the kitchen for a short discussion. I was alone in the place and had gained Saylor's trust to the point where I was allowed to help myself. I reached into the cooler and popped a Bud and nursed it for the next fifteen minutes while I listened to Ma Rainey on the deck.

Sherry emerged from the kitchen and began to gather up what looked to be her things, stuffing a romance paperback into her purse and then picking up a dusty umbrella from the side of the cooler. Her eyes were a little watery as she leaned in and kissed me lightly on the cheek before walking from behind the bar and then out the front door.

Saylor came out of the kitchen a little later and poured himself a straight shot of Mattingly and Moore. He adjusted the wire rims on his nose as if he were going to do something smart, but instead did something stupid and fired back the shot.

When he caught his breath he looked through me and said,

"God, I hate that." His face was screwed tight, but I guessed he wasn't talking about the speed-rail bourbon. "I knew she was giving away drinks to jack up her tips—all of 'em do it, even the honest ones—but there was money missing, five, ten a day, all this past month. I had to let her go, man; I didn't have any choice."

"Don't worry about it, Phil." I had pegged Sherry for a gonif the first day I met her but felt I had no duty to inform Saylor. I didn't owe him anything, not yet. "You still got Mai," I said.

He nodded weakly. "Yeah, and she wants more shifts. But she's got a temper, man, with me *and* the customers. I don't think I can handle that German wench in here all the time." His hands spread out. "I guess I gotta go through the process of looking for a new girl."

I looked at my beer bottle and saw a thousand more like it on a hundred more dark afternoons. Then I looked into the bar mirror and saw my lips moving. They said, "Hell, I'll bartend for ya, Phil."

He pushed his glasses up again and said, "You kidding?"

"Why not? The cases aren't exactly building up," I said with understatement, then told the biggest lie of the day. "Besides, I've done some bartending in my time."

Saylor thought it over. "I never had a man behind the bar here. Can't say any of these guys would notice the difference." I lit a Camel while he talked himself into it. "I guess I could give you a few shifts, try it out. You start tomorrow?"

"Yeah," I said with the misguided, giddy enthusiasm common in long-term unemployment cases. "Tomorrow."

On the way home I stopped at the MLK Library and borrowed a book on mixology called *Karla's Kocktail Kourse*, then took it back to my apartment in the Shepherd Park area of Northwest. The book was fine (except for those ridiculous *K*'s in the title) and entertaining with its modern fifties, triangularly matted illustrations, complete with hostesses serving drinks in June Cleaver dresses and the author's insistence on displaying cocktails set next to burning cigarettes. I studied into the night; my cat, confused by my diligence, alternately circled and slept on my feet the entire time. When morning came I was ready.

But I was never really put to the test. I found, with some disappointment, that the patrons of the Spot were hardly the type to call for Rob Roys or sidecars, or any of the book's other extravagant concoctions whose ingredients I had memorized. Neither were they, as Saylor had predicted, unhappy (or happy, for that matter) to see me behind the bar. Generally, their nostalgia for the Sherry dynasty faded with my first shift and their first pop of the day.

As the weeks went by I got quicker with the bottles and memorized most of the regulars' drinks. I snuck my own music onto the deck and received only a couple of belches, and kept the promise to myself never to drink on shift, which made that first one at the end of the day go down even better. I made few mistakes, though the ones I did make were memorable.

There was a guy I called Happy, partly because of what I am convinced was his inability to smile. Happy had hair like gray seaweed, a flat, veined nose, and heavily bagged eyes. He was taken to wearing baby-shit brown sport jackets with white stitching at the seams. The jackets appeared to have the texture of Styrofoam. Often he'd fall asleep at the bar with his hand limply wrapped around his drink glass. One afternoon he spit a mouthful of manhattan over the bar shortly after I served it to him. I looked his way.

"I asked for a manhattan," he mumbled loudly.

I thought of the only explanation. "Sorry. I must have used the dry vermouth instead of the sweet vermouth."

"Listen," he said with a fierce stare and a voice informed by sixty Chesterfields a day. "When I order a manhattan, I don't want *any* kind of vermouth, you hear? Pour an ounce of bourbon into a martini glass and drop a fuckin' cherry in it. Understand?"

I nodded that I did.

For the summer I had four shifts a week and accumulated

quite a bit of cash in the bottom drawer of my dresser. Ironically, I picked up some investigative work soon after I started at the Spot.

The first was a shadow job on the wife of a greeting-card salesman who suspected her of adultery. The salesman had out-of-town accounts and subsequently was away from home three days a week. I spent a good amount of time sitting in my Dodge at the parking lot of her office building in Rockville, smoking too many cigarettes and listening to what was becoming a decidedly boring, unprogressive WHFS. At noon I'd follow her and a couple of her friends to their lunch destination, then follow her back to the office. It wasn't until her husband left town, however, that she cut loose. On the day of his departure she left work early and drove to some garden apartments off the Pike. Two hours later she was gone and I was reading the name off her lover's mailbox. The next day they met at Romeo's apartment for a lunch boff, and I snapped his picture as he walked out the door to return to work. I gave the photos to the husband and watched his lips twitch as he wrote me a check for seven hundred and fifty dollars. It took the better half of a fifth of Grand-Dad that night to wash his broken face from my mind.

Shortly thereafter, the parents of a high school sophomore in Potomac signed me on to get to the bottom of what they hysterically perceived to be their daughter's growing interest in satanism. I hooked up with her fairly easily through her mall-rat friends and we had lunch. She seemed bright, though unimaginative, and her devil worship turned out to be no more than hero worship. She was into Jim Morrison and her ambition, man, was to visit his grave in Paris. In the conference with her parents I told them that in my youth I had survived a fling with Black Sabbath and early Blue Öyster Cult without killing a single cat. They didn't smile, so I told them to relax; in six years their daughter would be driving to law school in her VW Cabriolet and listening to Kenny G like all her other friends from Churchill High. They liked that better and stroked me a check for two hundred and a half. After that I resolved to be more selective in my cases (my bar shifts were keeping me solvent), but I'll never know if I would have held to it since in any case the phone, for the remainder of the year, neglected to ring.

Summer passed and then the fall. When I wasn't at the bar I spent my time reading, jumping rope, riding my ten-speed and, once a week, sparring with my physician, Rodney White, who in addition to being a reliable general practitioner was a second-degree black belt. Occasionally I kept company and slept with my friend Lee, a senior at American University.

The mayor's arrest on charges of possession was big news, though that event was more significant for the local media's shameful self-congratulatory arrogance and their inability to see the real story: the murder rate was at another record high and the gap was widening between the races, socially and economically, every day. But of course there was no story there, no angle. The colonizer and the colonized, just like the textbooks say.

This was also the year that I was to both lose and make two special friends. The friend I made was Jackie Kahn, a bartender at a woman's club called Athena's, located two doors down from the Spot. As I was walking past the windowless establishment one evening in late September, I noticed a flier tacked on the door concerning an upcoming "womyn's" march. I stepped inside and, ignoring a few mildly unfriendly stares, went directly to the bar and had a seat. The bartender gave me the once-over before she asked me what I'd have. She had short black hair and high cheekbones, and deep brown, intelligent eyes. I asked her name first and she said it was Jackie. I ordered a Bud.

After she served it she said tiredly, "Why do you want to come in here, make trouble or something? I mean, we don't mind getting a few guys now and then. But they're usually the New York Mary types, you know what I'm saying?"

"I'm a high school English teacher," I said, feeling a sudden rush from the two bourbons I had rocketed before closing the Spot. "I noticed a misspelling on your flier outside. You have *women* with a *y*. Just thought I'd point it out."

"That's the way *we* spell it," said a humorless type with slicked-back hair sitting to my left. I had the feeling this one didn't like me much. She confirmed it with her next suggestion: "Why don't you just move it the fuck on out of here, chief?"

"He's all right," Jackie said, surprising me. She was looking at me with a smile threatening to break across her face. "What do you *really* want?"

"A beer," I said, and extended my hand. She shook it. "My name's Nick. I bartend over at the Spot. Didn't feel like having that last one alone tonight." I chin-nodded to the table in the corner. "Thought I'd shoot a game of pool while I was in here. That all right, Jackie?"

"Sure." She nodded, then leaned in close and, with an amazingly quick read of my personality, said, "But do me a favor, Nick — don't be an asshole. Okay?"

I began to frequent Athena's fairly regularly after work for a beer and a game of pool. An ex-Brooklyner named Mattie would wait for me to come in and we'd shoot one game of eight ball for a five spot. Athena's was typical of most of the women's bars in Washington. It was owned by men who saw it only as an exploitable market niche and therefore tended to neglect it in terms of cleanliness and decor. But it was a place to go. To sensationalize the scene would be to give it too much credit; lesbian bars were the same as any other singles bars, with the identical forced gaiety and underlying streams of sadness. People met and fucked or resisted and went home alone.

Jackie and I began to spend time together outside of our jobs, going to the movies or having a beer or two at some of the saner places on the Hill. She was an accountant at a Big Eight firm downtown and moonlighted at Athena's for relaxation and to escape the masquerade that was apparently more necessary for gay women than it was for their male counterparts. Occasionally she'd poke her head in the Spot to say hello, and invariably one of my regulars would boast that he could "turn one of those 'rug munchers' around" if he had the chance. This was especially exasperating coming from guys who hadn't even been mercy-fucked by their own wives for years. As our friendship developed I began to pat myself on the back for finally having a close relationship with a woman that didn't involve sex. It had only taken me three and a half decades to learn. What I didn't know then was that Jackie Kahn would have the largest role in the single most important thing that I have ever done.

The friend I lost was William Henry. Henry was a deceptively quiet young man with an offbeat sense of humor who had migrated from the South to take his first job out of college as a reporter for a local alternative weekly. I met him when he sat in on a meeting where his tabloid's sales manager pitched me on buying space when I was advertising director for Nutty Nathan's. Though I didn't step up for any ads, Henry and I discovered from that meeting that we had very similar tastes in music. I hooked up with him downtown a couple of times — once to see Love Tractor at the Snake Pit and on another night to check out a hot D.C. zydeco band, Little Red and the Renegades, at the Knight's Work — but after my career at Nathan's blew up, I heard from him only through the mail. He was that type of friend who, without an explanation, would send me headlines from the *New York Post* or buy me unsolicited subscriptions to Australian biker mags, publications with names like *Chrome and TaTas*.

In July, William Henry was found murdered in his condo above Sixteenth and U, just around the corner from the Third District police station. He had been stabbed repeatedly with a serrated knife. A witness had seen a thirtyish man with a medium build leave the building at the time of the murder. The man was light-skinned and wore a blue T-shirt that appeared to have been stained with blood. The Metropolitan Police spokesman said in the *Washington Post* that an arrest was "eminent."

For a few days after that the *Post* ran a daily article on the slaying, returning to their favorite theme of Small-Town Boy Comes to Murder City and Meets His Fate. But when it was clear that the story would not have a pat ending, the articles stopped, and William Henry's killer was never found.

I WAS THINKING OF Henry when I stepped up to Boyle that night and gave last call. Buddy and Bubber were gone, as was Melvin. He had left when I put George Jones on the deck. The tape always sent him out the door. Darnell was in the kitchen, cleaning up. I could see his willowy torso in the reach-through and hear the clatter of china, muted by the sound of his cheap radio, as he emptied the dishwasher.

Dan Boyle placed his palm over the top of his shot glass to signal he was done, then drank the rest of the beer from the bottle sitting next to it. I asked if he wanted to put the night on his tab and he nodded, seeming to look both to my right and to my left simultaneously.

Boyle was square-jawed and built like a heavyweight prize-fighter, with stubbornly short, dirty blond, Steve McQueen–style hair, circa *Bullitt*. The age in his bleached blue eyes exceeded his thirty years. He drank methodically, and when he spoke it was through the tight teeth of an angry dog.

Many of the on-duty detectives who frequented the Spot wore their guns in the bar (it was, in fact, a police regulation that they do so), and most of them got tanked up and weaved out into the night without incident. But it wasn't Boyle's weapon (the grip of his Python always showed from beneath his wool jacket where it was holstered) that was disturbing, or the fact that he even carried one. He was clearly on the edge, and he was the last guy in the bar who I ever would have fucked with.

"Hear anything more on the William Henry case?" I asked him carefully. I bent into one of the three sinks and rinsed out the green bar netting.

"You knew him, didn't you?"

"Yeah."

"Haven't heard anything," he said. "But I'll lay you ten to

one your friend got burned for drug money. In this town, it all boils down to drugs. Let me tell you what it is. It's" — he glanced around the room — "it's the fuckin' boofers. You know what they ought to do about the drug problem in this city?" I didn't answer, having heard his solution a dozen times. "Take 'em out in the middle of the street and shoot 'em in the head. Public fuckin' executions."

I said, "Check on the Henry case for me, will you, Boyle?" He rose clumsily, nodded, and with a tilted, heavy gait made his way across the room and out the front door. A trace of snow blew through before the door closed.

The lights dimmed in Darnell's kitchen. He walked out, wearing a leather kufi on his head and a brown overcoat. Darnell was tall and bone-skinny and pushing forty. He had done time and from that had gotten a thick white scar from the back of his ear to the underside of his chin. The scar made him look tough but, whatever he had been, that part of his life was clearly over. He was soft-spoken and introspective now, and though it was obvious that he would never rise above his position in the kitchen, that futility did not prevent him from reporting to work every single day. He was, as one of my regulars had described him with special emphasis on the word, a man.

Darnell and I looked through the transom window and watched the steady diagonal fall of thick flakes, a picture that seemed unreal from our warm vantage point. Darnell, hoping for some company, said, "You headin' up my way?"

"I've got some work to do," I said. "Think I'll stick around, check my antifreeze."

Darnell looked at the pyramid of liquor on the wall and then back at me. "What you want to drink that nasty shit for? Shit kills your spirit, man." He shook his head and walked to the door, then turned. "You want me to lock up?"

"No, I'll get it. Thanks, Darnell."

"Check you tomorrow, hear?" He waved and then he was gone.

Dimming the lights even further, I finished wiping down the bar, placing all of the ashtrays but one in the soak sink. Then I slipped Robyn Hitchcock's *Queen Elvis* into the deck and listened to the quiet intro to "Wax Doll" as I poured myself two fingers of Grand-Dad. I brought the shot glass to my lips and with closed eyes tasted sweet velvet.

I opened my eyes to a shock of cold air and a memory fifteen years old. Billy Goodrich glided across the dark room and had a seat at the bar.

"Hey, Greek," he said. "Aren't you gonna' offer me a drink?"

TWO

THE FIRST TIME I met Billy Goodrich he was sitting on a wooden bench in Sligo Creek Park, rolling a huge spliff with the care and precision of an artisan. This was in the fall of my junior year, and my first semester at Blair High in Silver Spring. My grandfather had used a Maryland relative's address to get me in, alarmed as he was at my subpar sophomore performance in the D.C. public school system.

Billy yelled, "Hey, Greek," and I did a double take, surprised that one of the more popular students even knew who I was. "Come on over here and help me out with this number," he said.

We split the joint (the handshake of my generation) and then laughed awhile over nothing. After that we played one-on-one at the park courts for the rest of the afternoon and our friendship, with the uncluttered reasoning that accompanies those years, was sealed.

Billy Goodrich was one of the better-liked kids in school, though not for the usual reasons. He wasn't the best-looking or most athletic guy; neither was he the friendly intellectual who even the most brutal students grudgingly learn to respect. What he had was that rare ability to fit in at the fringe of every group—hippies, grits, geeks, jocks—without conforming to their constrictively rigid codes of behavior and dress. He did it with an infectious smile and a load of self-confidence that bordered on, but never slipped into, conceit. As I had always hung with Jews and Italians and other Greeks, he was also the first truly white-bread friend I had ever had.

The details of those years are unimportant and certainly not unusual. Billy had a '69 Camaro (the last year that car made any difference) with a 327 under the hood and Hi-Jackers in the rear. There was a Pioneer eight-track mounted under the AM radio and two Superthruster speakers on the rear panel. On weekend nights we drank Schlitz from cans and raced that car up and down University Boulevard and Colesville Road, trolling for girls and parties. On the nights when we got too drunk the cops would pull us over and, in those days, simply tell us to get on home. Our friends enacted roughly the same ritual, and amazingly none of us died.

I had part-time work as a stock boy, but on the days I had off, Billy and I shot hoops. Every Saturday afternoon we'd blow a monster joint, then head down to Candy Cane City in Rock Creek Park and engage in pickup games for hours on end. The teams always ended up being "salt and pepper," and the losers did push-ups. Billy had a cheap portable eight-track player, and on those rare occasions when we'd win, he would blast J Geils's "Serve You Right to Suffer" over the bobbing heads of the losing team. Eventually our overconfidence (and the desire to unearth the wet treasures that simmered beneath the red panties of our Blazer cheerleading squad) pushed us to try out for the varsity team, but Billy didn't have the heart and I, in truth, lacked the ability. The day we were cut we walked the path in the park and, with laughter and some degree of relief, split a bumper of beer and huffed half a pack of Marlboros.

After graduation Billy, who had already been accepted to an out-of-state school, took a construction job, and I continued to work as a stock boy at Nutty Nathan's on Connecticut Avenue. The prospect of another humid season carrying air conditioners up and down stairs was upon me, so when a customer I had befriended offered me the opportunity to tow his ski boat down to the Keys for two hundred bucks, I accepted. Billy's construction job was kicking his ass so he asked to come along. I secured a leave of absence from Nathan's with the help of my friend and mentor Johnny McGinnes; Billy simply quit. We made plans to stay in D.C. through the Fourth of July and leave the following day.

The summer of '76 was not just the tail end of my childhood, a fact of which even then I was vaguely aware, but also the end of an optimistic era for an entire generation. The innocence of marijuana had not yet, to use the most emblematic example, become the horror of cocaine, and the economic and political emergence of minorities hadn't yet been crushed by the moral bankruptcy of the Reagan years. But our Bicentennial celebration reflected none of this, and what I witnessed on Independence Night was simply the most spectacular party ever thrown in downtown D.C.

The next day Billy and I prepared to leave. We attached a hitch to his car (mine, a '64 Valiant with push-button transmission on the dash, never would have made it), changed his oil, and filled up the tape box. The tapes we were to return to most were Lou Reed's *Sally Can't Dance* (I can't hear "Kill Your Sons" now without the druggy heat of that summer burning through my memory), Robin Trower's *Twice Removed from Yesterday*, Bowie's *Station to Station*, Hendrix's mind-blowing *Axis: Bold as Love*, and the debut from Bad Company. We cut the black BAD CO. logo off that tape's carton and glued it, facing out, on the Camaro's windshield, to let any doubters know just who we were. There was also the odd business of a plastic grenade hung from the rearview, and a new bumper sticker that read MOTT THE HOOPLE: TELL CHUCK BERRY THE NEWS. For recreation we had copped, from Johnny McGinnes, an ounce of Mexican, a vial filled to the lid with black beauties, and half a dozen tabs of purple haze; there were also several packs of Marlboros scattered on the dash. We were eighteen years old and certain that the world's balls were in our young hands.

And so we took off. We put together four hundred dollars between us, and our plan was to travel around the South until the money ran out. Billy picked me up, and my grandfather stood and watched us from the front of our apartment house, tight-lipped and with his hands dug deep into his pockets, until we were out of sight. His shoulders were hunched up, and he grew smaller in the rearview as we headed down the block.

A half hour later we had secured the Larson on the hitch of the Camaro and said good-bye to the surprisingly trusting owner of the boat. We stopped once more for a cold six-pack, got on the Capital Beltway, and headed for 95 South.

That night we pulled into Virginia Beach and crashed at the place of a friend who was working in a pizza parlor for the season. In the grand tradition of resort employee living quarters, there were several burnouts staying in his two-room flat, where pot was always lit and the TV and stereo were always competing in loud unison. Since there were no cooking facilities, I can only guess that these guys ate pizza the entire summer. The decor consisted of a fisherman's net tacked to the wall (during our stay someone had hung a dead sea bass in its webbing) and a bright green carpet, which was stained alternately with puke and bong water. The next day we swam and then in the early evening Billy and I each ate a tab of purple haze and bought tickets to the B. B. King show at the local civic auditorium. We arrived and found we were the youngest and most sloppily dressed in the mostly black crowd of oldish fans, some of whom were sweating through their three-piece suits and evening dresses in the liquid heat. I began to get off on the acid during a tune where Mr. King sang, with his hands off Lucille and one fist clenched, "I asked my baby for a nickel / She gave me a fifty-dollar bill / I asked my baby for a sip of whiskey / She gave me the whole gotdamn still." Billy and I smoked joints for the rest of the show to notch us down, and the folks around us were all quite happy to join in. I kept a log on that trip, in which I critiqued B. B. King's performance in the following manner: he had "turned that shit out." Afterward a bespectacled guy wearing khaki shorts and a pith helmet accompanied us as we wandered from one late-night establishment to the next, fluorescently lit cafés that were indistinguishable in that they glowed and buzzed with identical intensity. We lost our friend sometime before dawn and ended up on the beach for what I thought was the most blazingly orange sunrise I had ever seen. Billy was sleeping by then, with his face in the sand, and I watched his body twitch as a deerfly continually had its way with his leg. I never once thought to brush it away.

We slept that morning and, after stopping to say goodbye to our host (he was scarfing down a slice of pizza as he waved us off), headed south. The drive lasted into the evening and ended when we pulled into a motel called the Pennsylvania on Twenty-first Street in Myrtle Beach, South Carolina. We hung out on the beach and swam the next two days in the piss-warm wavelets of the Atlantic. On the second night we felt rejuvenated enough to party and returned to it with a vengeance. By the time we got to the Spanish Galleon, the resort's most popular nightclub, which was packed with raucous innocents (in a way that only Southern bars can be), Billy and I were raped on beer and tequila and determined to score. We had by now developed a contest involving the number of women we could rack up on the trip (Billy dubbed it our "cock test"), and I immediately crossed a busy concrete dance floor where college kids were doing the shag to Chairman of the Board's "Give Me Just a Little More Time," and proceeded to slip my tongue into the mouth of a hideous but willing biker queen who had been standing by herself. From out of the corner of my eye I could see Billy laughing as I rolled my tongue in her cankerous orifice, and now, with spiteful determination, I led her out to the beach for the long walk down to the surf where I "made love" to her near the breakers. After I came in her doughy box her face changed from the merely ugly to the truly frightening, and when she demanded that I "fuck" her again, I obeyed, her oily black hair buried in the sand by my dutiful thrusts. Somehow I lost her in the Galleon and hitched to the motel, where an unrelenting Billy was waiting for me with an evil grin. For the next three days he teased me about the clap (and every time I urinated I could hear his laughter outside the bathroom door), but miraculously it didn't surface, and the next morning, my head pounding and down in disgust, we left Myrtle and continued south.

Our next stop was Charleston, the Jewel of the South, which at first glance promised to be a genteel blend of white-gloved belles and dripping cypress. We planned to visit Billy's friend Dan Ballenger, who for reasons I can't recall was nicknamed and preferred to be called Pooter. Pooter was an amiable squid who lived off base in a decaying suburb of the city. Pooter's cottage was small and not even air-conditioned with window shakers, so there was little else to do in that oppressive heat but lie around on his sticky green vinyl furniture and do bong hits while watching the Summer Olympics. This was the year the young man from Palmer Park took the gold medal in boxing, and I cannot remember anytime being quite so proud to carry the label of Washingtonian. On the second night of our stay Pooter took us to a shotgun shack of a bar on the edge of town where aggressively plain girls were employed to wear negligees and con the customers into buying them seven-dollar wine coolers. One of them, an emaciated, pimply little teenager, sat on my lap and then got pissed when I refused to step up for the drink. By now Pooter was nervous, as there were several sinewy, long-haired types scattered around the place who looked more than happy to dispatch wiseasses such as us. Billy made a point of finding the owner and telling him what a "classy place" he had, and that was when we all decided it was time to go. In the car Billy and I ate two more tabs of haze and drove to a Piggly Wiggly, where we stole a watermelon from the outdoor rack and, as a startlingly quick clerk chased us on foot, peeled out of the parking lot and into the thick night. The watermelon was as warm as the air and we dumped it after a disappointing taste. Then we found a movie theater and bought tickets to *The Outlaw Josie Wales*. After Joseph Bottoms's wonderfully acted death scene—"I was prouder than a game rooster to have ridden with ye, Josie"—I remember very little, since the acid kicked in and I focused, for the remainder of the film, on the colorful, dust-filled tubes of light that traveled from the projector to the screen. When the film ended we drove to the Battery, which seemed to be the only spot in Charleston that carried a breeze, and got high, and talked with a young man named Spit who claimed he didn't care for "ofay motherfuckers" but had no problem with smoking their weed. The whole time we were doing this, Pooter slept (I still don't know how) in the backseat of the Camaro, his head back between the Superthruster speakers that were now blowing thirty distorted watts of Hendrix out across the intra-coastal waterway. We slept that whole next day and, at six in the evening, said good-bye to a rather relieved-looking Pooter.

Soon after we hit the highway we agreed that we needed to clear our heads. Each of us swallowed a black beauty and then, as that cranial tingle began, we pulled over in Columbia and bought two large bottles of burgundy. After Columbia the speed tore in, and from then on it was all cigarettes, wine, open windows, and maximum volume (we blew one of the speakers that night, during Earl Slick's screaming guitar solo on Bowie's "Stay"). In Augusta we stopped for more wine, were thrown out of a rock-and-roll club for something Billy said to the doorman, then wandered into an all-black disco and danced with an amphetaminic frenzy until 3:00 A.M. (I was fairly proficient then in a jerky, popular dance called the Robot.) I drove the rest of the night, nervously picking at my thumb the entire way, which resulted in a good bit of blood on my hand by the time we reached our destination. We pulled into Atlanta at 6:30 in the morning.

The first hotel we saw was on Houston Street, and it was there, a ten-dollar-a-night wino flophouse, that we took a room. We only stayed in Atlanta a couple of days, finding it in general to be neither friendly nor safe, though I did get a date on the first night with a young, green-eyed strawberry blonde, a hawker for one of the clubs in the Underground. She had no intention of sleeping with me — she was too smart for that — but we enjoyed a quiet, air-conditioned evening together in her apartment, where she lent me the use of her blessedly clean shower. I think I reminded her of her brother from whatever small midwestern town she had mistakenly fled. The next day a junkie tried to pay Billy and me to pick up his "pharmaceutical" prescription for Quaaludes, and we came very close to doing it. We decided then to think about leaving, as our part of town was clearly no place for a couple of Yankee white boys, and of course there was the matter of the expensive boat parked in the lot behind the hotel. That night I sat almost naked in the window box of our room (the only spot that wasn't hellish), smoking cigarettes and thinking about home, while Billy stretched out in a bathtub filled with cold water. We left the next morning.

The trip to Key West was sickeningly hot and seemed to take the better part of two days. Once there, we dropped the boat off quickly to some middle-aged hippie and collected our two hundred dollars. We walked around the town but, our spirits drained, found its surreal trappings not to our mutual taste. There was a fully clothed, sun-blistered young man lying in the middle of Truman Street with pennies stuck in his eyes. That is what I remember of Key West.

An hour north on A1-A we smoked a huge, celebratory joint, which had me peaking just as we rolled onto the old Seven

Mile Bridge and gave me the most panicky few minutes I have spent on any stretch of road. Liberated from the boat, Billy's Camaro seemed to be mounted on mattress springs rather than shocks, and it was all I could do to keep the goddamn vehicle from becoming airborne as other similarly drugged and sailing individuals sped toward us, missing collision by what seemed like inches. When we got off the bridge we were both ready for a beer or two, and we stopped in Marathon at what looked to be a peaceful dive called Dave's Dockside. Never having experienced the novelty of a twenty-four-hour bar, Billy and I began a long, boozy evening in which we lost all but fifty dollars of our payoff money shooting pool. The whole thing ended around dawn when a pirate type (yes, wearing a black eye patch) took a swing at me for talking to his girlfriend. He was too drunk to connect, but suddenly our former friends all looked like bad-assed, raw-knuckled locals, and we walked out to the car and pointed it north.

After another day of hot, conversationless travel, we stopped in Daytona, for no reason other than to satisfy Billy's desire to drive his car on the beach. We checked in to a cheap motel and spent a sleepless night knocking biting, armored cockroaches the size of thumbs off our beds. After breakfast the following morning we were totally broke. We walked around and asked about work but understandably got no takers, as we were beginning to look like every other K-head biker in town. That night Billy, on sheer charm, picked up an Italian girl and got both a life-affirming blow job and a clean, cool place to sleep, while I settled for the spine-wrenching backseat of the Camaro. (For the rest of the trip Billy did not stop describing the determined look on the poor girl's face as she attempted to swallow, as he put it, "a month's worth of jizz.") The following day we half-heartedly tried to find a job in the one-hundred-and-two-degree heat, but by now we both knew it was over. Sometime after noon we simultaneously fell asleep or passed out on the sidewalk in front of a major hotel and were awakened two hours later by the cops, who threatened to book us for vagrancy unless we left town. We agreed but drove only a few blocks down the road, since at this point we had not even enough money for gas. At dinnertime I created a diversion in a convenience store by breaking a bottle of orange juice, while Billy grabbed candy bars, nuts, and several Slim Jims, and shoved them into his jeans. We ate this bounty seated at some memorial, which (we should have known) turned out to be the favorite cruising spot for Daytona's homosexuals. One of them, a birdlike boy our age who had the unfortunate, swishy mannerisms that Catskill comedians and conservative politicians so love to exploit, had a seat next to us and offered a small bit of money and a place to sleep if we cared to "indulge." We both answered with emphatic negatives, but when the kid persisted, Billy winked at me and told me to wait for him at the car. An hour later he returned with a wad of money in his fist and the explanation that he had persuaded the boy to give us a loan. When I asked him, with a smirk on my face, what he had to do to get it, Billy threw me up against the car with an explosion of fury I'd never suspected in him. We drove on and I didn't mention it again, but after that things were not quite the same between me and Billy.

There is not much to say about the next couple of days except that we found Route 10 and headed west. I do remember the surprisingly green and hilly terrain of northwestern Florida; and of the night we spent in Mobile, I have only the strange recollection of a downtown building painted black.

Sometime early in August we made it to New Orleans. I had Billy blast Robin Trower's "I Can't Wait Much Longer" ("I'll get my coat and catch a train / Make my way to New Orleans") through the speakers as we rolled into town. We chose to stay in a nine-buck-a-night cottage at a place called the Carmen D Motel on Chef Menteur Highway. The plump, elderly proprietors were rosy-cheeked and friendly, and there were chickens running around in the yard of willowy trees that the cottages surrounded. Billy and I found night work quickly on a movie theater cleaning crew. The manager of the theater was to lock us in at around midnight and let us out in the morning, but this was to last only one night. On that first night we smoked a couple of joints as soon as the owner had split and then decided, to the knowing looks and chuckles of our Mexican coworkers, that scraping chewing gum off the underside of seats just wasn't our thing. After that we resolved to stop thinking about work and simply enjoy ourselves until the money ran out. There seemed to be bars everywhere in that city, and in the next two weeks we did little more than sleep through the mornings, then spend the humid afternoons shooting pool and drinking Dixie. In one of those bars we met two sisters, older women named Viv and Julliette, who took a liking to us and then proceeded, for eighteen hours straight, to screw us raw in their respective beds. Billy had chosen Julliette (she was the better-looking of the two) but I was secretly happy to go with the redheaded Viv, who was witty and had a throaty laugh and full, buttery breasts. They had a name for that particular summer's high murder rate down there (I think they called it the Summer of Blood), but I cannot believe there is a place in this country so dedicated as New Orleans to the proposition of having fun. On our last night in town Billy caught one of the chickens in the yard, marked his leg with a twist tie, and fed him a hit of purple haze hidden in a piece of popcorn. Then we each had a tab, the end of our supply. Later, in our room, we began to trip our asses off while watching *The Wild Bunch* on our black-and-white set, howling as we mimicked the classic lines of dialogue, the images becoming progressively amorphic on the small TV screen set against the green wall, the corners of which by now had completely dissolved. On the stoop later, we sat and drank beer, chain-smoking cigarettes while talking about the road ahead. Our lone chicken was out there, traversing the yard in wild circles, wired to the hilt. Billy was distracted by this and remorseful to the point where he suggested we pack up and leave. I don't think he wanted to see that chicken dead, something that was certainly going to happen before morning. So we gassed up the Camaro, swallowed the remainder of our black beauties, and were out of New Orleans before dawn's first light. Twenty-four hours and twelve hundred miles later I was in my bed in the back room of my grandfather's apartment, and that is where I slept for the next two days.

The next week Billy reported to some ACC college in North Carolina, and I began classes at the state university shortly thereafter. We wrote a couple of letters in the fall, and then I saw him over Thanksgiving. The night we went out he was with one of his new fraternity brothers, a guy Billy called Digger Dog, and we went to a local pub where they talked about "brew" and "sport-fucking" and "DG girls" while I faded into my booth seat and got quietly drunk. High school friendships either die or continue in that crucial first semester, and ours simply didn't make it.

But none of that really matters. There is a photograph of Billy and me, taken by a tourist, that to this day is in an envelope at the bottom of my dresser. In the photograph we are sitting high up on a fire escape near Bourbon Street. Billy's hand is on my shoulder, and our hair is long and uncombed and past our shoulders, and we are both smoking cigarettes. There is that look on both of our faces, that look that almost shouts that it has all been grand and that it is never, ever going to end.

In everything that I have done since, and everything that I will ever do, there is nothing that will equal the wondrous, immortal summer that I experienced in 1976. Now Billy Goodrich had walked into my bar, fifteen years later, and brought it all back home.

THREE

HOW YOU DOIN', man?"

"Good," he said, nodding slowly as he smiled. "I'm doing good."

I stood there looking at him from behind the bar. He hadn't changed much. The blond hair was there, but it started farther back, and it was short and swept back. His face was still smooth and unlined, though there was a cool hardness now around his mouth and the edges of his azure eyes. He glanced at my shot glass, then up at me.

"Call it," I said.

"Anything in a green bottle. If you're buying."

I grabbed him a Heineken from the cooler and a Bud to go with my bourbon. Billy removed his jacket—he was wearing suspenders, a very bad sign—and folded it up on the stool to his left. Then he had a pull off the import.

"Well," I said, "you gonna tell me?"

"Tell you what?"

"How the hell you found me."

He furrowed his brow theatrically. "Who said I was looking for you? I was in the neighborhood...."

"Bullshit," I said, going over his clothing. "Guys like you are never in *this* neighborhood."

"You're right about that."

"Well?"

"I tripped over your name in the phone book, to tell you the truth." Billy paused. "I was in the market for a private investigator."

"And?"

"I called your answering service, and the girl said..."

"She's a grandmother."

"Okay, the *old lady* said I could get you down here. I was surprised she gave me the information so easily."

"She's the motherly type. Probably thought she was doing me a favor. Business has been slow, to say the least."

"Well," he said, "the whole thing was a shock to me. I mean, I ran into Teddy Ball a couple of years ago, remember him from high school?" I nodded, though I didn't really. "Anyway, he told me he heard you were some advertising bigwig for one of those electronics retailers."

"I was," I said, and let it go at that. "Now I do this."

"Hey, that's great," Billy said, in the tone of voice one uses when soothing a sensitive child. "If that's what you want, great."

"How about you, man? What are you up to?"

He shrugged with studied carelessness and said, "A little bit of everything. My Ten-Forty says I sell commercial real estate"—and here Billy winked—"but I have an interest in a couple of cash businesses in the suburbs. Restaurants, carryouts, you know what I'm saying?"

"Yeah, sure."

"Things are okay," he said, then looked at the remainder of his beer and finished it off. Billy held the bottle up. "How about another one of these Green Guys?"

I found him one and killed off the rest of my Grand-Dad, then poured myself another shot. While I did that I watched him nail half the bottle of Heineken. He looked up my way and stared at me for an uncomfortably long time.

"It's good to see you, Nicky," he said finally.

"It's good to see you too, man."

After that there was another block of silence. I had a taste of bourbon and chased it with some beer while he looked away. The music had stopped, but he was drumming his fingers on the bar. I moved down to the stereo and switched it over to WDCU, to give him something to drum about. They were playing Charlie Parker's "Lester Leaps In." When I walked back Billy was grinning. It was still an ingratiating grin but a little forced now, as if he were attempting to smile against a cold wind.

"So," he said, "I never would have figured you to end up as a detective."

"It just happened. Anyway, I'd hate to think I *ended up* as any one thing."

"You know what I mean."

"All too well. You meet somebody, right away, what's the first thing they ask you? 'What do you *do?*' I never know how to answer that. I mean, I do a lot of things. I'm a bartender, I read books, I'm a private investigator, I go to movies, I drink, I box, I listen to music, I fuck—which activity are they referring to?"

"I doubt they're referring to the last one." Billy shook his head and chuckled condescendingly. "You haven't changed one bit, man."

"Maybe," I said. "But you probably knew that. And you came down here anyway to ask for my help. Right?"

Billy finished his beer and replaced the bottle softly on the bar, then looked at me. "That's right."

"You want to talk about it?"

"I'd feel better if we went somewhere else." Billy had a look around the bar. "I mean, this place is so depressing. Don't you think it could use a few..."

"Plants?"

"Yeah, something."

"I don't know. I kind of like it the way it is."

WE WERE GLIDING NORTH on Fourteenth Street in Billy's sleek white Maxima, the glow of the dash lights rendering our complexions pale green. There was a car phone between the saddle leather buckets. The numbers on the car phone were also illuminated in green. A notepad filled with blank white paper was suctioned to the dash.

Billy had a pull off one of the road beers I had grabbed before locking up the Spot, then wedged the bottle between his thighs. I flipped through his CD selection and tried to find something listenable, but all he owned — Steve Winwood, Clapton, Phil Collins, the Who ("Hope I die before I get old," indeed — why didn't you, then?) — were forty-minute beer commercials. I closed the box and settled for the soft, intermittent rush of the Maxima's wipers.

Outside, the snow was drifting down in chunked, feathery flakes. Soft, radiant halos capped the streetlights ahead. Children were out, laughing and running on the sidewalks and in the street. One of them, a boy no older than eight who wore only a red windbreaker, threw a powdery snowball that hit our windshield and dissolved. I made a mocking fist and shook it at him as we passed, and he smiled and shook his own fist back. Billy locked the doors with a rather awkward, fumbling push of a button.

Just past Fourteenth and Irving we passed the remains of the Tivoli Theater. My grandfather had taken me there in 1963 to see *Jason and the Argonauts*, a film noted as the pinnacle of

Ray Harryhausen's work in stop-motion photography. The scene in which the skeletons come to life to do battle with Jason inspired some of the most frighteningly memorable, sheet-soaked nightmares of my childhood. The night of the film my grandfather and I had walked through a heavy snowstorm from our apartment to the theater. I can still feel the warmth of his huge and callused hand in mine as we made a path through the snow.

"Hey," Billy said. "Your papa still around?"

"*Papou*," I said. "He died a couple of years back."

"How about your folks? You ever hear from them?"

"No."

At my direction Billy pulled over and parked near the intersection of Fourteenth and Colorado. He double-checked all the locks before we headed down the block, turning his head back twice to look at the car as we walked.

"Relax, will you?"

"That's twenty-five thousand dollars' worth of car," he said. "I don't want to see it up on cinder blocks when I come out of this place."

"You worry too much," I said, but judging from the pale look on Billy's face, that bit of analysis didn't help. I pulled on the thin door and we entered Slim's.

Slim's was a small jazz-and-reggae club owned and run by a couple of East Africans, neither of whom was named Slim. At night there was always a live but unobtrusive band, and the Ethiopian food was top-notch. Slim's had a ten-dollar minimum tab, a quota I never once had trouble making, to keep out any undesirables. I stopped in once in a while on my way home and had a couple of quiet drinks at the bar while I listened to some of the cleanest jazz, mostly of the bebop variety, in town.

We crossed the room to a deuce in the back that was centered under a stylized portrait of Haile Selassie. Our waitress showed momentarily and took our order for two beers. Her name was Cissy. She was wearing a plain white T-shirt and blue jeans, and had beautifully unblemished burnt-sienna skin.

The band that night was the club's regular sextet — trumpet, sax, piano, drums, guitar, upright bass — whose members took turns soloing on practically every number. The turban-headed trumpeter was the coleader, though oddly the least talented of the group, and his partner was the saxman, an aging, bottom-heavy Greek I had seen around town who took his scotch through a straw. The youngest man of the bunch was the guitarist, and also the musician with the most potential, but obviously a heavy user. When he wasn't soloing he sat on a wooden stool with his chin on his chest, a crooked knit cap pushed over his brow, deep in his down world.

Billy and I sat through the rest of the band's set without speaking. Cissy had given us two unsolicited Jim Beam Blacks (a very smooth bourbon that is in fact too smooth for my taste) and served them in juice glasses halfway full to the lip. The band ended its set with a pumped-up version of Miles Davis's "Milestones." The young bartender put some low-volume Jamaican dub on the house stereo. Billy, who was starting to look a little pickled, leaned my way.

"Let's talk business," he said.

"All right." I pulled the deck of Camels from my overcoat and shook it in his direction. He started to reach for one but then waved it away. I slid one out, lit it, and took in a lungful.

Billy said, "I guess you've noticed the ring on my finger."

I nodded and said, "So?"

"This is about that."

"I don't tail wives or husbands anymore. I should tell you that straight up. My bartending job keeps me off that sort of thing."

"It's not what you think," he said.

"What is it then?"

"My wife has left me, Nick." Billy took the matches that rested on the top of my cigarettes and pulled one off the pack. He struck it, watched it flare, then blew it out. "She walked on her own accord. You'd call it desertion, I guess, if it was a man doing the walking."

"Kids?"

"None. We tried for a couple of years, but it wasn't in the cards."

I had a sip of bourbon then followed it with a deep drag off my cigarette. When I exhaled I blew the smoke past his head and tried not to look into his eyes. "Like you said, Bill, this is business. I'm going to ask you some questions that are personal...."

"Go ahead."

"This type of thing—and not to make it seem small—well, it happens every day. Hell, man, in a way it happened to me. So why hire a detective?"

"I'm worried about her," he said. "It's that simple. And since there's no evidence of foul play, the cops won't give it the time of day."

"You've been to them?"

"Yeah, I reported it the first day. They came around, asked me a couple of questions, I never heard from them again."

I had a last pull off my smoke and butted it. "What do you want me to do?"

"Find her, that's it. You don't even have to talk to her. Just report her location back to me, and I'll do the talking. If she doesn't want to come home, then at least I gave it a shot." Billy looked at me briefly and then looked away.

"What else?" I said.

"Like?" He nodded me on with his chin.

"Did she leave you for someone else?" Instead of answering, Billy finished the bourbon in his glass, an answer in itself. I signaled Cissy for two more. "Do you know him?" I asked.

"Yeah, I know him. He was a man I did business with." The waitress brought our Beams and two more beers. Billy and I lightly touched glasses, and I had a drink while he continued. "I met this guy as a client. I was showing him around town, some spots for a chain of carryouts he was thinking of opening. Anyway, I did him a couple of serious solids in terms of negotiating leases, that sort of thing. He liked my style, and he put me on the payroll of his corporation in a retainer capacity."

"You kept your job with the real estate company?"

"Yes."

"Kind of a conflict of interest there, wasn't it?"

"It depends on how you look at things, I suppose. I've learned some very creative ways of putting deals together, and I guess Mr. DiGeordano didn't want me doing that for anyone else but him."

"Joey DiGeordano?"

"That's right."

I whistled softly. "You got yourself pretty connected, didn't you, Bill?"

"You've heard of him, then."

"I read the paper," I said, leaving out the fact that my grandfather had known the old man. "The DiGeordanos have been in it once or twice through the years. They're what passes for a small-time crime family in this town. Nothing serious, by today's standards—a little gambling, some Jewish Lightning in the old days."

"I'm aware of those things," he mumbled.

"Keep going," I said.

"April and I—April, that's my wife's name—we socialized with Joey and his wife a few times early on. Right from the beginning I could see Joey had the eye for April. But that didn't bother me much. I mean, I was used to it. April is a very good-looking woman."

"Did they have an affair?"

"I can't prove it if they did," he said. "Let's say it was a suspicion I had."

"What was your relationship like when she left?"

"I thought it was good. We had our problems, but in general I was pretty content. And I was willing to work at it, that's the thing. Then I came home one day and she was just gone. Her closet was emptied and there was a note, and that was that."

"When was that?" I asked.

"A week ago yesterday," he said. "Wednesday."

"Anything unusual about the note?"

Billy considered that. "It came off a printer. I guess that's unusual, huh? A typed Dear John."

"Any idea why?"

"She ran the thing off on my computer. That was always a sticking point with her—I'd come home from work and immediately get on my computer and start running spreadsheets and figures. I guess I was pretty obsessed with making it and all that. Anyway, she certainly thought so. And the note was just her way of twisting the knife."

I thought that over and said, "What about Joey DiGeordano? Are you still doing business with him?"

Billy said, "Our business relationship has become strained. I can't exactly talk to him about it, even though I think he might have some idea where she is. That's where you come in."

I lit another cigarette and exhaled a thin gray veil that settled between us. "I'll need to know a few things about your wife. Her history, family, that sort of thing. A recent picture."

"Then you'll help me."

I nodded and said, "Yeah."

"Thanks, Nick." Billy shook my hand and held it for more than a few seconds. His felt cool. "I want you to understand that I didn't come to you for any friendship deals."

"There won't be any," I said. "I get two-fifty a day plus expenses, with a day's worth up front."

"No problem." A few strands of his moussed hair had fallen across his forehead, and he brushed it back. "Listen, man, I'm a little drunk right now."

"Me too," I admitted.

"Anyway," he said, "it's as good a time as any to apologize for all the years that went by. The thing is, Nick, I think of life as being more...linear than you do, you know what I mean? High school, college, career, marriage, family, retirement—and

I have no trouble leaving the last phase behind me when I start a new one. Anyway, when I went away to school, I could see you just weren't going to come along. I just don't want you to think I forgot about you, man. I never did."

"Don't worry about it," I said. "You're calling it straight. That's exactly the way it was."

The band was gathering for their next set. Billy reached for his wallet and said, "Come on, let's get out of here. I've had enough."

"You go on," I said. "I only live a couple of blocks away. I'll walk home."

"You sure?"

"Yeah."

Billy shrugged and left a twenty on the table. I let him do it and watched him button his coat. "I'll courier all that stuff to you tomorrow."

"Send it here," I said, and we traded business cards. His said WILLIAM GOODRICH.

"Thanks again, Nick."

I nodded and he walked away. As I watched him cross the room, I felt an odd sadness, that sense of irrevocable loss one feels upon seeing a friend who has changed so drastically over so many years. I recognized the feeling as little more than a burst of self-pity for my own youth, a youth that had quietly slipped away. But the recognition in itself didn't seem to help.

He was right when he said that I had chosen not to come along, but it was not really something I was sorry for. He had become that characterless, you-can-have-it-all predator that was everything I had come to hate. But somewhere in that cadaver was the long-haired kid who had called out to me one day in the park, and now he was calling out again. William Goodrich had hired me, but it was for Billy that I was taking the case.

I had another bourbon while I watched the last set, then settled up my tab. Out on the sidewalk, I tucked a scarf into my black overcoat and weaved north. The branches of the trees were heavy with powder, and the streets were still. The snow was ending, but its last flakes were still visible in the light of the street lamps. The snow made a sound like paper cutting skin as it fell. Tomorrow there would be a quick melt and a nightmare rush hour, a city of horns and tight neckties. But tonight D.C. was a silent, idyllic small town.

I turned the corner of my block and saw my cat huddled on the stoop of my apartment. I watched her figure slip down and cross the yard, a ball of black moving across a white blanket. Her grainy nose touched the fingertips of my outstretched hand.

FOUR

F RIDAY AFTERNOON'S LUNCH had been typically hectic.

Our regulars had arrived early, shuffling in and nodding hello with pleading doe eyes while I hurriedly sliced fruit and tossed bleach tablets into the rinse sink. The patrons were eager to start their weekend binges. Darnell's Fish Platter, a house favorite, began to get a lot of action, and at one point he was sliding the plates onto the platform of the reach-through faster than I could serve them. Ramon was lurking around somewhere, but, having blown a stick of sensimillion in the basement just before opening time, he was virtually useless.

That, however, had been the easy part of my day. When the rush ended I was left to baby-sit those few drinkers who had decided, as early as their first beer, not to return to work. Today this group of geniuses included Happy, who in his perfect world would someday be buried with one hand rigor mortised into a glass-holding C, the other in a horizontal victory sign, the fingers spread just wide enough to accommodate a Chesterfield; Buddy and Bubba, today arguing about boxing (confusing it with bullying) and splitting a pitcher with such intense closeness that they appeared to be joined at the hip; an alcoholic Dutch secretary named Petra for whom we exclusively stocked Geneve, a syrupy gin that was rumored to have the power to induce hallucinations; and, least tolerable of all, a fat federal judge by the name of Len.

The fact that Len Dorfman was a federal judge is a point worth mentioning only in relation to his repulsive personality. Len would swagger in after a tough morning on the bench, announce to our deaf ears that he had just "worked out" at the gym (I would wager any amount that he could not, if a gun were to be placed in his mouth, execute one sit-up), and order a Grand Marnier because, he claimed, he had "earned" it. After one snifter he would check over the clientele and begin to brag about all the "savages" he had put away that morning, adding with bluster that he had "thrown away the key." Then, like some third-rate Don Rickles ("Hey, if we can't make fun of ourselves, who can we make fun of?"), he would launch into his "I'm a cheap Jew" routine, a tired shtick that had everyone at the bar staring into their drinks in embarrassment. The fact that Len himself was Jewish made it, contrary to his belief, no less offensive. Finally, after his third round, he would begin to trash gays with a lispy, plump-mouthed imitation so filled with vicious self-hatred that there was no doubt in anyone's mind that Len was a man who had, on several occasions and probably in some bathroom stall in our very hallowed halls of justice, fallen to his soft knees and, with a fervor equal in enthusiasm to his flamboyant bar soliloquies, sucked cock.

He was doing that imitation when Dan Boyle walked into the bar. Boyle hated Dorfman, not for his ignorant slurs (they shared roughly the same prejudices) but for what he perceived to be Len's soft stance on criminals. Dorfman knew it and consequently settled up quietly and exited the Spot. The customers, even Happy, gave Boyle a round of applause.

I did my part and had a mug of draught in front of Boyle before his ass spread over the wood of his barstool. His eyes traveled up and lit on the stack of shot glasses. I separated the top one from the stack and set it next to his mug. Then I poured two inches of Jack Daniels into the glass.

"This one's on the house."

"You're the greatest," Boyle said.

"You Irish boys get so sentimental about your bartenders."

"Leave me alone. It's been a bad fuckin' day."

"Out on those mean streets, you mean?"

"Go ahead and laugh. After you walk a mile in my shoes."

"'Walk a Mile in My Shoes'?" I said. "Joe South, nineteen-sixty-nine."

"Huh?"

"Forget it."

I heard a sharp whistle and turned. Petra had done the whistling and now she was, with a perfectly angelic smile and the middle finger of her left hand pointed straight at the ceiling, flipping me off. Though she surely knew the meaning of that most universal symbol, some joker had convinced her one night that, in Washington's bars, this was also an accepted method of ordering a quick drink.

Boyle said, "I think that Dutch broad needs another hit."

I poured her a short one and while I was on that end drew a fresh pitcher for Buddy and Bubba. Buddy was a sawed-off little guy, and even while sitting straight, his wide shoulders barely cleared the lip of the bar. Now he was slouched and his blond head seemed to be sprouting directly up out of the mahogany. I placed the pitcher in front of that head. He nodded and then growled.

I changed all the full ashtrays into empties and moved back down to Boyle. He had taken off his overcoat and beneath that was wearing an old tweed with suede patches sewn on the elbows. As he turned to fold his coat on the adjacent barstool, I could see the bulge of his Colt Python protruding from the small of his back. I slid him another mugful of draught and washed out the empty in the soap sink.

"I checked into that thing for you," Boyle said.

"William Henry?"

"Yeah."

"What's happening?"

"Nothing, really. No new leads, not since the initial investigation."

"What do you think?" I said.

Boyle had a long drink from his mug, then wiped his mouth with the sleeve of his sport coat. "It's not in my jurisdiction," he said. "I only looked at the jacket last night."

"At a glance, then."

"At a glance? Your friend probably knew his attacker. There weren't any signs of forced entry. He had solid dead bolts on the door and an auxiliary lock; none of the jams were splintered. The ME's report said he was stabbed over twenty times with a serrated knife, like the kind your buddy Darnell uses in his kitchen. Henry was probably dead or in shock before the guy was finished knifing him."

"What does all that mean?"

"It could mean a lot of things. The intent was clear—he didn't want to wound Henry, he wanted him dead. It could have been a drug deal gone bad. Or it was a crime of passion. You know, a homo burn."

"A homo burn?" I frowned. "Come on, Boyle, what the hell is that?"

"We explore every possibility, Nick. That building he lived in, it had a history of homosexual tenants."

I sighed and drummed my fingers on the bar. "Keep going."

Boyle pointed to his empty shot glass. I reached behind me to the second row of call, grabbed the black-labeled bottle of Jack, and poured him some sour mash. He sipped it, chased it with some draught. "The main point I got out of the report, the angle I'd go for if I was looking into it, was how he got past the security guard in the lobby." Boyle winked. "That's, like I say, if I was going to look into it."

"What was the security guard's name, Boyle? The one that was on duty."

"I'll deny this if it ever gets out." I nodded and looked around the bar. Our regulars were drinking peacefully. A couple of them had solemnly closed their eyes and were mouthing the words to Joe Jackson's version of "What's the Use of Getting Sober? (When You're Gonna Get Drunk Again)" as it came through the speakers. Boyle said, "James Thomas."

I wrote down the name and said, "Any progress on the case?"

Boyle snorted and closed his eyes slowly as he sipped from the shot glass he held in his thick hand. When he was finished he put the glass down. "A case gets cold after a few days, Nick. And there's always something else. Right now we've got hookers gettin' whacked down in the Midnight Zone. Detectives working double shifts." Boyle drained half of what was left in the mug. "The thing you got to remember is, almost one out of two homicides in the District go unsolved. Pretty good odds for the bad guys, huh? You kill someone in this town, you got a fifty percent shot at getting away with it."

"What are you saying?"

"We're never going to find that boy's killer, Nick. That's a fuckin' bet."

"Thanks for the information."

Boyle leaned in and stared hard. He was attempting to focus his jittery pale blue eyes on mine. "If you need anything else, partner, you let me know."

"I will. In the meantime, I gotta be getting out of here." I wiped the area in front of him with my bar rag. "Believe it or not, I've got a date."

"I remember those days," Boyle said. "Dates. Now all's I got is rotten screaming kids."

"There's a solution to that."

"What would that be?" he said.

"Take 'em out in the street," I said, "and shoot 'em in the head. Public fuckin' executions."

ON THE WAY HOME I stopped and picked up my package at the office of my answering service on Georgia Avenue. After that I headed west a few blocks and parked the Dodge in front of my apartment. The afternoon sun had taken care of most of the snow. What was left was gray now and in mounds near the curb. My cat ran out as I stepped along the walk. She rolled onto her back and let me scratch her stomach. As I did this her left rear paw boxed the air convulsively. When her paw stopped moving I tickled the scar tissue where her right eye had been, then entered my place.

I changed into sweat clothes while the water boiled. Then I made coffee and took the coffee and my package to a small desk I had set up in my bedroom. I opened the package and spread its contents out on the oak top.

Billy Goodrich had organized his wife's file with all the efficiency and warmth of a client's prospectus. There was a cover letter and a photograph that appeared to have been professionally taken. I tacked that one to the bulletin board that hung over my desk. I glanced over the rest of the material—family and medical history, doctors, a résumé—and placed it back in the package.

After that I drove west and met Rodney White at a junior high gymnasium in upper Northwest. I did ten sets of abs and several sets of lat and tricep push-ups, then jumped rope while he taught his class. When he had dismissed his students we put on our sparring equipment and went to it.

"Move to the side, Home," Rodney said after I had taken a particularly vicious flurry of punches and squared off in front of him. "Just slide over, man, then make your move." He demonstrated, suddenly springing to the left, throwing mock jabs to my kidneys. I was facing away from him.

"What about doing that Hemingway thing, standing in there, going toe-to-toe?"

"Only in gladiator movies, Nick."

We sparred for another fifteen minutes, until my hands became too heavy to hold up in front of my face. Rodney White removed his mouthpiece and rubbed it dry on the arm of his gi.

"All right, that ought to do you for tonight." He pulled a towel from his bag and wiped the sweat from his forehead. "Say," he said. "Been a while since you've been in to see me, for a checkup."

I pulled out my own mouthpiece. A string of bloody saliva ran from the side of it and clung to my mouth. "A checkup?" I said, fighting for some air. "Doctor, I believe I could use one. Right about now."

A HALF HOUR LATER I was back in my apartment. I threw my wet clothes into the hamper, showered, shaved, dressed in a rented monkey suit, and fed and watered the cat. I got into my black forty-dollar Robert Hall overcoat and slipped a fresh deck of Camels into its breast pocket. Then I locked my apartment, ignitioned my Dodge Dart, and went to pick up Jackie.

JACKIE KAHN LIVED IN a two-bedroom condo with her lover, a woman named Sherron, in a three-story building on the edge of Kalorama. The D.C. guidebooks all claim that Kalorama means "beautiful view," from the Greek *kalo*. Not to split hairs, but *kalo* is actually the Greek word for "good." The word for beautiful is, phonetically, *orayo*, but I would never lobby for the change—Orayorama sounds a little like the gimmick for a fifties horror movie.

Jackie's building was an elaborate Grecian knockoff with egg-and-tongue molding that ran below the roofline, with an urn pediment centered above the stone portico. It was quite regal, and I supposed she was paying for it. I entered an unlocked set of glass doors and pushed her buzzer. After the usual formalities I made it through the second set of doors and took the gated, open lift to her floor.

Sherron opened the door on my first knock. She was wearing winter white pleated slacks and a black sweater with black buttons sewn along the top of the shoulder. On the front of the sweater hung a necklace of spheres that may or may not have been made of gold and that grew progressively larger as they converged at the center. She was taller than me and had wonderfully long legs, and in total she had the build of a Thoroughbred. I had seen reasonably intelligent men commit public stupidities in her presence.

"Can Jackie come out and play?"

"Come on in," she said in an accent laced with Puerto Rican.

"Thanks." I kissed her hello and caught the edge of her ripe mouth. She frowned and led me through a marble foyer to an airy living room painted primarily in lavender. There was a fire burning in a marble-manteled fireplace that was centered in the west wall.

"You look different dressed up," she said, her idea of a compliment. "Have a seat and I'll fix you a drink. Jackie will be out in a few minutes."

"Bourbon rocks," I said. Sherron left the room, and I watched her do it. After a few minutes she came back in and placed a tumbler filled with bourbon whiskey and cubes on a cork coaster edged with a silver ring. I had a long pull, tasted Wild Turkey, and set the glass back down on the tumbler. Sherron had a seat on the divan against the wall across from my chair. She looked me over as if I were a marked-down dress, then crossed one lovely leg over the other.

"So," she said. "Been peeping in any windows lately?"

"It's very pane-full." I drew out the last word so she could get it, but humor wasn't her shtick. In fact I had never seen her smile. I lit a cigarette because I knew she didn't like it and child-ishly bounced the match off the side of the crystal ashtray that was next to the coaster. Some smoke drifted her way and she made a small wave of her long, thin hand, like she was shaking off a bug. Mercifully, that was when Jackie walked into the room.

She was wearing an above-the-knee black evening dress with multicolored Mylar buttons down the front and gold piping around the neckline. Above the curve of the neckline was the top of her firm cleavage, the ridge of her sternum, and the tightly muscled traps of her shoulders. She had on patterned black stockings, and on the ends of those stockings were medium-heeled black pumps. There was a black patent leather belt that was tight enough to showcase her thin waist and the curve of her hips. Her black hair was swept up on one side and held in place by a thin diamond barrette. I thought I could see a bit of the flames from the fireplace reflecting off her bright brown eyes.

"How do I look?" she asked.

Sherron said, "Hot."

I said, "I'll say."

Sherron ignored that, and I finished the rest of my drink while they kissed. Sherron helped Jackie on with her cashmere coat, smoothed the front it, and walked us to the door. We said our tearful good-byes and then Jackie and I were alone and out in the hall. We walked to the elevator, called for it, and waited.

"You do look good," I said.

"So do you," she said. "You clean up very nicely."

"I don't think Sherron likes me too much."

"She's really nice, Nick. But you can lay on that Peck's Bad Boy act a little thick. And she's probably a little jealous. Wouldn't you be?"

"Yep."

The elevator arrived and we got into it. I closed the accordion gate and through it watched the marble staircase as it appeared to rise while we descended through its center.

"I used to love these things when I was a kid. The old Dupont Building, where Connecticut and Nineteenth meet at the Circle, had a gated elevator and a uniformed operator to go with it."

"Me too," she said. "I think this elevator was what closed the deal for me on this place."

"So who am I supposed to be tonight?"

"Anyone you want. Let 'em guess. These company Christmas parties get pretty rowdy, and I figured I could use an escort."

"Rowdy accountants?"

"Yeah. Once a year they're expected to cut loose."

"Sounds like my meat," I said.

"Do me a favor, Nick. Don't be an asshole."

THE PARTY WAS IN the penthouse of a new office building on the east edge of Alexandria and on the river, past National and just past Dangerfield Island. We parked Jackie's Subaru in the garage and, with a couple of foxy receptionists who had arrived at the same time, took the elevator up as far as it would go.

A mustachioed young man tediously took our coats when we stepped off the elevator. I retrieved my cigarettes and switched them to my jacket pocket, and we entered the party room. It was situated on the northeast corner of the building, and two of the walls were thick glass. The north view stretched past the lights of National to the Mall and the major monuments. The east view shot over Goose Island in the Potomac to Bolling Air Force Base and then into Anacostia and P.G. County.

The floor was shiny and veined to approximate black marble. There were several freestanding Corinthian columns scattered about the room that looked to be made of papier-mâché, their shafts painted a poinsettia red. Thick green ribbons were tied and bowed around the columns that I assumed had been rented for the affair. A swing combo situated on a narrow balcony was playing jazzy Christmas standards. The violinist had Stéphane Grappelli's style and tone down perfectly.

The room was already crowded and predominantly suited in black. Many of the men sported red bow ties with their tuxes, and most of the women were also in black, though there were a few seasonal reds and, at a glance, one blonde squeezed into gold lamé. I took Jackie's order and made a beeline for the bar.

The bar was set up in the left rear corner. As I approached it I saw the offerings grouped on the white-clothed table. The bottle with the familiar orange label, the gold lettering THE HEAD OF THE BOURBON FAMILY, and the gold oval-framed granite bust in the center that had a fitting resemblance to both LBJ and Buddy Ebsen was right out front, in all its eighty-six-proof Kentucky glory. I stood behind the other kids in line and waited my turn.

"Yes, sir?" asked a built brunet as I stepped up to the table. She had on a tuxedo shirt and a turquoise tie that was close to the color of the lenses in her wicked eyes.

"A vodka tonic, please. And an Old Grand-Dad, rocks."

She marked me with one long motherly look and poured our drinks. There was a pitcher set next to the bottles that was half filled with one dollar bills, probably her own. Good bartenders always place a tip receptacle on the bar and start it off with their own money. Wish fulfillment. I put two of mine in the pitcher, she thanked me with a wink, and I rejoined Jackie.

Jackie was with a tall man, and they were laughing about something as I handed over her drink. He was close to my age and his face was boyish, but his hair was steel gray. Two pieces of it, like the tines of a grilling fork, had fallen over his forehead, giving him the reckless look of, say, a young millionaire who raced cars.

"Nicky, this is John Wattersly. John, my friend Nick Stefanos."

We sized each other up and shook hands. "Good to meet you, Nick," he said in a smooth baritone.

"Same here."

"John's a senior," Jackie offered.

"Really," I said. "When do you graduate?"

Wattersly laughed and then showed me a warm smile that had probably opened plenty of doors for him during his climb. He seemed intelligent but not arrogant, and I sort of liked him, but he was certainly turning that smile in Jackie's direction an awful lot.

Jackie said, "I meant he's a senior manager. He's on his way to partner."

"I knew that, sweetheart," I said, and kissed her on the cheek as I squeezed her arm. Mine was now around her shoulder.

The next time Wattersly turned his head, Jackie ground the stiletto heel of her pump into the toe area of my shoe. The pain ricocheted off my Achilles tendon, sped up my calf, and watered my eyes. By the time Wattersly faced me again I had released Jackie and was wiping my face with a handkerchief.

"What do you do, Nick?" he said.

"International finance," I said.

"Interesting work. Who are you with?"

"Fitzgerald and O'Malley," I said, digging my grave as I pulled two names out of the air and stared at my shoes. "Gold bars, bullion, currency exchange." I winked. "That sort of thing."

I gulped half my drink as Wattersly winked back.

The evening continued to degenerate along those lines, but happily I was not alone. These accountants and their dates were certainly not averse to having a good time. Someone pulled the plug on the Christmas combo early on, and a boom box was set up, and everything from Motown to Springsteen to Depeche Mode began to turn the place on. There were also several art director types flitting about who, I was later informed, were members of the firm's in-house advertising department. Their leader was a popinjay who had grown his hair in front of his face precisely so that he could shake it out of that smug face with a casual toss of his head; he was running about the room taking clever Polaroids of the accountants whom he obviously thought he was so far above. After my fourth trip to the bar, I decided that it was a wonderful party and these were all very nice people and I was perhaps the wittiest individual in the room.

My responses to that ice-breaking question "What do you do?" began to range from the unlikely to the absurd. To Jackie's boss I was a university professor who was teaching a course this semester entitled Existentialism and Top 40. I explained that the course placed a special emphasis on the works of Neil Diamond (just "Neil!" to his legion of fans) and to his perplexed expression contended that "I Am...I Said" was one of the most deceptively simple yet brilliant songs of the last twenty years. To another executive I made the ridiculous claim to being the sole heir to the WHAM-O fortune. And to shut down a guy who would not stop talking to me about his son's high school football program, I proudly proclaimed, with a subtle flutter of my eyes, that I was studying to be a male nurse, explaining that I had chosen the profession "for the uniforms."

Late in the evening I followed the stunning blonde in the gold lamé dress to an area near the glass wall. One of my new accountant buddies had explained, with a remorseful shrug, that she was "with" one of the senior partners, a fact that may have frightened off most of the martinets in attendance but at this point did not affect me. When she was alone I touched her on the arm and she turned.

"Hi," I said.

"Hello," she said evenly, with the weary resistance born in beauties like her. Her push-up bra had set her lightly freckled, perfectly rounded breasts to a point where they touched and hung like trophies on the edge of her low-cut gown. She had a mane of wheat hair and a black mole above her arched lip. In the midsixties I had experienced one of my first erections while admiring such a mole on Anne Francis's lip during an episode of "Honey West," though at the time I did not even possess the beneficial knowledge of self-relief.

"I'm not an accountant," I said, and hit my bourbon. By

now I had forgone the ice, which was taking up far too much room in the glass.

"Really," she declared aridly. "What are you, then?"

"A mole," I said, still watching her lip. "I mean, as in spy. I was sent by an industrial espionage firm to infiltrate this party."

She caught the reptilian gleam of my eye. "Don't even think about it," she said, without the barest trace of levity, "unless you are a mole who happens to be very, very wealthy." Then she walked to the glass and turned her back to me, sipping her drink as she took in the view.

I was studying the arrogant little ball of her calf and the manner in which her dress was painted onto her luscious championship ass when Jackie walked over and stood by my side. Thankfully she was smiling.

"What's slithering around in that mind of yours right now?" she asked.

"The truth?" I said.

She nodded. "Yeah."

"I was thinking how, right now, I'd like to see her place her palms on that glass and lean over just a bit. How I'd lift up that dress, lift it with my forearms as my hands slid up the back of those tanned thighs. How I'd pull down those sweet panties, put one of my hands on the glass for support, and the other on her fine ass. How I'd enter that moist mound, not too gently mind you, hard enough to see her bite down on her lip and shut her eyes, shut her eyes slowly and peacefully like some Disney deer." I gulped some bourbon, rocked back on my heels, and exhaled. "So, in answer to your question, I was just thinking what I'd do with that if I had the chance. What were you thinking?"

"Same thing, brother," Jackie said with a low, sinister chuckle. "Different method."

ON THE WAY HOME Jackie and I stopped at Rio Loco's, a neighborhood Tex-Mex bar at Sixteenth and U and found a couple of stools in the back near the juke. Lou Reed's "Vicious" was just ending. Our blue-jeaned waitress set down a juice glass that contained two inches of Grand-Dad, and a mug of coffee for Jackie. We tapped receptacles and sipped our respective poisons.

"You mad at me?" I asked.

"Uh-uh. You were a hit tonight. A bunch of my friends asked me about you."

"Sorry about the kiss. The weird thing was, when Smiley was coming on to you, I was jealous."

"You're loaded," she said flatly. "So don't start analyzing things, not tonight."

"Right." I winked and had another taste. The juke was now playing "A Whiter Shade of Pale."

"There must be something missing in your life," she said, avoiding my eyes. "I mean there must be a reason why you drink like you do."

"Christ, Jackie, not now. There's work time and there's drinking time." I raised my glass. "Okay?"

"Yeah. Sorry. But I want to talk to you about something, something really important."

"Sure," I said, and put a cigarette in my mouth. Jackie lit a match, and I pulled her hand in until the flame touched the tobacco. I blew the match out with my exhale. "Let's talk."

"Not tonight. It's too important, like I said. I want your head to be clear when we discuss it."

"When, then?"

"You free for dinner Sunday night?"

"I guess so."

"Good," she said. "I'll pick you up at eight."

I KISSED JACKIE GOOD night and climbed into my icy Dart. It started after a few attempts and I pointed it northwest. There wasn't much action on the streets except for other drunks and cops too warm in their cars to bother. I parked in front of Lee's apartment building and listened to "Cemetry Gates" on the radio until it was finished. Then I ran across the hard frozen ground to her stairwell and rang her buzzer.

After what seemed like a very long while her door opened. She was wearing a brown-and-green flannel shirt and, from what I could tell, little else. She began to shiver as soon as the door was open. I had woken her up and she wasn't smiling. Her very green eyes had picked up the green off the shirt.

"Aren't you going to ask me in?" My tongue was thick and I was leaning on the door frame for support.

"It's late, Nick. I've got a final tomorrow."

"I'm sorry, Lee." I smiled hopelessly and felt my upper lip stick clumsily to my front teeth. "I thought..."

"I know what you thought," she said in a low voice that began to build. "There's lipstick on your cheek, hard liquor on your breath, it's three o'clock in the morning, and you've got a hard-on. You *thought* you'd slide on in here and relieve yourself, that's what you thought. Well, think about this. You mean something to me, Nick, in a strange way, but the next time you disrespect me like this, it's going to be the last time. Understand?"

Before I could tell her that I certainly did, the door was closing with a thudding finality. I stared at it for a minute and then walked back to my car. I drove around the corner to May's on Wisconsin where my bookie friend Steve Maroulis let me in the bar entrance. We had a nightcap together under the cruel lights of last call. I asked him a couple of questions about local gambling and wrote down the answers so I wouldn't have to ask him again. I think I downed another drink while he closed up and did the paperwork. It wasn't until the next morning, when I awoke fully clothed on a made bed, that I realized I had driven myself home.

FIVE

HERE WAS A story that used to be told around town concerning my grandfather and Lou DiGeordano that almost attained the status of local folklore, until the men telling it began to die off and it began to die off with them.

My grandfather, Nicholas ("Big Nick") Stefanos, came to this country from a village in Sparta just after World War I, leaving behind his wife and young son. Like almost three quarters of Sparta's male population in those years, he came to America to make a quick fortune and to escape the horrible rural poverty that resulted from the new government's disorder and indifference after the Greek War of Independence. He had every good intention of returning to Sparta, but as it happened his wife died from tuberculosis and his son was raised by relatives in the village. His son eventually married another young woman in the village and out of that union I was born. My parents sent me to the States at a very early age with the intention of joining me in a year or two, but again, as things happen, they never made it. Consequently I was raised by my grandfather in D.C. Having never known my parents, I can almost truly say that I've never missed them, though I'm sure some eager psychiatrist could bleed me dry with a lifetime of sessions and related explanations as to why I've become this person that I have.

Big Nick spent Prohibition living with relatives and driving a bootlegger's truck in upstate New York. I imagine he was also some sort of a strong-arm man, as he had the bulk, and I've heard several old-timers claim that he was quick with his clubbish hands. He himself told me, without remorse and in fact with a bit of light in his eyes, that he had done some "bad things" in those years to get by. I know he packed a pistol; an Italian .22 had blown up in his face around that time and given him a lifelong scar on his cheek, which explained his fondness for American firearms, witnessed by the fact that he carried a pearl-handled .38 Smith & Wesson in his jacket pocket until he died. There is a photograph of him in my possession that says more about those years than he ever could. He is in a dark, wide-lapelled pinstriped suit, and he's wearing a wide-brimmed hat. The hat is pulled down over one eye. There is a young blonde wearing a floral-print dress in the edge of the photograph, obviously an American woman, and she is looking up at him and laughing. It's easy to guess from his cocksure grin why that young man never returned to the village.

But something, some trouble maybe, made Big Nick decide to drift south and end up, with relatives again, in Southeast Washington in the thirties. He had brought some cash with him, and the cash staked him in a vegetable stand in the old Southeast Market. His life here was more austere, though reportedly he was a heavy drinker and enjoyed fairly high-stakes poker and occasionally games involving dice. One night, according to the story, he had a dream of his mother, alarming in itself, since Greeks in general did not believe it was likely to dream about the dead. In the dream she was behind the door of an apartment, and what he talked about with her is relatively unimportant. What he remembered when he woke up is that the number on the apartment door was 807.

The next day Big Nick put twenty bucks on 807 with a young numbers runner by the name of Louis DiGeordano. Little is known of DiGeordano's history before that day except that he was a Sicilian immigrant of my grandfather's generation who up to that point had not experienced the luck of Big Nick. He pushed a fruit-and-candy cart in the streets and lived near Chinatown in a two-room apartment with ten other relatives.

When the number hit, DiGeordano delivered the payoff to my grandfather. The hit was in the neighborhood of forty thousand dollars, a fortune in those days. The legend has it that when DiGeordano gave Big Nick the bankroll, my grandfather peeled off two thousand dollars and handed it to Lou. DiGeordano supposedly dropped to his knees (an embellishment, I think, that has been tacked on to the story over time), but my grandfather pulled him back up. It was a curious act of generosity that my grandfather never explained or claimed to regret.

Life after that took unexpected turns for both of them. My grandfather invested in a couple of downtown buildings and owned and operated a series of modest coffee shops until his death. He never flashed his money around, decreased his card playing over the years, and even quit drinking when I entered the picture. Lou DiGeordano opened his own carryout with the two thousand and began a loan-sharking business and an organized gambling operation that grew into a small, bloodless crime empire in D.C. that lasted well into the sixties. Lou was still alive, but his business had deteriorated and had been run into the ground, as businesses usually are, by his son, a man named Joey.

NOW, ON THIS BRIGHT, biting Saturday in December, I was driving my Dodge Dart south on Georgia Avenue with the window down, letting in as much cold air as I could stand in a vain attempt to slap away my hangover, and I was on my way to see the DiGeordanos. The cigarette I was smoking tasted like the poison it was, and I pitched it out the window. I tried a breath mint, but that was worse, and it followed the path of the cigarette.

I pulled over and parked on Georgia just past Missouri, in front of an R & B nightclub and across the street from a Chevy dealership and a Chinese restaurant facaded as a pagoda. Next to the nightclub was a pawnshop and next to that was Geordano's Market and Deli. The sign on the window was small, but there was a larger fluorescent sign below it advertising cold beer and wine to go. I walked around a man with mad black eyes who looked seventy but could have been forty. He was wearing a brown wool overcoat that was ripped open beneath both arms. The coat smelled, even with the wind behind us, of body odor and urine. The man said something unintelligible as I passed and entered Geordano's.

A small bell sounded as the door closed behind me. The air was heavy with the tang of garlic and spice. I went by tall shelves stacked with small red-and-blue cans and large gold cans of olive oil. Past the shelves were two coolers stocked with beer, fortified wine and sweet sodas, and past that a row of barrels with clear hinged lids containing various types of olives and spiced peppers. The barrels were lined across a Formica counter on which sat an old register. Beyond the counter was a work area and the entrance to a back room of sorts. In front of the entrance was a chair and next to that a steel prep table on wheels. Dried beans were scattered on the top of the table, and next to the table sat a burlap sack half filled with the beans. An old man was sitting in the chair, and he was looking closely at the beans on the prep table before he pushed small groups of them into his hand and dumped them into another burlap sack. He looked up at me as I approached the counter. Thin pink lips smiled beneath a broad gray mustache.

"Nicky," he said.

"Mr. DiGeordano."

I walked around the counter before he could stand and shook his hand. His grip was still strong, but the flesh was cool, and the bones below it felt hollow. His aging was not a shock—he was in his mideighties, after all, and I had seen him at my grandfather's funeral—but the frailty that went with it always was. He was wearing a brown flannel shirt buttoned to the neck and over that a full white apron. The apron had yellowed in spots, and there were reddish brown smudges of blood near the hemline where he had wiped his hands. He wore black twill slacks and black oilskin work shoes with white socks, an arrangement fashionable with kids sixty-five years his junior in some of the clubs downtown.

"I wasn't sure if this was your place," I said. "The name I mean. When did you drop the *Di?*"

"A couple of years ago," he said in the high rasp common in Mediterranean males his age. "Only on the sign out front. No use making it tougher on our customers to remember our name than it already is. We still get some of the old-timers, but mainly what we get is neighborhood people. Beer and cheap wine is our main seller. You can imagine."

I nodded and then we stared at each other without speaking. His eyes were brown and wet like riverbed stones. His hair was whiter than his mustache, full and combed high and then swept back. Deep ridges ran from the corners of his eyes to the corners of his mouth. The mouth was moving a bit, though he still wasn't talking.

"What are you doing?" I said, glancing at the table.

"Checking the beans for rocks," he said. "There's always a rock or two in the bag. You have to go through them by hand. A customer breaks his tooth on a rock, you got a lawsuit, you lose your business." He shrugged.

"Is Joey in? I'd like to talk to him if he has a minute."

"Anything I can help you with?"

"Nothing that serious," I said.

"In the office," he said, and made a small backward wave with the point of his index finger. Then he yelled for his son.

Joey DiGeordano stepped out momentarily. He was rubbing his hands with a towel, and he looked at me briefly before he looked over to his father. Joey wore a dark suit and a blue textured dress shirt more poly than cotton, with a plain lavender tie that was tacked to the shirt by a pearl button. He was street slender, and his hairline was identical to his father's, and it was pompadoured identically but was black and slicked with some sort of oil-based gel. The smell of a barbershop entered the room with him.

"Yeah, Pop."

"This is Nick Stefanos." Joey glanced my way again, this time with more interest. "Big Nick's grandson."

"How ya' doin'," Joey said in a tone that was inching its way up the scale toward his old man's.

"Good," I said. "You got a couple of minutes?"

"Sure," he said, and jerked his head just a little. "Come on back." I could feel the old man's appraisal as we walked by.

I followed Joey through a long storage room Metro-shelved with dry goods into a wider room that housed a metal desk and a couple of chairs. On the desk was a phone and an empty plastic in-basket and not much else. A calendar that featured a topless blonde holding a crescent wrench hung over the desk. Beyond the desk was a narrow hall containing a small bathroom and beyond that a padlocked door that opened to the alley.

A broad-shouldered lummox stained the bare wall across from the desk. He was also wearing a suit, but the suit did not hit the intended mark. His arms barely reached past his hips, his mouth was open, and his spiky haircut was some suburban hairstylist's idea of new wave. His eyes shifted beneath heavy lids as I entered the room.

Joey motioned me into a chair upholstered in green corduroy. I folded my overcoat on the back of it before I sat. He took his seat at the desk. He removed a pencil from a mug full of them and tapped its eraser on the edge of the metal desk. His olive skin was lightly pocked and his sideburns reached almost to the lobes of his ears. I had seen him in May's quite often, though we had never spoken. Usually he sat with a group of aging, scotch-drinking hipsters whose conversations ran from Vegas to "broads" to Sinatra and back again, guys who were weirdly nostalgic for a time and a place that they had never known. I placed his age at about forty-eight.

"Who's he?" I said to Joey, jerking my head slightly in the direction of the lummox.

"Bobby Caruso. You want some java?"

"Black," I said. "Thanks."

Joey signaled Caruso, the first time since we entered the room that he had acknowledged his presence. Caruso left but brushed my back with his heavy arm before he did it. I pulled a business card from my inside breast pocket and slid it across the desk until it touched Joey's fingers. He read it without lifting it off the table and then tapped the eraser on the desk as he looked back my way.

"What can I do for you, Nick?"

"I've been hired by Bill Goodrich," I said, "to find his wife." I let that hang in the air and studied his cool reaction. "He thought you might be able to point me in the right direction."

Joey chuckled and shook his head. He made a tent with his hands and didn't say a word, and then Caruso lumbered back into the room and set a small cup of espresso on the edge of the desk nearest my elbow. I nodded by way of thanks, and in response he tried to sneer, showing me some large front teeth that would have been attractive had they belonged to an aquatic rodent. I had a sip of the bitter coffee.

Joey said evenly, "I don't think I can help you."

"Bill Goodrich thinks you can." There was more silence as Joey and I stared at each other meaninglessly and without malice. Finally I said, "Let's talk about this, Joey. Alone."

Joey looked over my shoulder and moved only his eyes in

the direction of the doorway. I felt the heavy arm bump my back, harder this time, and then heard plodding footsteps fade. Joey used a thin gold lighter to fire up a white-filtered cigarette, then slipped the lighter into his suit pocket.

"Who's the sweetheart?" I said.

"Bobby's a young cousin of mine. I apologize for him. He's very protective of me and my father. Hangs around 'cause he's got visions of getting into 'the business.' Of course there is no business anymore. But I haven't been able to convince him of that."

"Keep him away from me," I said.

"You said you wanted to talk," said Joey, his dark eyes narrowing.

"Okay." I sat back. "Goodrich thinks you were having an affair with his wife. He doesn't seem too stoked about that, to tell you the truth. He just wants to make sure she's all right."

"What's your angle?"

"No angle. It's a job. Goodrich is paying me to locate her and that's it. It should be very simple if we all cooperate."

"How did you two hook up?"

"Old friends," I said.

Joey's eyes lingered on my wrinkled blue oxford and loosened knit tie. "I don't make you guys as peas in a pod."

"We were once," I said, and killed it at that. "How about you? How did you hook up with him?"

"Your friend's a very ambitious young man," Joey said. "He was persistent early on, calling me every day, trying to interest me in locations for carryout shops I was thinking of opening at the time. Finally I let him drive me around to look at some spots. I could see right away he was more interested in my business than in brokering locations. I guess Goodrich bought into all that fiction they print in the newspaper."

"It's not all fiction."

"No, but it *is* ancient history. The loan-sharking, the necessary arsons—they might as well have gone down a thousand years ago. We're involved in a little bookmaking here and there, and that's all — college basketball, and so on."

"So Goodrich was ambitious," I said, filling in the common blanks. "You met his wife over dinner, and he says you gave her the eye."

"Listen", Joey said, "I'll speed this up for you." He flicked an inch of ash to the linoleum floor and leaned forward. "I not only gave her the eye, my friend, I gave her this." Joey grabbed his crotch for emphasis and shook its contents. "All right? I gave it to her all over her beautiful body and anywhere else I damn well pleased. And all the while I had the distinct impression that your young friend was pimping his wife to me for just that purpose."

I shook a Camel from the deck. Joey leaned over with his gold lighter and set it on fire. I blew some smoke across the room that mingled with his. He slid the lighter back into his pocket.

"How so?" I said.

"Goodrich didn't care about that broad any more than I did, that's how so. I could see she had no class the first night I met her, and class is something I know a thing or two about."

I looked at the blond mechanic on the calendar and then back at him. "A thing or two at the most, maybe." The shot glanced off him, so I plowed on. "What was your deal with Goodrich?"

"I put him on the payroll as a real estate adviser. He was paid in cash, always in cash. It's something he asked for, and it's something guys like him can really appreciate. After a while their high salaries just become a blur of numbers. But cash — it's real, you can feel it in your hand, and it's dangerous, you know what I'm saying? Let's face it, there's no reason to be in business for yourself unless you can steal from the IRS. He wanted a piece of it. I gave him what he wanted, and I took what I wanted from his wife."

The comment lingered in the air like a bad odor. "Joey," I said, "do you know where April Goodrich is?".

Joey DiGeordano barked a short laugh that turned into a cough. When he was finished coughing he wiped his eyes with a handkerchief that he drew from the breast pocket of his suit jacket. Then he studied my eyes and grinned. "Big private eye," he said, and shook his head. "You really don't know a damn thing, do you?"

"Educate me," I said.

"I don't know where April Goodrich is," he said. "But I'll give you ten grand if you find her and bring her to me."

I considered that after a drag off my cigarette. "I thought you didn't care about her."

"I don't. But she's got something of mine."

"What would that be?" I said.

Joey said, "Two hundred grand."

I finished my espresso and had a last pull off my cigarette before crushing it on the floor. I heard Caruso's heavy breathing in the hallway and below that the faint tick of my wristwatch.

"You going to tell me about it?"

"Why not?" he said. "Everybody in town knows I got took for a ride. I have an apartment I keep downtown. I take my friends, girlfriends there, for parties, whatever. I also keep my bankroll there. Being in the cash business has its disadvantages. One of them is you can't use the banks."

"April knew about it?"

"Yeah. She was at the apartment on a regular basis for quite a while, and occasionally she needed cash. I didn't have a safe or anything, and I knew how much was there, so I figured it couldn't do any harm to let her in on it."

"You trusted her?"

"It wasn't so much as trust. She was a hillbilly piece of ass—from southern Maryland, for Christ's sake. I just didn't think she'd pull anything like that."

"Go on," I said.

"She had a key to my place. One night—"

"What night was that?"

"Monday, last week. She was supposed to meet me at the apartment. She *was* there—I called her at about six o'clock. But when I got there she was gone. So was the bread."

"How do you know she took it?"

"I *don't* know," he said. "Anything can go down, right? But my money's missing, and she's missing, and that's what I've got."

I thought things over. Bill Goodrich had said that April had disappeared a week ago Wednesday. The money was stolen on the Monday of that week. That left a day in between.

"Will you help me?" Joey said.

"I work for Goodrich," I said, rising from my chair as I put on my overcoat. "But if I find the girl, and she has the money, you'll get it back."

"Fair enough," Joey said. "But understand this. I've got people out looking for her. If they find her before you do, I can't guarantee they're going to be too gentle."

"People like Caruso?" I said, pointing my chin to the hallway. "He couldn't find his dick in the shower."

"Others too. There's a lot of people in this town, Nick, they owe me favors."

"So long, Joey."

"Be in touch."

"So long."

I turned and headed through the doorway. Caruso was off to the side, his back against the shelving. I don't know why he decided to make a play. Maybe he didn't like the way I talked to his boss, or maybe he just didn't like my looks. It didn't really matter. Guys like him always do the wrong thing, and they always keep doing it; he telegraphed his move by trying to look too casual. But casual hung on Caruso like his tight shiny suit. When I was one step away he jerked his arm up in my direction.

I grabbed the arm with my left hand and twisted it back. Then I boxed his ear with my open right hand and swung the elbow of that arm across his mouth. It sent him into the steel shelving with a force that rocked it back and knocked cans to the floor. I bunched his shirt and got up in his fat, sweaty face. A small amount of blood seeped off his gums and pinkened his beaverlike teeth.

"Now, listen, you fucking Guinea. You touch that arm to me again," I said, "and I'll cripple you. Understand?"

"Let him go," Joey said tiredly from the office to my right.

I looked to my left. The old man was in the doorway that led to the store, slicing me open with his watery brown eyes. I released Caruso's shirt and straightened my overcoat, shifting my shoulders underneath. Caruso exhaled and attempted a vicious stare but didn't say a word. I walked out into the store, sidestepping the old man. The old man followed. Finally I reached the front door.

"I'm sorry, Mr. DiGeordano," I said. "He had that coming."

"Not in my place, he didn't."

"I apologize."

"You have your grandfather's quick hands," he said. "But you don't have his class." Lou DiGeordano looked me up and down and made sure I saw it.

I pushed on the door and walked to my car, where I slid behind the wheel. I watched my hand shake as I touched the key to the ignition. The car came alive. I swung it out on onto Georgia Avenue and ignored an angry salutation of blaring horns.

SIX

SAY THAT AGAIN?"

Jackie Kahn said, "You heard me."

We were seated at a four-top near the kitchen in a restaurant called Giorgaki's on Pennsylvania Avenue in Southeast, a place that was decorated to approximate one of those sparse, white-stuccoed *cafenions* that are all over Greece. On the wall next to our table was a large framed photograph of the windmills of Mykonos. Waiters were hurrying through the outward swinging metal doors, and when they came out from the kitchen the excited shouts of argumentative Greeks came out with them. Jackie dipped her bread in the *tarama* that was dolloped next to the *tzaziki* on the appetizer tray and kept her eyes on mine as she tore a bit off with her teeth.

"I heard you," I admitted. "But why me?"

"You've got good genes. And you're…reasonably attractive."

Our African waiter arrived and set down a plate of marinated octopus just as Jackie spoke. He asked, in Greek more fluent and correctly accented than mine, if there would be anything else. I ordered an American beer and a retsina for Jackie. The waiter winked at me before he left. I squeezed some lemon over the octopus and had a taste.

"Knock it off, Jackie," I said as I swallowed a rubbery cube of octopus.

"There's nothing to knock off, Nick." Jackie rearranged the silverware around her plate and folded her hands. "Listen. I'm a person who's generally content. In that respect I'm very lucky. And I'm very comfortable with my sexual proclivity. I have a wonderful career, and I've found an extremely compatible person to share it with. There's only one thing now that I'm missing, and I see no reason why I can't have it."

"A child."

"Right."

"So adopt one," I said. "There's laws now that prevent discrimination against gay couples who want to adopt."

"I'm not interested in getting into some long, protracted process involving miles of red tape, or the expense that goes along with it. And like most people, I prefer to bear a child from my own blood, especially if I'm able."

The waiter brought our drinks and took our dinner order. Jackie asked for a country salad, and I ordered *souzoukakia*, a meatball dish in a spicy tomato sauce served over rice. He left and I had a pull off my beer, then studied Jackie's face.

"You're serious, aren't you?"

"Never been more serious, Nicky."

"How do I fit in?" I said. "So to speak."

Jackie smirked. "I thought that part would interest you."

"Only in the scientific sense."

"Uh-huh." She sipped her retsina and set down the glass. "Actually, the ball is rolling right now. A week from now I'm scheduled for a sonogram. If everything goes according to schedule—that is, if I'm ovulating—we could have intercourse next Sunday night."

"Intercourse? You make it sound so romantic."

"I just want to be efficient. It's not that the thought of being with you is so awfully repulsive."

"Now, stop. You'll make me blush."

"What do you think?" she asked.

I lit a cigarette and aimed the exhale away from her face. "Normally, I'd say something wise. But I can see you're not bullshitting me. I can tell you right off the bat that a guy like me has no business being a father."

"You wouldn't be, not in that way. I've had my lawyer draw up a waiver that would limit any parental rights you might have, even if you were to have a change of heart up the road. Of course I'd never stop you from seeing the child, if that's what you wanted."

"You've thought of everything."

"That's right," she said, and her eyes softened. "What else?"

"I'll tell you the first thing that came to my mind. Bringing a kid into this world—it's a huge decision, and sometimes it's one based entirely on selfishness. And I've got to admit, you know, as much as I wear my heart on my sleeve, who's to say that the fact that you're gay is not rattling around somewhere in the back of my mind?"

"What bothers you about it?"

"Are a gay couple going to make proper parents? I don't know. I don't know if it does bother me. I'm just being honest with you. I've gotta think about it. All of it."

"I didn't expect you to decide right here," she said. "But don't drag your feet. I've scheduled you for an appointment at the clinic on Wednesday morning. I want you to have a blood test, and I want them to check your sperm count while you're there."

"Don't trust me, huh?"

"If your sperm count's low, there's no reason to go through with it. As for the blood test, the fact is that I'm monogamous. And you're an active heterosexual. I'm not taking any chances."

"No chances, huh? Kind of takes the fun out of it."

"Fun?" Jackie said. "You'll find a way."

I DROPPED JACKIE OFF and drove north on Wisconsin through an alternation of flurries and freezing drizzle. The radio was on, a sports-talk program on WHUR. The caller was saying something derogatory about Larry Bird. He called and said roughly the same thing at about the same time every week. What he really objected to was the fact that Bird was white. But tonight I wasn't listening. I was thinking about Billy Goodrich.

I had called him at his house in Scaggsville after my meeting with DiGeordano. There had been a pause on his end when I told him about the money. The pause in itself could have meant a lot of things—shock, fear for his wife, a moment to strategize—and as I was waiting for his response, I realized my mistake. I should have brought the matter up in his presence; there are, after all, more clues in one face than in a hundred telephone conversations. In any case, when I hung up with Billy, he knew more than I did, and I knew nothing.

I found a spot near Lee's apartment in Tenleytown and killed the engine. On the way to her stairwell I hawked the remainder of a mint onto the brown lawn of the property. At Lee's door I straightened my overcoat and knocked twice. I watched my breath hit the metal door until the door swung open.

Lee had on a jade green shirt, buttoned to the top, the one that made her green eyes seem violently alive. The large brown speck in one of those eyes appeared hazel in the yellowish light of the stairwell. Her dark hair was drawn back, but a twist of it had come unbound and had fallen across her forehead and then down the side of her angular face. Her smile caused small lines to flower at the corners of her eyes.

"Hello," she said.

"Hi."

"How are you?"

"Sober. Get my flowers?"

"Uh-huh. Not very original. But the note was."

"You liked it?"

"Yeah," she said. "I got the part about you being a perfect slob. And the apology. But what are you now, an Indian? I mean you signed the note 'Tongue of Snake.' What's that got to do with the price of beans?"

"If you'd like" I said, "I'll just come on in and show you."

A moment later we were against the wall near the hall closet where, in a mindless rush, I penetrated her with my trousers heaped down around my shoes. Then, carrying her, still inside her, with a Chaplinesque waddle (my pants still binding my ankles) to the living room rocker, I set her down, pulled out, and with my chin scraping the perforated cane seat, her legs veed out over the Brentwood's lacquered arms, I chased the sliding chair across the hardwood floor, as I sunk my face into that slippery thicket of sweet brine, and showed her, with workmanlike pride, just what my tongue had to do with "the price of beans." During her first orgasm, her muscular thighs clamped down so tightly on my head that I thought for a moment she had dislodged some vertebrae. Her second spasm, marked by her cool dry lips and a visible shudder of her damp shoulders, was less dramatic. Then we were down on the floor and I was inside her once again, in an undulating crab walk that ended with her head tilted against the base of the sofa and me baying unashamedly, like the dog I was, at the low white ceiling.

Afterward we sat naked on the couch and drank a bottle of Chilean cabernet and listened to the "Reggae Splashdown" on HFS. We were both fairly quiet that night and both of us wanted it that way. The sex and the wine and our nakedness had thrown a calming blanket over us and the entire room. Somewhere in the evening I told her about Jackie Kahn's proposition.

"What are you going to do?" she asked. I searched for a trace of jealousy in Lee's voice, but there wasn't one. Instead there was interest and the genuine concern that I was not setting myself up for a brass-knuckled punch in the heart.

"She's going through with it," I said, "whether I agree to be the one or not. We're friends. I can't turn her down."

"How does it make you feel, to think you might become a father? Even though, you know, you're not really going to have the responsibility."

The chugging rhythms of Peter Tosh's "Legalize It" filled the room. I finished off the goblet of wine and placed it on the glass table in front of the couch. Lee leaned into my shoulder and I put my arm around hers. "There was a long while, after my marriage flamed out, I resigned myself to the fact that I was never going to have any kids. It's not an easy thing to come to terms with, believe me. Having kids always seemed to me to be the most elemental thing to do. But there's certain people maybe shouldn't have kids, even if they want to. I'm probably one of them."

"Cut it out," she said.

"It's not self-pity," I said. "What's the old expression? 'Kids shouldn't have kids'—Lee, that's all I'm saying. But when Jackie explained the deal, I've got to admit, I got excited. I can be a father, Lee. I *can* be. And I don't have to screw anybody up by doing it."

"You're just too hard," Lee said, and kissed me on the mouth. But she knew I was right, and she couldn't look me in the eye.

"I know who I am," I said. "That's all."

THE CLOCK ON THE nightstand read 4:39 when I awoke in Lee's bed. Lee's hip was warm against mine, and her breathing was like a faint wind slipping through the crack of a pane. I watched a tree's shadow shimmer across the bare white wall of her room. The shadow became more detailed as my eyes adjusted to the light. I thought about the weekend and felt my blood jump and knew then that it would be a while before I would return to sleep. I reached for the pack of Camels on the nightstand, found a matchbook, and struck a flame to the tobaccoed end.

The first lungful was toxic with sulfur, but I held it in and tried to watch the smoke of my exhale drift up toward the ceiling. What I saw was a subtle change of the spare light, like the slow movement of deep water on a moonlit night. I studied the lit end of the smoke and made a trail of it with a small circular motion of my hand. Lee woke and got up on one elbow. She put one small hand on my chest and with the other brushed the hair back away from her face.

"What's up, Nicky?" she said.

"Just thinking," I said. "The thinking woke me up, and now it's keeping me up."

"Thinking about what?"

I took a deep drag off the cigarette. "I had a run-in with this guy yesterday. This guy just happened to be Italian. Anyway, I belted him across the mouth. And after I did that I called him a name."

"What kind of name?"

"A Guinea. A dago. I don't remember."

"Go to sleep, Nicky. You didn't mean anything."

"Something like that always means something."

"Go to sleep."

"I got a feeling here," I said. "That this whole thing with Billy Goodrich—his wife, the DiGeordanos, all of it—there's something not right about it. Nothing ever good comes from situations like that, Lee. It's going to turn out bad."

SEVEN

WASHINGTON, D.C., IS laid out in quadrants with the Capitol serving as the point at which they all meet. Numbered streets progress, well, numerically, and run north to south. Lettered streets are arranged alphabetically and run east to west. At the border of each quadrant this numerical progression begins again. Thus it is nearly impossible to get lost in our nation's capital. Unless, of course, one hails from some hotbed of logic like, say, Baltimore.

I had parked my Dodge early Monday morning on Florida Avenue, facing west. Florida Avenue bisects the city at the fall line of the Piedmont Plateau. It is no accident that well-to-do whites live on the more stable high ground of upper Northwest, while moderate to poor blacks reside in North and Southeast; rather it is a geographic divination that seems to evolve in all the major cities of the Northeast. It is also no accident, then, though it can be said to have been mildly prophetic, that Florida Avenue once went by the name of Boundary Street.

I turned the collar of my overcoat up to warm my neck against the stinging wind and walked beside a retaining wall toward Sixteenth. On the wall was spray-painted, in red, STOP THE PHONY U.S. DRUG WAR IN PANAMA. At the corner of Sixteenth and Florida, on the opposite side of the street, was the apartment building gone condo where William Henry had lived and died. I gave it an uncritical eye as I waited for the light to change. The light changed, and I crossed Sixteenth and passed beneath a concrete archway, on which was painted the slogan CHE LIVES!. When I was through the archway, I was in Meridian Hill Park.

Meridian Hill Park could have been the most beautiful park in the city, a cross between a European palazzo and a garden. Neighborhood people in the pre–air-conditioned forties used to sleep here on summer nights and enjoy starlit concerts ranging from classical to swing. The park also had a grand view of downtown, until a high rise erected at Florida and New Hampshire avenues put an end to that. Sometime in the seventies the D.C. government renamed it Malcolm X Park, though since they had no legal right to do so (the Feds owned it), the place is still known officially as Meridian Hill. Most people who follow the teachings of Malcolm X agree that this is for the better, since Meridian Hill Park is now little more than a drug market.

I walked across a balustraded promenade that spanned an empty pool situated at the foot of a graduated series of empty fountains. I passed the large statue of James Buchanan on the east side of the park and climbed a set of concrete steps that led to the mall. On the wall that bordered the steps was painted the names of the members of a local gang called the Crew—Easy E, Duck Derrick, and Million $ Eric.

All of the activity that day was on the terrace at the crest of the park. Some kids were playing an informal soccer game on the grassy mall, where several posted signs forbid such activities. Though the air was quite cold, the game's participants wore light jackets, and a couple of them were in shirtsleeves. The curly-haired forward who was controlling the ball had his shirt-tail in his mouth as he dribbled upfield.

Everyone else in that part of the park was in the process of either buying or selling drugs. They were walking the perimeter of the mall—nobody was standing still—and there was the occasional brief hand contact as the deals went down. Some of the walkers were obviously cops, with their fatigue jackets and knit caps. Nobody, however, was being busted.

A Latino in a matching jean outfit with black shoes and white socks quickly glanced up as he approached in my path. He mumbled, "Sense! Sense!" as I shook my head and passed him on my way to the center of the terrace. At the front of the Joan of Arc statue, I stopped and leaned on the concrete wall that overlooked the fountains and the pool.

Some skateboarders with shaved heads were traversing the bowl of the last fountain in the grotto below. A boom box was set next to the bowl, out of which came a cut from local heroes Fugazi. A young man in a sweatsuit stood at the wall to my right, looked at me, and then yelled at the skateboarders, "I hope you break your muthafuckin' heads." Then he walked away.

I watched a thin figure emerge at the spot where I had entered the park minutes earlier. The man pointed a one-finger wave in my direction as he crossed the promenade. His hair had grown gray since I had seen him last, but there was still the quickness in his step. Winchester Luzon had kept our appointment.

I first met Winnie Luzon on my premier day as a stock boy at Nutty Nathan's on Connecticut Avenue, in early summer of 1973. I had wandered into the employee lounge at the back of the store, with a dust rag in my hand and a look of stoned innocence across my face. I had just been given my first words of direction from Phil Omajian, a sweet-natured down freak who was the store manager at the time: "Never walk *into* the stock-room without something in your hands, and never walk *out* of the stockroom without something in your hands." So I had picked up a rag and, coming down from the joint I had blown on my way to work (I hitched down Connecticut in those days, and invariably my patron driver would produce some weed — even strangers got strangers high in the early seventies), I entered the lounge with every intention of doing nearly nothing until my shift was done.

Luzon was sitting at Omajian's desk when I walked in, lick-ing the seal of a manila envelope. His pink tongue continued to slide along the edge of it as his eyes shifted in my direction. I was wearing a Nutty Nathan's T-shirt that day, the one with the old logo that made Nathan look like, in the words of one out-raged customer, "a goddamned mongoloid." (I could not have known then that years later, as advertising director for the com-pany, I would design a new caricature of Nathan that was less offensive but equally ridiculous.)

Luzon squinted through the smoke of his filterless ciga-rette and said, with the accent and brown hairless skin of a Fili-pino Charles Boyer, "You work here, kid?"

"Yes," I said, phrasing it as a question.

Luzon tossed me the envelope, rose from the chair, and produced a five from the pocket of his brocaded slacks, placing the bill in my hand. "Run the envelope down to the mechanic at the Amoco, a big cat named Spade. Black dude," he added redundantly. "On the way back pick me up a Mighty Moe from the Hot Shoppes. Tell Mary at the counter it's for Winnie — she'll toothpick an extra pickle to the top. Use the five and keep the rest for yourself. Hear?"

I nodded and did it. In fact, I delivered that package and picked up his food every day for the remainder of the summer. Though I knew there was something "wrong" in those enve-lopes, I was hardly concerned with questions of morality. If it was gambling chits (which I now know it to have been), well, gambling was something that was part of my life with Papou. And if it was drugs, then my opinion was equally neutral. Doing and moving pot was, after all, almost a duty for kids my age in those years. That was, of course, before cocaine crept into town and made the whole party a bloody nightmare.

Winchester Luzon was not the biggest character I met that summer (those honors go to the amazing Johnny McGinnes), and we never became too close. There was the wet-eyed Omajian, who drove me home on those sticky summer nights and waxed with a barbiturate deliberateness about the brevity of life: "Nicky, does it seem as if it's all moving so quickly?" (For him, it was—he died in 1975 of a massive coronary. The makeup men at Gawler's had, for once, done a fitting job when they froze a boyish smile across his ashen face.) Gary Fisher was the store's audio man, a good salesman who was fond of gadgetry and Colombian and who played Steely Dan's *Pretzel Logic* and a group called If in the sound room all day long. There was my friend Andre Malone, audio enthusiast and stone-free lover, fresh then with the bottomless energy and optimism of youth. There was part-time salesman Lloyd Danker ("Void Wanker," we called him, to his face), a zombified Jesus freak who was my tormentor. And of course there were the cashiers, Lisa and Lois, two young women whom I was to alternately feel and fuck in various locations of the store over the course of the summer. With all the giggly, pot-induced laughter, the music, the camaraderie of my sagelike new friends, and of course with all that sweet, sweet teenage lust, those dry humps against chipped wallboards in musty stockrooms, those rushed blue-balled moments at closing time, those achingly pungent smells of cheap musk and thick vaginal heat, it was natural that I couldn't wait to wake up on those hot mornings and head downtown for my next day of work.

Nevertheless, Winnie Luzon was a character. Everything about him, from his tight black poodle curls to his pointed, tin-man nose, to the crease on his slacks, to the toes of his Italian shoes, was sharp. He reminded me at times, especially in profile, as we watched the Watergate hearings that summer on the fifty television sets that lined the wall, smoke dribbling from his thin mouth as he slowly shook his head, of a cardboard devil.

Luzon had been fired late in August that summer, as I prepared for my junior year at a new high school. Omajian had found some clock radios in the Dumpster out behind the store, on a day when Luzon had uncharacteristically offered to empty the trash. Omajian reluctantly let him go, then ate a soper and drank some beers at his desk and brooded about it for the rest of the evening. I had not seen Luzon since, though Johnny McGinnes continued to cop from him on a monthly basis. It was from McGinnes that I had gotten Winnie Luzon's number.

Now Luzon was upon me, with the slight, gassy smile that twisted up on one side of his face. His hair was slick and still high and tight, though any hint of blackness was gone. I figured him at about fifty, but the seventeen years that had passed had turned him into an old man. His face was lined and swollen.

"What's going on, Nick?" he said as I shook his callused hand.

"Nothing much, Winnie. Thanks for coming."

"Hey, bro', you said nine o'clock at Joanie on the Pony, I'm here." Luzon pointed at the statue, with its broken lance. Joan of Arc's eyes had been painted red. "Shame what they did to her, huh? They fucked up this whole park, man."

"The dealers?"

"No, man, not the dealers. We do business here, we keep it clean. I'm talkin' about the fuckin' trashheads, bro'."

"You work out of here, Winnie?"

"Yeah," he said, then reached into his overcoat and drew a trademark white cigarette. Luzon lit it, coughed, then took a second drag. "I sell herb only, man, dime bags. The *Post* calls this a drug market, but nobody's selling crack, love boat, none of that shit. It's safe here, man, you want herb, you come up into the park, it's like the fuckin' Safeway, Holmes."

"You sell information too? McGinnes said you knew most of what was going on around town."

"Maybe for you, Nicky, I give it away. You were a good kid, man, you did me some solids." Luzon looked me over. "You put on some weight too. Some meat on those bones." His forehead wrinkled. "You wouldn't be no undercover man, would you?"

"I'm in business for myself," I said. "And anyway, I wouldn't blindside you, Winnie."

"Course not. Like I said, you were a good kid."

"I was sixteen."

"Sixteen. Shit." Luzon looked down at the wrinkled hand that held the smoke, then brought it to his mouth, as he stared over the wall at the skateboarders in the fountain below. "What do you want to know, Nicky?"

"The DiGeordano family."

"Yeah?"

"What do you know about them? Lately."

Luzon shrugged. "There's not much to know, man, not anymore."

"They a factor?"

"What?"

"Are they important? Are they still players?"

"Small players," Luzon said. "Very small. The old man's always had a numbers runner's mentality, never any big-time stakes. When the legal game happened, the business dried up for everybody but the big guys. Yours truly included."

"I know all about the old man," I said. "What about Joey?"

Luzon pursed his thin lips and slowly shook his head. "He's nothing. Hangs out at May's with all those other ring-a-ding-ding boys and dreams about the fifties. Places a few bets every so often, and sometimes he hits. Mostly track action. Long shots."

"I heard he got burned pretty bad recently," I said.

"On the odds?"

"Uh-uh. A woman."

"Oh, that," Luzon said, making a small wave with his hand. "I heard something too."

"You don't seem too surprised."

"It's not the first time a woman took DiGeordano to the cleaners. Joey D's been chasin' pussy all his life. Sometimes the pussy bites back."

"They say it bit back to the tune of two hundred grand."

Luzon chuckled. "Then that's some serious shit, Holmes."

"I'm looking for the woman who did it," I said.

"I guess Joey is too."

"That's right."

"You working for Joey?"

I shook my head. "The woman's husband."

"What's her name?"

"April Goodrich."

Luzon said, "I'll ask around."

"One more thing," I said.

"Talk about it."

"You remember hearing about that boy got killed across the street, earlier this year? At the Piedmont, in his apartment."

"White boy?" Luzon said.

"Yeah."

"Knife job, right?"

"Uh-huh."

"Heard some talk about it that day. Then the next dude got offed somewhere else, and that took its place in the conversation sweepstakes. You know how it goes around here."

"What was the word on the boy?"

"You saw the papers, just like me. Nobody knows anything, and if they did, who would they tell? I mean, what for? Just another punk-ass bitch, dead. We got our own problems, real ones, man." Luzon blew me a kiss and said, "He a friend of yours, man?"

"That's right," I said as Luzon's smile turned down. "And I'd like to know what happened."

"They say a light-skinned dude—"

"I read that already."

"Listen, Nicky. The only thing I know, they got the Piedmont locked down tighter than a schoolgirl, man."

"You've tried to get in, then."

Luzon looked up, sheepishly. "I've made some attempts, yes."

"What's your point?"

"That 'light-skinned dude in a blue shirt' routine—it's just smoke, man. That way the public thinks it's just a junkie kill, from the neighborhood. But no junkie got into that building unless he greased somebody's palm or unless that boy let him up. You see what I'm sayin'?"

"Yeah. Thanks, Winnie. See what you can dig up on that too, hear?"

"Sure, Nicky." Luzon shifted his feet and looked down at his shoes. "You positive you don't want no smoke?"

I drew a folded twenty from my pocket and my business card and placed them both in his palm. "Keep the weed," I said, "and call me."

Luzon eyeballed the card, smiled, and shook his head. "Good to see you again, Nicky. Or is it Nicholas?"

"Nicky," I said.

Luzon smiled again before he turned and walked smoothly back along the walkway that encircled the grassy mall. I eyed him until he became too small to watch, shoulders up with a white curl of smoke that seemed to circle around his head. If there is one thing I cannot reconcile, one inevitable, it is the slow, sad progression of decay.

WILLIAM HENRY'S BUILDING STOOD at the intersection of Sixteenth and Florida and was on the way to my car. I stepped behind the building and had a cigarette while I watched a delivery being made to the truck bay in the alley. An unsmiling man in a blue maintenance uniform checked the delivery in and then pulled the doors closed from the inside when the process was done. There were no outside handles on those steel doors and only one similarly fashioned door on the left side of the building. I crushed the butt under my shoe and walked around to the front.

The Piedmont was gray stone and six stories tall, with swirled detail work above each window. Black wrought-iron balconies had been added to the apartments at the time of their condo conversion, adding to the price tag but adding little in the way of practical use, since the balconies appeared to be only three feet deep. A couple of bicycles were chained to the railings, a few of which were strung with Christmas lights. I moved along the front walk to an open heavy glass door. Inside I encountered a locked set of similar doors and a black telephone on the gray wall. Next to the telephone was a slot for a magnetic card that I presumed would allow tenants to gain entrance. The telephone had no dial or numbers. I picked it up and heard a ring on the other end.

"Yes," said a large voice.

"Detective Stefanos," I said. "I'd like to ask you a couple of questions."

"Metropolitan Police?"

"That's right," I lied.

The phone clicked dead, and then a man as large as his voice walked across the marble lobby to the glass doors. This one was a hard two-fifty if he was a pound. He stopped on the other side of the door, folded his thick arms, and looked down into my eyes. The aluminum tag clipped to his shirt pocket read RUDOLPH. On the arm of his shirt, above the bicep, was sewn a red patch with the coat-of-arms logo of the Four-S Security Systems company.

Rudolph raised his eyebrows as I put my business card against the glass and quickly pulled it back. He pointed to the badge on his chest and then made a come-on gesture with his fingers. I put the card back up on the glass along with a ten spot that I produced from my slacks. Rudolph stared at me until I squeezed out another ten and put it behind the first one. He kept staring while he pointed once again to his badge and then at me. When I didn't produce one he walked away. He was still walking as I tapped my fingers on the glass.

Out on the street I buttoned up my black overcoat and found a pay phone on the corner nearest my car. I dropped a quarter getting the number of Four-S, then another dialing that number. After a few minutes I was directed into the office of personnel.

"How may I help you?" said an aging female voice.

"Jim Piedmont," I said, as I looked at William Henry's building across the way. "Bartell Investigative."

"Yes, Jim, what can I do for you?"

"I'm doing an employment check on a James Thomas, just on the essentials. Do you mind?"

"I'll help where I can," she said coolly.

"I just need to verify his current address. I have him at Fourteen-twelve P Street, in Northwest. Is that correct?"

"Hold on and I'll check," she said. I listened to the tapping of a computer keyboard while I wondered if there was any such address at Fourteenth and P. The woman got back on the line.

"I have him at Thirteen-forty-three Hamlin Street in Northeast."

"Over in Brookland area, right?"

"That I don't know."

"Can you tell me, Miss —?"

"Sheridan."

"Miss Sheridan, can you tell me the circumstances of Mr. Thomas's severance with the company?"

"No," Miss Sheridan said, "I can't."

"I understand," I said. "One more thing. I recently met one of your employees, a big fellow by the name of Rudolph."

"Yes?"

"I just wanted to tell you — he's doing one hell of a job."

"Thank you," she said.

"Thank *you*," I said, and hung up the phone.

I ripped a ticket off the Dart's windshield and threw it in the glovebox with all the others. Then I swung a U on Florida and headed across town to the Brookland section of Northeast.

EIGHT

JAMES THOMAS LIVED in a pale green two-story house with pine green shutters, on a gently graded piece of Hamlin Street between Thirteenth and Fourteenth in Northeast. The lots were large in this part of town, with wide yards whose once-grand homes were set far back from the curb.

My grandfather had still owned some Brookland property in the midsixties, when we would drive across town in his black Buick Wildcat once a month on Sunday to collect the rent. Papou's property was a brick warehouse on Ninth Street that faced railroad tracks that later were to parallel those of the Metro. The dark-skinned man we met each month was elderly and bald, except for two neatly trimmed patches of gray above each ear, and he paid my grandfather with a roll of twenties that he had ready as we pulled up to the lot. His name was Jonas Brown, and he ran a clean little auto body shop out of the space, and he called my grandfather "Mister Nick" and me "Young Nick."

After the riots, Papou sold the warehouse to Jonas Brown, and I had since rarely returned to Brookland. I remembered it as being as peaceful as any section of D.C., with its stately Victorians surrounded by huge clusters of azaleas in the spring. In my gauzy childhood visions, middle-class black families walked slowly down city streets, the men wearing striped suits and brown felt hats, the women in brightly colored dresses cinched with white ribbons, and Brookland was always Sunday morning.

So the drive that day down Twelfth Street, the neighborhood's main avenue, saddened me. A painfully thin, coatless woman stood at the corner of Twelfth and Monroe in what looked to be a chiffon Easter dress, her head bowed as she fought to remain upright against the strong, cold wind. At Michigan Liquors a young man in a thick red down coat stood talking into a pay phone, gesturing broadly with his free hand, his beeper clipped to the waistband of his sweatpants, the door open to his window-tinted Chevy Blazer that sat idling near his side. I noticed several other drug cars, Jags and Mercedes with gold wheels and spoilers and gold-framed licence plates, parked in the lot of the Pentecostal Church of Christ. The movie theater was gone, replaced by a chain drugstore. There were hair salons and dry cleaners and delis; outside their doors teenage boys heavily paced the sidewalks. At Lucky's Cocktail Lounge a warping sign depicted a logo of a forked-tongue Satan. Under the Satan a slogan was printed with red bravado: WHERE THE DEVILS PLAY, AND THE LADIES MAY.

I had parked my Dart two doors up from the Thomas residence, in front of a leaning Victorian that was fronted with stone steps leading up to a rotting porch. Two young men sat on those steps and watched me as I walked by. Ice T's "Drama" was coming out of their box. One of the boys smiled malignantly in my direction as the words "Fuck the damn police" rapped out of the speakers. All of the house windows were barred on this street, and the deep barks of large-breed dogs were alternately close and distant in the air. I walked on.

On the porch of the Thomas residence I knocked on a heavy oak door. After my second knock there were muted footsteps and the darkening of the peephole centered in the door. Then the release of deadbolts and the metallic slide of a chain. The door opened, and a tiny dark woman in a print housedress stood before me, looking up with quizzical, kindly brown eyes. Her hair was thin and white; her deeply lined features nearly aboriginal.

"Yes?" she said in a manner that wedded curiosity to trepidation.

"Is James Thomas in, ma'am?" I gave her my card along with my least threatening smile. She handed back the card after a brief inspection.

"That would depend on your business with him, Mr.....?"

"Stefanos."

"What is your business with him, Mr. Stefanos?" she repeated, with the greatest degree of forced unpleasantness that a woman of her frailty could muster.

"It concerns a case I'm working on," I said, adding, "I'm not with the police, ma'am."

She considered that as the December chill continued to intrude upon her house through the open doorway, along with the rap from the boom box on the porch of the house to her right. Her shoulders finally slumped in visible submission as she motioned me in. I thanked her and followed as she led me into a den furnished with throw rugs and faded overstuffed furniture.

Mrs. Thomas had a seat on the couch; I took mine in a cushiony chair. She folded a slim pair of hands in her lap after pulling the hem of her housedress down to her knees, then looked into my eyes. I don't know what she was looking for, or if the look was meant to intimidate me. It did. There were seventy years of hard life in those eyes, seventy years of churchgoing faith and hope in answer to deterioration and disappointment and death. The wooden clock on the fireplace mantelpiece ticked loudly in the otherwise silent room.

"I'd like to see your son," I said. "If he has a few minutes."

"Does this concern the young man's death at the Piedmont?"

"Yes, it does."

Mrs. Thomas sighed slightly but retained her posture. "The District police have gone over the case with us very thoroughly, Mr. Stefanos. I believe they were satisfied that my son had nothing to do with that boy's death."

"I'm not working with the police," I said. "So I'm not privy to what was said between them and your son. But I do have an interest in seeing that the murderer is found. William Henry was my friend, Mrs. Thomas."

Her hands moved together in a washing motion in her lap, as if it were her hands that were doing the deliberating. She looked away briefly and up the stairs, where I assumed James Thomas was residing. Then she looked back at me, her features softened but unresigned.

"When one person dies, his suffering is over, Mr. Stefanos. Those left behind often bear the weight of the hardship. I didn't know that Henry boy. The papers and the police said he was an innocent young man. Anyway, he's in the hands of the Lord now—neither you nor I can help him. But my son has been hurt enough. He's lost his job and he's lost all his self-respect. He sits in that room upstairs all day, and he doesn't come out, except for dinner and to walk down to the liquor store." Mrs. Thomas looked down at her lap. "I couldn't help that young man. It wasn't my job to help that young man. But it *is* my job to protect my son. And I don't want him hurting anymore."

"I didn't come here to hurt your son. I came here for a few simple answers. You believe in justice in heaven. I respect that belief, if a person can be satisfied with it. I can't. So I have to believe in justice on earth." I rose slowly, walked in her direction, and stood over her. "Let me have a couple of minutes with your son, and I'll be on my way."

"I'll ask if he'd like to see you," she said.

I stepped aside to let her pass and watched her ascend the

stairs. She held the wooden banister as she did it. Soon after that was the opening of a door and her voice, then a voice intermingled with hers that was low but gentle. In a few minutes she moved back down the stairs and stood before me.

"James will see you," she said. "Please don't stay too long." It was less a command than it was a solicitous request. I nodded and moved away.

At the top of the stairs was a half-shut beveled door stained dark cherry. Above the door a transom window was cracked open just a bit; a barely visible fall of smoke flowed out from the crack. I knocked on the door and pushed as I did it. Then I stepped into the room.

It was a bedroom, probably the same bedroom James Thomas had been raised in. The oak furniture was scratched; its copper hardware pulls had long ago tarnished. An ashtray spilling over with butts was on the dresser and another ashtray just like it was on the nightstand next to the unmade bed. By the nightstand was a wastebasket lined with a brown paper bag. The neck of a fifth leaned out from the top of the bag. James Thomas sat in a small wooden chair facing the window, a smoking Kool Long in his hand. There was a third ashtray balanced on one very thick thigh.

He stared out the window, took a long drag off his smoke, and said, "Come on in."

"Thanks." I removed my overcoat and folded it over my forearm.

"You don't need to be doin' that," Thomas said. "You won't be stayin' long. I said I'd see you because my mom asked me to. But now that I have, I want it short."

"That's the way I want it too, James." I had a seat on the edge of his bed. Closer to him now, I caught the stale stench of yesterday's cheap liquor seeping through his pores.

James Thomas turned his head in my direction. He was wearing a brown-and-orange-plaid flannel shirt that gapped at the buttons, stretched as it was from his barrel chest. His head was round, dark, and cubbish. He had not shaved in days, though his facial hair was faint and spotty. His eyes were watery and rimmed red, the full-blown badge of a burned-down drunk.

"Let's get to it," he said.

"All right." I handed him my card. He stubbed the butt in the aluminum ashtray that rested on his thigh, then blew smoke at the card while he looked it over. Thomas folded the card and slipped it into his breast pocket.

"So?" he said.

"I'm working on the William Henry case," I said.

"Workin' for who?"

"William Henry."

"Guess you don't plan on bein' paid," he said.

"*Somebody* got paid," I said.

Thomas shook a Kool from the deck on the windowsill and put the filtered end to his mouth. I produced a matchbook from my trouser pocket and tore one off the pack. He watched my eyes as I fired him up.

"Say what you got to say," he said.

"Okay," I said. "I'll keep it simple. I've looked over the file on the William Henry case. I've talked to some people in the neighborhood, and I've been to the Piedmont. Nobody gets into that building unless they live there or unless they've been invited. I even tried to buy my way in. It didn't happen. Not with the guy they've got on duty now."

Thomas's jaw tightened. "I told you to say what the fuck you got to say. Now, do it."

I stood and walked to the window. Out on the street was an old Bonneville, a white BMW with dark tinted glass, and a new maroon Buick Regal. I pointed to the Regal, looked at Thomas, and said, "That you?"

"Yeah."

"Not a tough call. I don't make you for a dealer—that eliminates the drug car. And that shit-wagon Pontiac isn't your style. No, a guy from your generation—what are you, early forties?—a guy your age who just came into some money would probably head right down to the car dealership, first thing, and pick out a brand new Buick. Cash on the line. Am I right?"

"Got me all figured out," Thomas said. "Nigger with some cash money, burnin' a hole in his motherfuckin' pocket. 'Nigger rich.' That what you and your boys say when you're sittin' around drinkin' brew, tryin' to feel all superior about yourselves?"

"That *is* your car, isn't it, James?"

"It's mine." Thomas hung his head and glanced down at the floor. His anger was there, but it was weak, with only the residual strength of a cut nerve. He sighed. "Company gave me what they call a 'golden handshake.' They let me go after the Henry case made the TV news. Gave me a bunch of money to go real quiet. So that's what I did. And now I got a new ride, all paid up." He looked at it through the window and lowered his eyes once again.

"How much did they give you, James? Twelve thousand? Fifteen? Because that's about what that car costs."

"Ain't none of your damn business what they gave me."

"It's easy enough to find out."

"Then go on and do it," he said angrily. I put on my overcoat and shifted my shoulders beneath it to let it fall. When I walked to the door I turned to face him.

"I am going to do it, James. But it won't change what we both know, right now. You didn't kill that boy. You didn't even have an idea that he was going to be hurt, or what it was all about. But you let somebody in the Piedmont that night for money, and because of it my friend got greased." I fastened the buttons of my overcoat. "You see the body, James? He was stabbed with a serrated knife. Stabbed in the chest and in the stomach and in the legs. Through the hand when he was holding it up, to protect his face. And in the mouth, James. Twenty times." I shoved a hand in my pocket. "You know the details— you've been swimming in a bottle of Early Times ever since.

When you're ready to crawl out, you reach for my card and you call me, hear?"

Thomas cocked his head and squinted. "What do you want?" he said slowly.

"Same thing as you," I said. "To sleep at night. And no bad dreams."

We looked each other over for a while. Then I closed the door behind me and descended the stairs. Mrs. Thomas was standing at the bottom, her hand resting on the scrolled end of the banister.

"I'll see myself out," I said with a nod. "I'm sorry for disturbing your day."

"Did you get the information you wanted?"

"Yes."

"My son didn't kill that boy," she offered with commitment. "I don't think he had one thing to do with it."

"I don't think so either. But he can point me in the direction of the ones who did." She walked me to the door, and once more we stood together. I asked her before leaving, "Do you know a Jonas Brown? He had an auto body shop down by the tracks."

Mrs. Thomas's facial features converged into an amalgamation of smile lines and rounded cheeks. "Yes, I know Mr. Brown quite well. He was in the congregation. He's been gone ten years. Now he's resting with the Lord."

"Good-bye, Mrs. Thomas."

"Good-bye."

Out on Hamlin, I put the key to the lock of my sedan. The boys on the steps next door were gone, though somewhere close a drum machine ticked out from a boom box. I loocked up and caught a glimpse of James Thomas.

It was the last I saw of him. He was framed behind the window of his bedroom in the second story of the house, expressionless as he watched me climb into the driver's side of my Dart. I lit a cigarette and stared at the growing end of ash, thinking of how things burn and fade, before I drove away.

NINE

THE HEALTH PRO Center was a bunkerlike structure that end-capped a ubiquitous strip shopping center in the South Gaithersburg area of Montgomery County. I had driven out Rockville Pike early Wednesday morning with a quarter-inch of frost on my windshield, an ice sheet that had only begun to dissipate as my car neared the outer loop of the Beltway.

Rockville Pike is a track of fluorescence and concrete and traffic signals, five miles of heaven for the nouveaux riches who live to shop. To be fair to Maryland, all metropolitan areas seem to breed such cultureless outlying strips. The state of Virginia, in fact, has its own Rockville Pike. On that side of the river they call it Tysons Corner.

The sky was lightening as the hour neared seven. My Dart chugged north against the traffic that was already beginning to build. Sometime after the Pike changed over to its interstate moniker, 355, I hung a left onto Shady Grove Road and followed that for another mile until I reached my destination. I pulled in, killed the engine, and walked across the lot to the doors of the bunker.

The glass doors were locked. I pushed a yellow button to the right of the doors and watched the barely lit lobby for some signs of life. After a few minutes of shuffling about in the cold air that by now had triggered an ache in my temples, a large man in a white smock waved from inside and strode toward me.

He unlocked the doors, and I stepped inside. The man was wearing jeans beneath his smock, the sleeves of which were rolled up to the elbow to reveal thick, hairy forearms. With his lumber-jack-meets–Gomer Pyle appearance (his smile matched that rube character's jaw-jutting grin), it was difficult to tell if he was on the medical or the custodial staff. I asked him for a cup of coffee.

"No coffee," he said, shaking his head slowly as he maintained that silly smirk. "It hinders the sample."

"Oh."

"Walk this way, please."

I immediately thought of the old gag, of course, but walking behind him in an elephantine manner would have been pointless, since there was no one around to serve as an audience, and at any rate it was way too early for that type of nonsense. I followed him down a corridor and asked, to his back, "Why did the appointment have to be at seven in the morning?"

"Policy," he said, stopping at an unmarked door, the smile fading for the first time. "We determined that most men find the procedure socially embarrassing. So we do it early in the morning, before anyone's around. As a matter of course."

He opened the door to a nondescript room that had a desk and a chair and a small Formica counter and cabinet arrangement. Beneath one of the cabinets hung a roll of paper towels. There were no prints on the white walls, and both the blinds and curtains were drawn, giving the whole deal the foreboding look of one of those emergency room side offices where doctors tell you, with studied evenness and with theatrically lowered eyes, that your loved one "didn't make it."

I followed the man into the room as he walked me over to the counter, where he pointed to (but did not touch) a capped plastic bottle sitting atop a magazine. A piece of tape with N. STEFANOS written across it was affixed to the jar.

"Just leave the bottle on the counter when you're done, and you can leave. There's paper towels if you need to clean up." His hick smile was beginning to appear once again.

"Are there any directions?" I said. "I mean, you're just assuming that I've done this before."

His smile was gone now. "Ninety-nine percent of adult men masturbate, Mr. Stefanos. And the other one percent," he said solemnly, "are liars." He walked to the door and kept his eyes on me as he closed it behind him. I'm not certain, but before he closed it, I believe he winked.

The first thing I did was check the lock. Then I walked over to the counter, dropped my trousers, and flung my tie back behind my shoulders. I unscrewed the lid on the jar, moved it to the side, and picked up the magazine. The title of it was *Girls Who Crave Huge Ones*, leading me to believe that if this was not one of the classier clinics in the area, it certainly had some very bizarre smart alecks working in the acquisitions department.

Between the ethnic young ladies in the front of the mag and the little scenario I was now developing in my mind (in which a checkout girl from my local market named Theresa lured me into the stockroom so that we could "log in" a shipment of olive oil), it wasn't long before my compass had begun to point north. But, flipping through the pages of *Girls Who Crave Huge Ones*, trying (rather feverishly now) to find that one perfect photograph that would send me flailing away into bug-eyed nirvana, I came upon (I mean, stumbled upon) a rather odd pictorial.

It was a series of Polaroid photographs of a certain aging rock-and-roll singer, a man who had cut a classic single in the fifties about the relationship between a backwoods young man and his guitar. Strangely enough, that single was never a number one record—it took a novelty hit, years later, called "My Wing-Dang-Doodle," to propel that singer to the top of the charts. And now, under the border-to-border headline of HIS WING-DANG-DOODLE, were several photographs of the totally naked singer, his arm around various young, equally naked women (their eyes masked in black to "protect their identities"), a lizardly lascivious smile on his aging face.

And what of his "Wang-Dang-Doodle"? Well, for one thing, it appeared to be longer and thicker than my own forearm. And the result was that this strange pictorial spread that had both grabbed my rapt attention and taken the bark out of my angry dog only delayed my mission at the clinic, so that it wasn't until fifteen minutes and several stop-and-go fantasies later (not to mention two more waddles across the room to check on that lock), that I tossed the paper towel in the wastebasket, cavalierly zipped up my fly, and walked with as much dignity as I could muster out to the lobby, where I signed out in a lined logbook.

"Everything go all right?" asked Gomer, who was now behind the desk.

"Like the Fourth of July," I said. "Do you mind if I smoke?"

The white-smocked man lowered his reddening face and pretended to go over some paperwork. He was slowly shaking his head as I walked out the door.

MY NEXT STOP WAS at the private office of another doctor, just a few miles away from the Health Pro Clinic, in a low-rise medical building south on the Pike. After filling out a new-patient form on a clipboard, on which I left both the insurance section and the emergency contact sections blank, I settled in among the mostly geriatric crowd in the white lobby and picked up a magazine.

I don't quite know how long I sat waiting, but I managed to

finish a fairly long magazine article in *Washingtonian*, written by a friend of mine from college named Marcel DuChamp. DuChamp had been a copywriter around town for years until he decided to be a man and put his name (well, not exactly *his* name—he was called Mark Glick when I knew him) and reputation on the byline. Copywriters, of course, have as much in common with writers as bowlers do to athletes, but at least M. DuChamp was making a go of it. The last time I saw him he claimed, with just a trace of bitterness, that at a party one could always tell the writers from the copywriters. The writers drink straight liquor and situate their frumpy selves in front of their host's bookshelves, while the copywriters stand together in a well-dressed circle with their well-dressed wives and tell "off-color" jokes. The wives of the writers, Marcel said, stand alone and stare with envy at the wives of the copywriters.

By the time I had finished Marcel's article, a somewhat severe middle-aged woman had emerged from a mysterious door and called my name. I followed her back into a hall, past a large scale and a wall-mounted Dictaphone, and into an office.

The office contained a table padded in maroon Leatherette that was half-covered with a strip of industrial paper. There was a folding chair next to the table, and several cabinets with thin drawers that I immediately knew contained all varieties of needles and clamps and other instruments that inflicted pain in the name of health care.

"Take your shirt off and have a seat on the end of the table, Mr. Stefanos," the nurse said. "Dr. Burn will be in shortly." She exited the room.

I undid the buttons on my shirt and made myself comfortable on the edge of the Leatherette table. The paper crinkled beneath me as I sat. As I waited, I mulled over how many children had been scared witless in anticipation of a visit with a man named Dr. Burn, and wondered why he, like my imaginative copywriter friend, didn't change his name to something less ominous.

But it wasn't long until the good doctor arrived, closing the door softly behind him. He was tall and lean, with the genetically regal gray temples of the profession and the glow of a man whose bronze hands were wrapped around a nine iron more often than they were around a stethoscope.

"Good morning," he said, looking over my blank chart.

"Dr. Burn," I said.

"What brings you in today?" he said.

"Just a blood test," I said.

"Getting married, are you?"

"Nope."

"Roll up your sleeve and make a fist," he said. I made a tight fist for the second time that day.

Dr. Burn hadn't looked me in the eye yet, and he didn't now, as he crossed in front of me and opened one of the thin metal drawers. He pulled a syringe out of its wrapping and wet some cotton in alcohol, then stood in front of me and dabbed the alcohol at the vein that was visible at the base of my bicep.

I looked away and felt a sharp sting, then I felt nothing. I said, "You get it, Doc?"

"No, I didn't, as a matter of fact," he said tiredly. "Your vein's a little tough. Do you drink very often, Mr. Stefanos?"

"Only on special occasions," I said.

"Right," he said; then I felt the sting again and turned to watch the burgundy black liquid fill the tube. Dr. Burn capped it off and handed me the plastic cylinder. I felt the sickening but reaffirming warmth of my blood through the plastic. "Hold this while I wash up." He returned after washing and took the sample from my hand. "What's the sample for?"

"I'm going to be a father," I offered, in response to his coercive gaze. "The mother wanted me checked out before we went through with the process."

"The process?"

"I'm a surrogate," I said, the words clipped with clinical sterility.

"That's very intelligent of her," he said, and added, before I could take it the wrong way, "and noble of you." He tapped his pencil on the clipboard. "But I'm curious. Why come to me for a simple blood test? Any of the in-and-out clinics would have done."

"That's true. In fact, I just came from a clinic where I could have had it done. But I wanted to speak to you. I was referred by William Goodrich."

"I saw that on your chart," he said. "Which is stranger still. William Goodrich isn't a patient of mine. His wife April is."

"I said I was referred by Billy Goodrich, Dr. Burn. I didn't say it was a medical matter." I buttoned my shirt and looked up at the doctor. "April Goodrich is missing. Her husband hired me to find her."

I handed the doctor one of my cards. He cleared his throat as he looked it over, then handed the card back to me.

"I'm afraid I can't discuss my patients with anyone without their consent. That is something that I think you can understand."

"Of course. But I'm not here to ask you if you know her whereabouts. I wouldn't ask you," I lied, "to compromise your professional relationship with your patient."

Dr. Burn had a seat on the folding chair and crossed one long leg over the other. He removed his reading glasses and placed them on the counter to his left. "Then what is this about? Is April in any danger?"

"I don't know. She may have just walked away and made a clean break from her marriage. Even if that's the case, I still intend to find her. It's what I was hired for. But if something's happened to her, it would help to know of any medical difficulties she may have. It could increase her chances."

"You mean, if she's been kidnapped."

"That's right."

"I would need to check this out with the police first, before I spoke to you. I assume they know."

"They have a record of her disappearance," I said.

Dr. Burn said, "I'll call you."

* * *

THE PHONE RANG SHORTLY after I arrived at my apartment.

"I spoke to the police," Dr. Burn said.

"Well?"

"Your story checks out."

"So? Is there anything I need to know on the medical end about April?"

"She's a healthy young woman," he said carefully, "as long as she watches herself."

"What's wrong with her, Doc?"

Dr. Burn chuckled without joy. "She's got a very minor problem, one that you would benefit from greatly," he said. "She's allergic to booze."

"No shit."

"Precisely."

"So April Goodrich can't take a drink."

"Not exactly," he said. "April is both corn- and grape-sensitive. Most liquor is out, of course, and it goes without saying that wine is too. The majority of rum sold in this country is shipped in hogshead barrels, blended with grape brandy before bottling. So that's out too. But rum bottled in Jamaica is a different story."

"You lost me."

"April can drink liquor that's free of corn or grape, and drink it she does, Mr. Stefanos — to excess. She's damn near what we used to call a Jamaican rummy."

"And if she drinks something else?"

"She knows not to. She'd get violently ill."

"Anything else?"

"Nothing on the medical end, as you say. Nothing else particularly unusual."

"What about on the personal end?"

"It's none of my business, of course" he said. "But I'll tell you this: on more than one examination, I noticed various…

markings about her wrists. Sometimes similar markings were around her ankles."

"What kind of markings?"

"Burns of a sort. Hemp or wire."

"You think she was tied up?"

"The markings would seem to indicate some sort of bondage, yes."

"April ever mention it? Complain about it?"

"No."

"Consenting adults, Doc. It's not my thing, but it's not illegal."

"Maybe not. But I met her husband once on a consultation, when they were considering having a child. Let's just say that I don't think April left home involuntarily. He seems to have had a proclivity for sudden anger, an anger perhaps that could have manifested itself in violence. Does that paint any type of picture for you?"

"It's vivid enough."

"Good luck, then," he said abruptly. "And good luck with fatherhood too. Your blood specimen was fine, by the way. Though you ought to take it easy on the sauce, as a general matter of health."

"It's under control," I said.

"I don't think so," he said.

"Thanks for the advice, Doc, and thanks for the information. You've been a big help."

TEN

THURSDAY'S *POST* WAS light on news but heavy with inserts. I read it that morning as I sat on my convertible couch, a mug of coffee resting on the couch's arm. My cat sat next to me, her thin body barely touching mine, licking her paws with deliberate, efficient zeal. Occasionally I reached over and scratched around the scarred socket that had once housed her right eye.

The headline of the Metro section screamed that the homicide numbers had exceeded the previous year's, with three weeks to spare before New Year's Day. Arsons and gay bashings were on the increase as well. Several related articles described the "faces behind the victims" of the street crimes that were now spreading "west of Rock Creek Park," a D.C. code phrase for whites. This from a newspaper that routinely buried the violent deaths of its black readership in the back of the section.

After my second cup of coffee I laid Dream Syndicate's *Medicine Show* on the turntable, cranked up the volume, and cleared the rocker out from the center of my bedroom. I jumped rope for the duration of the album's first side; for the B-side I did abs and several sets of push-ups. Then I showered, shaved, dressed, and had another cup of java and a cigarette. The cat slid out the door with me as I left the apartment. I tapped her head slightly before she scampered away into the depths of the backyard.

The platform of the Takoma Metro was empty at mid-morning. I caught a Red Line car and grabbed an early copy of *City Paper* that had been left beneath my seat. By the time I had finished the weekly's arts reviews, I was ready to transfer to the Orange Line at Metro Center. Six stops east I exited at Eastern Market and headed down Eighth to the Spot.

Darnell was standing by the door, waiting as I arrived, his hands deep in the pockets of his brown car coat. Next to Darnell was the tiny man-child Ramon, smiling his gold-toothed smile. Ramon had on a pair of Acme boots and wore a cheap cowboy hat with a red feather in the brim. Though there weren't many Western types left in D.C. (the garb was still mildly popular with Latins), there had been a short craze of it in the gay community centered around the 1980 release of *Urban Cowboy*. At that time it was nearly impossible to walk around the P Street area without witnessing a sea of cowboy hats. My friend Johnny McGinnes, never accused of being too sensitive, had dubbed the headwear "homo helmets."

"Gentlemen," I said as I pulled the keys from my pockets and put the correct one to the lock.

"Same shit," Darnell said. "Different day."

THE LUNCH HOUR WAS over, and pensive drinking had begun. A fiddle screeched, and Dwight Yoakam sang, "It won't hurt when I fall from this barstool...." Happy stared straight ahead, his hand gripping a rocks glass filled with Mattingly and Moore. At the sports corner of the bar, Buddy and Bubba were splitting a pitcher, while a pompadoured guy from Bladensburg named Richard blew smoke in Buddy's tight-jawed face and loudly insisted, "I'll bet you a goddamned C-note, goddamn it, that Tampa Bay did too make it to the fuckin' play-offs!" Melvin Jeffers's eyes were closed as he sat alone at the other end of the bar, mouthing the words along with Dwight Yoakam. I sipped a ginger ale and chewed ice from the glass.

Dan Boyle entered the Spot at three o'clock, had a seat at the bar, and exhaled slowly. His eyes, like a bashful old hound dog's, slid up the call rack to the Jackie D. I put a mug of draught in front of him and poured two fingers of the mash into a shot glass, placing the glass on a damp Bushmill's coaster. Boyle shut his eyes and drained the shot, then chased it with some beer.

"How's it goin, Boyle?"

"*Bad Day at Black Rock.*"

"Ernest Borgnine," I said. "And Lee Marvin."

"I'm not kidding, man. Been over at Edgewood Terrace all day, in Northeast. Twelve-year-old kid got blown away over a pair of Nikes. Shotgun load to the chest. You could drive a truck through the fuckin' hole. And the look on the kid's face by the time we got to him — twelve years old. I seen a lot of death, man. I seen too much death." Boyle rubbed his face with one large hand while I free-poured another shot. This one he sipped.

"You got a kid about twelve, don't you, Boyle?"

"A girl," he said. "It never gets any better, to see a kid get it, no matter who it is."

"Even when it's just a spade, right?"

Boyle had some more whiskey and some beer behind that, then focused his pale eyes on mine. "Don't be so fuckin' self-righteous, hombre." He was right, and I let him give it to me. I looked down at the bar until his voice softened. "Anything happening on the Henry deal?"

"Something will shake out."

"You let me know when it does," he said.

"Bet on it, Boyle. I will."

* * *

AN HOUR LATER ONLY Happy remained at the bar. A Chesterfield burned down in his right hand as he slept. For a while I watched it burn, then lost interest. Shirley Horn was smoothly pouring from the house speakers. Drinking music. I began to eyeball the Grand-Dad on the call rack and was contemplating a short one when the phone rang. I stubbed out my own smoke and picked up the receiver.

"The Spot."

"Nicky, that you?"

"Billy?"

"Yeah."

"It's hard to make you out, man."

"I'm on the car phone, on Two-ninety-five."

"What's up?"

"What's up with you? Anything on April?"

"Nothing," I admitted, then waited for his reaction. Hearing only static, I continued. "I was thinking of heading down to southern Maryland on Saturday. Talk to her family, see if she's been through."

"Want some company?"

"I'm a big boy."

"Sure you are," he said. "A big city boy—you'll be a fish on dry dock in that part of the country." Billy paused. "Me and April spent a lot of time together down there, Nick. And I've got a key to the trailer on her property. We can stay there tonight."

I thought about that. "I've got to make arrangements to have Mai take my shifts tomorrow. And I've got to go home, to feed the cat."

"Fuck the cat," Billy said with annoyance. "Listen, I'll pick you up in an hour, hear? I've got another sales call, then I'll swing by. We can go by my house first—there's something I want you to hear."

"I need warm clothes."

"You can wear some of mine."

"The ones with guys playing polo on them?"

"Turn 'em inside out, wise guy."

"All right, Billy. See you then," I said just before the click.

I glanced over at Happy to make sure there was still some paper left on his smoke. I dialed the number of my landlord and let it ring several times. No answer. Then I dialed Jackie's work number and made it through an army of secretaries before I got her on the line.

"What's going on, Nick?"

"Just checking in," I said. "Trying to picture you right now. What do you, got your wing tips up on the desk, leaning back in your chair?"

"Yeah, it's just a white-collar picnic around here. Come on, Nicky, I'm really busy. What's up?"

"I got a clean bill of health, Jackie. So I just wanted you to know that I haven't forgotten our date Sunday night."

"Somehow I didn't think you would," she said.

"What time?"

"Make it seven," she said.

"Okay. And Jackie—wear something provocative." I heard her groan. "Anything you want me to wear?" I added cheerfully.

"Not particularly," she said. "But there is something I don't want you to wear."

"What would that be?"

"That silly little grin," she said, "that you're wearing on your face right now."

"Right," I said. "Seven it is."

I hung up the receiver, walked over to Happy, dislodged the butt from his callused hand, and crushed it in the ashtray. It woke him up, or at least a half of him. One of his eyes opened and he looked into mine and mumbled something brusquely, something I couldn't make out.

"What?" I said.

"Gimme a fuckin' manhattan," he said. "That's what."

*   *   *

BILLY GOODRICH WAS THE picture of Young Turk affluence, D.C. style. In the driver's seat of his white Maxima, with his somber, subtly plaided Britches suit, suspenders, thinly striped shirt with spread collar, maroon-and-gold retro tie, and forty-dollar haircut, he oozed mindless ambition. Billy threw a glance in the direction of the passenger seat, where I was tapping the side of my index finger against the window.

"April called," he said, "and left a message on my machine."

"When?"

"Today. I called home for my messages and there it was."

I spread my hands. "Well?"

Billy said, "You'll hear it. We're almost there."

We had turned off 29 onto 214, a winding, gently rising road between the towns of Scaggsville and Highland. Only twenty minutes north of the District line over the Patuxent and into Howard County, the area was a mix of farmland broken by the creeping beginnings of development. Livestock dotted the landscape patched with last week's snowstorm as the sun burned down in the west. I lowered the passenger visor and sat back.

About a mile past a small shopping center that housed a pizza parlor and video rental store, Billy hung a right onto a gravelly two-lane road. He eased into a circular driveway and cut the engine. The sun had dropped now, leaving his house, a long rambler of brick and stone, in shadow.

"Nice," I said.

"I stole it," Billy said. "Come on."

We walked to his door, behind which we heard three deep barks and then some impatient crying from what sounded to be a large breed of dog. Billy turned the locks and a brown-eyed shepherd-Lab mix with a yellow coat appeared, her tail wagging slowly. She licked Billy's glove and smelled mine, and we entered the house.

I followed Billy through a marbled foyer and past a living

room elegantly but rather self-consciously appointed in Louis Quatorze furniture. The dog walked clumsily beside me, bumping my leg and looking up at me as she did it. We reached a kitchen done in white custom cabinetry with white appliances and a white Corian countertop ending in the shape of a modified mushroom cap.

"Take your coat off and have a seat," Billy said. "Want a beer?"

"Sure."

Billy pulled on the weighted door of the built-in refrigerator and withdrew a bottle of Sam Adams. He removed the cap with an opener and handed me the bottle. I had a pull of the cool, sweet lager and then another.

Billy said, "Listen." He went to a small oak table with scrolled feet, on which rested an answering machine, telephone, large notepad, and a Ball jar of pencils and pens. He pushed the bar on the answering machine.

A female voice began to speak on the tape. It was a calm voice, the words spoken plainly and without anxiety, with the upward inflection at the end of each sentence that is the vocal trademark of the mid-Atlantic South.

"Hello, Bill. . . . It's me, baby. You got my note I guess. . . . I guess the note kinda said it all. But I wanted to tell you, 'cause I figure you'd want to know . . . I figured you'd want to know that I'm all right, Bill. I went to see Tommy one last time and then I left, and now I'm . . . away. But I wanted you to know that I'm okay. Take care of Maybelle, baby, that's all I'm going to ask. . . . I'm not scared, Bill. . . . Take care."

Billy stopped the tape and hit the rewind. I stared at him as I listened to the whir of the machine.

"That her?" I said.

"Yeah."

"She sound all right?"

"She sounded real calm, buddy. Real calm."

"Who's Maybelle?"

Billy chin-nodded the Lab and said, "Her dog."

"And Tommy?"

"An old friend. An old boyfriend, I should say. In southern Maryland."

"Then we're headed in the right direction."

"I'd say so," he said unemotionally.

"You gonna play this for the cops?"

"Should I?"

"Don't erase it," I said. "But I don't think you need to bring them in again, not yet."

Billy nodded. "Relax while I get some things together. I'll be out in a few minutes."

When he was gone I walked to the kitchen's bay window and looked out into the dusk that was rapidly turning to darkness. Maybelle stayed with me and smelled the leg of my jeans. "That's my cat you're smelling, girl." I scratched behind her ears and rubbed the bridge of her snout. She licked my hand furiously, cementing our friendship.

Walking to the phone, I dialed my landlord. Still no answer. I finished my beer and tossed the bottle into a wastebasket that I found under the white porcelain sink. I drew another Sam Adams from the Sub-Zero and moved a chair to the bay window, where I drank it facing out into the night. Maybelle lay at my feet, breathing slowly.

Fifteen minutes later Billy emerged from the shadows of the hall and dropped a duffel bag at my feet. "Road trip," he said, smiling. "Like the old days, Greek."

"Right." I found a black cotton turtleneck and navy shakerknit sweater in the bag and put them on. Billy handed me a blue Hollofil jacket. I zipped that up over the sweater and transferred my smokes from my overcoat to the jacket pocket. I patted the pocket. "What about Maybelle?"

"My neighbors can walk her tomorrow."

"Let's bring her."

"She'll be a pain in the ass."

"She's April's. Let's bring her."

The mutt's tail was already wagging. Billy shrugged and the dog woofed and trotted to the front door of the house. We followed and Billy locked the door behind him. Out in the driveway we walked to the car, where Maybelle waited patiently for Billy to release the front seat of the Maxima. Maybelle leaped into the backseat as I entered the passenger side.

"Thirsty?" Billy asked as he ignitioned the car.

"I could stand it."

"We'll stop in the old neighborhood on the way out," he said, a trace of boyish mischief peeking through his smile. "For a short one."

Billy tapped on the brights as we pulled out onto the gravelly road. In the vanity mirror of the visor I saw Maybelle staring out into the blackness. Her breath formed crystal gray spiders on the tinted glass.

ELEVEN

A T 29 WE stopped at a deli for a six of Bud cans and drank two of those on our way into Silver Spring. Billy talked about the soft real estate market the whole way in, shaking his head solemnly between swigs of beer. He was wearing jeans and oilskin Timberland boots and a logoed, royal blue jacket over a heavy wool shirt. We kept the radio off, the low, steady hum of the engine the only sound around our silences.

Billy parked in Wheaton and cut the engine in front of Captain Wright's, near the intersection of Georgia and University. Captain Wright's had stood stubbornly at that corner through twenty years of modernization, and though it was in the geographical domain of the now-closed Northwood High, it had always been the hangout for students and "alumni" of Blair. Blair boys liked to think that their Territorial Wrights (as they called them) had evolved from the fact that the place was just too tough for Northwood boys, but in truth many of the bars in that part of the county, from Silver Spring to Aspen Hill, were roughly alike. It was a headbanger's bar, with the stale, vinegary smell of cheap liquor oiled into every wooden crack. A suburban boy on his way to a rotten liver could maybe get laid here, and if not, he could always skin his knuckles. The sign outside read CAPTAIN WRIGHT'S, but every teenager who gunned his glass-pack Firebird or muscle car Malibu up Georgia and University in the seventies had called this place, with some misplaced degree of affection, "Captain Fights."

I patted Maybelle on the head and cracked a window for her before we headed into Wright's. Over the door a plastic marquee announced that the Jailbaiter Boyz (from Frederick, no doubt, in that all the boogie/glam-metal outfits from that part of the state substituted their *s*'s with *z*'s) were the headliners that evening. We pushed on a thick door and left fresh air behind for stale as we entered.

The Jailbaiter Boyz, pale and strangers to exercise, were in midset, pounding out their deafening rendition of "Sweet Home Alabama." A confederate flag hung over the empty dance floor, surrounded by unaligned four-tops filled with flanneled and T-shirted young men drinking long-necked Buds and Lights. Few heads were moving to the music. We caught the perfunctory hard stares from the most insecure members of each group as we passed and made our way through the maze of tables to the dart room.

In the dart room several groups were in play. Some of the male players had their sleeves rolled up past their biceps and all had Marlboro hardpacks in their breast pockets. I recognized one woman as a high school acquaintance, her features heavy now and swollen from drink. She had been part of a group of wild ones who rode around in a lavender Gremlin on weekends, a car that Blair's males had collectively dubbed the Meatwagon. I had made out with her one night in someone's dark basement while Billy had had his way with one of her friends in the side room. I nodded to her, but she didn't know me, and I walked on.

In the back room Billy and I stepped up and leaned on the

bar. A wiry ex-wrestler from Blair named Jimmy Flynn was tending, where he had been since graduation. Flynn had always managed to make weight and go to the mat in the one-twenty-nine class; there wasn't much more of him now. He nodded and said, "I see you two jokers are still hanging out together."

Billy said, "And you're still pushing beer."

"Yeah."

"Give us two Buds, then."

"I'll have a bourbon with mine, Jimmy," I said.

"What'll it be?"

"Grand-Dad, if you've got it."

Flynn pointed to the unlit call rack. "Jack and Beam is what it is."

"The Jim Beam will do it," I said.

Billy put money on the bar and walked back toward the dart room, where I saw him move toward a woman in a half-length black leather coat. Her hair was as black as the coat, and she wore blue jeans and a loose purple sweater that didn't work at hiding her lush shape, if that was what she was after. She smiled at something Billy said, and he leaned into her slightly and returned one of his patented pretty-boy grins. I looked around the bar.

I knew one guy standing up, an alcoholic named Denneman who was memorable for having thrown up whiskey one morning in junior high first period industrial arts, thrown it up with stunning ferocity on the varnished oak of the center drafting table. His young porcine features had mutated into an obese mask of pink splotches and scars. Someone bumped my back—on purpose, I supposed—and I didn't bother to find out why. Instead I searched for a friendly face.

There was one—a guy I knew who had worked for years at the local Shell, sitting at a deuce away from the crowd with his girl, a plump young woman in a waitress uniform of white oxford shirt and black skirt. I grabbed my beer and whiskey off the bar and moved across the room to join them.

Thankfully, the guy's name was stitched across his shirt. "Hey, John," I said, shaking his hand.

"Nick, right?" He smiled crookedly but with warmth as I nodded. "Have a seat, man. This is my girlfriend, Toni."

Toni looked a little looped but still conscious and I shook her clammy hand as I sat. I was relieved to find that John was as genuinely nice as I remembered him, and the conversation stayed dead set on what type of Chrysler product I was driving now. But John had to go and screw things up by excusing himself to play a game of darts, leaving me to sit with Toni, who was becoming alarmingly more drunk with each rum and pineapple she was firing down.

Toni excused herself and stepped up to the bar. I waved my arm to get Billy's attention, but he was deep in conversation with the woman in black leather. And John, a lit cigarette drooping out the corner of his mouth, was playing his darts.

Toni returned with a bar tray, on which were set two rum drinks and another round for me. She served the drinks, left the tray on the sticky wood table, and slid the bourbon and beer in front of my forearms.

"Drink up," she said. "I can tell you like it."

I shrugged and had a pull off the fresh beer. The Jailbaiter Boyz were playing a Guns N' Roses cover amid some competing activity in the main room, most likely a spiritless fight.

"So, Toni. Where do you work?"

Toni made me pay for that innocent question by launching into a tirade against the management of the Brave Bull, a steak house around the corner on the mistakenly named Grandview Avenue. Then she got right up in my face (hers was now ghoulishly contorted) with graphically venomous descriptions of her unfortunate coworkers, and it became apparent that she hated all of them, save the Greek chef she called Uncle Baba, who was the "undisputed master" at carving "fuckin' sides o' beef" and "fuckin' cuts o' veal," a point that she argued with the vehemence of a litigator at the Nuremberg Trials.

"If you hate the place so much," I said tiredly behind a slug of Beam, "why don't you leave?"

" 'Cause I can't get a good job," she said indignantly, looking around carefully (as if there would be an African-American face within miles of Captain Wright's), " 'cause the colored women get all the good jobs."

"Where'd you get that idea?" I said, realizing as I did that I had made a huge mistake.

"Where? Where? I'll tell you where. I know it's true 'cause my ex–old man used to work for Montgomery County Social Services. That's how I fuckin' know."

For some reason I said, "Your ex–old man? Bullshit." And then I watched her fat little face turn red.

Seeing the hopelessness of the hole I had admittedly dug and then leaped into, I began to look around the bar for help. Toni wouldn't let it die, though, and she reached her flabby right arm across the table (her tricep was shimmying flatulently like one of Uncle Baba's cuts o' meat) and began to sock me on the shoulder with progressively harder punches, yelling, between each slug, "Huh? Huh?"

I realized then that she actually wanted to fight, and for a brief moment I indeed considered what a kick it would be to see her rubbery face cave in as I smacked her across the barroom, but John was a truly good guy, and then there was the tiny obstacle of the six-and-a-half-foot bouncer of indeterminate lineage in the black Harley T-shirt who was now eyeing me out the corner of his narrowed eyes. I finished my shot, then my beer, and set the bottle on the table.

"Have a nice night," I said, and went to recover Billy.

I pulled him away from his friend and gave him a nudge for the front door. Somebody at one of the tables near the dance floor yelled something at Billy, but when we glanced in that direction no one was looking our way. The Jailbaiter Boyz were destroying Free's "Fire and Water" as we headed out the door and into the cool, fresh air.

Billy was laughing as we climbed into the Maxima. May-belle's tail thumped the backseat. "You saved me, man."

"I saved myself," I said. "Who was the lady?"

"No lady." Billy shook his head as he started the engine and pushed a button for the heat. "I met her in here one night, about a year before I met April. Took her over to my car in front of Wheaton Guns, that night, and fucked her right in the parking lot. She made me pull out before I came—she didn't want to get pregnant 'again,' she said. Man, I shot off all over her leather jacket, the same motherfucker she was wearing tonight. She got some hankies out of the glove box, real calm, and wiped all that jism off, like it was nothing. And we just walked back into Cap'n Fights and had a couple more beers."

"You're a hopeless romantic, you know it?"

Billy chuckled. "She called me a couple of times after that. Described on the phone how she wanted to do all this funky shit to me—leather and shit—shit I'm just not into, man. So I didn't hook up. I never saw her again, until tonight. But I gotta love that jacket."

"A sensitive guy, Billy. To the end."

"That's me, Greek." He smiled. "How about another beer?"

"Okay."

"We're on a roll tonight, aren't we?" Billy handed me a beer and opened one for himself.

"Yeah, Billy. I believe we are."

I found WMUC on Billy's radio. They were just crashing into the intro to the Replacements' "Seen Your Video." I clock-wised the volume as we pulled out of the lot and headed south on University, toward the entry ramp to 495.

TWELVE

T HE MAXIMA CUT a swift southeast arc on the inner loop of the
Beltway. We followed and then passed taillights of various
geometric mutations, using the leftmost lane for the pass and
then returning to the center. Billy seemed to be holding his
booze fairly well, though the fact that he was driving did not
seem to influence his rate of drinking. He was on a tear, and I
was right there with him.

We exited at Route 5 and headed south, stopping at the
first bar we saw, a strip joint named the Fourway at a traffic
crossroads in Clinton, to cop a six of long-necks. I waited in the
car and kept an eye on the movement behind the fogged car
windows in the lot. Billy emerged from the bar, the thump of
bass briefly chasing him until the door behind him swung
closed, and hustled to the car. We popped the caps on two of the
beers, swung back out onto the highway, and once again drove
south.

The road went to four lanes with a wide, bare median, the terrain hilly at first and then flattened out. In the southeastern sky the bright yellow moon was full and large. We passed pickup cap depots and parts yards and outdoor ornamental pottery shops, broken by the odd stretches of undeveloped land. Ten miles of that, and the low lights of Waldorf appeared ahead.

Charles County's Waldorf stood where Route 5 met 301. It had once been a gambling mecca for Washingtonians who had a taste for the slots, but that had ended by law sometime early in the sixties. Scattered remnants of Little Vegas remained—the Wigwam "casino" had been converted for a while into a bakery, and now the peaked structure was nothing but an empty glass tepee—but Waldorf had been reborn initially as a five-mile stretch of car dealerships, Taco Bells, and strip shopping centers whose tenants consisted primarily of liquor stores, electronics franchises, low-end clothiers, knockoff booteries, and convenience markets. Now the area had entered another phase, as its predestined growth pushed it into the league of Washington Suburb. A mall at the south end of town, anchored by two mildly upscale retailers, had opened to much fanfare, bringing with it the legitimization of a ten-plex cinema and a new Holiday Inn.

But all the swirling logos and white-handled shopping bags could not mask the fact that Waldorf was still Waldorf—the memory of the abandoned 301 Drive-In still loomed like a decaying gray ghost over the highway, and it still took fifteen minutes to get an ice-cream cone from the geriatric hair-netted help at Bob-Lu's Diner. Then there was Reb's Fireplace (the sign had two silhouetted swingers dancing the night away over the tag line LET'S PARTY TONIGHT!), aptly named since it had become a raging inferno one night three years earlier and had remained undemolished, a charred shell and unforgivable eyesore to the occupants of the Volvos who cruised by nightly on their commute home to the planned "city" of Saint Charles.

Billy pulled the car into the next lot down from Reb's, where a nightclub called the Blue Diamond stood windowless and alone. The lot was filled with Ford and Chevy pickups, late-model American sedans, and Mustangs and Firebirds. We parked next to a black El Camino that had a blue tarp in the bed covering varying lengths of PVC pipe.

"What's going on?"

"One of April's haunts," Billy said. "She used to stop here on the trip home, and usually on the way back. Maybe someone's seen her."

I patted the dog, who had instinctively lain down when Billy cut the engine. We locked up and walked across the lot. A couple of young men exited the club as we approached. They didn't look at us, and they didn't hold the door. The Top 40 rock coming from inside faded and then blared out as I pulled the door open once again.

The Blue Diamond had two circular bars on either side of the room and a large dance floor in the middle, with a live band playing on a barely elevated stage in front of it. The band was finishing up their set with "Glory Days," the vocals buried somewhere in the heavily synthesized mix. A sea of acid-washed jeans, high-tops, and ruffled shirts moved on the dance floor. A glitzy banner behind the band announced that they were FRIDAY'S CHILD.

Two mustachioed bouncers, both twig-legged but heavy in the chest, checked our IDs. We moved to the bar and ordered a couple of domestics. I paid the tab and added a healthy tip, and the neckless bartender took both without a nod. Billy and I turned and leaned our backs against the bar.

No one spoke to us while we drank or even gave us a hard stare. Finally I turned to Billy. "Come here often?"

"I like it like cancer."

"We're way too old for this shit. Nobody even wants to kick our asses."

"I know," he said. "Let me ask around, then we'll split."

"That's my job."

"And you can do it. But I'll do it here. I know some of these guys."

"Go ahead."

I grabbed my beer off the bar and walked into the men's room. After I drained I washed up in a dirty sink and ran a wet paper towel across my face. When I walked out Billy was on the other side of the room talking to the barkeep. He was putting something back into his wallet while he talked. He nodded and headed back in my direction. I finished my beer and placed it on the Formica-topped bar as he arrived.

"Let's go," he said.

"Any luck?"

Billy shook his head quickly. "These brain-deads don't know a fuckin' thing."

We moved across the empty dance floor to the entrance-way. I noticed the blue vein of determination on Billy's temple, and I knew he was going to crack on the doorman, knew it like I knew the sun was going to rise, knew it from all the teenage years we had spent together in bars more dangerous than this. When we reached the door, Billy turned to the larger of the two bouncers and smiled.

"Thanks," he said. "We had a great time. And oh yeah" — Billy whacked his own forehead thoughtfully — "I meant to tell you when we walked in. I really like those jeans you're wearing tonight."

"Yeah?" the doorman said with hesitance.

"Yeah," Billy said, the smile turning down on his face. "My sister's got a pair just like 'em."

The doorman sighed and said, "You guys have a nice evening," holding the door open for us as we walked out. I zipped up my jacket as we moved across the lot.

"What the hell you do that for?" I said.

"It's his job to take shit."

"You always had to do that, Billy. You always were a mean drunk."

"Drunk?" Billy said, showing me his young-boy grin. "Man, I'm not even halfway there."

We climbed into the car, and Billy started it up while I fixed him a beer. Maybelle's nose touched the back of my neck. Billy caught rubber and tilted back his bottle as he pulled back out onto 301.

Waldorf ended abruptly, and then the highway was the same as it had been before—flat road and forest with the occasional strip shops, failed antique stores, and billboards. Billy kept the needle at seventy, and ten minutes later we hit La Plata, much like Waldorf only less. Past La Plata were last-chance liquor stores and low-rise motels with Plymouth Dusters and Dodge Chargers and Chevy half-tons parked in their gravel lots. Billy aimed the Maxima for a red-and-blue neon sign touting on/off sale as we both drained the last of our beers.

"You go in," Billy said, cutting the engine. "I'll pitch the empties in that can." He nodded to a rusted oil barrel open on one end that stood near the bar entrance.

We were parked in front of a wide, noncurtained plate-glass window. The bar—it had no name—was cinder block painted white. Through the window I could see a small group of men in their thirties and forties shooting pool. "I'll be right back."

I left the car, walked to a glass door, pulled it open, and entered. It was only ten o' clock, but the place was lit up like last call. I guessed they didn't go much for atmosphere—a look around the place confirmed it. There were three scarred pool tables standing on the industrial-tiled floor, with some metal folding chairs scattered around the tables. A jukebox was against the left wall, though it wasn't lit and there was no music playing. A narrow wooden bar stood against the back wall, also unlit, with a small selection of low-call liquor racked behind it.

There were two games being shot, and the entire patronage of the bar was grouped around the games. The men wore designer jeans circa 1978 and sweatshirts with the sleeves pushed back to reveal uniformly pale and hairy forearms. The few women in the joint, teased hair and also in jeans, sat in the folding chairs drinking beer and smoking cigarettes, the ashes of which they flicked to the floor. The men's cigarettes were balanced on the edges of the pool tables, lit end out.

I moved to the bar and on the way got a chin nod from one of the players, a nod that I returned. The woman behind the bar was blond and maybe fifty, with a raspberry birthmark on her right cheek.

"What can I get you?" she said in a businesslike but upbeat way.

"Two sixes of Bud bottles to go," I said, "and a pint of Old Grand-Dad. Thanks."

"Don't have the Grand-Dad. Something else?"

"A pint of Beam, then."

"The Black or White?"

"Make it the White."

She wrapped the bourbon and handed me the bag. "Let me go in the back and get you the beer." She winked. "Rather not pull it from here, have to restock the cooler later."

She left the bar and entered a walk-in to the left of it. I turned, rested my back on the bar, and looked out the plate-glass window onto 301. Billy was standing in the gravel next to the Maxima, looking down at the rush of his own steaming urine as he peed toward the window. His hair was unmoussed now, full and ruffled as I remembered it from his youth, and his mouth was slightly open, with that dumb look of stoned concentration he had perpetually worn as a teenager. I felt a sudden sting of guilt and looked away. I drew a cigarette from my jacket and lit it, keeping the hot smoke in and giving it a long exhale. Someone tapped my shoulder.

One of the pool players stood next to me. He had long black hair thinning on the top, and he was skinny and nearing forty. His small potbelly barely hung over the waistband of his Sergio Valente jeans.

"That your friend out there?" he said in a direct but not unfriendly way, pointing out the front window.

"Yeah," I admitted.

"I'd appreciate it," he said, giving a quick nod to a woman in one of the folding chairs, "if next time he wouldn't be so quick to show off in front of my wife."

"I'll tell him," I said.

He nodded and smiled. "You take care, buddy."

"You too."

I paid and thanked the woman behind the bar, put the bourbon in the larger sack, and moved toward the door. On the way out I smiled apologetically at the man's wife and got a smile back. Out in the lot I took a last drag, tossed the butt, put the beers in the backseat, transferred the pint to my jacket pocket, and patted the dog on the head. Two of the beers came out of the bag before I settled in.

Billy grabbed one, popped it, and tapped my bottle with his. He drank deeply and turned the bottle to admire the label. "That's what I'm talkin' about."

"You ready? Or you going to do a beer commercial."

"No, I'm ready. But I really had to let one fly."

"I noticed. So did all those folks inside."

"You talkin' about those rednecks?" Billy said, pointing in the window. "*Fuck* them."

WE CONTINUED SOUTH. THE road ahead was free of commercial activity and hilly once again as we neared the Potomac. I lodged my beer between my thighs and withdrew the pint of Beam from my jacket. I twisted the cap, broke the seal, and handed the bottle to Billy. He had his and then passed me the bottle as he chased it with some beer.

"That's good," he said, wiping his mouth with his shirt-sleeve. "Been a long time since I took whiskey from a bottle."

"Listen, Billy…"

"What?"

"I was looking at you, back there, pissin' on the highway. I saw you for a second, like it was you, man, fifteen years ago."

"Yeah?" Billy looked at me briefly with a blank smile and returned his gaze to the road.

"I'm trying to apologize," I said. "That's what I'm trying to do. I've been kind of ice cold, man, since you walked into the Spot. I expected things to be like they were with us, when we were kids—like *you* were. You understand?"

"You're drunk, Greek," Billy said, turning his face in my direction again. Half of his was lit green from the dashboard lights. "You *are* drunk, aren't you?" He smiled. "Or are you trippin'?"

"I guess I'm just drunk." I had a slow pull of bourbon, then beer. "Not trippin', though. Last time I did that I was with you. Right before you went away to school. Remember?"

Billy reached for the bottle. I put it in his hand. "That time in the park, right?"

I nodded, thinking back. The blurred dark limbs of trees rushed by against the night as I stared through the passenger window and recounted that night for Billy.

ON A LATE AUGUST afternoon, at the tail end of the summer of 1976, Billy and I had eaten a couple of hits of blotter that I had copped through the back door of Nutty Nathan's from Johnny McGinnes. We smoked a joint on the way down to Candy Cane City and once there began a round of pickup ball with a group of Northwest boys we had come to know. For the first hour we were on our game, but that ended when the acid began to seep in, and after a while our laughter caused us to drop out. I went home and took a shower, sneaking around my grandfather, unable to look him in the eye. Then Billy came by and picked me up in his Camaro.

That night had started like any other—we had no clue at first as to where we were headed, only that we were headed out. Neither of us talked about the buzz—that would have been uncool—but when Billy asked me to drive I knew he was tripping as hard as I was; he had never let me drive his car, even on his most twisted nights.

Billy was wearing straight-leg Levi's that night, rolled up once at the cuff, and one of those glitter-boy rayon shirts, from a store named Solar Plexus, in Silver Spring. The red lid of a Marlboro box peeked out over the top of the shirt pocket. On his feet were the denim stacks that he had bought at Daily Planet, a pair of shoes that he knew I had always wanted to own.

For some reason we ended up on Beach Drive in Rock Creek Park. I had begun to hallucinate mildly, but it was under control, and my driving up to that point had been okay. But then Billy popped *Eat a Peach* into the eight-track, and he turned up the volume, and when "Blue Sky" came on, and Dickey Betts moved into his monster guitar solo, I lost my shit. It was at that point that I was convinced that the car was going to lift up and fly right off the parkway.

I pulled over at a picnic area, Billy laughing over the sound of the tape, and he walked me down to a patch of dark, gravelly beach at the creek. I lay down by the creek and stared at the top branches of the oaks that lined the east side and listened to the rush of the brown water over the rocks and the loopy liquid guitar that was still flowing through my head. Then Billy took my shoes off and put his—the denim stacks I had coveted throughout our friendship—on my feet. And he talked to me for at least two hours. By then the branches had melted into the flannel gray of the sky, and there was a small throb in my stomach, and I had begun to come down.

"THAT WAS A NIGHT," Billy said when I was finished. "After that we went down to some hippie bar, right next to the Brickskeller at Twenty-second and P, second floor, got sober on alcohol. Some band was playing, some cat blazing on lap steel, right?"

I nodded. "Danny Gatton."

"How do you remember all that shit?"

"The funny thing is, I almost forgot. And the thing is, the thing you did for me that night, *those* kind of things are the only things worth remembering. Am I making any sense?"

"Yeah, pardner, you're making sense. Hang on." Billy eased off the gas and swung the Maxima into the turn lane. He pulled left across the highway onto Route 257. We passed a gas station and liquor store, then drove southeast, into a shroud of darkness.

THIRTEEN

W E FOLLOWED 257 for a quarter-mile, blowing by a hardware-and-bait shop lit only by a John Deere sign in the window. Then Billy abruptly veered left off the interstate, onto a roughly paved, unlit road that swept up into a grove of high shrub and pine, then opened to acres of flat field.

"Where we goin'? I thought April's property was off Two-fifty-seven."

"It is. Mount Victoria road parallels Two-fifty-seven. We'll come back out onto it at Tompkinsville." Billy winked. "Watch this, Greek," he said. Then he cut the headlights of the Maxima.

For a couple of seconds Billy and I were green, and every-thing outside the car was black. I grabbed the handle of the door and gripped it until the road ahead began to appear, slowly, in a bluish light. The moon was bright and almost directly overhead.

"You sure you want to do this, man?"

"Like we used to do, on that stretch of Oregon Avenue, down in the park."

"We knew that road."

"I know this one," Billy said. "Roll your window down, man, it's not too cold. Enjoy it."

I did, as Billy maxxed out the heater fan, then rolled his own window down. Maybelle came forward and laid her head partly on my arm, partly on the door, leaving her face out, letting the wind blow back her ears. She closed her eyes.

The sound of the heater meshed with the wind. I had a slug of bourbon and passed it to Billy. Through the glass of Billy's roof the moon shimmered above as if it were submerged in water. We passed a small gas station with an old Sunoco sign lit and suspended from two chains at the corner of a two-lane intersection, then moved on. No headlights approached from ahead or from behind.

Low trees began to appear on either side of the road, and the road grew darker. Billy saw something just ahead of his path, or maybe he didn't, and he laughed piercingly and swerved, and we drove onto a shoulder of loose gravel. There was a sharp, screaming metallic scrape. Maybelle yelped, and there were sparks, and I drew back my face just as something shaved it like a quick, cold razor. I turned and looked through the rear window, and saw a roadside mailbox uprooted and tumbling back onto the shoulder in the fading rouge glow of our brake lights. I checked Maybelle and she was all right, though now she was lying bellyflat on the backseat, her head resting firmly between her two front paws.

Billy's laughter was softly manic. I cackled with him and rubbed my right cheek, feeling raw skin but no blood. Then we were in a forest of pine, and there was almost total blackness, except for the light through the space between the tree line above, a light that snaked parallel with the road. Billy's laughter ebbed and he shifted his sight from the road to the tree line and back again, navigating the course while negotiating the serpen-

tine curves. At the bottom of a steep incline the road seemed to
end in a finality of shadow, but Billy turned the wheel sharp
right just as we seemed on the edge of the chasm, and then we
were suddenly out of the trees and on the flat blue road again,
the vast, open, moonlit fields on either side.

After another mile Billy tapped on the headlights, and we
merged back onto 257, turning left. I cracked two more beers,
handed one to Billy, and lit a cigarette for myself. We passed a
Methodist church and several bungalows with screened porches
set back from the highway, Pontiacs and Buicks parked in the
yards. A couple of markets that sold gas and liquor and lottery
tickets slid by. Both the markets and the houses were closed
and unlit.

Two miles later Billy turned right at 254 and accelerated
down a straight stretch of highway toward the lights of Cobb
Island. He slowed as we neared the water and drove by two crab
houses and bars on opposite sides of the road. The bar on the
right had lit Christmas lights strung around its low-rise white
facade, with lights that ran along the dock as well, out into the
channel beyond a gas pump and boat ramp. The road rose as we
crossed a bridge with cement rails that arced over the channel
and connected the mainland to the island. When we rolled onto
the island, Billy pulled the car into a lot past an IGF grocery
store and killed the engine in front of a small bar called the Pony
Point.

"A nightcap?" Billy said.

"How's my face?"

Billy grabbed my chin and turned my head into the light.
"You'll make it."

"Let's go."

We chugged the rest of our beers and put the empties in
the backseat, where Maybelle now slept. Out in the lot I tripped
stepping up over a concrete divider and felt Billy grab my jacket
and yank me back into balance.

"Keep your shit," he said. "Let's have some fun."

We stepped into the Pony Point. The place consisted of one small room paneled in knotty pine with a U-shaped bar extending out from the wall that divided the front of the house from the back kitchen. The bar was nearly filled. "Tight Fittin' Jeans" by Conway Twitty was shrieking out of the tinny jukebox. I felt heavy and slow as I moved toward the bar, but by now I had acquired that singular glow of imagined invincibility that is bestowed upon certain drunks during particularly blessed binges.

Billy and I found two empty red vinyl stools on the west end of the U and bellied up. A large jar of pickled pig's feet rested on the bar between us. I signaled the barmaid, a woman in her sixties with steel gray hair flipped on one side. She moved slowly to our curve in the U as she wiped an aquamarine bar rag across her hands. When she reached us she kicked her chin up just a bit to signal for our order. One of her spotted hands, with short, hard nails painted apple red to match the color drawn across her lips, rested on her hip. That hip, which still had a shape distinct from the rest of her, was slightly cocked. Grandma, with a fistful of rolled nickels.

"What can I get you fellas?"

"Two beers and two whiskeys," I said. "Make the beers Budweisers and the whiskeys Grand-Dad."

"I suppose you take your bourbon straight up," she said, and tilted her chin up once again to let her eyes look us over.

"Yes, ma'am."

She served the beers at once and rooted around the rack for a couple of shot glasses. While she did that, Billy and I tapped bottles and drank deeply. Then I had a look around the Pony Point.

On the east curve of the U sat three drunken men, their shoulders touching as if joined. The man in the middle was young, with a flattop and pale skin and an over-the-lip wisp of light brown hair masquerading as a mustache. He was bookended by two older men, one of whom was a well-worn version of flattop. Several beers sat in front of the three of them. The two older men looked quickly over to flattop and sang, in ravaged unison, "I'm gonna stick...like glue."

Flattop looked into my eyes from across the bar and yelled, with a crooked smile, "Tomorrow ah'm a fuckin' marine!" The Pony Point was filled with noise, but I could have heard the kid from out in the parking lot.

Our bourbons were served, and I raised my glass to Flattop before tapping Billy's and tipping the shot to my lips. The warm liquor slid down with slow-jazz ease. I savored the afterburn, then asked the barmaid her name.

"Wanda," she said.

"Wanda, buy those two older ones their next round. And give the soldier in the middle whatever he wants."

"Sure thing."

Billy said, "And we'll take a couple of those pig's feet, honey."

Wanda said, "You got it."

A hand wrapped around my arm. It was attached to a little man in a Cubs cap who was sliding onto the stool to my right. The man was not very old, but he had lost his teeth and on this night at least was not wearing the replacements. He used my arm for support as he adjusted his butt to the center of the stool.

"Thanks," he said, and removed the cap to wipe a fuzzy, rather bullet-shaped head.

"No problem."

"I see you're buyin'," he said matter-of-factly. He was trying to look up at me, but his gray eyes were missing the mark, shooting up toward the beamed ceiling.

"Why not? What are you drinking?"

"I'd love some whiskey. You like Conway Twitty?"

"No. But I dig Merle Haggard."

"My name's Ken."

I shook his hand and said, "Nick."

Wanda served our pig's feet on paper plates set next to

plastic forks and then poured Ken a shot of rail whiskey. Ken knocked back half of it posthaste and cupped his hand protectively around the glass as he set it down on the bar. Billy ignored the fork, picked up the pig's foot, and began to chew meat off the bone. I tasted a sliver of mine, rejected the texture, and pushed the plate in front of Billy. The juke was playing Dolly Parton's "Jolene." I lit a cigarette and ran my hand back through my hair.

Two men stood by the kitchen door at the far side of the room. One was heavy and dark-skinned and wore an eggshell apron stained brown around his waist. The other was tall and lean and wore Wrangler jeans and a brown flannel shirt unbuttoned once to expose a triangle of white T-shirt at the base of the neck. Both of them stared at me until I looked away. When I looked back their attention remained fixed. I turned to Ken.

Ken said, "You like Randy Travis?"

"Uh-uh." I said. "You ever listen to Gram Parsons?" Ken's eyes traveled back up to the ceiling as he thought it over and shook his head. "How about Rodney Crowell?"

"That's that boy married to Johnny Cash's girl, right?"

I nodded. "Had a great single on the country charts, seven or eight years back—'Ashes by Now.'"

"Yeah," Ken said. "I remember it. He's pretty damn good."

I turned my head to the left. Billy dropped what was left of the pink-and-yellow pig's foot to the plate and wiped a paper napkin across his mouth. He chin-nodded the two by the kitchen door. The tall one nodded back without emotion.

I said, "I don't think those two like us."

"They're all right."

"You know 'em?"

Billy had a long, even taste of the bourbon and winced. He set the glass back down on the bar. "Black dude with the apron's named Russel. Local boy, knew April when they were young. The tall hard guy's Hendricks—a state cop. Grew up in Nanjemoy on the other side of Three-oh-one. Rides out of La Plata but spends a lot of time around the island. Don't take it personal. It's me they don't like."

"Maybe I should talk to 'em."

"Suit yourself. Want an introduction?"

"No."

I killed my bourbon, stubbed my smoke, and picked up my beer. Ken suggested another round, but I ignored him as I pushed away from the bar and followed the curve of the U. I swerved by two old guys with winter sunburns and dirty hands and was clapped on the shoulder by one of Flattop's crew as I passed his back. His crossed eyes zeroed in on my chest as he sang, "I'm gonna stick... like glue."

The one with the apron, Russel, turned on his heels as I approached. By the time I reached the end of the bar, he had retreated into the fluorescence of the kitchen. That left me and Hendricks.

Hendricks looked in my eyes evenly and for a long time. I studied his as he did it. He had the clean, open face of a man who works hard every day and likes it. His eyes were dark blue, framed by short bursts of lines and set wide; his broad mouth stretched out across a stone jaw. I put him at about my age, though weathered by the elements.

"How's it goin'?" he said.

"It's goin' good."

"You about done nursin' that beer?"

"Yeah."

"Let's have another."

"Sounds good." I finished off the bottle. "But I'm buying, okay? Makes sense to buy the local cop a beer when you're in his county."

Hendricks grinned just enough to lift one cheek. "I won't stop you," he said.

"My name's Nick Stefanos."

"Hendricks."

I signaled Wanda with a sweeping victory sign and had her

serve another shot to Ken. Billy was off and talking to a huge bearded man in a Red Man cap who stood blocking the front door like a bear in overalls. The bearman's narrow eyes were obtusely pointed to the floor as Billy talked. When the beers came I raised mine to Hendricks and had a swig. The floor tilted somewhat beneath my feet. I wrapped a hand around the curved lip of the bar.

Hendricks said, "Which one of you lovers is drivin'?"

I pointed the neck of the Bud at Billy. "We're not going far. Sleeping at April Goodrich's farm tonight." I closed one eye a bit to focus on Hendricks. "You know her?"

"Knew her before she was named Goodrich," he said.

"Seen her lately?"

"That what you came down here for? Lookin' for April?"

"That's right."

"What's it about. Personal?"

"It is for him." I glanced quickly toward Billy and back to Hendricks. "For me it's a job."

Hendricks said, "You're no cop."

I shook my head. "Private."

Hendricks thought about that over a long, slow pull of beer. He placed the bottle softly on the bar, looked my way, and relaxed his shoulders. "So what happened to your face?"

I rubbed it and felt the swell. "To tell you the truth, I don't remember. We made a night of it, I guess."

"It's not a bad face," Hendricks said frankly. "But you can't tell a thing about a man when you meet him on a drunk. And right now I don't know nuthin' about you but your name. You want to talk to me, I'll be around the island tomorrow."

"Fair enough." I shook his hand.

"You take care, now."

Just then Hank Williams, Jr., roared out of the juke and Ken began to yell, from across the bar, "Bocephus! Boceeee-phus!" He was pointing at me and smiling and with one hand keeping the cap on his head as he bucked like a rodeo clown on the red vinyl stool. I weaved recklessly across the smoky bar, past Flattop and his send-off crew (his uncle or father appeared to be holding the young man upright now at the bar), and made it over to Billy. Ken was off his stool and at my side by the time I reached Billy and the bearman.

"Let's get out of here," I said.

Billy tried to focus one eye. A block of his blond hair had fallen over the other. "Had enough?"

"Yeah."

"One more stop, though."

"Where?"

"Place called Rock Point."

Ken let out a small whoop and I thought I saw the bearman break a tobacco-stained smile. I handed Billy some bills and he put those together with some of his own and left them all in a leafy heap on the bar. Wanda flicked her chin at him and then at me by way of thanks. Hank Williams, Jr., was still pumping out the bar-band jam as the four of us proceeded to fall out the front door. When I turned around for one final glance at the joint, Russel and Hendricks were standing in the entranceway to the kitchen. They were talking to each other, but they were looking dead straight at me.

THE FOUR OF US crashed like a wave into Billy's Maxima and headed north on 254. I handed a tape I had lifted from the Spot over the seat to the bearman and had him slip it into the deck. Steve Earle's "I'm the Other Kind" immediately boomed out of the rear-mounted speakers like some Wagnerian, biker-bar anthem. The bearman turned up the volume and clumsily moved his head to the beat. I watched it bob from behind like a hairy, floating melon. Ken sang the romantic wind-road-and-bike chorus (in between screaming praise about Earle's band, the Dukes—he called them the "Dee-yukes") and passed beers all around.

At 257 Billy turned sharply right, spit gravel, then recovered his course onto a crudely paved road that soon narrowed to one lane. We passed a shack of a general store—an old man in a down coat sat in a lighted telephone booth and waved as we drove by—and some screened bungalows set far back on properties bulkheading the Wicomico. The road ahead, veined now with deep fissures and cracks, seemed to narrow even further. And then, without warning of any kind, the road simply ended.

We parked the car in front of a steel guardrail serving as a barrier. To the right, on a raised plot of dirt and naked turf, stood a post office the size of a tollbooth. Billy and the bearman got out of the Maxima, and Maybelle scrambled over my legs to follow. Ken was next out, and then me. I felt the temperature drop sharply as my face met the winter wind that was coming out of the southeast and off the river.

Billy cut the engine and the lights; the music still played. I trailed the group—Maybelle had trotted off into a wooded area to the right—and climbed over the barrier, on which was posted a NO TRESPASSING notice peppered with buckshot. What was left of the concrete road continued, buckled and in pieces, on a downward slope to the river. The swells of the Wicomico shimmered from the light of the moon and moved diagonally toward the shore in rough cadence with the wind. South beyond the point the Potomac merged with the Wicomico in cold, deep current. I zipped my jacket to the collar.

Ken and the bearman stopped at the waterline; one of Ken's fists dug into his jean pocket, the other gripping the neck of the Bud. The bearman appeared to be rolling a joint—he was carefully twisting it now, his muttonchop hands working the papers very closely to his small eyes—and Billy, with the cheesecloth bladder that had plagued him since childhood, was pissing like a filly near a grove of sycamores on the edge of the gravelly beach. I drew the pint from my jacket and knocked back an inch of bourbon.

Down on the beach I joined Billy and passed him the bottle. He had his taste and then we both followed it with beer. The wind was lifting Billy's hair off his scalp and blowing it about his face. Music came from the road and through the trees—Steve Earle had yielded now to Neil Young on the tape. The feedback and grunge of twin Les Pauls and Young's wailing vocals pierced the rush of the wind.

"The road ends at Rock Point," Billy said out of nowhere, stating the obvious and pointing his beer bottle toward the river with uncharacteristic dramatic punctuation. "I used to come here all the time, that first summer when me and April got together. She didn't understand the attraction—to her it was the place where she and her friends came to smoke pot and drink and screw when they were growing up—but there was something to it for me. Something about the road running right into the fucking sea."

"What about now?"

"It went to seed," he said, adding, with a bitter edge, "like everything else in this life." Billy drank his beer and wiped the backwash on his jacket sleeve. "Rubbers and beer cans, and gooks fishing for spot. That's all this place is now."

I nodded in the direction of our new friends. "You know those guys?" The bearman had lit the joint and was stooping low as he shotgunned Ken, the Cubs hat now set far back on the little man's head. Ken had cupped his hands around the bearman's face to get it all, and the cloud of smoke emanating from their union was great and wide. Ken's head appeared to be on fire.

"I've seen 'em around the island before. Barflies." Billy looked at them and chuckled. "That's just what April'd be doing right now, if she hadn't met me. Gettin' high and hangin' out."

"There's more to this place than that. After all, she keeps coming back."

"Most people don't have enough sense to stay away from home, even after they outgrow it." Billy finished his beer. "Come on, man, let's get out of here."

"What about those guys?"

"They'll want to stay down here," he said. "Come on."

Billy and I walked back up the buckled fun house road and climbed over the barrier. Neil Young was shouting "Come On Baby Let's Go Downtown," backed by the primal electric rage of Crazy Horse; the wind kicked at our backs. I looked back to see if the bearman and Ken were following, but Billy was right—they had drifted. The bearman was doing a slow shuffle on the beach, and Ken had leaped out into the river to a slab of concrete that the tide had not yet covered. He was dancing some sort of whacked jig, and he appeared to be singing toward the sky.

We climbed into the Maxima, Maybelle appearing suddenly from the trees and taking her place in the backseat. Billy lowered the music and cranked up the heat, rolling the windows up as he did it. I looked back through the rear window. The music no longer reached his ears, but Ken continued to dance out on the concrete slab in the river. The bearman stood with his hands buried in his pockets, a stoned stare focused up at the full December moon.

THE GRAVEL ROAD TO April Goodrich's property was at an unmarked turnoff two miles back up 257. We followed it straight into a wooded area, and then it turned to hard dirt as it continued out into several acres of plowed field. The road ran through a field bordered by woods on three sides and on the fourth by a wide, still creek. In the center of the field stood a hickory tree, under which a small trailer was mounted on concrete. It had a poured concrete patio in front and a corrugated Plexiglas eave hanging over it. The road from there went back through the field and down to a dock that ran out and into the creek. We passed the trailer and drove down to where the road ended at an open boathouse that stood near the first planks of the dock.

Billy cut the engine and the lights. I could hear Maybelle's tail excitedly thumping the backseat, but beyond that there was just the deep silence that exists at night and only in the country.

"What now?"

Billy said, "Let's get out and feel the water. Finish the whiskey."

We exited the Maxima. Maybelle bounded out before us and ran out onto the dock. I waited for Billy to lead the way and then stepped out onto the vertical planks that bridged the severely eroded bank to the dock. Beneath my feet the wood was white with the excrement of gulls. The wind had abated here, though the air was damp and bitter.

The dock ended in the head of a T. I sat on a piling and buried my hands in my jacket pockets. Maybelle lay on her stomach to my right. Billy climbed down an aluminum stepladder that had been halved and lashed with thick rope to the pilings on the eastern corner. He was out of sight now, but I heard his hand splashing in the freezing water.

"Ice cold," his voice said. "Not frozen yet, though."

"I'm not comin' in for your ass if you fall in."

Billy climbed back up the ladder and said, "Sure, you would. If there's one thing I know, that's it." Billy rubbed his hand dry on his jeans and had a seat next to me. He leaned back on one elbow and pointed at my jacket. "Let's have a drink and a couple of those smokes."

"Sure."

I brought the pint and the Camels out from my jacket and rustled the pack in his direction. Billy drew one from the deck and put it to his lips. I fired his up, put one in my mouth, and lit it off the same match. The tobacco hit my lungs and I kept it there. I watched the silver exhale drift slowly in the motionless air like a ghost and spread out over the creek.

Billy took the Beam off the dock, uncapped it, and had a drink. He sighed comfortably and stretched like a waking animal. "Good night," he said.

Across the creek one prefab rambler stood in a clearing in the woods. Mounted atop a pole in front of the rambler was a spotlight that illuminated the property. A horse stood beneath the spotlight inside a small grassy area framed by a split-rail fence. The horse's breath, backlit and haloed, poured from its nostrils and widened into two even streams.

Some time passed. Billy pitched his cigarette out over the dock and into the creek. I followed the orange trail and listened to the quick, dull finality of the fire hitting water. Then I had a last drag of my cigarette and threw what was left of it in the direction of his.

"Your head's rolling," Billy said. "Let's go on up to the trailer."

I looked around at the dock. "Where's the dog?"

"You've been noddin'. I was waiting for that smoke to burn down into your fingers—would have let it too. But you woke up." Billy stood and reached for my hand. "Maybelle ran off. She'll be all right."

I stood with Billy's help. "We ought to find her. She'll freeze."

"Not cold enough. Come on, let's turn in."

We walked off the dock and onto the dirt road that cut through the field. Some clouds had drifted across the sky; the darkness seemed denser now. At the trailer Billy jiggled a key in the lock and opened the door. I followed him into the narrow space and closed the door behind me. Billy found a candle in a drawer and forced it into the neck of an empty bottle of Rolling Rock. He struck a match and lit the candle.

The trailer appeared smaller lighted. An old double-barreled shotgun rested in the hooks of a rack mounted above a narrow kitchenette. I thought I heard something move beneath one of two bunks that end-capped the trailer's interior, and raised an eyebrow in Billy's direction.

Billy smiled and shook his head. "If there's snakes in here, they're sleeping. Field mice, if anything."

"Oh."

"Here." Billy tossed me a rolled sleeping bag and pointed to the bunk where I had heard the noise. I ignored his direction and spread the bag out on the other bunk. Then I stripped naked and zipped myself in. I balled up shivering, waiting for the ache of cold to subside. The objects on the kitchenette and then the kitchenette itself began to move and float. I fell into an open-mouthed sleep.

I awoke some time later. A dull throb had entered my temple, and my mouth was glutinous and dry. There was a bit of natural light in the cabin now; dawn had begun encroaching on the night. I looked over at Billy.

He was up on one elbow, half out of his sleeping bag, smoking one of my cigarettes and staring into my eyes. His eyes reflected the flame of the candle that still burned in the green bottle. The lower right portion of his face was in shadow. We kept each other's gaze for a while — then I drifted back to sleep. When I opened my eyes, Billy was still staring. Now there was a cool smile across his smooth face. He dragged off the cigarette and thumb-flicked some ash onto a piece of foil set on the Formica counter that held the candle.

I said, "Something's not right, Billy. Let's talk about it."

"You're coming down off a drunk, that's all. You gonna be sick?"

"I don't mean that."

"What, then?"

"This whole thing." I sat up in my bunk and wiped the back of my hand across my mouth. "Who's Tommy?"

"Tommy?"

"The guy April talked about on the answering machine."

"Tommy Crane." Billy sighed. "Fuckin' pig farmer. Lives up Two-fifty-seven a few miles. April used to do him and maybe she still does. She said on the tape she was coming down here to kiss him good-bye. That's what we're doing down here, remember?"

"An old boyfriend, right? Like Joey DiGeordano. And that guy at the Pony Point, Russel — another old boyfriend. Maybe Hendricks too. All these old boyfriends — and you don't seem too shook about it, Billy. That's what the fuck is bothering me, man. It's been gnawin' at my ass since you hired me."

Billy squinted against his own smoke. "What's your point?"

"Do you love her?"

He looked down at the table as he butted the cigarette in the foil. His face had fallen into shadow, but when he looked back up again it was lit by the fork of the flame. "No, Nick, I don't love her. I'm not sure if I've ever been in love, to tell you the truth. But I'm sure I never was in love with her."

I struggled against a curtain of alcohol that now pushed down upon my consciousness. "I don't mind being a sucker, Billy—it's happened to me before—but I don't want to be *your* sucker, understand? We've got too much behind us, man, too many years."

"Sure," he said. "Let's clear it."

"You put April onto the DiGeordano heist, didn't you?" Billy nodded with hesitation. "Joey called it the first time I sat with him. He said you were pimping your own wife. I didn't want to believe him. Now I do."

Billy nodded again and lowered his eyes. "I'm sorry, man."

"You two were going to split the two hundred grand down the middle, then April was supposed to disappear. But April got wise. She booked with the full take and left you out in the cold. Now you want to find her and take back your share. That's what you really hired me for—right, Billy?"

"That's right, Greek," he said. "That bitch took what was mine, understand? And now I want it back." The shadow of the candle's flame danced across Billy's smile.

My eyes closed, watching him. The trailer darkened, and then it was black. I dreamed of high school, Billy, me, our teachers, our friends. Dead now, all of us.

FOURTEEN

THERE WAS A tightness in my chest, and in my sinuses the suffocating stench of stale smoke. I unzipped my bag and sat up naked on the edge of the bunk. My feet dangled, and I let my toes touch the cold linoleum of the trailer floor. I pushed the hair away from my eyes and rubbed my face for a long while. Then I dressed slowly, turned the knob of the trailer door, and stepped down onto the concrete patio, out into the light.

It was a clear and cold sunny day. Billy stood down by the bank, scrubbing Maybelle with a thick-bristled brush that he dipped in the brackish water of the creek. I zipped my jacket to the neck and walked across a field ridged with hard brown mud and a ground cover of freshly sprouted winter wheat. By the time I reached Billy, he was drying Maybelle with a yellowed towel. Maybelle shook off, snorted, and ran up the bank to greet me, her tail moving excitedly. I rubbed the top of her head as she pushed the side of her snout against my leg.

Billy's car was parked by the boat shed. A deep scrape was etched in the white paint and ran from the rear quarter panel to the mirror on the passenger side. I looked at it and then at Billy.

"I don't want to talk about it," he said. "I'm feeling bad enough, so let's not talk about it, okay?" I nodded. "How you doing?"

"A little rough," I said.

Billy put his fists in his pockets and tried to widen his eyes. "Want some breakfast?"

"Sure."

THE PONY POINT WAS open for business. We parked in front and left Maybelle behind. By now she had used her paws to form a bed from the yellowed towel.

A small bell sounded as we opened the front door and stepped inside. Wanda was behind the bar. She flicked her chin in our direction and threw us a tight smirk as she looked us over. I kept my eyes on my shoes and followed Billy to a booth.

A square-headed guy wearing a camouflage hat sat alone drinking coffee in the booth behind Billy's back. At the bar sat Flattop and his two older companions, beers in front of them all. They were still alive but barely conscious—one of Flattop's eyes had rolled up into his head while the other stared straight ahead. The uncle leaned his weight into Flattop, in an effort to keep them both upright. The other man was sleeping, his posture still erect, his hand wrapped around the body of the Bud.

I looked over at the hunter and then at Billy. "What's in season?"

"Rabbit," Billy said.

Wanda stood before us, her shapely septuagenarian hip slightly cocked. She tapped the pencil on the order pad and dished Billy with her smirk. "Bloody Marys?"

Billy said, "I'll have one in a mug."

I said, "Just coffee for me. And breakfast. Eggs over easy, with toast and scrapple."

Billy nodded. "I'll have the same."

Wanda wrote it down and then spun on her heels. She walked back behind the bar and tore the check off the pad, sliding it through the reach-through. I saw an eggshell apron fill the space and a brown hand grab the order. Flattop's uncle snapped his fingers with an on-the-one beat and sang, "I'm gonna stick... like glue."

"I'll be back in a minute, Billy."

I rose with difficulty and shook the dizziness from my head. At the bar I took a thick white diner mug from a stack and poured some coffee from the fullest pot heating on the Bunn-O-Matic. I had a sip standing there, then walked around the U of the bar to the kitchen's entrance.

Inside, Russel was standing over a large grill. On one side of the grill a dozen hand-packed burgers precooked slowly on the breakfast-level heat. Russel poured some grease from a coffee pot onto the other side. It spread into a pool the size of a dinner plate and began to sizzle.

"How's it going?" I said.

"It's goin'," he said without looking up. Russel took a thick black-handled knife from the rack and cut two slices from a wax-papered block of scrapple. He laid the scrapple carefully into the grease, then turned to face me.

Russel's hair was cut in a modified fade. His eyes were baby-round and olive green. Two black moles dotted the brown skin of his left cheek.

"I'm Nick Stefanos." I walked across the brick-colored tiles and shook his hand. His grip was tentative.

"I know your name," he said, and grinned slightly. "But I would have recognized you anyway. You're wearin' the same tired shit you had on last night."

"Didn't bring a change of clothes."

"Uh-huh."

He faced the grill again and turned the scrapple. I walked over to the opposite wall and leaned my back against a stainless-steel refrigerator. The kitchen was warm, and Russel had opened the back door. Some sun fell in through the wood-framed screen. Through the screen I watched a large black cat lick her kittens clean on a concrete porch. Beyond that, on a worn patch of brown grass, a three-legged German shepherd slept. I had a deep swig of coffee and lit a cigarette. The smoke of my exhale hovered and shimmered in the oblong wedge of sun.

"I'm looking for April Goodrich," I said.

"Hendricks told me."

"Can you help me?"

Russel used a spatula to retrieve the scrapple from the grill. He slid the scrapple onto a plate that he had lined with paper towels to absorb the grease. Then he broke two eggs using one hand, and another two after that. Russel carefully pushed the spatula around the white edges of the eggs.

"Depends on what you want to know," he said.

"Was she here?

He nodded. "She was down here."

"When?"

"About a week ago, I guess."

"When exactly?"

Russel thought it over, the spatula pointed upward like a barometer. "Middle of the week, about then."

"In this place?" I dragged on my cigarette and let the smoke drift.

"She doesn't come here," he said. "On the other side of the bridge, at Polanski's."

"Doin' what?"

"Drinkin' Jamaican rum," Russel said, chuckling. "Like she always do."

"Who with?"

His smile faded. "Tommy Crane."

"How'd they look?"

"Drunk. Crane had two beers in front of him and April was all over him."

"Why doesn't she do her drinking in the Pony Point? Avoiding you, Russel?"

"I don't think so," he said. "That was a long time ago. She's forgotten all about me, man."

"What about you?"

"Like I say, that was a long time ago."

"You still in love with her?"

Russel turned the eggs without breaking the yoke, then leaned his wide ass against the cutting board that fronted the grill. He crossed his arms and looked me over. "You ask a lot of questions, man."

"It's my job to ask questions."

He sighed and looked toward the wall. "I can't say if I was in love with her. I don't know. It's easy to confuse being in love with just lovin' the memory of a certain time. A certain time in your life, I mean. When anything's possible, all the shit's out in front of you. Before the world gets real, beats you down."

"Pretty philosophical."

"That's me. Two years at Howard, and that's what I got. Goethe, Sartre. Existentialism and the Absurd—the last class I took before I booked. Absurd is right. None of that shit had a goddamn thing to do with what's reality."

I looked at Russel's apron and then into his intelligent eyes. "What are you doing down here?"

He chuckled. "How's D.C.?"

"You know how it is."

"Where you live?"

"Shepherd Park."

"Uptown."

"Uptown, and east of the park."

"Yeah, I know how it is, all right. Rough two years I spent

up there—for a country boy. In D.C. I wasn't nothin' but a 'bama." Russel relaxed his shoulders. "So that's what I'm doing here. I like this place. I like to walk at night, and I like to fish and I like to hunt. And I like my animals, man." He glanced out the screen door. "My cats and my dogs."

"You seen April since that night at Polanski's?"

"Uh-uh," he said, shaking his head.

"Why's she hooked up with Tommy Crane?"

"April likes the wheel, and Crane's holdin' serious weight. That boy's damn near a legend."

"I don't follow."

Russel said, "If Crane had any more dick, he'd be wearin' three shoes. You follow now?"

I had a last drag and pitched the rest of my cigarette out through the gap in the screen door and into a mound of dirt. Russel lifted the eggs off the grill and dropped them onto two plates. He added the scrapple and some buttered toast from a stack, then placed both plates on the platform of the reach-through.

"Your breakfast is up, man."

"Thanks for the information."

"You got honest eyes. I didn't talk for you, though. And I sure didn't talk for that gray husband of hers. If April's runnin' from him, then I wish her luck. But her hangin' with Tommy Crane can only come to bad."

"I'm going out to his place now, to talk to him."

"Then you take care," Russel said. " 'Cause that's one crazy motherfucker."

BREAKFAST WORKED. I HAD two more cups of coffee, then voided my rotten bowels in the men's room and washed up. When I walked out, Billy, who still looked somewhat ashen, took my place in the sole stall. I made a go-cup of coffee at the bar, thanked Wanda, and stepped out into the parking lot for some clean air.

Hendricks was sitting in his unmarked Ford, the powerful engine idling. He stepped out of the white car without cutting the ignition and strode slowly in my direction. He was in his brown uniform now, though his general appearance hadn't changed. He had looked exactly the same the night before—like a cop.

"So," he said, hooking his thumbs through the belt loops of his slacks. "How you feelin' today?"

"Better now. Thanks."

"Nothin' a good breakfast can't cure, right?"

"Russel's a good cook."

"Best in this part of the county."

I glanced at the .357 Smith & Wesson that was holstered on his hip. The lacquered walnut stock gleamed in the sun. "I see you favor the four-inch barrel."

Hendricks frowned with interest. "Now, how you know that, Stefanos?"

"My grandfather was an S & W man. So I heard enough trivia over the years for some to stick. Your gun's squared on the butt—and they only square it on the four-inch. Smith and Wesson rounds the butt on the three-inch barrel."

"That's right." Hendricks patted the holster. "It's not that the barrel size makes a damn bit of difference to me. But it makes a hell of a better...impression if you have to draw it."

"You have to much, down here?"

"It happens," he said. "But I can't say I favor this one at all. Fact is, the son of a bitch sights low. Much as I try to correct, I hit a full foot higher than I aim."

"Aim low, then."

"Thanks for the big-city tip." Hendricks winked, looked over my shoulder, and smiled with satisfaction as he followed Billy's labored trek from the door to the Maxima. I heard the engine start behind my back.

"I better get going," I said.

"Where to?"

"See if Tommy Crane's around. He was drinking with April at Polanski's a week ago. Maybe he can tell me where she went."

Hendricks said, "You don't want to be messing with that guy, if you can help it."

"Russel said the same."

"Well, he knows. Crane nearly beat the life outta Russel one night at Rock Point, for nothing at all. I was doing a routine drive-by and ran right up on it. By that time Russel was on the ground spittin' blood and froth, and Crane was still kickin' in his ribs."

"I'll watch myself."

"I'm not kidding," Hendricks said.

"I'm not either," I said. "This is just a job to me. And I don't want to die."

BILLY AND I CROSSED the bridge over the channel and turned left onto 257, then followed the highway for two or three miles. At a steepled church Billy turned right and drove back southeast toward the Wicomico. The road was narrow, though smoothly paved. Billy slowed at a gravel road on the left that broke into a thick forest of oak. He was turning in when I told him to cut the engine. Billy parked on the gravel road.

"What is it?" he said.

"Crane live back in there?"

"That's right."

"How do you know? You been here before?"

"Long time ago, when me and April were first coming down here. She introduced me; I didn't know there was anything between them." Billy looked me over. "What's wrong with you, man?"

"I don't want any surprises, that's all. I want everything up front before I talk to this guy." I cracked my window and stared straight ahead. "Joey DiGeordano told me that April took the money on Monday last. You say she took off on Wednesday. What happened in between?"

Billy glanced at his lap and brushed air off his leg. "We celebrated."

"Where?"

"I don't know. What difference does it make?"

"Tell me everything you did between the time she glommed the cash and the time she left you."

Billy sighed with annoyance. "All right. The night she came home with it, we stayed in. We paced a lot, didn't sleep much. The next day I worked and April stayed home. That night— Tuesday night—we went out. We were getting a little nervous then—about having all that cash, about when DiGeordano's boys were going to get around to come looking for it. And we planned to leave town the next day, cool our heels, whatever. Fact is, we didn't have a plan." Billy paused as he cracked his own window. Some sweat had appeared on his forehead. "Anyway, like I say, we went out. To a movie."

"What'd you see?"

"I don't know, some bogus action flick at the Laurel Ten. You know, the new one, with the guy's got a ponytail."

"What about after that?"

"We went out for a few."

"Where?"

Billy thought it over and waved a hand in my direction. "I can't remember the name, a chain joint. One of those phony Irish names, they have drinks comin' out of machines. Right in front of Laurel Mall. O'Tooligan's, MacManley's, some shit like that."

"April get drunk?"

"She always gets drunk."

"She get drunk enough to give you any idea she was going to split?"

"She was drunk enough. But no, she didn't say a word."

"And she left the next day."

"That's right. I went to work, and when I came home she was gone."

"No note, right? I mean, that computerized Dear John you told me about, that was all bullshit, right, Billy?"

Billy narrowed his eyes. "I apologized already, last night. You've busted my balls enough, don't you think? I've got nothing else to tell you."

"All right," I said, pointing down the road. "Let's go see Crane."

FIFTEEN

TOMMY CRANE'S COTTAGE was in a half-acre clearing about a quarter-mile through the woods. Fifty yards from the house was a cinder-block structure larger than the cottage. We parked the Maxima beside a red F-150 truck on a plot of hard sand under a single oak that stood next to the cottage.

I pointed to the cinder-block structure. "What's that?"

"Pig compound. He houses and feeds them in there. Slaughters 'em in there as well, from what I can remember."

I thought things over. "Crane probably won't let me in his house, if he's got something to hide. At the very least, maybe I can get in to use his bathroom. If he does let me in, I'm going to need as much time as I can in there alone, to look around. Do your best and keep him occupied, even if it's only for a few minutes. You'll know when to do it. But for now, just stay in the car, okay? I don't need any distractions up front."

"It's all you now, man. Go on."

I climbed out of the car and pushed Maybelle's head back in—she was trying to slide out with me—before closing the door. A fat sound, the movement of animals, came from the direction of the compound. The air felt colder as I passed beneath the naked branches of the oak. The branches cast shadows like black arthritic arms on the hard earth.

I stepped up onto a wooden porch whose planks were painted gray. There was a screen door and after that a solid one. I pulled open the screen door and knocked on the other.

The door unlocked quickly, and Tommy Crane stood before me. He was wearing a blue chamois shirt over a thermal under-shirt, and loose-fitting jeans. Over the shirt was a black down vest that bulged on the left side of his chest. On the side of his hip a knife was secured in a thin brown-leather sheath. The knife's handle was wrapped tightly with black electricians's tape. The long blade of the knife took up the balance of the sheath. The sheath ran halfway down Crane's thigh.

"Yes?" Crane said. The voice was controlled and uncom-fortably gentle—for a man his height and weight, it didn't fit. His tan hands were long and densely veined, and his rawboned wrists filled and stretched the cuffs of the chamois shirt. The wrists had the thickness and mass of redwood.

"My name's Nick Stefanos."

"That supposed to mean something to me?" Crane squinted and scratched his black beard. A wire-thin scar veed deeply into the right side of the beard.

"I work for Billy Goodrich," I said, turning my head briefly in the direction of the Maxima. Crane looked toward the car and saw Billy in the driver's seat, then looked back at me. There was lack of interest and mild annoyance in his thin black eyes. I shifted my feet to simulate discomfort as I handed him my card. "Mind if I come in?"

He gave the card a contemptuous glance. "For what?"

"I'm looking for April Goodrich. I understand she was down here and she was with you."

"She was down here," he said, and as he said it he stepped out onto the porch and closed the door behind him. Crane ran one hand through his thick black hair and pulled the bulk of it back behind his ears. Then he hitched up his jeans and puffed out his broad chest. "You want to talk to me, come on, but make it quick. I got work to do, and plenty of it."

Crane skipped the steps, jumped down off the porch, and landed walking, taking long strides toward the pig compound. I looked quickly at Billy. Billy shrugged, and I followed Crane.

I trailed him to a wood gate, where we butted through and stepped into a small grassy area enclosed by a barbed-wire fence. The wire was wrapped and tied at six-foot intervals to knotted wood posts driven deeply into the earth. We continued toward the cinder-block structure to an opening cut to accommodate an average-sized man. The structure was topped unevenly by a cor-rugated tin roof laid over asbestos sheeting. A thin periscopic chimney rose out of the roof, and gray smoke drifted out through the chimney. The wheezy animal sounds grew heavier as we approached the gate that was hinged to the opening.

Crane pushed on the gate and strode in, lowering his head to clear the top-frame of the entrance. I followed him into a dark, concrete-floored area of roughly eight hundred square feet. The entire structure was elevated to provide for a concrete feed-ing trough that ran around the sty and was accessible from the outside. On the left wall two farrowing pens were lit and warmed by infrared lamps, and in those pens two sows lay on their sides. Several piglets suckled the sows' teats from behind a set of steel rails. On the right wall were sleeping compartments where slats of timber had been cross-nailed inches above the cold concrete. In the rear of the sty a copper circular trough was mounted on a brick base. A fire burned in the center of the base and the putrid steam that rose from the liquid boiling in the trough entered a hole that led through the chimney. Next to the cooker was an iron drinking trough. Next to that a black hose lay dripping and coiled on the concrete. On the wall behind the troughs several butchering knives rested in the hooks of a punchboard. Beside the punchboard was an exit, exactly the size of the opening through which we had entered. The ropes of a pulley dangled from the rafters, above it all.

Crane kept walking. He lowered his head once more and stepped outside through the rear opening. I followed. Now we were in another fenced enclosure with twice the area of the yard in front. Bales of hay were lined end-to-end around the bottom of this fence, and a few dozen pigs and weaners of varying litters were lying on their sides on the worn grass, butted up against the hay. It was colder in the yard than it had been in the sty, but the sun was bright and the air was bracing and clean.

Some of the pigs had risen at the arrival of Crane, and they began to move about the yard. They alternately snorted and squealed. A white pig larger than the others moved slowly in our direction. The rest remained against the bales. I nodded toward them. "They like the feel of that hay?"

"Not really," Crane said. "Pigs like the sunshine, but they hate the wind. Hate it damn near worse than they hate anything. So they come outside for the sun and get behind the bales. Now one of those sows—that one over there"—Crane pointed to a large Middle White in the corner of the yard—"she's lyin' back because she senses it's her time to die. I haven't fed her for twenty-four hours, for the reason of the mess the killin' makes if there's food in her belly, and that just adds to her confusion. But she knows, boy. She knows."

A huge white pig came within ten feet of us and then turned and waddled off back toward the others. He had long deep sides and a strongly curled tail, and he appeared to be smiling. His huge balls hung low and nearly touched the ground.

"That must be the king," I said.

Crane snorted and smiled. His capped teeth were even and gray. "Yeah, he's the cock star. You get a Large White boar with a set o' nuts like that, boy, it only comes once in a lifetime. You can cross him with anything—Blacks, Middle Whites—the whiteness of his meat transports, makes great butcherin' pig." Crane looked lovingly at the boar. "I imagine he services fifty, sixty sow a year. Eats like a sumbitch too—seven, eight pounds a day—but he earns it."

"Pig-keeping your only business, Tommy?"

Crane squinted. "Askin' questions yours?"

"No. I work in a bar in D.C."

"Then there's your answer. Man does different things to get by—hustlin' drinks is just one, I guess. I do some hauling, small-engine repair—lawn mowers, go-carts. Stuff like that." Crane ran his hand back through his hair once more and looked me over. "Like I told you, I got work to do. What do you say we cut all this in half?"

"I'm for it." I looked quickly past Crane to the car. I could only see half of it from that vantage point, but the half I could see included the driver's seat. Billy wasn't in it. I returned my attention to Crane. "Talk about April."

"The truth?" Crane grinned like a disease. "April and me been doin' the crawl for years now," he said. "She didn't love me, and she didn't love her husband. But she liked what she got here more than she liked what she was gettin' at home. You see what I'm sayin'?" I shifted my feet. "Anyway, she finally had enough of your friend Slick, and she split. On her way out she came to say good-bye."

"When was that?"

"Early last week. I don't remember the day."

"How long did she stay?"

"One night."

"She say where she was going?"

"West."

"That's pretty vague, Tommy."

"It's the way she wanted it, friend."

"Would you tell me where she was if you knew?"

Crane rolled his tongue around the inside of his cheek and slowly shook his head. "No."

That finished it for now. We stared each other down to no effect amid the mass of pigs that had by now closed in around us. Then Billy appeared from inside the sty and walked out into the yard.

"Hello, Tommy," he said.

"Goodrich."

Billy turned to me. "You getting anywhere?"

"No." I shoved my hands in my jeans and looked around the yard with studied indifference. "Look," I said. "You guys talk it out, all right? I gotta take a leak."

Before Crane could stop me I had negotiated myself through a mobile maze of pigs and had entered the sty. I moved quickly out and into the front yard. Maybelle was barking inside the car—her nose had made wormlike marks on the window as she pressed against it—but I ignored her and jumped up the steps and onto the porch. I looked behind me to see if Crane had followed—he hadn't bothered, or Billy hadn't let him—and turned the handle of the front door. The door opened and I walked inside.

The first thing I saw was a small living room. There was a battered couch upholstered in faded blue and a heavily varnished table fashioned from the cross section of an oak. On the table was a blue bong, and next to that lay a small mound of green piled in the inverted top of a shoe box. Behind the couch a Roger Dean print was mounted and framed on a yellow wall. On the opposite wall a nineteen-inch Zenith was elevated on a particle-board cart, and next to that stood a rack stereo. The tall black speakers of the system bookended the Zenith. I walked through.

At the end of a narrow hall were three doors. One was opened to Crane's bedroom. Through the crack of the second I could make out a bathroom. The third door was locked. I entered Crane's bedroom.

The bedroom window gave a view of the entrance to the compound. Crane and Billy had moved back from the yard and were in the sty now. Billy's royal blue jacket was visible through the gate, and next to that the duller blue of Crane's shirt. Only their torsos showed in the darkness of the sty. They appeared to be standing very close to each other. I moved quickly past the window and to the dresser.

Crane's dresser was topped with loose change, an eel-skin wallet, some odd porcelain figures of black birds, and a porno mag. The cover of the porno mag—*Bang-Cock Blossoms in Tie-Land*—featured a smiling Asian woman with pink lipstick. I glanced back through the window, then checked Crane's wallet. Slid between the wallet's stained plastic covers were two photographs of two different women, neither of whom I recognized. In the billfold was a ten and three ones. I closed the wallet and placed it back on the dresser.

The dresser drawers contained Crane's underwear, T-shirts, and socks, and in one there was an assortment of lingerie. I went through each drawer quickly, running my hand beneath the clothing, finding nothing. When I was done with that I looked back out through the window. Billy was out of the compound and walking heavily toward the car. There was a particular anger on his face, a genuine anger that I had seen on him only once.

I ducked the window and moved back out into the hall. The locked door was still locked. I entered the bathroom and flushed the head. Then I ran cold water into my cupped hands and splashed it on my face. There was towel rack next to the sink but no towel. I opened a wall cabinet and pulled a white washcloth off the top of the stack. Small silver objects came out with the washcloth and fell to the tiled floor. They made a metallic sound as they hit. I bent down and scooped three pieces of jewelry—a ring and two earrings—up into my hand. I put those in the pocket of my jeans. Then I replaced the washcloth, stepped quickly out into the hall, walked through the living room, and bolted out the front door and onto the porch. The frantic cry of an animal mingled with the whir of the wind.

Billy was in the driver's seat of the Maxima, staring straight ahead. I moved to his window and made a roll-down motion with my hand. He pressed his thumb to a togglelike switch, and the window slid down.

"Gimme a smoke," he said. Some red had bled into the azure blue of his wide eyes.

"Sure." I shook one from my pack. Billy took it by the filter and pushed the lighter into the dash. "Crane tell you anything, Billy?"

Billy bit down on the cigarette as he lit it and spit some smoke out the window. He shook his head. "That son of a bitch knows where she is, Nick."

"I know."

"Well?"

"Stay here. I'll give it one more shot."

The crippled black shadows of the oak pointed toward the compound. I followed their direction. The frenzied animal scream increased as I pushed past the gate, walked across the yard, and entered the sty.

Crane was by the back door. He had tied the ropes of the pulley to the hind legs of the white sow. She hung suspended above an empty trough, her head jerking as she wheezed and screamed. I stood before Crane.

"We're taking off," I said.

Crane jerked his hand inside his black vest and pulled out a .38 snub-nosed revolver with a nickel finish. He passed the short barrel across my chest as he moved it to his right hand. I felt the blood drain from my face and then a flush of raw anger as I watched Crane smile. He rested the muzzle of the .38 between the sow's eyes.

"You look a little shook, Stefanos. Ain't you never seen an animal slaughtered?"

"I've never seen a man like it so much," I said.

Crane's smile turned down. He looked toward the sow and back at me. Then he ran his left hand down the sheath strapped to his leg. "What I like is the efficiency, friend. Only takes one shot. Then this stickin' knife, straight in ahead of the breast bone, six inches deep. They die quick, believe me, and they bleed right out into the trough. No mess."

I said, "If April doesn't show up in a few days, I'm coming back down here to talk to you, Crane. Got it?"

Crane lowered the .38 and held it by his side. He looked me over slowly. "I don't see a man who can back that up. All's I see is a two-day drunk. It's over, pal. April's gone. Now, you get gone too."

He began to raise the pistol. I backed up and walked away and didn't look back. Out in the air, I breathed deeply as I headed for the car. Billy reached across and opened the passenger door. I slid into the cold leather seat and stared ahead.

"Well?" Billy said.

"Nothing," I said as the sow's scream ripped the air. "Close your window, okay?"

Billy hit the toggle and the window closed tight, sealing out the death cry from the sty. "What about in the house? You find anything?"

"Nothing," I said, touching the jewelry through the pocket of my jeans. "Come on, man, let's get out of here. Let's go."

Billy started the engine. As we neared the trees I heard the dull thump of a pistol shot, then tasted the bilious remains of alcohol and breakfast surge up in my throat. I swallowed it and shut my eyes. There was only the hum of the engine then, and the steady sob of Maybelle from the backseat. I pushed the lighter into the dash and fumbled in my jacket for a smoke. We followed the gravel road back through the trees, heading west for the highway.

SIXTEEN

HIGH GRAY CLOUDS chased us into D.C. Billy and I didn't
speak much on the way in. An hour and a half after we left
Crane's property, we parked the Maxima in front of my apartment in Shepherd Park and cut the engine.

Billy looked out at my yard and exhaled with control. "So
what's next?"

"You tell me. You want me to keep going, I'll do it."

Billy's said, "You gotta push Crane, is what you gotta do.
You know that, don't you?"

I shifted in my seat. "Maybe just pushing a guy like him
won't do much. I need something on him."

"You see anything in his house?"

"I saw a lot of things. But I didn't know what I was looking for."

"What did you see?" When I didn't answer, Billy raised his

voice. "Come on, man, I'm paying you....I'm paying you to tell me."

"All right, Billy," I said evenly. "Here it is. Crane's a green-head. He's also into porn—rough trade. April's doctor told me there was evidence she'd been tied up—that wasn't you, right?" Billy shook his head and opened his mouth stupidly. "So it was Crane that was giving it to her the hard way. Want me to keep going?"

He nodded. "Yeah."

"I found some clothing in his dresser, maybe all belonging to the same woman. And I saw some jewelry. April wear much?"

"Jewelry?" Billy pushed some blond hair off his forehead and thought it over. "Well, her wedding ring."

"What else?"

"A cross. A gold cross on a gold chain, with a small diamond in the center of it." He paused. "And a ring on her other hand, on her pinky finger. A ruby in a silver antique setting."

"She wear that stuff all the time?" I said.

"Most of the time, yeah." Billy looked in my eyes. "You find any of that at Crane's?"

I shook my head and looked away as I did it. "No."

Billy put his hand on my shoulder. "Listen, Nicky..."

I pulled away from him, opened my door, and put a foot to the curb. "Don't worry," I said. "I won't drop it."

"Call me," he said.

"I will."

I watched his car turn off my street. Then I walked around the side of my landlord's house and picked up the mail off the stoop that was my entrance. I called for my cat as I unlocked the door and stepped inside.

The red light on the answering machine blinked next to the phone on the table that end-capped my sofa. I moved to the machine and pushed down on the bar, then listened to my messages as I looked over the general solicitation that was my mail.

The first message was from Jackie Kahn. She called to remind me about Sunday night, and to "bring a bottle of red, and not that cheap Spanish shit." Dinner was at 7:30, she said, adding, "Be here by seven." The second message was from a collection agency. I finished glancing at the mail during that. The third message was from the security guard, James Thomas.

Thomas's confession was rambling, soaked in the moaning self-pity that comes only at the final inch of a deep night of whiskey. I got what I could from the quiet pauses and the long, low sobs that followed. The sound of a man gone to the bottom is more frightening than the tears of any woman, and I was only thankful that I wasn't there to see it, to see his cubbish head lowered into his thick hands and the spasmodic, infantile shake of his broad, round shoulders. "I did what you said I did....I took the money, and...now I'm fixin' to take more....I'll be gone after that....I want you to know I didn't kill that boy.... That boy sure didn't deserve to die....The man from the orange and red—"

The tape ran out. When it did, my apartment went silent. Then, through the silence, I heard the faint cry of my cat.

I followed the sound out into the backyard. She called out weakly once more when she felt me near, and that's when I saw her. She was caught in the latticework, where I had found her years before, after the cat fight that had taken her right eye. This time some thick wire my landlord had used as patch had done it; a piece of it had entered her paw and gone deeper as she had moved into it, trying to get away. Now she was lying in the dirt next to the lattice, breathing rapidly and staring ahead glassily. I bent down and tickled the scar tissue of her lost eye and stroked behind her ear. As I did that I pulled the wire from her paw. She stiffened and stopped breathing as one rooted yellow toenail came out with it.

I tore a piece off the tail of my shirt with one hand while I stroked her with the other. Then I wrapped that around her paw and cradled her up into my arms. I ran with her to my Dart and got behind the driver's seat and cursed the engine when it failed to start. When it did start I gunned it to the animal hospital at the District line on Georgia Avenue, landing on my horn several times to clear traffic along the way. My cat felt cool and hard in my arms. I talked to her all the way in, but she never once looked up in my direction.

Two hours later a young attendant wearing jodhpurs and a flannel shirt brought her out. I signed some papers and then the young woman put my cat into my arms. She was limp but warm now. Her paw was bandaged and her head drooped off my forearm.

"What do I do?" I asked the young woman.

"Just take care of her," she said coldly. She stared me down and I let her do it.

"For the paw, I mean."

"Change the bandage and put Neosporin on the puncture before you do it." She gave me the long face again. "The paw's not the problem. How long was she out there, without food or water?"

I looked away. A row of animal lovers sat against the wall and stared collectively with pursed lips in my direction. "About a day, I guess," I mumbled.

"She was dehydrated, and near frozen. You're lucky her heart didn't burst."

I felt my own heart jump. "Sorry," I whispered to the young attendant, then put an edge on it. "Want to spank me?"

She blinked and sighed. "Just take care of your cat, okay?"

I thanked her and turned. Someone called me a dick as I slinked out the front door.

THAT NIGHT I HAD a slow bourbon and listened to the message from James Thomas. Occasionally I checked on my cat—I had placed her in a cardboard box, on a white blanket next to her blue foam ball—who remained awake and calm but pointedly uninterested in my presence. Later I laid Gil Scott Heron's *Winter in America* on the turntable and had another bourbon. "A Very Precious Time" came on, and with it a heavy melancholic buzz. A third bourbon didn't change that. I picked up the cardboard box that held my cat, put it at the foot of my bed, and went to sleep.

ON SATURDAY AFTERNOON I drove out to Laurel with the heater of my Dart blowing cool air toward my numb face. The temperature had dropped severely overnight and remained somewhere in the high teens. I passed through a studentless College Park and then into the warehouse district of Beltsville. As I neared Laurel, the thick traffic reflected the last shopping weekend before Christmas. At a tree stand, a fire burned in an iron barrel. Near that a father tied a Douglas fir to the roof of his station wagon while his kids chased each other around the car. Loudspeakers were lashed to poles, and through the speakers came the echo of canned carols.

I parked the Dart near Laurel Mall and walked to a place called Bernardo O'Reilly's that stood in the mall's lot. Once inside I was greeted by a young brunet hostess. She was wearing shorts and a white oxford with green suspenders over the oxford. The suspenders had buttons pinned on them from top to bottom, and on the buttons were "wacky" sayings redundantly punctuated with exclamation points.

"Welcome to Bernardo O'Reilly's," the hostess said with a cheerfully glued-up smile, but her eyes had no depth. "One for lunch?"

"One for the bar."

"All righty," she said.

"Okeydokey," I said.

"Right this way."

I followed her, dodging baby carriages, shopping bags, and perky waiters and waitresses dressed the same way as the hostess. There was the hood of a '50 Chevy mounted on the wall and next to that antique Coca-Cola ads and Moxie signs, and the mounted heads of wooden Indians. Bernardo O'Reilly's looked less like a bar than it did a garage sale run by Keebler elves.

I nodded my hostess off as I removed my overcoat, but she was already skipping toward a table where the entire wait staff had gathered to sing "Happy Birthday" to a woman in a pink jogging suit. I had a seat at the empty bar.

There were two young bartenders. Both wore green suspenders, and both had green bow ties to match. The larger of the two stood in front of me. He was heavyset, leaning to fat, and he had a modified crew cut that seemed to be the Laurel rage. The little tuft of hair that remained on the top of his head had been gelled up.

"What can I get you?" he said. A button on his suspender said HAVE A REAL COOL YULE.

"Just a Coke, please."

"Would you like to see a menu?"

"No, thanks."

He pointed to a machine behind him that had a tap protruding from the front of a clear plastic plate. Behind the plate something swirled like a brown and white pinwheel. "How 'bout a Coke-a-Doke?" the bartender said.

"What the hell's that?"

He looked at me through a sour smile. "Rum and Coke. You know, frozen."

"A regular Coke'll do it," I said. "And don't do anything cute to it, hear?"

He nodded and came back with my drink. I placed my card next to the coaster (which advertised COKE-A-DOKE) where he set the glass. He picked up the card and looked it over. His mouth dropped open and his lips moved as he did it.

"You wanna talk to the manager?" he said. "Is that it?"

"No. I can talk to you if it's all right."

"What about?"

I reached inside my overcoat and pulled out the photo of April that Billy had sent me and placed it on the bar. The bartender glanced down but didn't touch the photo. "She was in here about a week and a half ago," I said, "on a Tuesday night. Drinking at this bar, I think."

"I don't work Tuesday nights."

"Who does?"

The bartender jerked his thumb toward the service area, where his partner was garnishing some frozen drinks on a tray. "He does. He works the main bar at night and service bar on the weekends."

"Ask him to come over here for a second, will you?" I pulled my wallet and from that a five. I placed the five on the bar and pushed it into my friend's hand. "Thanks."

"Sure thing."

Bartender Number One walked over to Bartender Number Two to talk things over. As they talked, Bartender Number One dropped the five into an empty pitcher that was their mutual tip jar. I listened to the Beach Boys' pathetic "Little Saint Nick" on the house stereo while some whistles screamed and boingers boinged in the background, probably signaling someone else's birthday. The place made me want to puke something, preferably Coke-a-Doke, directly on the bar.

Bartender Number Two walked my way. He puffed out his narrow chest and lowered his voice. "How's it goin?"

"Good." I tapped the photo once on the bar. "She was in here Tuesday night last week, with a friend of mine."

"What's this all about?"

"It's about another five, for you and your buddy."

Number Two looked around and leaned over the bar. "You're talkin' about a ten then, am I not right?"

"If ten can make you remember."

He looked over the photo and back at me. "What'd your friend look like?"

"My age and size. Blond hair."

"Drinkers, right?"

"You tell me." I put the ten on the bar and kept my hand on it. He studied the photograph.

"Okay. They were in that night. The reason I remember is 'cause Tuesday's rum night. You know, we do a special on it, get a premium back from the local distributor. Anyway, it doesn't draw much of a crowd, but this particular lady" — he touched his finger to the photo — "she put away almost a liter of Bacardi Dark herself that night. Man, she could really pound it."

I took my hand off the bill. Number Two pulled it off the bar, folded it, and slipped it into the breast pocket of his oxford shirt. "How much for the Coke?" I said.

"On the house," he said, and winked as I put on my overcoat. "If you don't mind my asking, why are you after those two? They done anything wrong?"

"No," I said. "Nothing wrong. Just a man and his wife, gettin' a load on for the holidays. Thanks for the information."

"No problem. Have a real cool yule."

"Right."

ON THE WAY HOME I stopped at Town Hall in College Park for one beer that turned into four and two hours' worth of pool with a biker named Robert. The sky was dark when I walked out. I drove down Rhode Island Avenue and cut across Northeast to my apartment in Shepherd Park.

My cat was lapping water from her dish when I entered my apartment. I spooned some salmon into her food dish and tapped the can with the spoon. She abandoned the water for the salmon. In my bedroom I hit the power button on my stereo — Weasel was still on, moving from the Kinks' "Father Christmas" to the Pogues/Kirsty MacColl duet, "Fairytale of New York" — and I let it play. Out in the hall I opened the closet door and searched until I found a two-foot-high plastic Christmas tree with retractable arms, buried in the clutter. I dusted off the tree and set it up on the small table in my living room.

After that I made coffee and poured some whiskey in it and took it out to my couch. I drank it to the fade-in of the Pretenders' "2000 Miles." When I woke up, my cat was sleeping in my lap. I talked to her for a long while as I scratched behind her ears. Then I picked her up and carried her into my bedroom, where I put her in the cardboard box. The clock on my nightstand said 2:14 A.M.

I undressed and removed my wristwatch and laid it on my dresser. Next to the watch were the earrings and the ring from Tommy Crane's cottage. I picked up the ring and looked closely at the silver antique setting. Then I absently rubbed the tiny ruby that was set like a spot of blood in the middle of the ring.

I switched off the light and got into bed. I thought of April and Billy, and of Tommy Crane. The next time I looked at the clock it read 4:05. I sat up in bed, reached for my cigarettes, and lighted one off a match. A half hour later I sat up again and put fire to another one in the dark.

SEVENTEEN

JACKIE KAHN'S ACCORDION-GATED elevator rose through the center of the marble staircase and stopped with pneumatic ease. My footsteps echoed on the marble floor that led to her door. I knocked once on the door. It opened and Jackie leaned in the frame.

She was wearing a mustard-colored bathrobe. Something black and lacy showed from beneath the collar of the bathrobe. She smiled. "Nicky."

"Hey, Jackie."

"You're mighty punctual tonight."

"That's me. Johnny-on-the-Spot. Here." I handed her a bottle of Chilean cabernet. She inspected the label.

"Looks fine," she said with a nod.

"Gran Torres, 1982."

"Come on in."

I stepped into the condo and removed my overcoat in the

marble foyer. Jackie hung it in a hall closet, and then I followed her into the living room. A Yule log burned in the fireplace set in the lavender west wall, and in the dining room a beveled glass table was set for two. On the center of the table one lavender candle was lit. Jackie kept walking and I followed as I talked to her back and watched the shimmer of her thin calves.

"Where we going?"

"To the bedroom, pal. We've got a date, remember?"

"Sure, I do. But this is all happening so fast." Jackie stopped walking, turned, and rolled her eyes.

"Dinner's almost ready. Let's do it, okay?"

"Do it?"

"Yeah."

"How about a drink first?"

"Nope."

"Hinders the sample, right?" Jackie didn't answer.

We moved into her bedroom. It was a futon-and-halogen-lamp affair with a fireplace on the wall adjacent to the bed. She had built a small fire, and the halogen lamp was dimmed to its lowest degree. Two Bose 301s were mounted in a teak wall unit behind the bed. Chaka Khan was doing "Everlasting Love" through the speakers. I nodded to the speakers.

"Chaka a relative of yours?"

"She spells it differently," Jackie Kahn said. "Quit stalling, Nick. Let's make a baby."

Jackie undid her robe and sat facing out on a sky blue towel that she had spread on the edge of the futon. She spread her knees and leaned back, resting her palms on the futon. The black lace teddy she was wearing ended at her midriff. Below that was her flat abdomen and below that faint tan lines where her panties would have been. The muscles of her inner thighs rippled and then met in one beautifully manicured vee of cleanly shaved pudendum. I felt slightly dizzy as the blood in my head quickly headed south.

"You plan on doing this through osmosis?" Jackie said.

I shook my head, closed my mouth, gulped, and removed my shirt. I tripped climbing out of my slacks, then did the one-legged hop as I pulled off my socks. Chaka Khan screamed as I took off my underwear and dropped it in the pile with the rest of my clothes.

"Okay, I'm ready."

Jackie smirked. "You only look half-ready."

"It would help if you'd say something romantic."

"How about grabbing that Vaseline off the nightstand?"

"That's a start," I said.

I retrieved the blue-and-gold jar from the nightstand, removed the top, and dipped two fingers into the petroleum jelly. I walked toward Jackie with a cupped hand and a smile of crocodilian sensitivity.

Jackie said, "Hold it right there, soldier. I'll do that."

I nodded bashfully and handed her the jar. Jackie scooped out some Vaseline and massaged it into her vulva with two index fingers. When one of the fingers disappeared knuckle-deep into her vagina, the dizziness returned, and I glanced down to see my dick jumping about like some rude marionette.

"I think I'm about ready now," I said.

"Well, you look it. Come on."

I moved forward, and we did the dance. Except at the moment of entry, when she grudgingly let a parted-lip wince cross her face, Jackie remained quite expressionless throughout. Twice during our "lovemaking" I greedily reached inside her negligee to feel her breasts, and both times she mechanically slapped my hand away. That slowed things down a bit, as did my lame attempts at humor ("Jackieee," I shouted at one point, "oh, Jackie, oh, Jackie, uh-Ooooh!"), but when I finally closed my eyes and began to enjoy the great pureness of sensation, the shortness of breath, and the last tongue-biting, eyes-rolled-up-into-the-head preejaculatory seconds, then everything in the room, everything in the world in fact, was better than fine.

When it was over I removed my sweaty forehead from

Jackie's dry shoulder. The edges of Jackie's deep brown eyes crinkled as her smirk twisted up on one side. She brushed a hand back through her short black hair and leaned back on the futon.

"Well?"

"Well, I can't tell for certain, of course," I said. "But it sure *felt* like the mother load." Then I cocked my head thoughtfully to one side. "Was it beautiful for you?"

"Nicky," she said. "You are *such* an asshole."

JACKIE HAD GRILLED SWORDFISH steaks on the Jenn-Air and served them topped with a mustard, butter, and dill sauce. We ate them with grilled new potatoes and a green salad lightly seasoned with oregano and pepper and garlic vinegar. I had a sip of the cabernet and Jackie did the same.

"Nice wine," she said.

"I'm a hero, then. I thought the red might not go with the fish."

"A myth. The red goes fine. As for being a hero, I'll tell you in a couple weeks."

"That when you find out?"

"Uh-huh."

"Well, if it doesn't happen this time — you know, I'll always be there for you." I slid an oily nod toward her bedroom, and Jackie laughed.

"If it doesn't work out, I'll try the insemination route next time, thanks."

I put my wineglass on the table. "It wasn't all that awful, was it?"

"No, it wasn't all that awful. But I didn't enjoy it, if that's what you mean. I went through my entire youth and my twenties not *enjoying* it, as a matter of fact." Jackie had a taste of fish and closed her eyes briefly as she chewed and swallowed. "When I finally did admit to myself what I really wanted, there was a long period of curiosity, and then some guilt, and after that acceptance. And now I just feel right. And happy."

"Well, then I am too," I said. "Happy for you. We're friends, right?"

Jackie smiled radiantly in the light of the single candle that stood between us on the beveled glass table. "You are a good friend." She leaned in on her forearms. "So I was wondering if you could scare up the energy to give it another shot after dinner. For insurance. I know I'm ovulating—I've been on Pergonal to stimulate it, and I can feel it, like a little tickle down there." She looked toward her lap and back at me. "What do you think?"

"It's been a while since I've Done the Deuce."

"Is that a yes?"

"It is."

I LEFT JACKIE'S AROUND midnight and drove out of Kalorama, up Connecticut and west to Wisconsin, where I turned right and headed uptown. Christmas lights were strung in the windows of the bars and in the pizza parlors that served AU students in that part of town. I listened to the Cure's "Pictures of You" and kept listening after I had cut the engine of my Dart in front of Lee's apartment. When the song was done I climbed out of my car and turned the collar up on my overcoat as I took the stairs to Lee's.

She answered on the third knock after a check through her peephole. I straightened up as the door opened. Lee wore black jeans and a hip-length, army green sweater. The sweater picked up the green from her eyes.

"Hi, Nick." She smiled weakly and looked behind her toward the living room, then back at me.

"Hi. Can I come in?"

"I don't think it's such a good idea," she said.

"Got company?"

Her features softened. "Yes."

"Talk to me for a minute?"

Lee looked behind her once more and nodded. She checked the lock and closed the door, and stepped out with me into the yellow light of the stairwell. Her arms folded up and she began to shiver. I took off my overcoat and draped it over her shoulders. The hem of the coat nearly touched the ground. Lee looked up.

"How'd it go tonight?" she said.

"It went okay."

"I'm sure you found a way to make it interesting. Anyway, I didn't expect to see you tonight." She turned her head and nodded at the door. "Obviously."

I shuffled my feet. "Listen, Lee. I'm not drunk.... I didn't come over here tonight to bother you. I just wanted to talk, maybe spend the night. Just sleep with you."

Lee looked down at the overcoat that was billowing at her slippered feet. "Sorry, Nick. About my friend in there" — Lee motioned her chin — "it's nothing serious really, he's just a friend."

"You don't have to tell me anything."

"Well, I want to. And I want to talk. I've been meaning to call, to tell you."

"Tell me what?"

Lee looked down again and then raised her head. She brushed some of her brown hair off her face. "This isn't a good time, I know. But I'm graduating in January, in a couple of weeks. And after that... I've decided to leave town, Nick."

"For how long?"

"I don't know. My parents have been bugging me all year, 'What are you going to do after graduation?' I guess they're probably right. My father wants me to do some paralegal work, he's got a job lined up for me. I'm going back up to Long Island. It's not like I'll never be back. Who knows, right?"

"You'll figure it out," I said. "You'll do fine."

"Thanks." Lee put her arms under mine and locked her hands behind my back. She kissed me lightly on the base of my ear. "How's it going for you?"

"Things are moving."

"Yeah?" She smiled. "What about your friend's wife? You find her?"

"I'm close, I think."

"Anything on your friend Henry?"

"I'm getting close on that too."

"What happens to you after that?"

I chuckled unconvincingly. "Short-term goals for me, Lee. You know that."

Lee kissed me on the lips for a long while. I didn't want her to pull away. I didn't want to lose the warmth of her face, or her smell. When she backed up, her eyes were wet. It could have been the bitter air, but I wanted it to be the loss.

Lee handed me my overcoat and smiled. "Bye, Nicky. I'll call you. Soon."

"So long, Lee." I turned and walked down the stairs to my car.

I stopped once more that night around the corner at May's, for a bourbon and a glass of beer. Steve Maroulis was behind the bar. Before I left I placed a ten-dollar bet with Maroulis on a horse named Miss Emmy and then drove back by Lee's. The windows of her second-story apartment were dark now. I headed for Military Road and drove home through empty streets.

EIGHTEEN

THE NEXT DAY I replaced Mai behind the bar at three o'clock. Monday night was the worst shift of the week, and it was traditionally hers, but Mai was making me do penance for my trip to southern Maryland. I stuffed my blue bar rag into the waistband of my jeans, smoothed it out on the side of my hip, and passed through the service entrance to the bar.

Happy sat on his favorite stool, staring straight ahead into the bar mirror, one hand around an up glass, the other holding a lit Chesterfield. Mai stood at the service bar and drank a shift Heineken while she talked to me about some unfortunate young marine she was dating. I stocked the backup liquor beneath the rack and nodded occasionally as she talked.

A guy named Dave drank coffee and sat alone at the end of the bar, reading a pulp novel called *Violent Saturday*, by W. L. Heath. Dave was the Spot's reader—every joint had one—who never drank anything stronger than black coffee. I suspected he was an on-the-wagon alkie who simply liked the nostalgia of sitting in a bar, but I never confirmed it. The only time he ever spoke to me was when I tried to empty and clean his overflowed ashtray. "Don't do that," he had said quietly, gripping the side of it. "Dirty's the way I like it."

When Mai left I put Bob Marley's *Kaya* on the house deck and turned up the volume. I poured myself a cup of coffee, lit a Camel, and folded my arms. In the rectangular cutout of the reach-through I could see Ramon in a boxer's stance, toe-to-toe with Darnell, who had raised his long arms, exposing his midsection. Ramon punched Darnell's abdomen with a left and then a right. Darnell smiled and slowly shook his head.

That was how the afternoon and early evening passed. Buddy and Bubba came in, whispered quietly to each other, and split one pitcher before leaving with a sneer in my direction. Len Dorfman stopped by for a late Grand Marnier and talked loudly about a "savage" he had locked up that day, until a hard stare from Darnell sent him out the door. And Boyle came by for a draught beer and a shot of Jack.

Boyle mumbled about "the fucking streets" and his "fucking kids" throughout his round. I left him, and when I stumbled back from the walk-in with two cases of Bud in my arms, he was gone. A damp five-dollar bill lay across the Cuervo Gold coaster next to his empty shot glass. I restocked the cooler to Let's Active's *Cypress* while Darnell mopped the kitchen and hosed off its rubber mats. When I was done I slid a worn copy of *London Calling* into the tape deck and hung the dripping clean glasses upside down in the rack above the bar. Then I drained the sinks and wiped everything down and poured two inches of Grand-Dad into a heavy shot glass. I opened a bottle of Bud, stood it next to the shot, had a taste of both, and lit a smoke. An unlatching sound came from the direction of the front door.

A man and a woman walked in and took the two steps down into the bar area of the Spot. A stream of cold air flowed in with them. The man walked slowly and deliberately, and stopped in front of the bar, running his hands through the waistband of his tan polyester slacks. The woman stopped two feet behind him and stared. The heavy drama of cops was present in each choreographed movement.

"You Stefanos?" the man said.

"That's right."

"Too late for a drink?"

"As a matter of fact, it is," I said genially, keeping my arms folded. "I'm about closed. Just waiting for my friend in the kitchen to finish up."

The woman spoke in a low dull voice. "He's finished now. Tell him that, and tell him we want to be alone." She had military-short brown hair and round Kewpie-doll lips. Her pocked cheeks had been camouflaged with rouge.

"Detectives, Metropolitan Police," the man said, and quickly opened his coat to reveal a badge suspended from his breast pocket. "I'm Goloria, and this is Wallace."

"Detectives?" I said, feigning surprise, looking them over. Goloria wore a stained London Fog raincoat over a brown plaid sport jacket. Wallace had on a gray wool skirt with a cotton oxford and a vinyl Members Only jacket worn over that.

"Just tell your friend to leave," Goloria said, "so we can talk."

"Now?"

"Tell him."

I walked back to the kitchen. Darnell was finished and dressed for the weather, his brown overcoat buttoned and his leather kufi tight on his head. He had been standing in the dark, looking at us from the reach-through.

"Better get going," I said.

"You sure, man?"

"It's all right. They're cops."

"That don't mean a *fuck*in' thing. You ought to know that."

"Go on, Darnell. It's all right."

Darnell walked out and passed without looking either of them in the eye. He closed the front door tightly as he left the

Spot. I emerged from the darkness of the kitchen and took my place behind the bar. "The Guns of Brixton" 's thick bass came from the house speakers. Goloria and Wallace had taken seats at two adjacent stools. Wallace lit a smoke and put her black vinyl handbag next to the ashtray in front of her. Sitting there, her shoulders appeared to be broader than Goloria's.

Goloria said, "What are we listening to?"

"The Clash," I said.

He turned to Wallace and raised his thin eyebrows mockingly. Then he turned back to me. "Turn that shit off and fix us a couple of drinks. When you're finished, come around the bar and let's have a talk."

"Sure. What'll it be?"

Goloria looked up at top call and squinted. "Crown Royal on the rocks, with a splash. Wallace'll have the same. Okay, Wallace?" Wallace nodded.

I moved to the stereo and hit the STOP button on the deck. After that I filled two rocks glasses with ice and free-poured the whiskey. I topped it with a spurt of water from the gun, and set both glasses down in front of the cops. Then I drained my Grand-Dad and kept my eyes on Wallace as I did it. I grabbed my bottle of Bud off the bar, walked around to their side, and stood behind them. They swiveled their stools around to face me.

"What can I do for you?" I said.

Wallace blew some smoke in my direction, and Goloria sipped whiskey while we looked each other over. He was on the low side of forty, but his long narrow face had a cancerous gauntness. His mouth hung open and his lids drooped as he studied me. He looked somewhat like a hound.

"Ste-fa-nos."

"That's right."

"Greek?"

"Yeah."

Goloria rubbed a bony finger along his ten o'clock shadow and grinned. The rubbing made a scraping noise in the bar. He looked at Wallace. "Wallace, I've known a few Greeks in my years on the force. Hardworking people. Restaurant people, mostly. A few professionals, here and there. But never a Greek detective. That's strange, isn't it?"

"That's right," Wallace deadpanned. "It's strange."

"Well, maybe not so strange," Goloria said quickly, "when you think about it. I mean, the Greeks never did mind taking on the dirtiest jobs—not if there was a buck in it for 'em. Hell, you can't even get niggers to do restaurant work anymore."

"What's your point?" I said.

"My point is, being a detective—a private detective that is—it's dirty work. And it's usually work where you can pick up a quick dirty buck. So I figure it's not too different for a guy like you to be in the private detective business."

" 'Cause it's dirty," Wallace said.

"I figured that out," I said. "You two practice this before you walked in?"

"Shut up," Goloria said, and then flashed me a smile of sharp carnivorous teeth. "Okay?"

I swigged from the neck of my beer, swallowed, and sighed. "What do you want?"

Goloria said, "You've been out in my district asking questions about a woman named April Goodrich."

"What district is that?"

"The Third."

"I'm looking for her," I admitted.

"Well, now you can stop. I've got that covered, understand?"

I said, "Let's skip all the bullshit. What we're really talking about here is the reward money that Joey DiGeordano put out on the street. Am I right?"

Goloria said, "Say that again?"

Wallace eased herself down off the stool and stood on the wooden floor under the smoky light of the conical lamp. She opened the clasp of her vinyl handbag. Goloria set down his drink, rose, and slowly straightened out his raincoat against his chest with both hands. I backed up a step. The Spot was quiet and suddenly very small.

I looked at Goloria. "I'm not in it for the reward money. So I'm saying that I'm not in your way. That solve our problem?"

"I don't know a Joey DiGeordano," Goloria said.

"I thought maybe you did," I said, watching Wallace knead something inside her handbag.

"What else you think?" Goloria said.

"I thought for a second, maybe you were just a little bit Greek." My eyes narrowed as I felt the warmth of the Grand-Dad. "You know. Dirty."

"He told you to shut up," Wallace said unemotionally.

"Sorry," I said. "Detective Gloria?"

"It's Go-loria," he said, taking a step toward me.

"Right. Anyway, I apologize. But you two have just got me a little confused. Being with you here, see, I just can't figure out" — I scratched my forehead — "I just can't figure out which one of you two's got the swingin' dick."

"I do," Wallace said, and there was a metallic flash as her brass-knuckled fist swung and connected across my jaw. On the slow trip down I felt a dull ache and after that a jolt of pain. I landed on my elbows as cold beer emptied out across my chest, and I looked up. The two of them stood there, silhouetted against the light of the conical lamp. Their figures glided across a backdrop of smoke and white stars. I rubbed my jaw and squinted up in their direction. A small puddle of blood washed around in my mouth. I swallowed it and coughed.

"Now I think you get it, right, Stefanos?" It was Goloria's calm voice. I kept my mouth shut. He waited and spoke again. "Well, here it is anyway, for the record: I don't want you playing detective anymore in my district. You got nothing to do with the Goodrich girl anymore. You got nothing to do with *anything* in my district anymore, understand?"

Wallace chuckled and kicked my foot. "He understands. Sure, he does."

Goloria made a head movement toward the door. "Let's go, Wallace." They began to turn.

I stopped them with my voice. "Hey," I said weakly. "You forgot to pay for your drinks."

Goloria withdrew a wallet from the seat of his polyester slacks and balled up a few one-dollar bills. Then he walked back and stood over me and dropped them on my chest. They bounced off and fell beside me to the floor.

"Merry Christmas," he said.

I stayed on the wooden floor and listened to their shuffling footsteps and to the opening and closing of the front door. I remained there in that position for another ten minutes of silence. When I stopped feeling dizzy I got up on one knee and jiggled my jaw and wiped nausea-sweat from my forehead.

Five minutes later I was in Darnell's kitchen with my head in the washbasin, a steady stream of water running down my face. I stared into the blackness of the drain and thought things over for a long while.

Afterward I dried off with a towel and walked back to the service bar. I poured a shot of whiskey and threw it back, then picked up the telephone and got Mai's number from information. I dialed that number and Mai picked up on the fourth ring.

"Hallo."

"Mai, it's Nick."

"Nick, that you? It doesn't sound like you. You drunk?"

"Drunk? Yeah, just a little." I coughed and cleared my throat. "Listen, Mai, I need you to do me a favor."

"A favor. Shit, Nicky, don't ask me to take your shift tomorrow. It's Christmas Eve." Mai whispered into the phone. "I promised my soldier boy we'd spend all day together. He's here right now."

"This is the last time, Mai, I promise. I've got to go out of town for the day. Believe me, it can't wait."

"You don't sound so good, Nicky, honest to God." She thought things over. "If it's really important—"

"It is. Listen, I owe you."

"You're damn right you do," she said rapidly, but the edge was out of her voice. "Anyway, maybe if I come in tomorrow, Phil will remember to hand me my Christmas bonus. Fat chance, huh?" She laughed broadly. "By the way, where you going, back down to the country?"

"Southern Maryland." I dabbed blood off the side of my mouth with a bar rag.

"Got a girl down there?" she said demurely.

"A girl?" I said, lighting a cigarette. "I'll find out. Tomorrow."

NINETEEN

THE NEXT MORNING I packed my nine-millimeter Browning and a full clip into the trunk of my Dart and drove south on 301 in the direction of Cobb Island. The temperature was in the teens, but there was no wind and my Dart cruised effortlessly down the highway beneath a steel sheet of clouds. At Waldorf I cracked a window and huffed a Camel, and in La Plata I stopped for a burger and a Coke. A half hour later I was on the Island and sitting on a brown Leatherette stool in a nearly empty Formica-floored room that doubled as the dining area and bar of Polanski's.

The bartender's name was Andy. Andy had a brush cut and wore a green V-necked sweater over a white T-shirt that was exposed both at the neck and at the base of his great belly. His double-knit pants were chocolate brown and cinched with a wide black belt. Black work boots covered his long feet.

Andy shook my hand and said, "Now we've been introduced. What can I get you?"

"A draught beer," I said.

Andy plunged his thick knotted hand into the cooler and withdrew two glass mugs. He gripped the handles of both with one hand as he tapped out the beer and put a head on it without wasting more than a few drops. I looked at the two beers and then around the empty Polanski's. Andy placed both beers in front of me.

"There you go." He leaned a scabbed elbow on the bar and studied the crescent-shaped bruise on my jaw.

"Maybe I have that look," I said with a crooked smile. "But one beer'll do it for me today. Thanks."

Andy frowned and looked a bit hurt. "It's Tuesday, man!" He pointed behind him to a glitter-drawn sign that itemized the daily specials. "Two-for-one beers every Tuesday — best damn day of the week around here, 'cept for the weekends."

"Just one for me today, Andy, thanks." I pushed one of the mugs and slid it in front of his arm. "You have it."

He shook his head. "Too early for me, pardner." Andy took the mug by the handle and poured it out into the last of three sinks behind the bar. He walked down to the service end and began building a pyramid of shot glasses that he stacked on a piece of green bar netting.

I nursed the draught through a cigarette and stared into the bar mirror. Andy played a Tammy Wynette Christmas tape and stayed on his end of the bar. When my mug was empty I walked across the room to a pay phone near the men's room. In a worn directory I found the number to the Pony Point. I dropped a quarter in the slot and punched in the number and when Wanda picked up I asked to speak to Russel. She put the receiver down. I listened to Tammy Wynette on my end and Randy Travis on theirs until Russel picked up.

"Yeah," he said.

"Russel, it's Nick Stefanos." There was a silence. "The detective from D.C., looking for April Goodrich."

"I remember you," he said. "What you want?"

"You know how to get in touch with Hendricks?"

"Sure," he said. "Same way you would—dial nine-one-one."

"Come on, man," I said impatiently. "You know how to get him direct, don't you?"

Russel said, "What's up with you, man? You don't sound too cool."

"I'm fine," I said. "Listen, Russel. Call Hendricks—this isn't for me, it's for April—and tell him to get over to Tommy Crane's place"—I looked at my watch—"in about a half hour."

"I can get him," Russel said carefully.

"You going to do it?"

Russel paused. "Sure, Stefanos. I'll do it."

"Thanks." I hung up the phone.

I walked back to the bar and dropped a five on it and thanked Andy as I put on my overcoat and slipped my smokes into the side pocket. Then I left Polanski's and stepped across the asphalt lot. The air was colder now and there was a wind, and the steel clouds had deepened to slate. I climbed into my Dart and fired the ignition.

TWENTY

FOLLOWED 257 to the steepled church and hung a right onto the road that led to Crane's property. At the gravel entrance I cut left into the break of the oak forest. The trees were leafless but the overhang of their heavy branches darkened the road. In the clearing I stopped my car beneath the single oak that stood near Crane's cottage. Crane's F-150 wasn't there. I cut the engine.

Outside the car, I removed my overcoat, folded it on the driver's seat, and closed the door. I fastened the top button on my wool shirt and called out Crane's name twice. For several minutes I listened to the sound of animal movement in the compound and waited for a human response. When there wasn't one, I walked across the hard earth and hopped up onto the porch of Crane's cottage.

I opened the screen door and knocked on the solid door behind it. From behind the door I heard nothing. I stood there in the cold and stamped the porch with my work boots to circulate blood into my feet. Five minutes later there were still no signs of life, and I tried the knob on the door. It turned and I looked behind me, and then I stepped into Crane's cottage.

I yelled his name. With the door closed, there was only the occasional creak of the old house conceding to the rush of the wind. The smell of bong water and sulfur cut the living room. I walked to the oak-trunk table and touched my finger to the resin in the bowl of the bong. It was cool, as were the butts in the ashtray next to it. I wiped sweat and ash off my hands and onto the thighs of my jeans, and crossed the living room to the narrow hall. I passed the open bathroom door and stood in the doorway to Crane's bedroom. A Westclox alarm ticked loudly from his night table. From the doorway I looked out one window to the compound and out the other to my car beneath the oak. No sign of Crane. I called out his name once more and stood there, listening to the clock. Then I turned and walked back down the hall to the door that had been locked four days earlier.

I tried the knob. The door was still locked.

I jiggled the knob and quickly put a shoulder to the door's body. The frame cracked and split in the right corner, but the door didn't open. I said Crane's name again, but now it was only habit, and this time I didn't wait. I moved one step back and jammed the sole of my work boot into the area just below the knob, and the door kicked open.

I stood at the top of a dusty flight of irregular wooden stairs. The bottom of the stairs ended in darkness. I grabbed a loose banister and skimmed it as I walked down toward the cellar. A moldy, botanical smell rose up as I descended. At the last step I searched for a switch, rubbing my hand across a cold cinder-block wall clodded with dirt. I looked back once and saw color-less light at the top of the stairs. I felt no switch, but I kept inching forward.

A string brushed my face. I found it with my hand and pulled down. It clicked without result. I ran my hand up the string and touched a bulb caked with dirt. I wrapped my hand around the bulb and turned it clockwise until there was light.

I stood on a dirt floor in a root cellar that ran the length of the cottage. Rusted farm implements—wooden rakes, a fence-post digger, and a sledgehammer—leaned against the east wall. In the far corner several open-topped brown paper bags sat in rows, where bulbous plants had begun to sprout stalks like emaciated, grasping hands.

Two thick black snakes were stretched out sleeping next to the bags, their heads resting like rubber fists against the cinder-block wall.

My heart rate accelerated, and I looked back up the stairs. When I turned my head back I saw another door set in the third wall. The snakes appeared to be sleeping. I eyed them as I walked over to the door.

The door had been secured with a padlock fastened through a hasp. I put my ear to the cool wood and heard the steady hum of an appliance through the door. I stepped back and listened. There was still no movement above in the cottage. I walked to the east wall and grabbed the sledgehammer by the wood handle and returned quickly to the door. I swung the hammer once and tore the hasp off its hinges. Then I kicked open the door.

Inside, a carefully arranged room was carpeted in red. A mattress lay in one corner and a camera set on a tripod pointed down at the mattress. The walls of the room had been paneled in sound-treated tile. On one wall hung oak shelves filled with black videocassette cases. In one of the shelves a television rested beside a VCR. On another wall several mounted photographs depicted acts of sodomy and rape. Many of the photographs were simply closely cropped shots of women's faces. The faces reflected fear and pain.

A portable humidifier sat on a table and hissed steam into the room. Next to the table the coils of an oil heater glowed red. The room smelled of oil and incense.

I scanned the videotape selection. The cases were unlabeled, as were the tapes within. I walked back to the doorway and looked up the stairs, then returned to the bed and threw back the sheets. The mattress cover was clean. I felt the mattress and then lifted it. A brown leather briefcase lay beneath it on the red carpet.

I grabbed the briefcase by the handle and pulled it free from the bed's frame and dropped it on the floor at my feet. I fumbled with the catch—it wasn't locked—and opened the hinged top. I looked inside and ran my hand along its contents. Then I closed the briefcase and got up off my knees and walked quickly from the room, past the snakes on the cinder-block wall and the tools and the bags containing rooted plants, and up the stairs to the landing, through the narrow hallway to the living room, where I ran now, out the front door and off the porch and across the hard earth to my Dart parked beneath the oak.

I jangled my keys and fit one into the trunk and raised its lid. Inside, my nine-millimeter sat loaded and wrapped in oilskin. I set the briefcase next to it and slammed the trunk shut. Then I looked for my ignition key as I moved to the driver's side of my Dart. I had opened the door of it when I noticed a tall man leaning in the entranceway of the sty, fifty yards away.

His arms were folded and he was staring at me with a grin. Some of his thick black hair had fallen in front of his eyes. Tommy Crane pulled the hair back behind his ears.

He said, "Can I help you, friend?"

I looked into the car and fingered the ignition key. I might have made it, though maybe not—Crane was quick, I had seen it in his walk—but it didn't matter, because by then I had already decided to push it. Billy Goodrich had hired me to find his wife; I had only found the money, so for me it wasn't over. I closed the door and stepped away from the car.

"I didn't see your truck," I said with what I knew was an unnatural smile.

"I can't hear you," Crane said.

"I said, I didn't see your truck."

"I lent it to a friend." Crane was wearing his black down vest over a red chamois shirt. He made a sweeping gesture with his hand. "If you want to talk, come on. We can do it in the sty, but I don't have time to fuck around. I got work to do."

I looked behind me to the empty gravel road that led into the dimness of the woods. Then I looked back at Crane. "Okay. Let's talk."

I walked toward the sty. By the time I reached the hinged gate, Crane had ducked inside. I cleared the lip of the entrance without lowering my head and stepped into the cinder-block structure. The concrete floor was freezing, and the cold traveled up and numbed my calves.

Crane was by the back exit, standing in front of the punch-board that held the butchering knives. He had picked up the black hose that had been coiled beside the copper trough. Liquid boiled inside the trough, and beneath it burned an orange pile of embers. The rank smell of swill filled the sty.

I moved toward Crane and passed a litter of piglets feeding from a sow beneath the warmth of an infrared lamp. Another sow lay alone in a farrowing pen. I could see the balance of the pigs through the exit in the yard out back. Some were down behind the bales of hay. The rest were moving slowly about, wheezing and snorting as they bumped one another with their snouts.

Crane fingered the brass nozzle of the hose and tightened it with a white-knuckled turn. "So," he said, looking at the nozzle. "You came back."

"I said I would."

Crane slid his hand down off the nozzle and wrapped his fingers around the black rubber. "Sayin' it's one thing. The other day, you didn't look like you had the stones." He squinted. "What changed your mind?"

"A dirty cop, back in D.C."

Crane studied my discolored jaw. "A cop, huh?"

"That's right. He told me to stay off the case. But it didn't really matter that he was a cop. He was just another guy, looking to get a piece of April Goodrich. It happened like that her whole dumb life. And I think the last time it happened, it happened here."

Crane said, "How you figure, friend?"

"It wasn't too tough." I walked around Crane and leaned my back against the punchboard. It gave me a view through the entrance to the yard outside. I could see most of my car, and beyond that the empty gravel road that ran into the woods. My car sat alone beneath the oak. I thought of Russel and the warmth of his kitchen, and the care he gave to his animals. I wondered if he had picked up the phone and made the call.

"April headed west," Crane said.

"No," I said, "she didn't." Two large black pigs stood blocking the exit to my left, and Crane had squared off in front of me.

"Then where is she?"

I shifted my weight. "Here, somewhere. She came down with a briefcase full of money she stole, from back in town. You killed her for the money. Or maybe you killed her for the kick. Either way, Crane, you killed her."

Crane said, "You crossed the line now. You better be able to prove what you're sayin'."

I reached into the pocket of my jeans, pulled out the silver antique ring with the ruby stone, and held it out. Crane's black eyes widened. I said, "Here's my proof."

"That's a stupid trick," Crane said. "And it's one you're gonna die for."

He swung the hose. The brass nozzle clipped my shoulder. I felt the sting and tucked my chin into my chest and pulled my elbows in, my balled fists in front of my face. I backed up and Crane swung again, making contact across my forearm. I grunted as the nozzle broke the cushion of muscle and reached the bone.

The black pigs screamed from the doorway. Crane made an animal sound and bared his clenched gray teeth as he brought the hose up over my head. It came down with force, but I moved to the side, and the nozzle chinked the concrete. Before he could bring it back up I pushed him off balance with an open palm, then came quickly out of my stance and fired off a left to his lower back and then a hard right into his kidneys, aiming two feet deep. Crane dropped the hose and doubled down to catch his breath, and when he did I moved in front of him again. I had time to rear back on this one, and Crane didn't even blink as he watched my punch come straight in and connect square on the bridge of his thick nose. The nose gave like dry sponge, but it only moved Crane back one step. He straightened up and walked toward me, blood inching down over his lip.

I stumbled and fell back. Crane grabbed me by the shirt and pulled me back up. There was blood now streaked across his teeth, and in his eyes a mechanical rage. He shook me and then without releasing his grip quickly moved me backward with a shove that sent me into the punchboard. Knives loosened and fell to the concrete. I groped for the handle of the largest one as it bounced but got my hand around its steel blade instead. I heard pigs wheezing and I heard Crane laugh as he kicked my hand and pinned it against the punchboard. I felt the edge of the blade bite the skin of my fingers, and I watched my hand release the knife, and I saw the clean, even slice and then the blood.

Adrenaline brought my knee violently up into Crane's balls. He grunted and his eyes jerked skyward, and I shot my hands up between his and broke out of his grip. He threw a wild round-house. I ducked it, then shifted to the left and came up in a boxer's stance and combinated again with a left and then a right to his back. Crane screamed and spun with a hammer fist that hit my ear like a club and knocked me to the ground. I was up quickly and shaking my head clear when he grabbed me and ran me into the punchboard again. My forehead hit first, and as he pulled me back the sty was spinning and the sounds of Crane and the pigs were in the distance. I was pushed out the exit then, and I fell to my knees in the hard mud, and Crane put a boot to my back. I rolled over and stared at the moving gray sky as squealing pigs brushed my arms and walked with manic clumsiness across my chest. I was still trying to make the sky stop moving when everything suddenly turned to night.

It was day again. I raised myself up on one elbow. The pigs were now back along the fence. I moved my arms at the joint and then my legs. Nothing was broken, and nothing felt right. I wiped blood from my palm onto the leg of my jeans and stared at the ground until I could focus on the ridged mud. When I looked up I saw Crane taking long strides through the sty in my direction. The snub-nosed .38 was in his hand.

"I should have killed you straight up," he shouted, still walking with purpose. "Makes no difference now."

I didn't try to move. I took a deep breath and smelled the air, and I remembered that it was Christmas Eve. Crane ducked his head and exited the sty. I thought of my grandfather, and of his hand around mine, the two of us, walking at night through the snow. Crane stood over me and cocked the pistol's hammer and pointed the .38 at my head.

He said, "No mess, friend."

There was a roar. Crane's red shirt ripped apart in the middle of his chest, and his black vest waved out as if it had been blown by a sudden gust of wind. Blood and bone jetted out and rained down. Crane threw the .38 aside and did an airy two-step dance. His eyes rolled as he fell to the ground and landed at my side, his arm draped across my chest. The arm jerked in spasm. I pushed it off me. Then I looked in the direction of the sty.

Hendricks was standing in the exit. Smoke curled out of the barrel of the .357 that he held at his side.

I wiped chunks of Crane off my face with a shaking hand. I looked at what was left of him. His mouth was open and his gray teeth were sunk into the mud. The large white boar hobbled by and stopped and inspected Crane's inert body. Something like a smile was on the boar's snout. I looked at Hendricks and nodded. Hendricks nodded back.

"April's dead," I said.

"Then Crane had it comin'."

"Maybe so," I said. "But you didn't have to kill him."

Hendricks smoothed out the brim of his hat as he holstered the .357. "I was aiming for his legs," he said, with a shrug. "Sight's way off on this goddamn Smith and Wesson." A slight gleam appeared in his eye. "Gotta get that son of a bitch fixed. Know what I mean?"

TWENTY-ONE

HENDRICKS WALKED SLOWLY back to his car and radioed for an ambulance. While we waited for it he had a seat beside me in the mud and asked for the details. I handed him April's ring and described everything I had seen in the cottage, with the exception of the brown leather briefcase. Hendricks listened closely. He never once looked at Crane or touched the corpse.

When the ambulance arrived I left the keys to my car with Hendricks and was gurneyed and rushed north to La Plata General. I spent the next three hours in the emergency room, mostly next to a moaning, liver-spotted old woman who had stumbled and broken both wrists on what was probably her last Christmas Eve. She complained about her daughters who lived in Pittsburgh and never called, even at Christmas, and I sat there and let her complain. I had eaten a couple of Tylenol 3s, and I wasn't feeling all that bad. But a taste of whiskey would have made things a whole lot better.

The bearded doctor who finally saw me had the look of a lawn and garden department manager. He cleaned out the cut across the inside of my hand and wrapped my fingers together with tape over a gauze bandage. After that I was ushered off into a busy room and laid on a cold table, where an unsmiling brunet with shapely but occupationally cumbersome breasts took several X-rays of my bruised arms and shoulders. Everything turned up negative.

I asked for "something stronger," but the good doctor ignored me as he pushed his wire-rimmed glasses back up over the bridge of his nose and wrote out a prescription for more Tylenols. When I was released I walked out to the parking lot alone. Hendricks leaned on the trunk of my Dart. His white car sat idling next to mine.

I followed him to the station in La Plata and sat at a nondescript metal desk in a room that had a gated chain fence run along its interior. Hendricks asked me the same questions he had asked earlier, and I tried to duplicate my answers exactly. When it was over I asked if I was to be charged with anything, and I asked if my name would be released to any of the local media. He answered no to both questions, and I thanked him again and wished him a good Christmas. He did the same, and as he handed me the keys to my car I shook his hand and said good-bye.

Two miles up the road I pulled off onto the shoulder, got out of the car, and walked back and unlocked my trunk. Inside was my automatic, and next to that the leather briefcase. I closed the trunk and got back into my car and stopped at the next open bar and had a beer and two shots of Jim Beam, then drove back to my apartment in Shepherd Park.

My landlord was waiting for me at the door with my annual Christmas present, a fifth of green-seal Grand-Dad. I gave him a hug and a kiss on his dark brown cheek, and picked up my cat on the way in, rubbing the scar tissue in the socket of her right eye as I carried her. My landlord followed me. I poured two slugs of

Grand-Dad into juice glasses and shook two Tylenol 3s into his palm, and two into mine, and we washed those down with the bourbon. Two hours later the bottle was nearly empty, and I had the English Beat's *I Just Can't Stop It* on the stereo, full blown, and my landlord and I were dancing wildly around my living room while my cat watched calmly from her roost on top of the radiator. It was Christmas Eve, and I guess I had a right to celebrate, but I wasn't thinking about the holiday. I was thinking that I had come close this time, that I had seen the empty black eye, and I had walked away. I was thinking how good it felt to be alive.

HENDRICKS PHONED ME FROM southern Maryland two days later. A dog search of Crane's property had failed to turn up any sign of April Goodrich. The cottage had been combed as well, with no result. Only when Hendricks screened the tapes from the root cellar did he find the evidence.

The collection had consisted of the standard rough trade pornography, with a few snuff films in the bunch. On the tail end of one, some home video footage had been cut in.

"You sure it was her?" I said carefully to Hendricks.

"Yeah," he mumbled. "You don't want to know the details, Stefanos. Let's just say he did her like one of his pigs. Tied up, with one bullet to the head."

I thought about it and closed my eyes. Hendricks coughed once on the other end of the line. I said, "That kind of thing can be faked, Hendricks. Any reason to think..."

"No reason. Listen, Stefanos—I've seen the tape, you haven't. What I saw can't be done with trickery, or special effects. April Goodrich is dead. Now, I don't know the motive, except that Crane surely was one sick son of a bitch. But it doesn't matter now, does it?"

"I guess not," I said, thinking of the money.

"I called her husband," Hendricks said.

"I know. I spoke to him myself."

"How's he doin'?"

"How would you be?" I said.

"Right," Hendricks said.

"There's a service for her tomorrow, outside of town."

"I never get that close to D.C."

"Bad things happen in the country too, Hendricks."

"Bad things happen everywhere," he said tiredly. "You take care."

THE MEMORIAL SERVICE FOR April Goodrich was held in a small Baptist church in Beltsville, just south of Laurel. April had no family, and none of her former friends were in attendance. The group consisted of Billy, his parents, me, and a pale, anemic minister. I kept three pews back from Billy and his family and watched Billy the entire time. He stood with his hands folded, expressionless throughout.

Outside the church I shook Billy's hand and began to walk away. Billy told his parents to wait on the front steps and followed me across the gravel lot to my Dart. He caught me as I was putting the key to the driver's side lock.

Billy thanked me for coming, and for seeing everything through to the end. Then he asked if I had "found anything" that day at Crane's.

I shoved him back with both hands. Billy fell onto the gravel. He sat there looking up at me, and we stared at each other for what seemed to be a very long time. Finally I got into my Dart, started it, and pulled out of the lot.

In the rearview I saw him stand and brush the dirt from his billowing cashmere overcoat as he watched me drive away. Billy's parents were behind him, staring at us both. They held each other on the steps of the church, wondering what kind of horrible thing had finally happened, just then, to end it between their son and his old friend.

TWENTY-TWO

THE DAY AFTER April's service I took the Metro to Gallery Place and had lunch at the District Seen. A bartender in combat fatigues served me a club sandwich and a cup of vegetable beef to go with it. I washed that down with a Guinness, and then another while I read that week's *City Paper* and listened to De La Soul on the house deck. When bicycle messengers started to crowd the place, and Jaegermeisters were served, I settled up my tab.

Out on the street I walked down Seventh, opened a common-entrance glass door, and took the stairs that led to both a portrait gallery and the offices of *DC This Week*, the alternative weekly that was itself a more hard-news alternative to *City Paper*. I entered the door marked DC THIS WEEK.

A young woman in rimless glasses was sitting at a desk, talking into a headset as she clipped art on a rubber mat. She looked up as I walked in, and raised one finger in the air to hold me off. I waited until she had released her call.

"Yes?" she said.

I placed my business card in front of her on the mat. As she looked it over I said, "I'd like to speak to your editor, if he has a minute."

"Do you have an appointment with Jack?"

"Nope." I smiled. She didn't.

"What's this abou — what's this in reference to?"

"It's about my friend, William Henry."

She relaxed, took off her glasses, and rubbed her eyes. "You knew William?"

"Yes."

The woman slid her glasses back on and punched a finger at the switchboard. "I'll see if he's in."

I stood with my hands in my overcoat pockets and listened to her mumble into the phone. Other phones rang from beyond the makeshift barrier that nearly encircled her desk, and in between their rings the tapping sounds of several keyboards meshed with a dublike bass. The multitalented receptionist removed her headset and stood up.

"Follow me," she said with a come-hither gesture.

I walked behind her through a room where several tieless young men and young women typed on word processors. In the corner of the room a man with no hair on the sides of his head but plenty on top leaned over a drawing table and drew a line down a straightedge. A small boom box sat on a makeshift ledge above the drawing table, and out of the box Linton Kwesi Johnson spoke over a throbbing bass and one scratchy guitar. None of the people in the room looked up as I passed.

The receptionist stopped at the first door on a row of small offices and opened her palm in direction. I thanked her and stepped into the office. A woman stood up from behind an oak desk.

She was my height, with full-bodied, shoulder-length red

hair that had fine threads of silver running through it in several key places. Her cream satin blouse was open three buttons down and tucked into a short olive green skirt. A wide black belt was wrapped around her waist. Black stockings covered her legs, and on her feet were a pair of olive green pumps. Her thin face was lightly freckled, and the freckles were the same shade of those that were liberally sprinkled across the top of her chest. Lipstick the color of her hair was drawn across her wide mouth. Her eyes were pale green. She extended her hand. I shook it and held it until she pulled it gently back.

"You're Jack?" I said.

"Jack can't see you," she said. "My name's Lyla. Lyla McCubbin. I'm the managing editor."

"Nick Stefanos."

I handed her the same card I had given the receptionist, removed my overcoat, and had a seat in a high-backed chair across from her desk. Lyla sat back down and studied the card.

Her office was a clutter of newspaper and computer paper. Beside her desk was a word processor with green characters on the screen. A section of an article she was editing on the computer had been blocked off in black. Three Rolodexes, a black phone, and a blotter-style desk calendar crowded the top of her desk. Behind her on the white wall hung the office's sole photograph, a picture of a fair-haired child standing between her parents, a young hippie family at a Dupont Circle rally, circa 1969. The child had freckles across her face, and she was holding her father's hand. A Walkman rigged to an external speaker sat next to the computer, softly playing King Crimson's "Matte Kudasai."

Lyla folded her hands in front of her on the desk. "Rolanda said you wanted to speak to someone about William Henry."

"That's right."

"What about?"

"His murder."

"What have you got to do with it?"

"I'm looking into it."

Lyla took a pencil out of a leather cup and tapped the sharp end on her blotter. "Who are you working for?"

"Myself," I said. "And Henry."

Lyla's phone rang. She kept her eyes on mine and let it ring a few times before she picked it up. "Tell him I'll call him back." She replaced the receiver and studied my face. "So," she said finally. "You're a private dick."

"'A black private dick. With a sex machine for all the chicks.'"

"'Shaft'?"

"'You daamn right.'"

Lyla threw her head back and laughed. It was an easy laugh, from way down in her throat. I liked the way it sounded and the unconscious way her mouth opened wide when she did it.

"Well," she said, "at least I know that we're from the same generation."

"Yeah," I said. "I saw *Shaft*, first run, at the Town Theatre, on Thirteenth Street. 1971. My grandfather took me—against his better judgment."

"The Loews Palace on F Street," she said. "That was my first downtown film experience. A Liz Taylor double bill, no less. *Butterfield Eight*, and *Cat on a Hot Tin Roof*."

"So you're a real Washingtonian."

"All my life."

"Me too," I said.

Lyla replaced the pencil in the cup, smiled, and leaned back in her chair. The movement made her camisole shift beneath her satin blouse, and I watched the rise of her freckled breasts. She crossed her left leg over her right. The muscles in her thighs became defined with the action. I shifted in my chair to get a better look. She watched me do it, and neither of us flinched.

"You came here to talk about William Henry," she said.

"Right."

"Any progress on the case?"

"Not with the police. Apparently things got cold, real quick. I managed to dig up some stuff on my own."

"What kind of stuff?"

"You asking questions now?"

"Sorry," Lyla said. She brushed some lint off the side of her skirt. "It's a habit. You and I are basically in the same business, right?"

I nodded. "I used to read your bylines when you were still doing investigative. Before they hired Henry and bumped you up to managing editor."

"William Henry improved on my work," she said. "He was a damn good reporter."

"He was a good friend too."

"Yes, he was." Lyla stared off toward the blank white wall to her left. "Jack had hired him, in a private interview. So on his first day of work, when he walked in, none of us knew what to expect. Anyway, he comes in, and here's this trim, compact guy, on the short side, with long sideburns—they weren't stylish then—and one of those Ben Bradlee striped shirts, with a rep tie. His hair was receding too, remember, and he wore wire-rims, which only added to that Ivy League schoolboy look." Lyla ran a finger along the top of her lip. "So you can imagine that all of us so-called alternative types here didn't trust him at first. But right away he had us all loosened up—that little son of a bitch had the driest sense of humor, and the finest heart, of anyone ever walked through that front door."

"His death," I said. "It wasn't a random murder. That lead, about the light-skinned guy with the bloody shirt, seen leaving his apartment—I think that was basically bullshit, a plant of some kind."

Lyla leaned in and said, "Tell me about it."

"The information I got was that the murderer was let up into Henry's apartment, by the security guard who was on duty that night."

"Who gave you the information?"

"The security guard."

"Then you should be talking to him."

I shook my head. "He's gone. He's been gone, since he left the message and admitted that he was bought. I finally got hold of his mother—she says he left home a few days ago and hasn't been back since." I winced inadvertently at the memory of her broken voice as she said it, knowing full well that he'd never be back.

Lyla settled in her chair. "So that brings it back to us. How can I help you?"

"What was Henry working on here when he died?"

"Nothing," she said. "The funny thing is, he had just filed his last story, a week before his death. That week, he took a few days off, though he was in and out of the office, every day. But the cops asked Jack about all that. They took all his notes, and his diskettes."

"The cops?"

"The two investigators that were assigned his case."

"They talk to you?"

Lyla nodded. "I didn't have anything to tell 'em professionally. As for their personal questions, I just didn't answer. I had the impression they weren't going to follow up on the murder anyway."

Lyla watched me think things over. When I looked up, she was looking into my eyes, and her mouth was open, just a little. I felt something happen between us then, but I moved on.

"It's possible Henry was working on something you didn't know about, isn't it?"

"Sure. He played his cards close to the vest, when he wasn't on a specific assignment."

"He keep backup diskettes on his notes?"

Lyla said, "Yep."

I said, "You give those to the cops too?"

"Uh-uh."

"Any chance you'd print out those disks for me?"

"A real good chance," she said.

"I'd appreciate it."

Lyla rang Rolanda and had her retrieve Henry's diskettes from the file room. Rolanda entered with a container, and Lyla instructed her to use the laser to print out the last two months' worth of work. Rolanda, who seemed a bit overworked, sighed a bit during the instructions. When she left, Lyla said, "It'll be a few minutes."

I nodded to the photograph on the wall. "That's you, right?"

"Yeah. My parents were beatniks, and then they were hippies. They were a little old for it, even then. But for them it wasn't a fad. I was raised to believe that if you had to go against the grain and suffer a little bit to change things, it was worth it, if it made a difference. Even a small difference."

"You're doing it."

"I'm trying."

I said, "How close were you with Henry?"

Lyla's pale eyes widened a bit. Off guard, but only for a second. "You mean," she said, "was I sleeping with him?"

"Approximately."

"Well, it's none of your business, Stefanos. But just to get things on the table—no, I wasn't." She smiled, but not at me. She was thinking about Henry. "But hell, I would have, in a heartbeat. And it's not as if I didn't try. Once, when I got him drunk, I even asked him."

"He was gay."

"Sure, he was. But he didn't wear it on his sleeve. It was only one part of what he was. And since he didn't talk about it much, I mean, I didn't know if he was...exclusive about his gayness or not. Straight people are pretty naive about that kind of shit, aren't they? Anyway, I liked him, and at the very least, I thought it was worth a shot."

"The cops thought his murder might have been a crime of passion, at first. You know any of his lovers?"

Lyla shook her head. "Not personally. I did meet this guy once, a bartender, when William and I were drinking at the Occidental, in the Willard. The bartender's name was Michael— a gorgeous guy, but stiff. I didn't like him. William was a bit in the bag that night, and he told me that the two of them had dated."

"Anything worth checking out?"

"I would say no. But I don't know how your business works. How you get your information, how things shake out."

I shrugged. "I talk to a lot of people and things happen."

Lyla looked at my bandaged hand and then up at the deep purple crescent on my jaw. "They certainly do."

"Not as often as you'd think."

"You a drinker, Stefanos?"

"Now it's your turn to get personal."

"You look like a drinker."

"I know what it tastes like."

"No need to be defensive," she said. "I like a man who can take a drink."

After that we sat without speaking. Her homemade tape was playing Richard Thompson's *Gypsy Love Songs*. The time went by like that, and the silence wasn't uncomfortable. I liked her looks, and her honesty, and her intelligence. I liked everything about her.

Rolanda entered the office with a manila folder filled with papers. I took the folder and thanked her, and stood to put on my overcoat. Lyla McCubbin wrote a phone number on the back of her business card and pushed it across the desk. I slipped the card into the cellophane cover of my cigarette pack. She took my card and placed it in the front compartment of her desk drawer. Then she stood and shook my hand.

"I hope this helps."

"I'll let you know what happens. Thanks."

Lyla leaned on one foot. She let her other foot out of her olive green pump and ran her stockinged toe around the shoe's instep. Then she crossed her arms and twisted her lovely mouth up into a lopsided smirk. "Call me. Okay, Stefanos?"

I said, "I will."

TWENTY-THREE

I WALKED EAST on Pennsylvania Avenue. The temperature had fallen with evening, but I was warm with the buzz of new energy against the night. At the National, older couples were exiting cabs, dressed and eager for Andrew Lloyd Webber's latest scam on the theatergoing public. In Freedom Plaza tourists walked hurriedly past a man playing flute. The man stood coatless in front of an empty wax cup.

At Fourteenth and Penn I entered the leaded glass doors of the Occidental Restaurant in the Willard Hotel. I walked through a long hall, past black-and-white portrait photographs— Pat Schroeder and Carole Thompson on my right, George Bush and Harry Truman on my left—and down a flight of stairs into the bar area of the restaurant. Cole Porter played as I descended the stairs. I felt like Fred Astaire, with a two-day beard covering a bruised face.

I took off my black overcoat and hung it on a rack, transferred my smokes to the inside pocket of my Robert Hall sport coat, and had a seat at the bar. The seat I took was next to a black-haired Jewess who was picking at an appetizer plate of peppered scallops and squid on a bed of romaine lettuce. She held her fork as if it were hot. Next to her sat another young woman with large, expensive jewelry and a tiny nose that cost more than the jewelry. They were probably grabbing a bite to eat before heading a few blocks uptown to the Spy Club, where rich boys would buy them drinks from the proceeds of their trust funds. I gave the Occidental a look.

The room was all dark wood and candles, deuces primarily, young affluent couples with pale skin who looked pleasant in the light. In the bar area, three businessmen were hitting on a rather plain-looking woman who was wearing a dress that appeared to be decorated with a doily. On the far side of the bar, a distinguished elderly couple sipped their martinis and stared straight ahead. At the service bar, the manager fingered his Brooks Brothers tie with one hand and his brush mustache with the other. I signaled for the bartender.

The bartender walked over and stood square. He buffed the spot in front me with a clean white cloth, though the spot was already dry. His name tag said MICHAEL, my first bingo in a very long while.

"Welcome to the Occidental," he said with a white-toothed smile. He had the handsome but vacuous blue-eyed look of a military cadet, and he was built low to the ground, broad-shouldered and thick. "How can I serve you?"

I had seen him pour a half ounce of scotch into a rocks glass overflowed with cubes and serve it to an unfortunate man on the other end of the bar. I said, "You can serve me an Old Grand-Dad. Neat. And put a cold bottle of Budweiser next to it."

Michael's smile went away but not his chipper tone of voice. "It would be my pleasure," he said, and drifted.

By the time he returned I had lit a cigarette. Michael placed my drink on the bar with a thud. About a dollar's worth of bourbon splashed out over the lip of the glass.

"Thanks," I said.

"Cheers!" Michael said, and walked away.

I drank my Grand-Dad and chased it with beer. From the corner of my eye I saw the black-haired young woman fan away the smoke of my cigarette. I had one more deep drag, crushed the butt in a clean ashtray, and had a look at the bar.

The bar blended mahogany and oak with an inlay of brass. The runoff board was shiny copper, and free of bar netting. The liquor wall was subtly lit and backed by an immaculately beveled mirror framed by miniature marble columns. "Stardust" played on the house stereo. I signaled Michael for another round.

Michael returned with my bourbon and beer. "Cheers," he said tiredly.

"And to you," I said as I slid my business card along the top of the bar until it touched his fingers.

He looked it over. His eyes shifted toward his manager, then back at me. He was still smiling, but the smile was tight. "So what?" he said in a low, calm voice.

"Remember William Henry?"

Some color drained from his face, but he held on to the smile. "It's my business if I do," he said.

The woman next to me slipped down off her stool and ripped the receipt from the body of her credit card voucher. "Thanks, Michael," she said, stealing a contemptuous glance at me before winking in conspiracy at Michael.

"It's been my pleasure," Michael said. The woman and her bobbed friend left the bar. Michael watched them until they had vanished at the top of the stairs.

I sipped bourbon. "Can we talk?"

"No."

"Why not?"

"I'm busy."

"I'm busy too. Answer a couple of quick questions. After that you won't see me again."

"What kind of questions?"

"About William Henry."

Michael shifted his shoulders. "I don't know anything about him."

"You were his lover."

Michael frowned. "I went out with him, one time. Like I told you—that's my business."

"Sure, it is. And you can bury it, or go tell it on the mountain, for all I care. It makes no difference to me. But the cops are following up on that angle. I can give them your name, if you'd like. Or you can tell me what you know."

Michael made a head motion that encompassed the entire bar. "Listen, pal," he said softly. "If I didn't need this gig, I'd tell you to fuck off, right now."

"I don't think so," I said, looking him over. "Anyway, you do need it."

He loosened his shoulders. "I'll give you one minute."

"Fine. What was your relationship with Henry, the night he died?"

"It was over, way before that."

"How long before?"

"Months."

"He have many friends, besides you?"

"No idea."

"He ever talk about anything, about being in any danger, while you knew him?"

"No."

I sighed. "You're not thinking too hard."

"I'm answering your questions," he said behind a smirk.

"And I'm trying to find my friend's killer."

"What happened to William was a shame," Michael said without a trace of sincerity. "He was a nice guy, but that's all he was. I'm telling you, you're going down the wrong street. Our relationship—it didn't mean anything, understand?"

"I'm beginning to."

Michael gave me his hard look. "So why don't you just pick your things up and leave?"

I dropped fifteen on the bar, rose, and put on my overcoat. "You're real tough," I said. "You know it?"

Michael looked around for his manager, who had gone into the kitchen. He leaned over the bar and whispered through a clenched jaw. "Maybe I'll see you sometime, out on the street."

I smiled and said, "It would be my pleasure."

I POURED A CUP of coffee, walked it into my bedroom, and had a seat at my desk. My cat followed me in and dropped on her belly, just resting against my feet. I turned on the gooseneck lamp that was clamped to the side of my desk and opened the manila folder that contained William Henry's notes. The notes were entered by date. I read them chronologically over the next two hours, then read them again, this time highlighting several names and passages that recurred throughout.

When I was done, I removed the third of the notes that were related exclusively to Henry's last filed story and placed them back in the folder. What remained was cryptic and, in several spots, frustratingly coded. But seemingly at random, two genderless names continued to appear: Pyshak and Bonanno.

I had one more cigarette and butted it halfway down. I washed up, undressed, and read a little until my eyes began to get heavy. My cat dozed on the blanket at my feet.

The words *Pyshak* and *Bonanno* drifted through my head as I fell into the dark arms of sleep.

TWENTY-FOUR

THE NEXT AFTERNOON I sat at the bar of the Spot with William Henry's notes spread before me. A telephone and the area white-page directories rested on the bar, near the notes. The Spot's reader, Dave, sat at the other end of the bar, his head buried in a slim novel. A coffee cup sat in front of him, and a lit cigarette burned in an ashtray next to the cup. Mai was on the long shift. She tried to talk to me about her latest military conquest while I looked over the notes. I kept my attention on my work.

There were no Pyshaks in any of the three metropolitan directories, but there were several Bonannos. I spent two hours placing calls to every one of them. Many had answering machines, on which I left no message. To the ones I reached I took the long shot of asking to speak to William Henry. I was hoping for a fumble, or a hang-up, or some sign of recognition. What I got was bewilderment, and a dead end.

Happy hour—a colossal misnomer at the Spot—soon came,

and the regulars began to file in. Buddy and Bubba swaggered to the sports section and were followed shortly by Richard, who was immediately in their collective face over an '86 Super Bowl point-spread dispute. Melvin Jeffers had a seat alone and ordered a gin martini ("extra dry, darlin'"), and asked Mai to change the music over to something more "upbeat." Mai slid an old Michael Henderson tape into the deck and served Melvin's drink. Henderson's "Be My Girl" began to croon from the speakers.

After two verses of that, Dave collected his paraphernalia and got off his stool. On the way out he stopped behind my back and tapped me on the shoulder. His reading glasses hung on a leash across his broad chest. He placed the glasses back on his nose and scratched his gray-and-black beard as he looked over my notes.

"Workin' on a puzzle?" he said with the deep rasp of a heavy smoker.

"In a way." I leaned back and rolled my head to loosen my neck. When I turned around, Dave was still standing behind me. I didn't know what he wanted, or why he was waiting there with a fixed, dogged stare. But Dave read books, and he hadn't had a drink in years. That put him miles ahead of everyone else in the joint, including me. "Have a seat," I said.

Dave touched the right stem of his glasses and bellied up. I signaled Mai for Dave's dirty ashtray, and she retrieved it from his favorite spot and placed it in front of him. Dave lit a smoke and fitted it into the groove of the tray.

"What's got you stumped?" he said.

I told him about the case, and about the two names, and about the calls I had made. Dave stared at the names for a few minutes. Then he turned over one of the sheets of notepaper, withdrew a pen from the plastic holder in his breast pocket, and began writing down words in two parallel columns. Afterward he let the glasses off his nose and set the pen down on the notepaper. He pushed the paper along the bar until it rested in front of me.

I looked the words over and said, "What'd you do?"

"You said the notes appeared to be in code, partially at least."

"I said I didn't understand them—it's not the same thing."

Dave said, "So you're sure *Pyshak* and *Bonanno* are persons' names."

"Not entirely. What do you think?"

Dave tapped the filter on the cigarette that was wedged in the ashtray. He let it burn there and looked at me. "I think *Bonanno*'s a name. It's common enough. And when you break it out phonetically, and syllabically, screw around with it a little"— he pointed to the column of words on the right—"you come up with nothing."

My eyes traveled to the column on the left. "Go on."

"Now do the same thing with *Pyshak*," Dave said, twitching excitedly, putting his glasses on again and adjusting them on the tip of his nose. "Look what you get." He ran his finger down the column of jumbled *Pyshak* mutations—*Piss Hack, Pishe Ak*— and stopped at the last two words. The words read *Pie Shack*.

"It's a business," I said.

"It's a possibility," Dave said, smiling.

I smiled back, getting ahead of things. "A bakery?"

Dave shook his head and watched me from the corner of his eye. "Think, Nick—the relationship to Bonanno. How many Italian bakers you know?"

I thumped my fist on the bar until it hit me like a stone. "Pie Shack," I said quietly. "As in pizza pie."

"If I was you," Dave said, "that's where I'd start."

THREE PIE SHACKS WERE listed under Pizza in the Spot's year-old, tattered copy of the yellow pages. I wrote down the addresses and phone numbers and then had Mai place the bar's sticky black Rolodex in front of me. I withdrew the cleanest business cards of several food and beverage distributors, put them in my wallet, and grabbed some related price books that had been left behind by various salesmen. Then I lifted my overcoat off the hall rack and exited the Spot.

I stopped uptown at my apartment for a shower and a shave, and to feed my cat. Out of the shower, I dressed the cut on the inside of my hand and left the bandage off. I put on jeans and a black V-necked sweater over a white T-shirt, and slipped my Doc Martens oxfords onto my feet. Before I left I stroked my cat's head until her eye closed. She slinked across the room to her dish. Her eye was still closed as her pink tongue lapped water from the dish. I closed the door silently and walked out into the night.

The air was misty and cold. Halos ringed the streetlights on Sixteenth as I drove south. I hung a right at U Street and parked my Dart near the firehouse. The engine coughed a bit as I cut it. I locked up and crossed over to the south side of the street, where several bars and carryouts were grouped on this farthest corner of Adams-Morgan.

I checked the address from the list in my overcoat pocket and walked west. I passed Rio Loco's, the Tex-Mex bar that Jackie and I patronized with frequency. I passed an open but empty frozen-yogurt parlor and a pizza-and-sub shop named the Olde World. Just past that stood a bankrupt "art bar," and next to that the Pie Shack. Or, as I realized as I neared its boarded entrance, the Pie Shack's burnt remains.

A red condemnation sticker from the fire department hung crookedly on the front door. The plate-glass window that fronted the store had been busted out, replaced by iron bars. Cupping my hands around my eyes, I looked through the bars. The interior had been swept out, with remaining equipment, booths and counters pushed irregularly into one far corner. The ceiling had fallen through, leaving wires and fixtures dangling into the space. The interior walls were sooty and charred black. Nothing but a burnt shell. I backed away and retraced my steps, walking east on U.

A few doors down stood the Olde World, fluorescently lit

and open for business. I entered and leaned my elbows on the Formica counter. Next to me at the counter was a long-haired man wearing a fringed leather jacket. He held in his hand a slice of pepperoni with extra cheese, and he studied it with interest between bites. There were no employees behind the counter, but through the door that led to the kitchen I heard the laughter of two young men over an LL Cool J single. I tapped my palm on the knob of a bell that sat next to the electronic register.

One of the young men emerged from the kitchen, still laughing as he downstepped out, yelling back to his partner about some "serious bitch" that had been in earlier that evening. He stopped at the counter, looked over my shoulder onto U Street, and said, "Yeah."

"Let me get a slice of cheese."

"Anything to drink?" Still looking past me.

"Just the pizza."

The young man turned his head back to the kitchen and yelled, "One slice o' plain, Dopey." He turned back to me. "Dolla-fifty."

I handed him two ones. He bobbed his head to "Round the Way Girl" and mouthed the chorus, shutting his eyes soulfully as he rang me up and slapped the change onto the counter. "What happened to that place two doors down, the Pie Shack?"

The young man shook his head, stopped mouthing LL Cool J, and shrugged. "Motherfucker burned, man."

"When was that?"

He shrugged again. "Don't know. Before I came to work here."

"When was that?" I repeated.

"Near six months," he said, and spun back into the kitchen. There was more laughter, then he bounded back out with my slice and dropped it on the counter in front of me. I thanked him, but by the time I got the words out he had disappeared into the back. I ate the pizza in silence, standing at the counter, next to the man in the fringed leather jacket.

Out on the street a Ford Escort came to a screaming halt in front of the Olde World. An orange-and-red cardboard sign logoed identically to the sign that hung above the Olde World's entrance was fastened to the roof of the Escort. The baseball-capped driver double-parked and jumped out of the car, a black thermal cover cradled in his arms. He ran past me and dashed into the entrance of the shop.

I stood on the street for a few minutes with my hands in my overcoat pockets and watched the activity. Outside Rio Loco's, a shirtsleeved man in his twenties wearing a fraternity cap leaned against the brick facade and vomited at his feet. I walked around him and entered the bar. The place was packed with college kids and neighborhood regulars. Some of the college kids were grouped near the back of the bar, loudly singing "New York, New York," drowning out the juke. My regular waitress saw me from across the room and fetched me a Bud from the service area near the kitchen. I leaned against the wall and drank it standing up, then placed the empty on the bar with a five spot pinned underneath. Fifteen minutes later I was in bed in my apartment, making plans to visit Pie Shack Number Two early the next day.

THE SECOND PIE SHACK listed in the yellow pages was located on Sligo Avenue in Silver Spring. I drove up Georgia the following morning, passed under the railroad bridge, and turned left on Sligo. Just beyond a used bookstore and a body garage, I parked my Dart in front of the address written in my notes.

The Pie Shack was there, but it was closed, with black bars on the front window and a red fire sticker attached to the door. One block down, near the corner of Sligo and Fenton, stood the Olde World carryout. I grabbed my price books off the seat beside me and climbed out of my Dart.

The wind blew my knit tie back over my shoulder as I walked. I smoothed it down when I reached the glass door of the Olde World, and stepped inside. The layout was the same as in Adams-Morgan—a small waiting area, two or three tables with red vinyl chairs, and a Formica counter.

A thin, young dark-skinned man in his early twenties sat on a stool behind the counter, reading what looked to be a textbook. The man had sharply defined cheekbones and a small, pinched nose. Some Caribbean music played softly from a trebly speaker in the kitchen.

At my entrance the young man stood and closed the book. I put my own book on the counter and smiled.

"Can I help you?"

"I hope so," I said in a chipper tone.

"What can I get you?"

I placed a business card in front of him. The business card was from Variety Foods, and the name on it was Ron Wilson. "Ron Wilson," I said, still smiling as I shook his hand. "Variety Foods. And you are?"

"My name's Elliot," he said with an island lilt, putting a palm up in front of my face in a halting gesture. "Before you get into your pitch, man, let me tell you that you're talking to the wrong guy."

"Who should I be talking to?"

"The main office is out of our store in Northwest. They do all the buying from there."

"Write that address down for me, will you?" I handed him my pen and a torn piece of paper out of the notebook. While he wrote it, I said, "What happened to the Pie Shack, down the street? I was supposed to make a call on them today."

Elliot passed me the notepaper. "You got some old information, man. The Pie Shack's been closed for a long time, since right before we opened. Electrical fire is what I heard."

"Who do I talk to in your main office?"

"Guy named Francis. Frank. Runs the operation."

"Thanks," I said as I shook his hand once again. "By the way"—I nodded toward the kitchen—"who are we listening to?"

"The Mighty Sparrow, man." Elliot smiled. "The Sparrow rocks."

"He does. Thanks again." I walked toward the door.

"Hey," Elliot said from behind my back. "Don't work so hard, man—it's New Year's Eve."

I waved back at him and walked out onto the sidewalk. Back in my Dart, I cracked a window and lit a smoke. Across from the pizza shop, two Ford Escorts sat parked, signs strung to their roofs. I studied the delivery cars. The orange-and-red lettering of the signs' logos matched the orange-and-red logo on the Olde World's facade.

James Thomas's voice filled my head: "I want you to know I didn't kill that boy.... That boy sure didn't deserve to die.... The man from the orange and the red..."

The orange and the red.

I pitched my cigarette out the window and spit smoke as I retrieved the address that Elliot had written out for the Olde World's office. Then I checked it against the address of the third Pie Shack. By then it was an exercise. I knew that they would be on the same block, and I knew without question that the last Pie Shack would be empty, burnt, and abandoned.

I pumped the gas once and turned the ignition key. Six cylinders fired and I pulled away from the curb.

TWENTY-FIVE

THE OLDE WORLD headquarters stood in the street-level space of an office building at the southeastern corner of Twenty-first and M. I parked my Dart in the lot behind a movie theater and restaurant at Twenty-third and slid the white-shirted attendant a couple of bucks for the privilege. At the restaurant's back door a Latino busboy sat on a black railing, smoking a joint. He took a hit, held it in, and followed my path with his gaze as I crossed the lot.

I walked east on M Street. Downtown had begun to empty out for the holiday. An early rush hour thickened the streets, leaving few pedestrians afoot. Underdressed homeless men shared the sidewalks with blue-blooded attorneys in plain charcoal suits and with women dressed unimaginatively and mannishly in their pursuit of success. The West End balanced poverty and ambition, granite and spit, money as new as the morning paper and glass-eyed hopelessness older than slavery.

At Twenty-second I checked the location of the third Pie Shack. A synthetic-diamond store now stood at the address. If there had been a Pie Shack, and it had burned, it had burned a long time ago.

I kept walking until I reached the door of the Olde World. When I got to it, I stepped inside.

The layout was the same as all the others. This time a man in his thirties with Mediterranean features stood behind the counter. He was writing something in a spiral notebook when I walked in, and as the entrance bell above the door sounded he slipped the notebook into a space below the register. I smiled and placed my Variety Foods business card on the counter.

"Afternoon," I said. "Ron Wilson, Variety Foods. And your name?"

"Cheek."

"Cold enough out there for ya today?"

"Yeah," he said.

"Colder than a brass monkey's balls, right?"

Cheek rolled his eyes in exasperation and sighed. "What can I do for you?"

"Is the owner or manager in?"

"He's in," he said in a high voice, and touched the paper hat that was stained at the rim with the oil of his hair. He wiped a smudge of grease off one thick eyebrow that ran unbroken over his deeply set brown eyes. "But he don't see salesmen without an appointment."

"What's his name?"

"Frank."

"Do me a favor." I leaned on the counter, buddying up. "It's New Year's Eve, and this is my last call of the day. Hell, it's my last call of the year, and I've got to make my numbers." I winked. "Go back there and tell Frank that there's a guy out here, he's willing to sell anything on his price sheet for fifty percent better than what he's buying it for anywhere else."

"Fifty off?"

"Five-oh."

"He still won't see you," Cheek said.

I said, "Give it a shot, huh?"

Cheek moved into the kitchen and stayed there for quite some time. I waited with my price book under my arm. When a customer entered and the door chime sounded, Cheek returned from the kitchen. He licked the graphite tip of his pencil before he wrote the customer's order on a green guest check pad, then he turned and walked back into the kitchen. I stayed put and five minutes later Cheek was back with a square, flat box of pizza. He rang the customer up and slammed the drawer closed as the customer headed out the front door. Cheek began to reenter the kitchen when I stopped him.

"What about Frank?" I said cheerfully.

Cheek turned around and pushed the paper hat back on his damp head. "He says he'll see you for a minute, if what you got's legit. But only for a minute. He's busy."

"A minute's all it will take. Thanks."

Cheek waved me back. "Come on," he said.

I followed him behind the counter, through a doorless frame, and into the kitchen. The kitchen was open and bright with a track of fluorescent tubes that lighted it from front to back. On the north wall stood a large baker's oven, its door down. A thick young expediter with curly brown hair, long in the back and shaven on the sides, peered into the oven. He checked the pies inside and then flung the door up and shut. Beside the oven, warming lights glowed red over a two-level steel table, and on the shelf above the lights sat an institutional microwave oven. Next to the microwave a Sony box with removable speakers was set on DC101. The righteous freak-out of Van Halen's guitar careened throughout the room.

A large stainless-steel prep table was situated in the middle of the room, and on the opposite wall a cold salad bar abutted a sandwich block, both refrigerated underneath. Several black-handled knives of various sizes were racked above the sandwich block. Next to the block a four-foot-wide stainless-steel refrigerator stood upright and stopped inches from the ceiling. On the third wall sat two deep stainless-steel sinks, with a rinse hose suspended above. A tall, wiry man with slick black hair and a severely pocked face stood before the prep table in the middle of the room, ladling sauce into a pie shell. Neither he nor the expediter looked up as I passed into the kitchen.

Cheek raised his hand and said, "Wait here."

I stopped walking and cradled my book. The thick young expediter moved quickly behind me to the sandwich block and pulled a knife off the rack. He retrieved some onions from a plastic container below and deftly began to peel and slice them on the board with the knife's serrated edge. The pock-faced man pushed tomato sauce around the pie shell with the bottom of his ladle in slow, careful circles. Cheek entered a small office in the back of the kitchen. I watched him do it.

Two men sat in chairs in the office. I could see their pants legs — one wore black twills, the other khakis — and the wooden legs of the chairs in which they sat. Some smoke drifted out of the office door. I listened to Cheek's high voice, and a deeper one after that, and then the khaki legs unwound and the man inside them stepped out of the office with Cheek.

He was an average man of average-to-heavy build, with a blue work shirt tucked into the khakis and a dirty apron tied over half of both. There was a plastic foam cup in his right hand and the ass end of a cigar in the fingers of his left. He plugged the cigar in the side of his saliva-caked mouth and stopped walking a foot shy of my face.

"What ya got," he said. Booze was heavy on his breath.

"Deals," I said, my salesman's smile glued ridiculously high. "Unbelievable deals, Frank." I extended my hand. "Ron Wilson, Variety Foods."

Frank put his hand to his mouth, unplugged the cigar, and had a gulp of scotch from the plastic foam cup. "Let's skip all the bullshit, okay? Cheek said you had something good, and it's

New Year's Eve, and to tell you the truth I'm already half in the bag. So let's see what you got, quick, before my mood changes and I make you come in on order day like every other slob."

"Sounds good to me," I said. "Where should we go? In your office?"

"Uh-uh." Frank's head tipped like a bell in the direction of the sinks. "Over there."

I followed him and watched the office as I walked. Smoke still leaked out from behind the door. At the sink I set my black book on the drain platform and opened to a random page. Black-and-white photographs of canned goods ran top to bottom on the left quarter of the page, and corresponding price columns took up the balance.

"I assume you use all of these goods," I said, lightly running the tip of my forefinger down the column of photographs, studying the gimmick as I spoke. The dollar amounts lessened as the purchase quantities increased.

"We use a lotta shit," Frank said as he pulled the scotch cup away from his lips. He had chewed small crescents of plastic foam off the rim. "What's the deal?"

"Like I told Mr. Cheek, fifty off." I looked around for Cheek's support, but he was back out front.

"Fifty off what?"

"Our best price on the sheet," I stuttered through the smile. The smile had atrophied now to a twitch.

"Bullshit," Frank said. A cloud of cheap cigar smoke hung between our faces. "What's the catch?"

"No catch," I said with wide eyes. "New Year's special, onetime order. No limit. You get acquainted with our business, we make a new friend."

The bluesy intro to Jethro Tull's "Locomotive Breath" played through the Sony. Frank had another slug and belched. The belch watered his eyes and caused his lips to part like two pink slugs.

"One thing I always say, Winston."

"Wilson. Ron Wilson."

"One thing I always say. If it's on sale today, it can be on sale tomorrow. Right?"

"Maybe so," I said. "But I sure would like to write an order before the clock strikes twelve."

"Never happen," Frank said. "I'm not that kind of sucker. Nice try, though. Always ask for the sale." He rocked back on his heels. "Look me up after the New Year, hear?"

"I will. Thanks." I extended my hand again, and again Frank ignored it. Instead he turned his head back toward the young expediter.

"Turn that shit down!" he yelled, pointing at the boom box. Then he waddled back like a man carrying something odious in the seat of his pants and shut the door behind him.

The thick young expediter moved to the Sony and reduced the volume by a hair. I closed my book, put it under my arm, and walked through the kitchen toward the lobby. The tall, wiry, pock-faced man glanced up and looked me over as I passed. His eyes were small and heavily hooded, all black pupil, whiteless as a snake's. I felt them on me as I exited the kitchen.

TWENTY-SIX

OUT ON THE street I walked quickly back to my Dart. I put the price book in the car and retrieved a heavy wool sweater from the trunk. I removed my tie and put the sweater over my shirt, and my overcoat on top of them both.

On my way back I stopped in a deli named Costaki's and bought the largest go-cup of coffee they sold. I tore a hole in the plastic lid and sipped the contents as I walked south on Twenty-first. I kept low passing the Olde World and just beyond it cut left down a narrow alley.

The alley ran between Twentieth and Twenty-first. A tan building stood east to west on the south side of the alley, with two green dumpsters positioned and spaced against its side. A doorway cut into the building next to the dumpster closest to Twentieth. I walked down the alley and stepped up onto the curb and stood in the doorway. I could see the Olde World's back entrance from the doorway, on the north side of the alley.

Nothing much happened after that. Steam rose from the hole in the coffee lid, and the traffic sounds from the right and the left began to soften. I had a cigarette and smoked it down to the filter. A couple of women walked across the alley and quickened their pace when they saw me in the doorway. A bundled bicycle courier rode by, and then a gray Step-Van, both without incident. An hour passed and dusk darkened the alley.

At 7:25 a brown Mercury Marquis drove by slowly and stopped in the alley at the Olde World's door. From the shadow of my doorway I watched an obese man in a brown coat get out of the Marquis and open the trunk. He removed what looked to be two filled pillowcases and carried them up to the door, where he rang the buzzer. Hands appeared shortly thereafter from behind the door. The hands grabbed the pillowcases, pulling them inside. The obese man in the brown suit walked back to the trunk and closed it, then reentered the driver's side and drove out of the alley.

I lit another cigarette. By eight o'clock no one else had driven in or out of the alley. There was little sound now, except for the rustle of paper and debris that the wind blew and lifted in tight, violent circles.

I jogged back to my Dart, started it, and drove over to Twenty-first, where I parked facing south on the street, in sight of the Olde World's window. I turned the radio on and switched it to WDCU. I listened to a Coltrane set, and one by Stan Getz. In the middle of the Getz set, the lights in the Olde World's window went out. I turned the ignition key on my Dart.

A black Lincoln passed my car and stopped in front of the Olde World. The young expediter who had retrieved the car got out of the driver's seat and left the engine running. A heavy man in his fifties with bushy gray sideburns walked out of the Old World and moved toward the car. A live cigarette in an alabaster holder dangled between his fingers as he walked. Black twill pants legs showed beneath his double-breasted black overcoat. The heavy man climbed into the Lincoln and drove away. Before he did it I wrote his D.C. license plate number in my notebook and checked my wristwatch. The time was 8:35.

The expediter zipped his green army jacket and walked north on Twenty-first, toward Ward Park. Frank and the tall pock-faced man emerged from the Olde World right after that. Frank had an inch of cigar in his mouth and a plastic foam cup in his hand, and he wore a corduroy car coat. The tall man had changed into gray slacks and a long gray overcoat a shade darker than the slacks. The two of them walked to a silver blue Lincoln parked three car lengths ahead. Frank unlocked the door and got behind the wheel. The tall man waited in the street until his side unlocked, then climbed into the shotgun seat. They pulled away from the curb. I yanked the column shift down out of neutral and felt it engage.

The Lincoln turned down the alley and at the end of it made a left onto Twentieth. When the taillights disappeared around the corner of the building, I followed. At New Hampshire Avenue the Lincoln cut right and headed northeast. At Georgia it turned left and shot straight north, and at Kansas Avenue it turned right again and resumed its northeastern path.

Kansas was wide and clean and residential, and free of cops. The Lincoln accelerated and stayed at fifty. I kept back two hundred yards the entire trip, running three reds along the way.

The Lincoln cut right at Missouri, crossed New Hampshire, and continued on at the top of North Capitol. Missouri became Riggs, and the Lincoln veered right down a slope that began South Dakota Avenue. We headed southeast then, paralleling Eastern Avenue at the Maryland line. At an arm of Fort Totten Park in Northeast, as the garden apartment complexes decreased, near an industrial section of concrete yards and waste-disposal sights, the Lincoln turned right on Gallatin, along a grove of widely spaced trees. I kept on, easing my foot off the gas.

A quarter-mile past a home for unwed mothers, the Lincoln turned left onto an unmarked, unpaved road and slowly drove into a break of trees. I continued past and in my rearview watched the taillights fade. I stopped the Dart in front of an isolated row of brick colonials on Gallatin and killed the engine.

I pulled my arms out of my overcoat, put lined leather gloves over my hands, and left the coat behind me on the seat. Out of the car, I ran quickly across the road, through a hard field, and into the grove of evergreens and willows. A dim yellow light glowed in the direction of the Lincoln's path, and I cut toward it diagonally through the trees, with slow, careful steps. As I neared a wide clearing, I stopped and crouched down behind the trunk of a scrub pine. My breath was visible in the yellow light ahead. Through it, I watched the Lincoln come to a slow stop.

The light topped a leaning lamppost. Next to the lamppost a bungalow stood far back at the edge of the clearing. The woods continued on behind the bungalow. The silver blue Lincoln sat parked next to the black Lincoln that had been driven by the man in black twills. Lights glowed from inside the bungalow.

Frank and the pock-faced man climbed out of the silver blue Lincoln. Frank walked over to the black Lincoln and unlocked the trunk while his partner, tall and unmoving, stood by. Then Frank pulled the two pillowcases out—the pillowcases the expediter had transferred earlier to the trunk when he had retrieved his boss's car—and shut the lid. They crossed the yard and stepped up onto the bungalow's porch. The wooden porch gave and creaked beneath their weight.

The two of them entered with the turn of Frank's key. A square of light spilled out as the door opened. After it closed, the porch darkened, and then there was only my breath against the light of the lamppost, and the headstone cold of the woods around me. I waited awhile to let some nerve seep in. When I thought I had it, I looked behind me once, and again. I swallowed spit and crept low, like a prowler, away from the pine and out into the clearing.

I stopped behind the trunk of the black Lincoln. Soft music

hopped with the intermittent surge of horns played from inside the bungalow, but the clearing was quiet. I could hear my own breathing and feel the rubbery thump of my heart against my ribs. I pushed away from the car, staying low, and stepped up onto the porch, crawling heels-to-ass to a spot below the front bay window.

I raised my head until my eyes cleared the bottom of the window's frame.

It was a Sears bungalow from the 1920s, modified into some sort of private casino. The walls of the first floor had been removed, leaving one large room with a door leading back to the kitchen. Two twenty-five-inch televisions sat on the left wall, and two different basketball games were being broadcast on the sets. A round card table covered with dirty green felt stood in the center of the room, with six wooden swivel chairs placed around it. Red, white, and blue chips were strewn about the table's green top.

On the back wall an oak bar ran between the kitchen door and a wood staircase. The kitchen door was open, and the staircase led to a dark landing. Two closed doors were outlined in the shadows of the landing.

One high-backed stool stood at the far end of the bar. Behind the bar Frank poured scotch into a rocks glass filled with ice. The checkered walnut stock of a .38 Airweight showed above the waistband of his khakis, where it was secured by a snap in a nylon holster. Frank replaced the scotch in a small group of medium call bottles illuminated by a naked-drop light from above. A small dirty mirror hung on the cedar paneling behind the bottles. A compact stereo with squat black speakers stood next to the bottles.

The heavy man in black twills stood with a drink in his hand in front of the two television sets, shifting his head slowly between the two games. The blue light from the sets danced across his unemotional, heavy-lidded eyes. The tall, pock-faced man was bent over one of the pillowcases, with his hand inside.

He withdrew a fistful of small white slips of paper, and he turned and said something to Frank, and both of them laughed. A mangled smile turned up on the heavy man's face as well, but he kept his eyes on the games.

The pock-faced man turned his head back down toward the pillowcase on the floor. It was then that I studied his face for the first time. The scars only covered the right side, and they were chunked deep, and red. The left side of his face was tightly smooth, with street-pretty definition. I lowered my head and crawled away from the window, off the porch.

A small, curtained window was positioned on the right side of the bungalow. I walked lightly past it, to the rear of the house. A narrow set of painted wood stairs led to the back entrance of the kitchen. From the bottom of the stairs I could see a tubular fluorescent light hung on the white plaster ceiling. A string switch dangled from the light. I walked up the stairs, my hand sliding up a loose splintered rail, and looked through a sheer lacy curtain.

Through the tiny kitchen, past the main room, and out the front bay window to the yard, a set of headlights approached from up the road.

I jumped off the steps and hit the ground running. I saw the headlights pass across the house and traverse the ground at my feet, and I heard myself grunt as I sprinted blindly into the woods. Willow sticks lashed my face, and there was the sound of branches snapping at my feet, and the sound of the branches adrenalized my legs, and I turned right and ran harder and faster, as if a fire were chasing me up a flight of stairs. I kept running until I reached the broken grove of willow and pine.

I stopped for breath, looked behind me once more, and ran out of the grove, across the hard field and the road, back to my Dart. I gunned it and drove up Gallatin to the Maryland line at Chillum, where I cracked the window and lit a smoke, hanging a left and then another just after that, back into the District.

The streets were shining and noisy, filled with loud, swerving vehicles and juiced-up, hard-luck cops on the worst beat of the year. I dodged them all, driving beneath a pearl moon, my fingers tight around the steering wheel, all the way back to my apartment in Shepherd Park.

I TURNED ON THE lamp switch next to my couch on the way to the liquor cabinet in my kitchen, where I withdrew what was left of my green-seal Grand-Dad. My cat circled my feet as I poured the bourbon into a juice glass, and kept circling as I tossed it back. I swallowed the whiskey, leaned over the chipped porcelain drain board, felt the burn, and waited for the warmth to wash over my face. I poured another shot and let the liquor slop out of the bottle's neck. Some of it spilled out onto the porcelain. The rest filled half the glass. I had a sip this time and walked out of the kitchen with the glass in my hand to the couch in my tiny living room.

I balanced the glass on the arm of the couch, picked the telephone up off the rug, and placed it in my lap. My cat jumped up on the couch and touched her nose to my arm, then jumped down and walked off, tail up, to the bedroom. I dialed Winnie Luzon.

Winnie picked up on the third ring. "Talk about it," he said.

"Winnie."

"Yeah?"

"Nick Stefanos."

"Nicky! Happy New Year, Holmes."

"And to you, man." There was some sort of tinny disco in the background, and the laughter of a woman.

"So what's up, Nick?"

"Partying tonight?"

"You know me, man, tonight the shit is *ser*ious."

"I won't keep you, then. Got a couple of questions, though, if you can spare a minute."

"Hold on." Winnie put his hand over the mouthpiece and yelled something I couldn't make out. When he got back on the line the music had been cut, and the woman was talking rapidly in Spanish, her voice fading as she walked away. I heard a match strike and the crackle of lit paper, and Winnie's exhale.

"We talk now?"

Winnie said, "Sure."

"Listen—you ever hear of a place called the Olde World? Pizza and subs, down in your neighborhood, Sixteenth and U?"

"Down near Rio Loco's, right?"

"The same."

"Yeah, sure. Good pizza, man."

"You know the owners, anything about 'em?"

Winnie took in some smoke and held it. I could envision the glaze in his eyes, and the shrug. "Uh-uh."

"There was a place near the Olde World, another pizza joint, called the Pie Shack."

"The Pie Shack—that's that place burned."

"Arson?" I said.

"That was the rumor."

"Any real word on that?"

"Nothing in stone."

"How about the name *Bonanno*, that mean anything?"

"Bonanno?" Winnie said. "It's a Guinea name, Nick, common as Smith."

"So it doesn't click."

"Uh-uh. This about that Goodrich thing, the thing with Joey DiGeordano?"

"That's taken care of," I said.

Winnie went silent for a minute or so, then snapped his fingers into the receiver. "Hey, Nicky, that reminds me, man. You had some heat come around, asking questions about you, in Malcolm X."

"What kind of heat?"

"Two cops. Detectives I do business with, now and again."

"You sell them information?"

"When I have to, yeah. But this one, I don't like the way he looks, or the way he talks. I don't sell him nothin'."

"What was he asking?"

"About your friend, the one got slashed in the Piedmont."

"William Henry."

"Right. This joker wanted to know if you been around, askin' about your friend."

"You tell him anything?"

Winnie paused. "Don't embarrass yourself, Nick."

"Thanks, Winnie." I had a sip of bourbon and let it settle while I thought things over. "What'd this cop look like?"

"Skinny and mean. Like a wet dog."

"He give his name?"

"Goloria."

I put fire to a Camel and rolled the bourbon around in the glass. "And his partner?"

"Lady cop, with nuts."

"Wallace, right?"

"That's right. Ring a bell, Nick?"

"It's beginning to," I said.

"Listen, man, I gotta go." Winnie's voice lowered to a whisper. "Don't want to piss off the pussy, Holmes. Know what I'm sayin'?"

"Go on, Winnie. Have a good time, man."

"Stay safe, Nick." The phone clicked dead.

My landlord was having a small party upstairs. I listened to the thump of bass and the sound of feet moving on hardwood floors. My cat emerged from the darkness of the bedroom and hopped back up onto the couch. She waited for me to move the telephone aside, then crawled onto my lap and kneaded it until she tucked her paws in and dropped down on her belly.

I lit another smoke and finished my bourbon. A blanket of gray had settled in the center of the room. I butted the cigarette and turned off the lamp next to the couch, letting my head ease back as I ran my fingers through the fur of my sleeping cat. The last thing I heard was an ebb of laughter from above, the swell of music, and the muffled screams of old friends and lovers.

TWENTY-SEVEN

Hello?"

"Mr. DiGeordano?"

"Yes."

"Nick Stefanos."

"Nick, how are you? Happy New Year."

"Thanks, same to you."

"What can I do for you?"

"I apologize for calling you at home on the holiday, but I need to ask a favor."

"You want to speak to Joey?"

"No, sir, it's you I'd like to speak to."

Louis DiGeordano cleared his throat. "Go ahead," he said in his high rasp.

"Not over the phone, if you don't mind."

"Is this about the Goodrich girl?"

"Some of it is," I said. "Most of it's about something else."

DiGeordano's voice went in and out as he mumbled for a bit. I sat on the couch at my apartment, sipping coffee. He put his mouth closer to the line. "The family's coming over for New Year's dinner," he said, "at five. I suppose I can meet you this morning, for a short while."

"How about in about an hour? Say, eleven o'clock?"

"Fine."

"Hains Point, is that okay? Parking Area Six. You know where that is?"

"Do I know it? Nick, it was me that took you to Hains Point for your first time, nearly thirty years ago."

"Can I pick you up?"

"No, I'll have Bobby drive me. See you at eleven."

I waited for another dial tone, then rang Darnell. He lived alone in the Shaw area of Northwest, with only a mattress on the floor and a small table and chair set in a bare-walled efficiency. The holidays were rough on guys like me, rougher on guys like Darnell.

Darnell said, "Yeah."

"Darnell, it's Nick."

"Nick, what you doin', man?"

"Headin' down to Hains Point. Want to come along?"

"Hains Point? While the hawk flies? Shit."

"I've got to meet a man. It won't take long. But it's a nice day, thought you might want to take a drive. Matter of fact, thought you might want to drive."

"You know I ain't driven a car since I checked outta Lorton. Don't even have a license, Nick."

"Come on, Darnell—what're you going to do today, sit around, watch beer commercials in black and white? You don't even drink."

Darnell thought it over. "I can drive?"

"Yeah."

"You swing by my way?"

"In a half hour."

Darnell said, "Right."

WE CAUGHT THE PARK off Thirteenth at Arkansas and took the express route downtown. Heavily clothed joggers bounded colt-ishly through blocks of sunlight on the path to our right, the wind at their backs.

Darnell wore his brown overcoat, his matching brown leather kufi tight on his head. He drove my Dart with one hand on the wheel, his left elbow resting on the window's edge. Darnell had brought his own tape—Sly Stone's *There's a Riot Goin' On*—for the ride, and he slipped it in as soon as he had slid glee-fully into the driver's seat. He had rolled down the window right after that, and I had let him do it without objection, seeing the involuntary, childlike grin on his face, though it wasn't a day for open windows. The bright sun barely dented the cold front that had fallen into town overnight.

We passed the Kennedy Center and drove along the river to East Potomac Park, winding finally into Ohio Drive. Darnell eased off the gas as the road went one-way, a line of naked-branched cherry trees to our left, the golf course to our right. After another quarter-mile, at Parking Area Six, Darnell pulled the Dart into a small lot that faced Washington Channel.

There were few cars circling the park, and only one—a red Mercedes coupe with gold alloy wheels—in the lot. In the light I could make out the outline of a shaven head behind the tinted glass of the coupe's driver's side. I rolled my own window down and pushed the lighter into the dash. When the lighter popped out thirty seconds later, I used it to burn a Camel.

Darnell rocked his head and softly sang the chorus to "Thank You for Talkin' to Me Africa." He turned the volume up a notch and looked across the channel to the restaurants and fish stands that lined Maine Avenue. I blew a jet of smoke out the window and watched it vanish in the wind.

"Nice day," Darnell said, breaking away from his own song. "Thanks for askin' me out. You been decent to me, man, and I appreciate it. To most people, it's like I'm invisible."

"Thought you might like to drive."

"Been a while," he said, staring toward the water. The sun made sailing shards of glass on the channel. "Funny how a simple-ass thing like a drive down the park"—he stopped, shook his head, and smiled weakly. "Drivin's what got me my bid in Lorton in the first place, you know that?"

"I heard you got caught up in something."

Darnell laughed shortly and without pleasure, then shook his head. "More than caught up, Nick. I knew what I was doin', in the way that any kid knows he's gettin' into somethin' wrong, knows it but can't stay away."

"What happened?"

Darnell rubbed a skeletal finger down the bridge of his long, thin nose. "Round about the mid seventies, I was runnin' with this Southeast boy. I knew he owned an army forty-five, used to brag how he bought it off some vet in the street. One day, he asked me to drive him down to see this girl he knew, down his way. I was known in the neighborhood as a guy who knew cars, see, knew how to make 'em move. I did it, even knowin' he was on somethin', talkin' more bullshit than usual that day, actin' strange. Anyway, on the way down he told me to pull over in front of some market, down off Minnesota Avenue. I parked out front, left the motor run—he said he'd be back right quick—and then this stickup boy I was runnin' with, he started shootin' that forty-five of his inside, shootin' that motherfucker all to hell."

I dragged off my smoke and flicked ash. Darnell stopped, took a long breath, and continued. "The way it ended, some-body died, and the police were all over the joint straight away, and they ran in and killed that boy too. I stayed in the car, didn't even try to run, knew it was over then, let them pull me out, my hands up, let them push my face right into the street." He glanced in my direction but averted his eyes. "Later on, they told me that boy was hard on the Boat. Had enough green in him to knock down a horse."

"You paid up," I said.

"I did, man. More than you know."

A black BMW pulled into the lot and stopped alongside the Mercedes. The driver, a young man wearing a black jacket with a large eight ball embroidered across the back, stepped out and gave the world a tough glance. The Mercedes' door opened and a man not yet twenty wearing a parka with a fur collar put his foot out onto the asphalt. They shook hands elaborately, and then the driver of the BMW walked around the passenger side of the Mercedes and got in. Both doors closed, leaving only an armor of tinted glass.

Darnell said, "What do you think that's about?"

"Couple of young professionals. Doctors, maybe, or lawyers. Right?"

"Nick, man, what the fuck *happened* to this town?"

"I can't tell you what happened. Only that it did."

Darnell leaned closer to me on the seat. His eyebrows veed up and wrinkles crossed his forehead. "Remember 1976, man? The way people acted to each other, everything—the shit was so *positive*. Groups of kids on bicycles, blowin' whistles, ridin' in Rock Creek Park. The message in the music—Earth, Wind and Fire, 'Keep your Head to the Sky.' Even that herb-smokin' motherfucker George Clinton, Parliament, 'Chocolate City'— 'You don't need the bullets, if you got the ballots, C.C.'—you remember that, Nick?"

"I remember."

Darnell sat back and spoke softly. "When I got out, in '88, it was a new world, man. There wasn't no hope, not anymore— not on the street, not on the radio, nothin'. Nothin' but gangster romance."

I looked in the rearview and said, "Here comes our man."

A black 1974 Eldorado turned in to the lot and pulled three spaces down from our car. The engine cut, the passenger door opened, and Louis DiGeordano slowly climbed out. He looked in my direction and titled his head toward the concrete walk that ran around the park at the water's edge. I nodded and stepped out of the Dart.

"I'll be back in a few minutes, Darnell," I said before I closed the door.

"I'll be waitin' on you right here," he said.

I buttoned my overcoat. DiGeordano was down on the walkway, facing southeast toward the brick edifice of Fort McNair. I walked to the driver's side of the Caddy and watched the window roll down. Bobby Caruso sat behind the wheel.

He filled a shiny suit, the French cuffs of his shirt four inches ahead of the sleeves on his jacket. His hair was gelled and spiked, and the fleshy rolls of his neck folded down over the collar of his starched shirt.

"What is it?" he said, his face stretched in a constipatory grimace.

I leaned on the door. "That day in the market, when we went at it."

"I remember. What about it?"

"I called you a name that day. I want to apologize for that."

Caruso relaxed, letting the boyishness ease into his face. He looked then like the kid he was, dressed for the P.G. County prom. "Forget about it," he said.

I shook his hand and walked away. Caruso yelled, "Hey, Stefano," and I turned. "That shit you pulled on me that day, with your hands—where'd you learn it?"

I smiled. "From my doctor."

Caruso smiled back, showing his beaver teeth. "I thought doctors were supposed to help people, not hurt 'em."

"Take care of yourself," I said, and walked across the grass, through the thin branches of a willow to the concrete walkway, where I stood beside Louis DiGeordano.

"Let's walk," DiGeordano said. "Shall we?"

DiGeordano put his hand on the two-tiered rail that ran

along the channel, and began to move. I walked beside him, taking a last pull off my smoke.

He was wearing a gray lamb's-wool overcoat with a black scarf over a suit and tie, and a matching felt fedora. The brim of the fedora was turned down, with a slight crease running back to front in the crown. A small red feather was in the band, the same shade of red as the handkerchief folded in the breast pocket of his suit. A liquid wave of silver hair flowed under the hat, swept back behind his ears.

DiGeordano smoothed the black scarf down across his suit and pulled together the collars of the overcoat, against the wind. "Those two in the parking lot," he said. "You see them?"

"Yes."

"*Titsunes*," he said. "Drugs, guns, and *titsunes*. That's what this park is now. That's what this whole city is."

"I don't know. I come down here in the summer, ride my bike down here quite a bit. I see a little of that. But what I mostly see is families having picnics, getting out of the heat. Old men fishing, couples holding each other, sitting under the trees."

"It's not like it was."

"It's exactly like it was. It's people, enjoying their city."

DiGeordano looked across the channel and shook his hand in the air as he walked, the wag of his fingers meant for me. "You don't know what I'm talking about, Nicky," he said. "You're not old enough to remember."

"I guess not," I said, deferring to his age, though in one sense he was right. We lived in the same city, but a million miles apart.

He put his hand back in his side pocket, his brown eyes squinting now in the wind. "We always walked this side of the park, in the old days, every Sunday. The Potomac side, looking toward Virginia; it gets too much wind, and too much spray from the chop."

"You said you were with me and my grandfather the first day I came down here."

DiGeordano's pink lips turned to a smile beneath his gray mustache. "Yes. This was very early in the sixties, you were maybe five years old. Nick had bought a cheap fishing pole for you and baited it with a bloodworm. You were holding the pole—he was holding it, really, standing over your shoulder— and a perch hit the line. Nick yanked it from the channel and removed the hook, and this little perch, it was no bigger than the palm of your hand, it flipped off the walkway and back into the channel." DiGeordano laughed deeply. "You were wearing a pair of denim overalls with a red flannel shirt underneath, and I'll never forget you chasing after that fish, trying to scoot under the railing. Nick grabbed you by the straps of your overalls and pulled you back—he laughed the rest of the day about it, talked about it at our card games, how you tried to go in after that fish. He talked about it for years."

I stopped walking and put my hand on his arm. "I need your help, Mr. DiGeordano."

He looked me in the eyes, shrugged, and made a salutatory motion with his hand. "Anything."

We walked on. A low, thick cloud passed beneath the sun. Its slow shadow crossed the channel in our direction. "Do you remember a murder last year, a young white man in his apartment on Sixteenth Street, a reporter for a small newspaper in town?"

DiGeordano withdrew a lozenge from his overcoat pocket, unwrapped it, and popped the lozenge into his mouth. He clucked his tongue, staring ahead. "Yes, I remember it. It was in the papers, every day. Then nothing."

"That young man was a friend of mine," I said.

"Go on."

"He was researching a story on a pizza place called the Olde World and a man named Bonanno at the time that he was killed. I think the people that run the Olde World have an arson business and gambling operation as well, and I think my friend was murdered because he got too close."

"Bonanno's a filthy pig," DiGeordano said.

"You know him?"

"Of course."

I stopped and struck a match, cupping one hand around it, lighting another cigarette. Then I blew out the first sulfurous hit and ran a hand through my tangled, uncombed hair. DiGeordano leaned his back against the rail and looked at my unshaven face. "You're deep into this," he said, "aren't you?"

I took a fresh drag off the smoke. "Bonanno's a fat man, bushy gray sideburns, right?" — DiGeordano nodded — "and there's two more with him, a guy named Frank and a tall man with bad skin. Who else?"

"No one else," he said tiredly. "Bonanno and Frank are small-time hoods out of Jersey. The tall man goes by the name of Solanis. Contract mechanic, from Miami. They say he killed a cop and drifted north. Caught some buckshot in the face while he was drifting. Bad business, that — killing cops, and outsiders — it isn't done. Very sloppy. They're not going to last."

"What are they into? Organized gambling?"

DiGeordano chuckled. "Not too organized, from what I hear. As far as bookmaking goes, they don't know shit from apple butter. They still work from chits, for Christ's sake, and notebooks."

"So what's their game? Arson?"

"Their game?"

"They moved their shops near a string of pizza parlors called the Pie Shack, and every one of the Pie Shacks got burned out. That can't be a coincidence."

"It's not," he said. "But arson's not their source of income. Neither is gambling."

"What is, then?"

DiGeordano said, "Pizza."

I dragged off my cigarette and looked out into the water. The cloud had passed, leaving the channel shiny and brilliant in the noon sun. "Tell me about it."

"It's simple," he said. "The pizza business is very profitable. Bonanno moved into proven, established neighborhoods and burned out the competition. Solanis was there to make sure there weren't any belches. The guy who owned the Pie Shack simply left town, and felt lucky to leave alive. Bonanno puts a couple hundred thousand in nontaxable income in his pocket every year. The gambling is their kick, and the business end of it just covers their losses. No drugs, prostitution, nothing like that—just a bunch of hoods, selling pizzas."

"What about the law, the fire people?"

DiGeordano shrugged. "Bought."

I flipped the remainder of my cigarette out into the channel. "A cop by the name of Goloria, and his partner, a woman named Wallace, they paid me a visit a while back."

"Goloria," DiGeordano said.

"That's right. Things got rough—he said it was about April Goodrich, but something wasn't right. Is Goloria connected to your son Joey?"

"No. My ties with the law in this town go farther back, and higher than that. We don't have to get down in the shit with cops like him. He tried to approach us, once. I sent him on his way."

"He's been talking to people I know about the young reporter's murder."

"That's not a surprise—I would think he'd be a little nervous that you're looking into it."

"Why's that?"

DiGeordano ran his fingers along the brim of his hat. "Goloria's in with Bonanno."

I leaned on the railing and looked down into the gray channel. A dead catfish floated on the surface, near a large sheet of packaging paper. I felt feverish and dizzy in the cold wind, and I unfastened the top buttons of my overcoat as I turned to DiGeordano. "Who killed the reporter?" I said.

"You should have talked to me from the beginning," he said. "There's still very little going on in this town that gets by me. I know you disapprove of me, and my son. I can only tell you that in all my years, I never shed any innocent blood, in anything I did. In fact, there was very little violence at all. That's why I can't stomach what's happened to this city. People like Bonanno—they're vampires, but fragile as dust. Their own ignorance exterminates them. Do you understand?"

"Who killed the reporter?" I said again. The wind whistled through our silence, and water slapped the concrete.

"The knife job," DiGeordano said. "That's the signature of Solanis."

"That's what I needed to know."

"Before you act on this," he said, "you'd better think things over."

"I'm fine," I said. The cold wind stung my face.

DiGeordano studied me. "There's something else?"

I nodded. "There's one more piece of business."

"You're talking about my son's problem, with April Goodrich." DiGeordano waved his hand slowly in front of his face. "Like I said, nothing gets by me. You found the girl, and she's dead. Isn't that right?"

"Yes. But there's more to it."

"Such as?"

"Have Caruso pull the Caddy next to my Dart," I said, pushing away from the rail. "I've got something to show you."

I WORKED EARLY SHIFT at the Spot for the next four days. At the end of each shift I changed clothes, drove out to Gallatin in Northeast, and parked my car in front of the row of brick colonials. Then I walked into the woods and waited for them to arrive at the Sears bungalow, and on each of the four nights, they showed with the pillowcases filled with gambling chits, at roughly the same time. Occasionally there were visitors, interchangeable ruddy-faced men in dark clothing who drove through the woods in Buick Electras and Pontiac Bonnevilles and stayed for a few quick, stiff drinks. But always at the end of the night there were the three of them — Bonanno, Frank, and Solanis.

ON THE FOURTH NIGHT, a Wednesday, I returned to my apartment, poured a drink, phoned Dan Boyle, and told him everything I knew.

ON THURSDAY AFTERNOON BOYLE walked into the Spot with a gym bag in his hand and took a seat at the bar. He put the bag at his feet, ordered a draught, and asked for it in an icy mug.

"What's in the bag, Boyle?" I said as I wiped down the bar.

"You'll find out soon enough." Boyle put a Marlboro to his lips and pointed a thick finger past my shoulder. "This beer's gettin' lonesome," he said. "How 'bout a hit of that Jack?"

TWENTY-EIGHT

BOYLE DRANK SLOWLY AND silently through happy hour. Buddy, Bubba, and Richard sat at the far end of the bar and drained a pitcher, their shoulders touching. Melvin Jeffers sang ballads softly through two gin martinis before walking out with a cheerful wave, and Happy knocked back several Manhattans as he dented a deck of Chesterfields. Ramon and Darnell stood in the kitchen, Ramon demonstrating his proficiency with a switchblade knife. I leaned against the call rack, my arms folded across my chest, moving occasionally to empty an ashtray or fill a pitcher. John Hiatt's *Bring the Family* played through the house speakers.

By eight o'clock, Buddy, Bubba, and Richard were gone. Buddy had sneered on his way out, doing his Tasmanian-devil-with-stretch-marks walk, and Bubba had followed, scratching his head. Happy had fallen asleep at the bar, a half-inch of hot Chesterfield wedged between his yellowed fingers. I phoned him a cab and walked him outside, and put the cab on his weekly tab.

When I returned, Boyle had gone to the head. I retrieved two bottles of Bud from the cooler and buried them in the ice chest. Darnell was in the kitchen placing dishes in the soak sink, his back to Ramon. Ramon touched his knife to Darnell's back and pushed on the blade. Darnell turned with a balled fist. Ramon laughed and pursed his lips in a kiss, but stepped back. I poked my head in and asked them to keep an eye on the bar while I shot down to the basement for some beer.

The Spot's dirt-floored basement was long and dusty and lit by a single naked bulb. I went down a narrow set of wooden stairs and walked through powdered poison. Rat tracks were etched in the powder, and the smell of death hovered in the room like a heat. I set up two cases of Bud and a case of Heineken on top of that and got under all of them, lifting with my knees. By the time I reached the top of the stairs and reentered the bar, a line of sweat had formed across my forehead.

Boyle was back on his stool, his hand around a mug of fresh draught. A Marlboro burned in the ashtray, next to the draught. I set the beer at the foot of the cooler and locked the front door.

I returned to the cooler and pulled out all the cold Buds and Heinekens. Then I ripped open the cardboard cases and stocked the warm beer on the bottom of the cooler, placing the cold beer back on top. I slid the cooler lid to the left, closing it. Boyle asked for another shot of Jack. I poured it, replaced the bottle on the shelf, walked back down to the deck, and slipped in Winter Hours' EP, *Wait till the Morning.* The rumble of "Hyacinth Girl" came forward.

On the walk back toward Boyle I dimmed the rheostat and took the lights down in the bar. I pulled a Bud out of the ice by its neck and popped the cap. I set it on the bar next to a heavy shot glass and poured Grand-Dad. Boyle raised his glass and tapped it against mine.

"Here's to you, Boyle."

"And to you."

I closed my eyes and felt the bourbon numb my lips and gums and the back of my throat. I waited for the warmth to fill my chest and followed it then with a deep pull of beer. The beer was cold and good, and a chip of ice slid down the neck and touched my hand as I drank. I placed the bottle back on the bar and bent down over the three sinks and began to wash the last of the night's glasses.

Boyle said, "You ready to talk?"

I looked into the foamy wash sink as I plunged a collins glass over a black-bristled brush. "Go ahead."

Boyle lit a cigarette and dropped the match into the ashtray. A wisp of smoke climbed off the match. "What you told me last night," he said. "It was an awful lot to swallow. So I did some checking today, called in some favors, ran plates—the whole shooting match."

"And?"

"Goloria was on the William Henry case from day one. He collected the evidence from the newspaper where Henry worked, and he buried it, and he probably bought or threatened a phony witness to testify to that 'light-skinned man in a blue shirt' crap. The Pie Shack arsons are all listed as electrical fires. Somebody got bought there too."

"What about Wallace. She in on it?"

"I don't think so. Goloria's her hero, and they're fuckin' the hell out of each other—that's no secret—but aside from her being a strange bird on the edge, that's as far as it goes. Believe it or not, I think she's an honest cop. She just happens to be in love with a disease."

I finished grouping the clean glasses on the ridged drain area of the sink. Then I hung them upside down by their stems in the glass rack above the bar. I watched Boyle as I worked. He sipped his mash, and as he lifted his glass to his lips the lapels of his Harris tweed jacket spread apart. The stock of his Colt

Python angled out from the shoulder holster lashed to his chest. A second holster hung empty below the opposite arm.

"Anything on Bonanno?"

Boyle put his glass down on the bar and switched his hand to the beer mug's handle. "The plate numbers you gave me checked out. Both Lincolns are registered to the Olde World. Bonanno's down as the owner. No criminal record on Bonanno locally, or on Frank Martin."

"And Solanis?"

"He's what you think he is. I called a DEA buddy of mine, on a hunch. Solanis was an enforcer in the Miami drug trade, and he's on the Fed's hot list. Took out an undercover cop." Boyle's skittish blues eyes settled on mine. "Knife job."

I shook a cigarette out of Boyle's pack. Boyle produced a Zippo from his jacket pocket and thumbed open its lid. I leaned toward the flame, hit it, and took in a drag that burned deeply into my chest. My smoke found his and drifted up through the misty cones of light that opened out from the lamps above.

"You tell your DEA buddy that Solanis was in town?"

"No."

"How about the Metro cops?" Boyle shook his head and gave me a twisted smile. "Why not?" I said.

Boyle said, "You called *me*. Thought you might have something else in mind."

I turned to the left and saw Darnell and Ramon, their heads framed in the reach-through, looking at Boyle. Ramon stepped away, and I watched him hand Darnell his closed knife, passing it palm to palm. Darnell slid the knife into his back pocket.

Ramon walked out of the kitchen, his coat in his hand. He nodded to me with his chin and walked to the front door. I let him out, locked the door behind him, and returned to the bar. I pointed to Boyle's glass.

"You ready?"

"Yeah."

I topped him off, then had a pull of Bud. "Island of Jewels" 's clean guitar filled the room. Boyle ran a hand through his short dirty blond hair.

"What you got in mind, Boyle?"

Boyle smiled. "What *you* got in mind?"

"I'm not sure." I looked at him carefully. "You said you'd help, and now I need it. I think you're honest, and I think you've got a cast-iron set of nuts. And I think you're a little bit crazy, Boyle."

"Sure I am," he said. "But how crazy are you?"

"I'm here," I said, "and I'm listening."

Darnell shut the kitchen light down and stepped out into the room. His kufi was tilted crookedly on his head, and he had folded his brown overcoat over his arm. He placed the overcoat on a stool and leaned his mantis arms on the service bar.

Boyle's eyes shifted to Darnell, then to me. "Just you and me on this."

"I want him to stay," I said.

"He's a con," Boyle said.

Darnell said, "You got a problem with that, redneck?"

"*Do* you?" I said.

Boyle smiled as he looked Darnell over. "He's all right, you know it? I like this guy."

I sipped bourbon and placed the shot glass on the bar. "Then let's get to it."

"Okay," Boyle said. "Here it is. I can turn all this information over to the proper channels, and maybe something will shake out. Maybe they'll bust Bonanno on a tax rap or even the arsons. Maybe Solanis will go down on the murder charge, but that's a long shot too—you can believe the knife he used is long gone. And without that security guard, maybe Goloria will go up on charges, and maybe he'll walk. A shitload of maybes."

"You saying that's one way of doing it?"

"That's the straight way."

"What's the other way?"

"It depends on what you want, Nick."

I pulled another beer from the ice, uncapped the neck, and glanced into the amber bottle. "I figure Solanis is going to burn, sooner or later. But there's something wrong when outsiders can come into this town and get rid of an innocent man, and there's sure as hell something wrong when one rotten cop helps them do it." I looked straight into Boyle. "You know what I want."

"I figured that," Boyle said, leaning forward. "So I set things up. I called Goloria this afternoon. I told him we wanted to meet."

Drops of water fell from the glasses suspended in the rack above, darkening the mahogany of the bar. I finished the rest of my bourbon and dragged on my cigarette. Darnell pushed his hat back on his head. "What'd you tell him, Boyle?" I said. "Exactly."

"That you knew about the arsons, and the murder. That you told me you knew. And that you wanted to see them and talk things over."

"When?"

"I didn't say. Goloria got all quiet when I laid it out for him, didn't want to talk about it on the phone. But here's a bet — that crooked bastard will be at that house in the woods tonight to discuss it, and so will Bonanno. And the others."

I tilted the beer bottle to my lips, drank deeply, and wiped the backwash from my chin. A lull came in the tape, and the Spot grew quiet. I looked at Boyle and Darnell, and I wondered how it had happened that I had ended up with them, wondered what had brought us together like thieves in the night, in a shitty little bar in the southeast part of town. The thought of Tommy Crane crossed my mind, and how close I had come. But that thought passed. I felt my buzz swell, and I smiled, knowing then that it was done.

"What's the plan, Boyle?"

Boyle butted his Marlboro. "You and me walk right into that house, start a fire under their asses, and make the arrest. From what you tell me, there's enough there for a bookmaking charge straight away. But I think we got a shot at some confessions too. Once we get into it, let it develop."

"How?" I said.

"You carry a gun, Stefanos?"

"I own a nine. I don't carry it."

Boyle reached down and pulled the gym bag up and placed it on the bar. He yanked back the zipper and put his thick hand into the bag. "A nine, huh?" Boyle dropped a nine-millimeter semiautomatic on the bar and spun it so the grip pointed toward me. "Then this ought to do. Beretta, ninety-two. Fifteen in the clip."

I picked it up, hefted it in my palm, and released the magazine. It slid out, into my hand. I heeled it back in, checked the safety, turned, and lined up the front and rear white-dotted sights on the stereo system at the end of the bar. Then I lowered the pistol and placed it back on the bar.

"Where'd you get this?"

"From a suspect," he said.

I nodded in the direction of the bag. "What about you?"

Boyle said, "I'm already heeled." He pulled back the collar of his Harris tweed jacket, showing me the Python. Then he reached into the bag and retrieved a five-shot .38 Special, slipping it into the empty holster below his left arm. "Now I'm real good."

Darnell pushed away from the service bar, stood up, and cleared his throat. "You'll be needin' a driver," he said.

I looked at Boyle. "That okay with you?"

"Yeah."

I finished my beer, left the empty on the bar, and shoved the Beretta barrel down against the small of my back, behind the waistband of my jeans. Darnell shifted his shoulders into his overcoat, and Boyle buttoned his raincoat over his tweed. I switched the lights off from behind the bar. The neon Schlitz logo cast a blue light in the room.

Boyle said, "How 'bout grabbing a bottle, for the ride."

I reached into the stock under the call shelf and pulled out a fresh bottle of Jack. Boyle raised his hand. I tossed the bottle over the bar, and he caught it by the neck. Then he broke the seal and had a drink.

Darnell gave me a sidelong look. "You sure about this, man?"

"He knows what he's doing."

"Goddamn right I do," Boyle said. "It's time for some fucking justice." He ran a hand through his tight curly hair and slipped the bottle of Jack into his raincoat pocket.

I set the alarm and locked the door. The three of us walked out into the night.

TWENTY-NINE

W E TOOK THE Dart northeast across town. Darnell kept the speedometer just over the limit and signaled at his turns. The radio stayed off. Boyle sat in the back, drinking steadily and asking me questions about the layout of the bungalow. I answered from the shotgun seat and drummed my fingers on the dash, staring straight ahead.

Darnell took Missouri to Riggs and dipped down onto South Dakota. After a few miles of that he cut left on Gallatin Street and drove along the edge of Fort Totten Park. We passed the break in the grove of trees and slowed a few hundred yards down the street, stopping in front of the row of brick colonials. Darnell cut the engine.

Few lights were on in the windows of the houses to our right. The street was dark and quiet, tucked in for the night. I heard the chamber spin and shut on Boyle's Python, and the sound of gunmetal scraping against leather.

Boyle said, "We walk in, Nick, straight up the road and to the house. Okay?"

"Then what?"

"This isn't going to be a surprise. They're expecting us, though maybe not so soon."

"How do we play it?"

"Like a shakedown, at first. Like we want a piece of what's going on."

"You start it off, Boyle."

"Right." I could hear the plastic cap unthread and the slosh of liquid as Boyle tipped the bottle to his lips. "You'll catch the rhythm, as it goes. When I get a confession out of Solanis, I'll draw down on 'em, make the arrest."

"You deputizing me?"

"Fuck, no. You're a witness. Don't be afraid to pull that Beretta, though, if the shit starts raining down."

I could see Darnell to my left, staring at me, trying to get my attention. I drew the Beretta, eased a cartridge into the chamber, and replaced the pistol behind the waistband of my jeans. Then I unlocked my door and spoke to him, looking away. "If you hear it start to fly apart, Darnell, pull the car around at the break in the trees. Got it?"

Darnell nodded. Boyle had another long drink, capped the neck, and dropped the bottle on the seat. He and I stepped out of the car and shut the doors. We walked down Gallatin toward the unmarked road, the wind blowing back our coats.

At the gravelly break in the trees, we turned right. I heard the slam of a car door, recognized the sound of it, and turned my head. Darnell's reedy silhouette stepped across the field and vanished into the woods. I nudged Boyle, but he stared straight ahead. We continued down the road, toward the light of the house. The liquor still warmed me like an ember; it took the edge off the fear that was churning in my gut.

The Lincolns were parked out in the clearing, cast yellow under the light of the lamppost. On the porch of the house a figure moved toward the door. The door opened and a square of light spilled out onto the porch, and then the door closed again and the light vanished. The figure remained on the porch.

"You see that?" Boyle said.

"Yeah."

"Whoever it is, he just put his head in and told them they had company."

I adjusted my eyes to the light as we neared the house, gravel splitting beneath my feet. "It's Frank Martin," I said.

"Martino," Boyle said. He chuckled and shook his head. "Martin. Fuckin' goombahs and their names."

We brushed past the Lincolns and moved toward the porch. I left my hands in the pockets of my overcoat as we walked up the steps. Frank's arms hung loosely at his sides. His corduroy car coat was open, exposing the khakis and a dark blue shirt. The Airweight was in the nylon holster, unsnapped, tucked into the side of his khakis, and Frank made no effort to hide it. He touched his fingers to the grip, then let his hand fall back at his side. We stopped on the porch in front of him. Frank looked at me.

"Salesman, huh? I knew you weren't no fuckin' salesman. No such thing as fifty off." A big band sound with a vocalist came softly through the front door.

"Can we go in?" I said.

Frank looked at Boyle for the first time. "You've got heat under your coat—I can see it. Take the guns off and leave 'em at the door."

"I'm a cop," Boyle said, his voice deepening a note. "I wear a gun, and it doesn't come off. We came to talk to your boss. You want to start somethin' before we get into that, start it now."

Frank swung both hands nervously, careful not to swing them near the Airweight. He looked away from Boyle and put his hand on the knob of the front door. Frank turned the knob and opened the door. "Go on."

Boyle stepped first, and I followed. Sinatra was the vocalist, and he was singing "It Happened in Monterey" at a low volume through the Sony's black speakers on the bar. Goloria was sitting on one of the chairs near the two blank television screens, his bones etching their angles on a cheap brown suit. A tan shirt and a yellow-and-brown rep tie hung beneath the suit. The tie was crooked at the knot.

Solanis stood behind the bar, wearing a black sport jacket and a tieless deep red shirt, buttoned to the neck. His buckshot scars matched the redness of the shirt, but the rest of his face was finely lined and almost serene, his black hair damp with gel and lazily combed back. He moved the swizzle stick around slowly in a rocks glass filled with scotch whiskey and watched Boyle move into the room. I closed the door behind me and withdrew my hands from the pockets of my overcoat.

Goloria stood quickly, touched the knot of his tie, and slid four fingers of the other hand behind his belt. "Boyle," he said nodding. "We didn't expect you so soon. You should have called. We could've set a time, when we could all talk together."

"Where's Bonanno?" Boyle said.

"Not here."

"I can see that. His car's out front."

"He got picked up by friends," Goloria said. "What can we do for you?"

Boyle moved toward Goloria and stopped a few feet away. I walked over to the card table. Solanis watched me do it, a restful smile growing on his face. I picked some red chips up off the table and ran them around in my fingers, glancing up the stairs to the landing. The lights were out and the landing was deep in shadow.

"How's the wife and kids, Goloria?" Boyle said.

"Same as yours, I guess. Same as anybody's."

"And Wallace?"

Goloria paused to narrow his eyes. "You want a drink, Boyle? You look to me like you could use a drink. Jack's your pleasure, isn't it?" He glanced over toward the bar and grinned with effort. "Solanis, fix Detective Boyle here a Jack Daniels."

Boyle said, "Keep your hands on the bar. I drink with my friends. This is business." Solanis's face remained expressionless as a stone.

Goloria rubbed the heel of one brown shoe against the instep of the other. "Tell us what you two want."

"Stefanos wants what I want," Boyle said. I didn't know where he was going with it, and I don't think he did either, but he had their attention. Standing there, a head taller than Goloria, his feet spread wide and firm on the wood floor, Boyle was like a bull, staring them down on their own turf.

"You've got to get clearer than that," Goloria said.

"All right," Boyle said. "Stefanos came to me with the details of your operation. He knew the reporter that was looking into it, and he got curious. Pretty soon the Pie Shack arsons and the bookmaking came to the surface."

"So?"

"You always were a piece of shit, Goloria." Boyle took a step forward but kept his voice low and even. "Shaking down bartenders, threatening informants, that's one thing. Making book and setting fires, that's another. It depends on where you draw the line. I draw the line at all of it. You got no problem with turning your head and getting your palm greased, that's up to you I guess—as long as nobody gets hurt."

"Keep talking."

"Solanis over there—murder one on the reporter. You buried the evidence, and you planted some that was phony."

Goloria sighed and ran one finger down a crease in his gaunt face. "You still haven't told me a fuckin' thing, Boyle. Now I'm going to ask you again—what do you want?"

Boyle said, "Low as you are, Goloria, you're still a cop. I'm not about to turn you in, if there's any other way."

"You talking about a payoff?"

"I'm talking about options."

A heavy dull sound pushed in from beyond the front door. Goloria and I turned our heads in the direction of the sound;

Boyle stared ahead. The song from the box ended and another one began, Sinatra's "I've Got You under My Skin." Goloria grinned and turned his attention to the bar. "Turn it up, Solanis," he said, snapping his fingers. "This one really jumps."

Solanis walked slowly to the Sony and hiked up the volume. I heard movement from the second floor and looked up, but there was nothing, and then the sound of the movement was drowned out by the music. When I looked back Solanis was walking back to his spot behind the bar, staring at me.

I stared back and said, "We've got a problem here."

Goloria said, "We don't need a private cop in this, Boyle. It's between you and me."

"What kind of problem you got, Stefanos?" Boyle said, smiling a little now, ignoring Goloria, getting into the rhythm he had talked about.

"The security guard," I said, feeling that rhythm, and a warmth in my face.

"What about him?" Solanis said, his voice dry as a December leaf.

"Shut up," Goloria said, turning his head to the bar. The Nelson Riddle arrangement swelled in the room, horns rising, Sinatra bending his vowels as he jumped back into the verse. I put my hands on the belt loops of my jeans, hiked them up, and ran my right hand around the waistband to the back, feeling the checkered points of the Beretta's serrated grip. I rested my thumb on the grooved hammer.

"If I'm going to get involved in this," I said, "there better not be any loose ends. I talked to that security guard myself. He's a broken-down drunk. He'll talk, eventually." In my peripheral vision I saw motion from above. I kept my eyes on Solanis.

Solanis smiled. "He won't talk."

"I told you to shut up," Goloria said.

"Maybe you better let me handle it," I said.

"No need," Solanis said, the smile gone now, a sudden

emptiness in his black eyes. "I took care of him, the same way I did that reporter." The black eyes narrowed. "That nigger screamed when I gave him the knife. He screamed like a girl."

"Goddamn it, Solanis, shut up!" Goloria said.

Boyle crossed his arms and reached into his coat. Then he drew his guns, pointing them at Goloria. Solanis's hand slid under the bar, and he began to crouch down.

I pulled the Beretta and thumbed back the hammer.

Goloria whitened and said, "Take it easy, Boyle," and as he said it his own hand jerked toward the inside of his brown suit.

Boyle said, "I'll see to your wife and kids, Goloria," and he turned one gun on Solanis, and that's when everything blew up at once.

Solanis dropped just as Boyle fired the Python. A strip of oak splintered off the bar and bottles exploded from the shelf.

I saw the movement again from above on the landing, and I looked up. A man stepped out of the shadows and swung a sawed-off in my direction.

I dived, and then there was thunder, and the card table heaved up at my side and seemed to come apart. Something tore away at my cheek. I squeezed the trigger on the nine as I fell, aiming in the direction of the landing, the Beretta jumping in my hand, my knuckles white-hard on the grip. I saw a figure tumble and fall through the smoke of the muzzle and the ejecting shells, and then I saw a man in black twills convulsing at the base of the stairs.

Boyle walked across the room, firing both guns into Goloria, alternating shots from the Python to the .38. Goloria was covering his face with his hands, and one of his hands was without fingers now, and he was dancing backward, shaking his head furiously like he was coming out of water, fighting for breath. Goloria's knees buckled and he toppled onto his back, his hands crossed now as if tied at the wrist. The heels of his brown shoes kicked at the floor.

Boyle dropped the .38, turned toward the bar, and switched

the Python to his right hand. He yelled, "He's coming up, Stefanos!" and Solanis stood straight from behind the bar, the dreamy smile on his face, his eyes wet and black, a .45 in his hand.

Solanis howled and fired blindly in my direction, the round fragmenting the arm of a wooden chair beside me. Boyle shot Solanis once in the chest. The slug threw him hard against the liquor shelf and the mirror, and Solanis's back was blown out, his blood and cartilage spraying the mirror. Pieces of the stained mirror shattered and flew off, and Solanis fell to the floor.

Sinatra sang from the box.

Boyle said, "Cover the front door."

I pointed the Beretta there, keeping both shaking hands on the grip. I looked down at the blood on my shirt. The blood seemed to run from my cheek.

Boyle moved through the gun smoke, his arm extended, the Python at the end of it, and walked behind the bar. He pointed the barrel down at Solanis and clicked off an empty round.

Boyle turned, switched the radio off, and went to Bonanno at the foot of the stairs, kicking the shotgun across the room. He bent at the knees, pressed a finger to Bonanno's neck, then holstered the Python inside his jacket as he stood. He didn't bother to check Goloria.

"Dead," Boyle said. "All of 'em."

"I took one in the face," I said.

Boyle rubbed his nose as he walked to my side. I sat on the floor and held the Beretta at the door. Boyle crouched down and looked me over. He put two thick fingers to my cheek, and pulled something away. There was raw pain, and the pain blinded me for a short second, and then it went away. Boyle focused his pinball eyes on the fragment of red poker chip he held in his hand.

"You'll live," he said.

I rubbed my cheek and surveyed the ruins. "Jesus Christ, Boyle."

"You can lower that gun. Martin's long gone. You better get going too."

"What are you going to do?"

Boyle said, "Fix it."

I dropped the Beretta to the hardwood floor. Boyle drew a handkerchief from his jacket and rubbed my prints from the gun as I stood. He moved to Goloria and placed the automatic in the hand that still had fingers, and he wrapped the fingers of that hand around the grip. Then he drew the Python and the .38 and walked around the bar to Solanis. Boyle bent down, and when he came back up the guns were no longer in his hands. I knew then what he was going to do. Boyle looked at me with impatience.

"Get going," he said, turning to put his hand around a bottle of Jack Daniels that stood with a few remaining bottles on the liquor shelf. He undid the cap.

I nodded, said nothing, and walked out the front door. Standing on the porch, I saw a set of headlights pointed in the direction of the Maryland line on Gallatin Street, and I heard the faint wail of sirens. I looked down at the base of the porch. In shadow, Frank Martin's body lay like a large crumpled bird, the head twisted at an odd angle to the shoulders. A vague black line ran open beneath his chin.

I looked back through the lace curtains of the porch window, to the heavy figure with the bushy gray sideburns heaped at the foot of the stairs. Boyle was standing over Bonanno, the sole of one shoe resting on the dead man's chest, the bottle of Jack tilted back to his lips.

I stepped off the porch and walked through the trees, toward the lights that burned at the end of the gravel road.

THIRTY

B OYLE FIXED IT.
        In the three days that followed, an article ran daily on the front page of the *Post*'s Metro section, detailing the violent events that transpired in the house near Fort Totten Park. Every day that week, when I arrived for my shift at the Spot, a newspaper was left for me by Darnell, folded behind the register to the story's page.

Darnell had not spoken one word on the ride back that night, had never mentioned the name Frank Martin, and he would never speak about any of it again. With Boyle it was the same, though he could not enjoy Darnell's anonymity. Boyle's daily entrance at the Spot invariably created a nervous flurry of whispers from the regulars. The papers had made him out to be the city's premier badass, a Wyatt Earp–style lawman in a town whose initials had come to stand for Dodge City. No one took a stool next to Boyle at the bar again.

By the time of the last article, some basic facts had been embedded in the public's mind: Two detectives, Boyle and Goloria, had gone into a house without backup and had attempted to arrest a group of low-level bookmakers headed by a man named Bonanno. After the gun battle, in which Bonanno, his cohorts, and Goloria were killed, Boyle came upon evidence, through the notes of a young reporter killed months earlier, linking the group to a series of arsons, which in turn connected them to the reporter's own murder. The murderer turned out to be a cop killer named Solanis, wanted in several states by the FBI.

As for Goloria, he had died a hero, and he was given a hero's burial, with separate features on his career in the *Post* and on the local TV news. His family was the recipient of a full pension, along with several remunerative gifts from local police associations and booster clubs. In one of the pictures that ran in the newspaper, Goloria's wife and children stood graveside, the veiled wife holding a handkerchief to her grimacing face. Behind her in the picture, posture-straight and stone-faced, her badge clipped to her breast pocket, stood a stoic Detective Wallace.

A CARD ARRIVED AT my apartment a few days later. The envelope was postmarked D.C., without a return address, and the card was plain white. Inside the card was a short note, in handwriting I didn't recognize. The note read, "Nice work, Stefanos. And thanks." It was signed, "A Fan."

I threw away the newspaper clippings on the case shortly thereafter and kept the card.

A COUPLE OF WEEKS passed. February announced itself with a sunny, seventy-degree day. Two days after that a front traveled down from Canada and dropped a foot of snow on the area, and the cold air that hovered above for the next week kept the snow in place. Temperatures inched back up into the forties, and after another week the snow was gone.

On one of those dull gray days in late February, as I was sifting through the mail at the Spot, I opened an envelope addressed to me from Billy Goodrich. Inside the envelope a check had been made out in my name for services rendered.

The bar was slow that day, and it gave me time to sit next to the register and consider the check. As I did, I looked into the bar mirror, stared at my reflection between the bottles of Captain Morgan's and Bacardi Dark, and I thought about the night that Billy Goodrich had walked into the Spot, and how I had been staring into that same mirror, between those very bottles, that night.

The moment gave me the feeling that there was something dangling, something left to do. I stared harder, and my eyes began to burn from it, and I heard someone ordering a drink from far away, but now I wasn't listening.

I turned the bar phone toward me and punched Billy's number into the grid.

"Hello."

"Billy, it's Nick."

Billy paused. "Nick, how you doin'?"

"Good."

"You get my check? I sent it—"

"I got it."

"It's okay, isn't it?"

"It's fine."

Billy cleared his throat. "What's up, Nick?"

"We got some unfinished business, Billy."

There was another pause, longer this time. I listened to the sounds of the Spot. "I've been waiting for your call," he said.

I said, "It's time we settled up."

"That's what I want too."

"Where and when?"

Billy thought things over. "Down at April's property, at Cobb Island. That's where it is, right?"

"That's right, Billy. That's where it is."

"You working tomorrow?"

"I'm off."

"I'll pick you up, then, at your place. About eleven?"

"Eleven's fine."

"See you at eleven."

"All right."

I hung the receiver in its cradle, waited for a dial tone, and phoned Hendricks at the station in La Plata. When he told me what I needed to know, I said good-bye, and stood there for a long while, running my finger along the thin scar on my cheek, a permanent reminder of the bungalow on Gallatin Street.

I went to the men's room to wash my face. When I was done I stood outside the bathroom door, rubbing my hands dry on the blue rag that hung on the side of my jeans. I walked back into the bar and finished off the remainder of my shift.

THIRTY-ONE

ILLY'S WHITE MAXIMA pulled up in front of my apartment the next morning at eleven sharp. On the way out the door I scratched the soft area behind my cat's gnarled ear, felt her head push into my hand, and watched her eye slowly shut. I left her outside on the stoop with a dish of salmon mixed with dry meal and locked the door behind me.

The sun that day was weak, high above an unbroken sheet of gray clouds, and I zipped my jacket to the neck. I walked to the Maxima and opened the passenger door, sliding onto the leather seat. Billy offered his hand, and I shook it.

"Where's Maybelle?"

"I took her back to the pound," Billy said. "I'm not a dog lover to begin with, you know that. Anyway, she was never mine."

Billy wore his logoed royal blue jacket with blue jeans and Timberland boots. His hair was long now, blond and disheveled, almost exactly as it had been fifteen years earlier. But there was a stretched quality to his smooth face, a pained tightness around his azure eyes.

"Let's stop for some coffee, Billy, on the way out."

"Sure," Billy said, looking me over. "You can take that jacket off, man. I've got this heat workin' pretty good."

"I'm finc," I said. "Let's get going."

We drove down North Capitol, cutting east around Union Station, following Pennsylvania to Branch Avenue, past car dealership row at the commercial hub of Marlow Heights, then down Route 5 through the ruin that was Waldorf. The road flattened as 5 became 301, the strip malls and antique dealers breaking the brown, leafless countryside.

Billy pulled over in La Plata for a couple of burgers, and a few miles farther on we stopped again at the unmarked pool hall that advertised on/off sale. I bought a pint of Jim Beam from the woman with the raspberry birthmark and made a phone call from inside the bar and then returned to the Maxima. Billy gunned it back onto 301, and we continued south.

At 257 Billy turned left across the highway, passing the hardware-and-bait store with the John Deere sign in the window. We stayed on the highway this time, Billy keeping the Maxima at sixty-five. He hadn't spoken much on the ride down, though the silence was not uncomfortable; there was little between us left to damage. I pulled the pint of Jim Beam from my jacket, cracked the seal, and had a taste. I offered the same to Billy.

"Too early," Billy said.

"Suit yourself." I looked out the window at a row of evergreens blurred against a brown stretch of tobacco land and pasture. I had another drink and tightened the white cap onto the neck of the bottle.

Billy downshifted at the gravel road that marked the entrance to April Goodrich's property and turned left. We took the road into the woods and out through the open field, toward the creek.

Billy coasted and came to a stop beneath the hickory tree that stood next to the trailer.

"We can walk from here," he said.

"Walk where?"

"Into the woods, right?"

I looked out toward the creek. "Whatever you want, Billy."

Billy said, "Wait here. I'll be right out."

Billy got out of the car and went to the door of the trailer, where he used his key to enter. I watched him step inside, and after a while I got out of the Maxima and closed the passenger door.

I stood with my hands in my jacket, facing the creek. A circle had opened in the sheet of clouds, and a tubular shaft of sunlight shot through the circle, illuminating a section of the creek. Some barn swallows darted through the light, just off the dock. The clouds closed and the light was wiped away. I heard the trailer door shut, and I turned.

Billy stepped across the concrete patio, the old Remington shotgun from the trailer cradled in his arms. He stopped, reached into his pocket, and withdrew two shells. He shook the shells next to his ear, heard the rattle of buckshot, and thumbed the shells into the shotgun's broken breach.

"We going hunting, Billy?"

"No," Billy said. "Guy got killed on this property, two years back, in those woods. Fuckin' rednecks get drunk, shoot at anything. I don't walk back in there without this shotgun, not anymore." He nodded toward the line of trees, three hundred yards west across the field. "We'll go in over there."

"I'm with you. Let's go."

We walked over the winter wheat ground cover, through pockets of mud spotted in the hard earth. The sun broke through again and retreated. In the open field the wind was damp and cold, and it blew Billy's hair back on his scalp.

At the end of the field we cut right and walked along the tree line, passing a matted deer carcass in a ditch at the edge of the woods. Fifty yards later there was a break in the brush and trees, and we took it. I looked behind to get my bearings; the trailer, the hickory tree, and the car sat dwarfed on the open land, very far away.

The trail narrowed and dipped, and ended at a thin stream that ran down toward the creek. We followed the stream northwest, deeper in the woods, to a marshy area, where tadpoles swam through leaves beneath the last of the winter's ice, and then on through a section of high grass that had been flattened by sleeping deer. After that the ground became a bed of soft needles, and we were in a forest of oak and tall pine, the thickness of the pine trees broken by the occasional holly that grew underneath. We walked through the forest for nearly a mile, until it seemed as if we were deep inside of it, and we reached a small clearing near another marsh. Billy said then that we should stop, and I had a seat on the trunk of a fallen oak that had begun to rot before the freeze.

I pulled the bottle from my jacket and took a slug of warm bourbon. I swallowed it, breathed deeply, and smelled the air. "Where to now?" I said.

Billy said, "You tell me." He was standing in front of me, fifteen feet away, his legs wide, his boots planted in the damp leaves and pine needles, the shotgun across his arms. "You said it was down here."

"It?"

He frowned. "Don't fuck with me, Greek. Not today. I lost my wife because of some cockeyed scheme that went all wrong. I can't bring her back. But I have to be real now." Billy looked a little past my eyes. "If I let this go, then it *was* for nothing. I'm talking about the money, Nick. It's out here in these woods, isn't it?"

"Who told you that? Tommy Crane?"

Billy's face became tight with anger. "What's that supposed to mean?"

I stood and slid the pint into my side pocket, unzipping my

jacket halfway down. A flock of crows glided in over the trees and landed in the clearing. "Settle down, Billy. We'll get back to that. You want to talk about the money, fine. Let's get that out of the way."

"Go ahead."

"You were right about one thing. I found the suitcase in Crane's root cellar, the day Hendricks took him out."

Billy squinted. "Where is it?"

"I used it," I said.

"Used it how?"

I pushed some hair off my eyes and shifted my weight. "To save your ass, Billy. I met Louis DiGeordano at Hains Point a few weeks ago, and I gave him the money. He owed me a favor, going back a long time ago. I asked that there wouldn't be any retribution against you, for what you tried to pull on his son. He agreed."

Billy's shoulders hunched and shadows fell beneath his eyes. He rubbed his hand over the barrels of the shotgun. "I didn't need that kind of help from you," he said, looking at the ground, moving his head slowly from side to side. "That money was dirty. It didn't *belong* to anybody. I didn't hire you to give that money away."

"I know that, Billy. I know exactly what you hired me for."

"I hired you to find my wife, and that's it."

"You knew where your wife was," I said. "You knew it all along. You knew it the night you came to me in the Spot, the night you asked for my help. She was already dead, Billy. She's buried in these woods right now."

"What's that?" Billy said softly. "You sayin' I killed my wife?"

"No. Tommy Crane killed April. You didn't put the gun to her head. But you were part of it."

Billy's finger curled around the trigger of the shotgun. "You got everything all wrong, Nick."

"I don't think so," I said. "I should have seen it when I

woke up in the trailer. You were down by the creek, washing Maybelle with a brush. She had gone off and spent the night in the woods, and she had found April." I moved to the side, away from a branch that partially blocked my view of Billy. "April had taken the money and left town—that part of what you told me was true. You knew she'd head right down here and see Crane. I think you phoned Crane and tipped him off about the cash. You probably told him to get it from her, and then there'd be some sort of split between the two of you. But Crane killed April— maybe because she resisted, or maybe just because he wanted to watch her die. When it was over, Crane decided to keep it all himself—he didn't need you anymore, and he could always use blackmail if you tried to get rough."

A forced, sickly smile spread across Billy's face. "You're way off," he said.

"No," I said. "I'm not. You didn't hire me to find your wife. You hired me to shake down Crane for the money. You knew I wouldn't give up on it. You knew it because we were friends, and our being friends meant something." I looked him over. "You were really slick, Billy. Those photographs you sent me, of April. They weren't pictures of April at all. It wasn't much of a risk on your part—I wouldn't have shown them to anyone who knew her, there wouldn't have been any need. And April's jewelry—you planted it in the bathroom of Crane's cottage while I was with him in the sty. The bathroom was the one room of his house I had told you I'd be in. When I confronted Crane with the ring, he told me that it was a stupid trick. It didn't hit me at the time, but that's exactly what it was—a trick you used, with a duplicate ring, to get me back down to Crane's. If it worked, fine. If it didn't, and Crane took me out, then there was no loss there either, right, Billy? I'm willing to bet that when the cops dig April up, that ruby ring will still be on her finger."

"This is bullshit," Billy said. "You've got no proof of any of this. None."

"I've got proof. April was killed on Tuesday night—I

confirmed it with Hendricks. The date and time of her death were displayed right on the videotape. And Crane was seen with April, earlier that night, at Polanski's. Crane had two beers in front of him on the bar, and Tuesday's two-for-one night. But you told me you went drinking with your wife on Tuesday night, at Bernardo O'Reilly's."

"You confirmed it yourself. You went there and—"

"Shut up, Billy. Shut up and let me finish. The bartender at Bernardo O'Reilly's said you were with a woman that night who polished off nearly a fifth of rum, all by herself."

"That's right," Billy said. "Rum was April's drink. It's all she could keep down."

"April was grape-sensitive. That means she could only drink rum that was bottled in Jamaica. The woman you were with in O'Reilly's was drinking Bacardi Dark." I spoke slowly. "That's Puerto Rican rum, Billy."

Billy swung the shotgun in my direction. I reached into my jacket and drew the Browning from its holster, locking back the hammer. I pointed the gun at Billy's chest.

"Break that Remington," I said. "Break it and throw the shells to the right. Then toss the shotgun to the left."

A watery redness had seeped into Billy's azure eyes. "Nick, you don't think—"

"Do it," I said, my voice rising. Billy separated the shotgun from the shells and threw them onto the leafy earth. Behind him the crows lifted out of the clearing and flew over the trees.

"So," Billy said. "This is how we end it."

"That's right."

Billy dug his feet into the leaves and looked up at the tops of the trees, then back at me. "I would have been square with you from the beginning, Nick. That was my intention—to get your help in getting my money back from Crane, with a piece of it going back to you. But from the first minute I hooked up with you, I could see it wasn't going to be like that." He stared down at his boots. "The world isn't all good or all bad, like you think.

It's somewhere in between. The ones who come out of it all right are the ones who pull from both ways."

"Skip the bullshit," I said, my knuckles bloodless on the automatic's grip. "Our friendship—any friendship—it's the only thing that sticks. Everything rots, but that's always supposed to be there. You used it, man. You ruined it."

Billy looked me over and shook his head. "You better wake up," he said. "You think anything I did when I was nineteen means anything to me? You talked about that time in the park when we tripped, when I gave you my shoes. You talked about it like it was important. Shit, Nick, I barely even remember it. That might as well have been two different people that day. It's got nothing to do with this."

"It's got everything to do with this."

Billy buried his hands in the pockets of his jeans. "Then that brings us back to now."

I straightened my gun arm. "I'm not letting you walk, Billy."

Billy said, "I'm walkin'."

"Don't try it, Billy. I'll shoot you in the back."

"No, you won't." Billy smiled. "I'm walkin', Greek. I'm walkin' back to my car. You're going to let me, and you're going to give me some time to do it. After that, everything's fair."

"Don't, Billy," I said, my voice shaking.

"So long, Nick."

He turned. I shouted his name once, keeping the gun pointed at his back. I held it there until his royal blue jacket faded in the thickness of the forest. Then I lowered the gun to my side. A few minutes later the crows returned to the clearing. I holstered the Browning, sat on the trunk of the oak, and pulled the Jim Beam from my jacket.

Billy was right—I couldn't have squeezed that trigger on him, ever—but he was only half right. He wasn't going to walk. I had called Hendricks earlier that day, from the pool hall on 301.

There are only two ways off the peninsula that ends at

Cobb Island — by highway or by water. Billy didn't own a boat. Hendricks was waiting for him, the big cop-car engine idling out front of the hardware store, where 257 meets 301.

THE WOODS GREW DARKER as I finished the pint. I rose off the trunk and walked toward the deep gray light, through another stretch of woods to the highway. A long-haired young man in a Chevy truck stopped as soon as my thumb went out, and he drove me onto the island, letting me out at the Pony Point.

For the next three hours Russel and I sat together, drinking with slow and steady intent. Hendricks showed at dusk and joined us at the bar until closing time. At the end of the night the three us made a wordless toast, and after that Hendricks drove me all the way back to my place in D.C.

I offered him my couch, but he declined. I said good-bye, moved across the yard, and walked around the side of the house. At the stoop, I reached down to stroke the ball of black fur that was lying on the cold concrete and felt the push of a tiny nose against my hand. I put the key to the lock and turned the knob. The two of us crossed the threshold and stepped into the darkness of my apartment.

THIRTY-TWO

I TOOK ON no new cases in the months that followed. At Billy's trial, sometime in April, I was asked to testify as to the deceptions he had initiated relative to the cover-up of April Goodrich's murder.

The state went for conspiracy to commit murder, hoping to ensure a conviction on a lesser charge, and I answered their questions. Billy wisely claimed that the money in question had been gotten through gambling, eliminating the involvement of the DiGeordano family in court. I went along with that part of it, allowing Billy to play that particular string out to the end.

On the final day of my testimony, I walked from the courthouse and did not return. Hendricks phoned a few days later and told me that Billy had been given a two-year sentence for conspiracy after the fact. Billy and I had not made eye contact once during the hearing; he was gone from my life.

*   *   *

TWO DAYS LATER, ON a Saturday afternoon, I was driving my Dart down the Dulles Access Road, the windows rolled down, the spring sun whitening the road. Jackie Kahn was beside me on the passenger seat, and Sherron was seated in the rear. Their luggage had been shoehorned into the trunk. The Smithereens' "Behind a Wall of Sleep" played loudly from the radio, just covering the sputter of the engine beneath the hood. I lit a cigarette and watched Sherron's face in the rearview.

She frowned. "You sure this piece of junk's going to make it, Stefanos?"

"Mopar engine," I said. "You can bet on it. What time's your flight?"

"In about twenty minutes," Jackie said.

I goosed the accelerator and swerved into the left lane.

We reached Dulles International Airport ten minutes later. I dropped Sherron and Jackie at the terminal and told Jackie to meet me at the gate.

I parked the Dart and walked across the lot, toward the main terminal's great arced wall of glass. Inside, I checked the arrival/departure board, then made my way to the gate through a block of servicemen and European tourists. The steward had made the final call for boarding, and the line had dwindled to three. Jackie and Sherron were standing at the end of the line, the tickets in Jackie's hand.

"Think we cut it close enough?" I asked as I reached them.

"Didn't know that Dodge could break eighty," Sherron said. She wore a double-breasted designer suit, and her lips were painted a lovely pale pink.

Jackie looked at Sherron and made a gentle nod toward the gate. "I'll be right along. Here." She handed Sherron her boarding pass.

Sherron put a hand to Jackie's shoulder and gave me a kiss on the cheek. "Take it easy, Stefanos. You come visit, okay?"

"I will."

Sherron walked stylishly through the gate. She looked back once and smiled in my direction, and capped the smile with a wink. When she rounded the corner, I turned to Jackie.

Jackie wore a smock-and-pants arrangement that day, a colorful handbag draped over her shoulder. Her short black hair was combed forward at the sides, flapper style. Small gold coins hung from her ears, and her brown eyes seemed translucent in the light.

"I'd better go," she said.

"You'd better."

"Got a lot to do when I get there."

"I'll bet. You've got, what, two or three weeks before you start your new job?"

"Something like that. It'll give me a chance to explore, get comfortable."

"San Fran's a nice town, what I hear."

"I couldn't turn down the offer," she said. "And, with what's coming up" — Jackie stopped to run a hand across her stomach — "I thought a new start was in order, all the way around."

I dug my hands into my pockets. "You know I don't want you to go."

"Sherron wasn't just being polite," Jackie said. "We want you out there, Nick. You're welcome anytime."

"I plan on it," I said. "In the meantime, write. And send pictures."

The steward began to attach a rope at the gate. Jackie stood on her toes and kissed my mouth. She pulled away and touched a finger to my cheek.

"I trust you," I said. "You know that?"

Jackie smiled. "You did good, soldier."

She squeezed my hand and walked away.

Later I stood at the window and watched her plane lift off. It gained altitude, made a wide arc, and flew west. When the plane was only a dot of black entering the clouds, I walked back through the main terminal, out into the parking lot. I found my car and sat in it for a while, watching the sunset, and the flow of foot traffic and cars. A chill cut the air. I started the Dart, pulled out of the lot, and headed back downtown.

MAI PLACED A COLD bottle of Budweiser on the bar when I entered the Spot. I walked to the stool that was centered beneath the blue neon Schlitz logo. I bellied up and wrapped my hand around the bottle. The joint was empty.

Mai stocked beer in the cooler while Darnell washed the last of the night's dishes. I could hear the clatter of china and see his long brown arms against his stained apron through the reach-through as he worked.

"Slow night?" I said to Mai.

"Yep," she said, her plump little hand buried in the cooler, her blond hair pinned up in a pretzel-shaped bun. "A long night watching Happy stare at the cigarette burning in his fingers."

"Sounds thrilling."

"I did get a seventy-five-cent tip out of it, though."

"Then it was worth it." I saw some sweat roll down the back of her neck and felt the guilt. "You got plans tonight, Mai?"

Mai pulled her arm out of the cooler and faced me. She wound a twist of blond back behind her ear and showed me some teeth. "Got me a new soldier boy, Nicky."

"Why don't you take off, then, take a hot bath, get ready. I'll close up."

She smiled and straightened her posture. "You mean it?"

"Go on, get out of here."

Mai untied her tip apron dexterously and tossed it behind the register. She kissed me on the cheek, yelled good-bye into the kitchen, and skipped out the front door. I followed her, locked up, and walked back in.

I slid an old wave mix—Squeeze, Graham Parker, and Costello—into the tape deck. I listened to that while I finished restocking the cooler. When I was done I wiped down the bar, drained the sinks, and laid the green bar netting out in the service area to dry. I put most of the cash in a metal box and placed it underneath the floorboards, and left the register drawer open with a few ones and a five in the till. Then I grabbed an empty shot glass, the bottle of Grand-Dad off the call shelf, and a fresh Bud, and set them all up on the bar next to a clean ashtray. I placed the deck of Camels and a pack of matches beside the ashtray, had a seat, and settled in.

Darnell came out of the kitchen an hour later, tucking the tails of his beige shirt into his work pants as he walked. He stood next to me, leaned one foot on the rail, and unwound his long arms, resting them on the bar. I finished my fourth shot of bourbon and poured another to the lip of the glass.

"Private party?" Darnell said.

"Uh-uh."

"Mind if I hang?"

I gestured toward the empty stool to my right. "Have a seat."

Darnell sat and picked up my bottle of beer. He looked at the label, studied it, and placed the bottle back with the shot glass. I cupped my hand around both, a low, even tone encircling my head, entering my ears.

Darnell said, "You look pretty far away, man."

"I guess I am."

"Trouble with the ladies?"

I concentrated, looking at myself in the bar mirror. I had been thinking about Jackie at the beginning of the night, and then Billy Goodrich. But afterward my thoughts had gone much further back, long before the day I had met Billy on the bench in Sligo Creek Park. More skeletons, come to life.

"No," I said. "I was thinking about this Greek boy I knew way back. A kid named Dimitri."

"Never heard you mention him."

"He's been gone," I said, "a long time." I had a drink of

bourbon, rolled it around the glass, and followed it with another swallow. I chased that with beer and rested the bottle on the bar, keeping my fingers on the neck. Costello's beautiful country import, "Shoes without Heels," flowed through the speakers.

Darnell said, "Talk about it, man."

I looked into my shot glass. "I met this kid Dimitri, playing basketball in the church league, when I was seventeen. He was from Highlandtown — Greektown — up in Baltimore. We came from different places, but our friendship clicked for some reason, real fast. We started hanging out together, I'd drive up to Baltimore to see him, he'd take the bus to D.C. This kid was tough, big shoulders, but he had this smile.... He had a lot of life, you know what I'm saying?" Darnell nodded, watching my eyes in the mirror. "That summer, we used to crank up J. Geils's *Bloodshot*, dance out front of his row house, the tape deck set up right on his stoop. So when Geils came to the Baltimore Civic Center, you know we were the first ones with tickets, the first ones at the show." I paused. "Dimitri was wearing this hat that night, sort of like a Panama hat, but gangster style. And J. Geils came on — this was the *Ladies Invited* tour, they opened with the first track off the LP, 'The Lady Makes Demands' — and turned the place out." I poured another inch of Grand-Dad into the shot glass, downed it, and exhaled. The glass left a ring of water on the mahogany bar. "Somehow I lost Dimitri in the crowd. But later, from my seat above, I recognized him by his hat, pushing his way up to the front of the stage. That show was bumpin', man." I paused, picturing the crowd, girls in halter tops, a cloud of marijuana hovering in the arena. "Anyway, when Dimitri finally came back to the seats, he wasn't wearing the hat — when I asked him where it was, he said he had handed it to Peter Wolf, on the stage. I told him he was full of shit, and Dimitri didn't argue about it — that wasn't his style. He just smiled."

Darnell said, "What happened to that boy?"

I moved my face around with my hand and pushed hair

away from my eyes. "A couple weeks later he got into a car with a couple of Polish boys from the neighborhood. He didn't know the car was stolen. They were driving down the Patterson Parkway, and a cop made the car, and the driver tried to outrun the cop. He flipped it doing seventy. Dimitri went through the windshield. He was in a coma for a week, and then he died. The boys who stole the car walked away with scratches."

Darnell said, "You don't need to be thinkin' about that tonight, Nick."

"Listen"—I smiled and shook my head—"that's not the end of the story. Six months later I pick up an issue of *Creem* magazine, off the newsstand. Inside, there's a story on the J. Geils Band, and on the facing page there's a photograph of Peter Wolf. He's wearing Dimitri's hat, Darnell. And the caption underneath says, 'Lead singer Peter Wolf wears a hat given to him by a fan at a Baltimore concert.'"

"That must've tripped you out."

I had a sip of bourbon, put it down, and drank deeply of the beer. "Dimitri went out like a fuckin' champ."

Darnell frowned. "You don't believe that, Nick."

"You're wrong," I said. "Dimitri checked out at the top of his game. The way everybody should." I lit a cigarette, blew smoke over the bar, and let it settle. "He never had to watch himself get old in the mirror. He never had to hold a fucking gun on his friends."

Darnell looked at the drink in front of me and straight back in my eyes. "Man, you're the one that's wrong. That shit you're drinkin, it's got you all twisted up inside." He put a hand to my arm. "I'll tell you what that boy never got to do. He never got to walk his woman down the aisle. He never got to hold his baby up to the sky. He never got a chance to taste the good *or* the bad. You better see that, man. If you don't, you're lost."

I reached for my drink. Darnell pushed the glass away, out of my reach.

"I'm all right," I said.

"I'm drivin' you home."

"Let me sit here for a little bit."

"I'm drivin' you home," Darnell said. "Come on."

I steadied myself, my hand on the bar. "I'm all right."

"Let's go, man."

I focused on Darnell's eyes. "You lock the place up. Okay?"

"I'll take care of it," he said, getting under my arm.

We walked together to the front door. A cool blue light burned behind us in the room, and smoke rose off the ashtray on the bar.

I STOOD IN THE shower and slept on my feet. The water temperature fell, and when it did, the coolness of it woke me. I exited the stall, dried off, combed out my hair, and dressed in a black sweatshirt and jeans. My cat followed me into the kitchen, circling my feet as I brewed a cup of coffee.

I took the coffee out into the living room and had a seat on the couch, resting the cup on the couch's arm. I sat there and drank the coffee, stroking the cat on my lap. I did that for a while, and then the phone rang. The cat jumped off as I picked the phone up from the floor and placed it in my lap. I put the receiver to my ear.

"Hello."

"Stefanos?" It was a woman's voice, unidentifiable but familiar.

"Yes."

"You never called me."

"Who is this?"

"A fan," she said.

I thought about that, and I remembered the note. Then I thought some more about the voice. "How's it going?" I said.

"It's goin' good. Why didn't you call?"

"I'm not the aggressive type."

"You got aggressive pretty quick on the William Henry case."

"What's that?"

"I read the *Post*," she said. "I figured you were behind it somehow, though I don't know how you finessed it." I let her talk. I liked the sound of her voice. "Don't want to discuss it, huh?"

"Uh-uh."

"You drunk, Stefanos? You sound a little drunk."

"Tired," I said.

"Well, it is late. So I'll get right to the point. Listen, I was wondering—you didn't call, so I thought I'd take the initiative here—I was wondering if maybe you wanted to take in a double feature tomorrow night, down at the AFI."

My cat sat on the radiator, watching me twist the phone cord around my hand. "What's on the bill?" I said.

"Some shoot-em-up out of Hong Kong, and a Douglas Sirk melodrama. *Magnificent Obsession*. Something for you, something for me."

"No Liz Taylor?"

"Nope," she said. "And no Isaac Hayes."

I grinned. "Sounds good to me. You buy the tickets, I'll spring for whatever comes up next. Okay?"

"Okay. I'll pick you up at your place," she said. "About six-thirty."

"You know where I live?"

"Your number's on the card. I crossed-referenced it to your address in the Hanes Directory."

"You're a hell of an investigative reporter."

"See you tomorrow night, Stefanos."

"Right."

I got off the couch with the phone in my hand, and I stood in the center of the room. A Dinah Washington number played from my landlord's apartment above. I danced a few steps and put the phone down. My cat watched me and blinked her eye.

I took the coffee cup to the kitchen and found the note that had been signed "A Fan" on the plain white card, in the basket where I dumped my overdue bills. I walked with the note to my bedroom, and I opened the top dresser drawer.

I wasn't certain that night as to why I kept the note. Call it a feeling, listening to the woman's voice on the phone, that something right would happen next. But as spring became summer, I began to understand.

That was the summer that I first noticed the texture of the crepe myrtle that grew beside my stoop, the summer I woke each morning to the sweet smell of hibiscus that flowered outside my bedroom window. That was the summer that a tape called *The La's* played continuously from my deck, the summer that a Rare Essence go-go single called "Lock It" raged from every young D.C. driver's sound system on the street. And that was the summer that I held hands in the dark with a freckly, pale-eyed redhead with the perfectly musical name of Lyla McCubbin.

Under a shoe box filled with trinkets from my youth, in the bottom of the dresser drawer, lay the envelope that held the few memories I had chosen to hold on to through the years. I placed the white card into the envelope, behind the photograph of me and Billy Goodrich sitting high on the fire escape in New Orleans. I slipped the envelope back under the shoe box and closed the drawer. My cat walked slowly into the room and settled at my feet.